Praise for Carolyne

"Carolyne Aarsen delivers a spunky heroine…
fun story…[and] a warm romance."
—*RT Book Reviews* on *Finally a Family*

"A heart-achingly tender story of how different
people depend on relationships bound by blood
to influence their capacity to love."
—*RT Book Reviews* on *Cowboy Daddy*

"Another delightful romance…sure to bring a
smile to your lips."
—*RT Book Reviews* on *Twin Blessings*

"Aarsen delivers a touching story… [With] the
occasional bursts of humor you have a terrific
[tale]."
—*RT Book Reviews* on *Any Man of Mine*

"Carolyne Aarsen just keeps getting better and
A Hero for Kelsey is proof of that."
—*RT Book Reviews*

Carolyne Aarsen

CATTLEMAN'S COURTSHIP

and

COWBOY DADDY

HARLEQUIN® LOVE INSPIRED®CLASSICS

If you purchased this book without a cover you should be aware that this book is stolen property. It was reported as "unsold and destroyed" to the publisher, and neither the author nor the publisher has received any payment for this "stripped book."

Recycling programs
for this product may
not exist in your area.

ISBN-13: 978-0-373-60142-4

Cattleman's Courtship & Cowboy Daddy

Copyright © 2015 by Harlequin Books S.A.

The publisher acknowledges the copyright holder
of the individual works as follows:

Cattleman's Courtship
Copyright © 2010 by Carolyne Aarsen

Cowboy Daddy
Copyright © 2010 by Carolyne Aarsen

All rights reserved. Except for use in any review, the reproduction or utilization of this work in whole or in part in any form by any electronic, mechanical or other means, now known or hereinafter invented, including xerography, photocopying and recording, or in any information storage or retrieval system, is forbidden without the written permission of the editorial office, Love Inspired Books, 233 Broadway, New York, NY 10279 U.S.A.

This is a work of fiction. Names, characters, places and incidents are either the product of the author's imagination or are used fictitiously, and any resemblance to actual persons, living or dead, business establishments, events or locales is entirely coincidental.

This edition published by arrangement with Love Inspired Books.

® and TM are trademarks of Love Inspired Books, used under license. Trademarks indicated with ® are registered in the United States Patent and Trademark Office, the Canadian Intellectual Property Office and in other countries.

Printed in U.S.A.

HARLEQUIN®
www.Harlequin.com

CONTENTS

Carolyne Aarsen and her husband, Richard, live on a small ranch in northern Alberta, where they have raised four children and numerous foster children and are still raising cattle. Carolyne crafts her stories in an office with a large west-facing window, through which she can watch the changing seasons while struggling to make her words obey. Visit her website at carolyneaarsen.com.

Books by Carolyne Aarsen

Love Inspired

Refuge Ranch

Her Cowboy Hero
Reunited with the Cowboy

Hearts of Hartley Creek

A Father's Promise
Unexpected Father
A Father in the Making

Home to Hartley Creek

The Rancher's Return
Daddy Lessons
Healing the Doctor's Heart
Homecoming Reunion
Catching Her Heart

Visit the Author Profile page
at Harlequin.com for more titles.

CATTLEMAN'S COURTSHIP

I have learned to be content whatever
the circumstances.
—*Philippians* 4:11

I'd like to dedicate this book to Linda Ford, my friend and critique partner. You rejoice with me and weep with me and help me struggle with stories. Especially this one. You are an inspiration and an encouragement. I couldn't do what I do without your help.

Chapter One

Panic spiraled through Cara Morrison as she stared at the cowboy standing with his back to her looking at a chart on the wall of the vet clinic.

Nicholas Chapman. The man she was once engaged to. The man she thought she didn't care for anymore.

He wasn't supposed to be back in Alberta, Canada. He was supposed to be working overseas.

And she wasn't supposed to be reacting to her ex-fiancé this way.

The familiar posture, the slant of his head with its broad cowboy hat, the breadth of his shoulders, his one hand slung up in the front pocket of his faded blue jeans all pulled at old memories Cara thought she had pushed aside.

Bill, the other vet, was out on call and her uncle had chosen this exact time to grab a cup of coffee, leaving the clinic in her capable hands, he had said. If she'd known who the next client would be, she wouldn't have let him leave!

Nicholas turned and Cara's heart slowed for a few

heavy beats, then started up again. She sucked in a quick breath as her mouth went dry.

Gray eyes, the color of a summer storm, met hers in a piercing gaze. Eyes she had once looked into with love and caring. Eyes that once beheld her with warmth instead of the coolness she now observed.

"Hello, Cara. I heard rumors you were back in town." Nicholas pushed his hat back on his head, his well-modulated voice showing no hint of discomfort.

The last time she saw him, three years ago, he wasn't as in control. His anger had spilled over into harsh words that cut and hurt. And instead of confronting him, challenging him, she had turned tail and run.

And she and Nicholas hadn't spoken since then.

Her friend Trista had assured her Nicholas was working overseas on yet another dangerous job.

Yet here he stood making her heart pound and her face flush.

"I'm visiting my aunt and uncle for a week," she said, forcing a smile to her face, thankful the trembling in her chest didn't translate to her voice. "After that I'm heading to Europe for a holiday."

"What made you decide Europe?"

Okay, chitchat. She could do chitchat.

"My mother spent some time in Malta."

"Ah, yes. In her many travels around the world."

Cara frowned at the faint tone of derision in his voice. Though Cara had wished and prayed that her mother would stay with her instead of heading off on yet another mission project, she also had wished she shared her mother's zeal.

"She did some relief work there," Cara said. "I'd like to visit the orphanage where she worked." She folded her arms over her chest. "And how are things with you and your father?"

"We're busy on the ranch," he replied. He drew his hands out of the pockets of his denim jeans and placed them on the counter.

The hands of a working man. Cara fleetingly noticed the faint scars on the backs of his hands, a black mark on one fingernail.

His eyes bored into hers and for the smallest moment she felt like taking a step back at the antagonism she saw there. But she clung to the counter, holding her ground.

"And how are you enjoying Vancouver?" he asked.

"I'm moving."

Nicholas raised one eyebrow. "Where to this time?"

"I've got a line on a job in Montreal working for an animal drug company in a lab."

He gave a short laugh. "Didn't figure you for a big-city person working in a lab."

"The job is challenging." She gave a light shrug, as if brushing away his observations.

At one time this man held her heart in the callused hands resting on the counter between them. At one time all her unspoken dreams and wishes for a family and a place were pinned on this man.

She couldn't act as if he were simply another customer she had to deal with. "What can I do for you?" she asked, going directly to the point.

He gave her a smile that held no warmth and in spite of her own hurt it still cut.

"I need to vaccinate my calves before I put them out to pasture."

"How many doses?" she asked, sliding the large

glass refrierator door open and pulling out the boxes he asked for.

"Anything else?" she asked, favoring him with a quick glance, hoping she looked far more professional than she felt.

"Yeah. I'm sending a shipment of heifers to the United States. I need to know what I have to do before I send them out."

"From your purebred herd?"

Nicholas nodded, reaching up to scratch his forehead with one finger. He often did that when he contemplated something, Cara thought. She was far too conscious of his height, of the familiar lines of his face. The way his hair always wanted to fall over his forehead. How his dark eyebrows accented the unusual color of his eyes. How his cheekbones swept down to his firm chin.

He looks tired.

The thought slipped past her defenses, awakening old feelings she thought she had dealt with.

She crossed her arms as if defending herself against his heartrending appeal.

"I'm sending out my first shipment of heifers along with a bull," he continued. "If this guy likes what he sees, I could have a pretty good steady market."

"You're ranching full-time now?" Cara fought the strong urge to step back, to give herself more space away from the easy charm that was causing her tension.

Nicholas frowned, shaking his head. "After I ship out the heifers I'm heading overseas again."

"Overseas?" She'd been told that, but she didn't know the details. Guess working offshore rigs wasn't dangerous enough, or didn't pay enough. "Where will you be?"

"A two-month stint in Kuwait. Dad's still able to take care of the ranch so I figure I better work while I can."

"And how's your leg?" she asked, referring to the accident he suffered working on the rigs just before their big fight. The fight that had shown Cara that Nicholas's ranch would always come before anything or anyone else in his life. Including her.

Nicholas eyes narrowed. "The leg is fine."

"Glad to hear it."

Before they could get into another dead-end discussion, Cara pulled a pad of paper toward her. "As for the heifers you'll be shipping, you'll need to call the clinic to book some tests." Was that her voice? So clipped, so tense? She thought after three years she would be more relaxed, more in control.

She reached for a pen but instead spilled the can's contents all over the counter with a hollow clatter.

Of course, she thought, grabbing for the assortment of pens. Nicholas Chapman shows up and hands that could stitch up a tear in a kitten's eyelid without any sign of a tremor suddenly become clumsy and awkward.

"Here, let me help you," he said as he picked up the can and set it upright.

For the briefest of moments, their hands brushed each other. Cara jerked hers back.

Nicholas dropped the handful of pens into the aluminum can, then stood back.

Cara didn't look at him as she scribbled some instructions and put them in her uncle's appointment book. "I made a note for my uncle to call you, in case you or your dad forget." She didn't want to sound so aloof, but how else could she get through this moment?

He took the paper she handed him and, after glancing down briefly at it, folded it up and slipped it into his pocket. "I could have phoned for the information, but I was in town anyway."

He'd heard she was around, but was seeing her as much of a shock to him as to her?

He grabbed the bag, murmured his thanks then left. As the door swung shut behind him, relief sluiced through her.

Their first meeting had finally happened.

Maybe now she could finally get past her old feelings for him and get on with her life.

It had been three years since they'd broken up over the very thing they had talked about. His blind devotion to his ranch and his commitment to working dangerous jobs that paid high wages, which all went back into the ranch.

When she found out he'd broken his leg on one of his jobs, she'd been sick with worry. After his accident, she'd pleaded with Nicholas to quit working the rigs. But he hadn't even entertained the idea.

When he'd left, when he chose the work over her, she'd left, too.

She'd come back to Cochrane periodically, but only when she was sure he was gone. So they had never talked about her sudden departure and they had never met each other face-to-face. Until now.

Cara wished she could do exactly what Trista, her best friend, had been telling her ever since she left. Get over Nicholas. Start dating.

Trouble was she had no interest in dating. She never did.

As a young girl, she had moved every couple of years as her mother sought the elusive perfect job. Each move meant pulling up roots and breaking ties.

Then, at age fifteen, she moved in with her aunt and uncle in Cochrane. Determined to make something of herself, she applied herself to her studies and worked summers in her uncle's vet clinic.

It wasn't until she graduated medical school and started working at her uncle's clinic full-time that she met Nicholas and truly fell in love for the first time. They dated for six months and got engaged.

And six months later they broke up.

Though she knew she had to get over him, seeing him just now was much, much harder than she'd thought it would be.

One thing was sure, Cara couldn't stay, knowing she'd run into Nicholas again. Her reaction to him showed her that quite clearly.

She'd stay the weekend and go to church with her aunt and uncle. Then, on Monday she would be on the phone to a travel agent getting her ticket changed as soon as possible.

Nicholas adjusted his corduroy blazer, straightened the tie cinching his collared shirt and shook his head at his own preening.

Since when, he asked himself, *did you get so fussed about what you look like when you go to church?*

Since he knew Cara Morrison would be attending. He had almost changed his mind about going this morning. He had to trim horses' hooves and check fences, but at the same time he felt a strong need to be at church. When he worked rigs, he couldn't attend at all, so he when he had a chance to worship with fellow believers, he took it.

He turned away from his image in the bathroom mirror and jogged down the stairs.

His father was rooting through the refrigerator and looked up when Nicholas entered the kitchen.

Dale Chapman still wore his cowboy hat and boots. Obviously he'd been out checking the cows already this morning. He was a tall, imposing man and, in his youth, had been trim and fit.

Now his stomach protruded over the large belt buckle, a remnant from his rodeo years that had taken his time and money and given him a bum back and a permanent limp. Though his hair was gray, he still wore it long in the back.

"What's with all this vaccine?" He pulled out one of the boxes Nicholas had purchased yesterday.

"I thought we were out."

Dale Chapman narrowed his eyes. "I heard that Morrison girl was back in town," his father said as Nicholas pulled out the coffeepot and found it empty. "Is that the reason you went to the vet clinic?"

Nicholas shrugged off the question, wishing away a sudden flush of self-consciousness as he pulled the boiling kettle off the stove and rinsed off an apple. Not the most balanced breakfast, but it would hold him until lunchtime.

"If you think she's going to change her mind you're crazy," Dale said as he pulled a carton of milk out of the fridge. "She's not a rancher's wife and we all know how that can turn out."

Nicholas ignored his father's little speech as he poured grounds and hot water into the coffee press. Though it had been fifteen years since Nicholas's parents' divorce, Dale had mistrusted women ever since. And that mistrust had seeped into his opinion of Cara. His father's negative opinion of Cara Morrison hadn't been encouraging when he and Cara were dating. When Cara broke off the engagement, Dale had tried and failed not to say "I told you so" in many ways, shapes and forms.

"How long she around for this time?" his father asked, pouring the milk over his bowl of cereal.

"Didn't ask."

"Probably not long, if she's like her mom."

Nicholas didn't say anything, knowing nothing was required, and he wasn't going to get pulled into a conversation about Cara.

He thought he had been prepared to see her again. Thought he had successfully pushed her out of his mind. Hadn't he even dated a number of other girls since Cara?

Again he could feel the miscreant beat of his heart when he turned and saw her standing behind the counter, almost exactly as she had the first time they had met.

That first time he'd seen her, he'd been enchanted with her wide eyes, an unusual shade of brown. The delicate line of her face. She had looked so fragile.

But he knew better.

He'd seen her covered in mud, rain streaming down her face as she helped deliver a foal. He'd seen her do a Cesarean section on a cow in the freezing cold, seen her manhandle calves that weighed almost as much as she did.

Cara Morrison was anything but fragile.

And he was anything but over her.

She left without a word, he told himself. *She couldn't even break up with you to your face. She ran away instead of facing things. Get over it.*

So why was he going to church knowing he might see her?

Because he wasn't the kind of person to run away or get chased away.

He had some pride, he thought, finishing off his apple and tossing the core into the garbage can. And because, when he stayed away from church, his heart felt empty and his soul unnourished.

He said a quick goodbye to his father and ran to his truck. He was already running late.

Half an hour later a helpful usher escorted him to one of the few empty spots in the building. He sat down, got settled in and ended up looking directly at the back of Cara Morrison's head.

He glanced around, looking for another place to sit, but then the minister came to the front of the church and encouraged everyone to rise and greet their neighbors.

Nicholas immediately turned to the person beside him and then Cara's aunt called out his name. Was it his imagination or did Cara jump?

"So good to see you here," Lori Morrison said, catching his hand. He shook Lori's hand and then, with a sense of inevitability, turned to Cara.

She gave him a tight smile but didn't offer to shake his hand. "Good morning, Nicholas. Good to see you again."

"Is it?"

The words came out before he could stop them.

Well, that was brilliant. Nicholas watched Cara slowly turn away from him. Why couldn't he be as cool as she was? Why couldn't he return her greeting instead of running the risk of antagonizing her again?

Now she stood with her back to him, the overhead lights catching glints of gold in her hair. Three years ago she wore it short, like a cap. Now it brushed her shoulders, inviting touch.

He crossed his arms, angry at his reaction to her. It had been three years. It was done.

And Nicholas spent the rest of the church service alternately trying to listen to the minister and trying to ignore Cara Morrison.

He was successful at neither.

Finally the minister spoke the benediction. The congregation rose for the final song. As soon as the last note rang out and the minister stood at the back of the church, Nicholas made his escape.

He had his hand on the bar that opened the exterior door when he heard someone call his name. His first impulse was to ignore whoever called him. And he would have managed if the helpful person behind him hadn't tapped him on the shoulder.

"I believe Mrs. Hughes wants to talk to you," his neighbor said. He pointed out a thin, short woman waving at him from the top of the stairs in the foyer.

Nicholas smiled his acknowledgment and, with a sigh of resignation, walked back through the crowd of people in the foyer.

He had his hand on the handrail of the steps and looked up in time to see Cara walking down the stairs past Mrs. Hughes.

Cara caught his eye, then glanced quickly away.

Right behind her stood her uncle, Alan Morrison.

Nicholas caught Alan's piercing gaze. It was as if he were making sure Nicholas didn't "hurt" his precious niece yet again. Nicholas wanted to reassure him that as far as Cara was concerned, he had gotten the memo long ago.

Then Nicholas saw a look of puzzlement cross Alan's

face as his step faltered. Alan's hand clutched the hand-rail on his right side as he cried out.

Then, as if in slow motion, he crumpled and folded in on himself.

Cara turned. Her aunt Lori screamed.

And as Nicholas watched in horror, Alan Morrison fell heavily down the rest of the stairs.

Nicholas was the first one at his side. Cara right behind him. "Call an ambulance," Nicholas shouted to the people who now milled around.

"Stretch him out." Cara pulled on Alan's arm, falling to her knees beside him. "Straighten him out and open his coat."

Alan's face held a sickly gray tinge, his eyes like dark bruises, unfocused, staring straight up.

As Nicholas unbuttoned Alan's suit jacket, Cara placed her hand above his mouth then, bending over, put her mouth on his and gave him two quick breaths.

Her fingers swept his neck, pressing against it.

"No pulse," she murmured.

"I'll do the CPR, you take care of the breathing."

Nicholas counted to himself, one and two, pressing down on each count. Cara was bent over her uncle's head, breathing for him.

Nicholas felt vaguely aware of the people around them as they worked, Lori crying, someone else telling people to move away.

But for Nicholas, the only thing that existed was the two of them fighting to save Cara's beloved uncle's life. A tiny cosmos among the shifting crowd around them.

He didn't know how long they worked. It seemed like a few moments, a brief snatch of time.

Yet by the time someone called out to make room for

the paramedics, the tension knotted his shoulders and the hard floor dug into his knees.

"I'll take over, sir." Hands pulled him back as others caught the rhythm he had maintained.

Nicholas caught the glimpse of two uniformed men and he got slowly to his feet, his legs tingling as the blood rushed back to them.

Another paramedic strapped an oxygen mask on Alan's head, manually pumping life-giving oxygen into him.

Cara sat back, her hands hanging slack by her side, her eyes huge in her pale face.

Nicholas tried to work his way around Alan to be at her side. But someone else took her by the shoulders. Lifted her up. Held her as she visibly trembled.

That's my job, my place, he thought, feeling ineffective and surprisingly possessive as someone else stroked her hair in comfort.

In a flurry of activity the paramedics had Alan on a stretcher and then wheeled him out the doors.

Beyond the double doors Nicholas saw the whirling lights atop the ambulance and the enormity of what had just happened struck him.

"Cara. Go with him," Nicholas heard Lori Morrison called out.

Cara glanced around, looking confused at the sound of her aunt's voice.

"Please," Lori pleaded. "I can't. I just can't."

Nicholas found her this time and gave her a gentle push in the direction of the ambulance. "I'll take care of your aunt. You go. Be with your uncle."

He gave her shoulder a quick squeeze before she whirled away, running after the paramedics.

Nicholas hurried to Lori's side. "I'll take you to the hospital," he said, slipping his arm over her shoulder. "We'll meet Cara there."

Lori only nodded, clutching his arm.

He steered Lori to his truck and soon they were speeding down the highway to the hospital, trying in vain to keep up with the ambulance. Lori sat curled against the passenger's-side window, a silent figure clutching her coat, her face strobed by the flashing red lights of the ambulance they were following.

While he drove, Nicholas sent up a quick prayer for Alan Morrison and for Cara, praying the ambulance would get to the hospital on time.

Chapter Two

Sorrow, huge as a stone, lodged in Cara's chest. Tears threatened, but she held them back. In the past couple of hours her aunt had cried enough for both of them.

She wanted time to rewind. She wanted to go back when her uncle was still walking around. Still talking and telling his terrible jokes.

Not strapped to a gurney with a paramedic working on him while they raced to the hospital in the swaying ambulance.

Myocardial infarction, the paramedics had said. Heart attack.

How could a heart suddenly decide to stop working? What triggered it?

Images flickered in her mind. Uncle Alan wheezing as he lifted a box. His unusually high color.

Though he only worked part-time, Cara knew he'd been under stress lately. The practice had been extremely busy and Alan was called more often to fill in on the large animal work.

Another vet, Gordon Moen, was supposed to be com-

ing to help out, but he wasn't arriving for another three
weeks.

Too late for Uncle Alan.

The stone in her chest shifted and tears thickened her
throat.

*Please, Lord, don't take him away, too. You already
took my mother, please spare him.*

Then she caught herself.

God didn't listen to prayers. How many had she sent
up that her mother would come back to her? Would put
her first in her life?

Had God listened when she prayed Nicholas would
choose her over his work? Over his ranch?

Sometimes she wondered if her prayers were selfish
but she believed that anyone else in her situation would
want the same things.

Aunt Lori always said God moved in mysterious ways.
Well, they were certainly mysterious to Cara.

Cara rolled her head slightly, chancing a glance at
Nicholas, who had stayed at the hospital. The knot of
his tie hung below his open collar of his rumpled shirt.
She couldn't help the hitch of her heart at the sight. He
looked more approachable now, more like the Nicholas
she remembered.

As if aware of her scrutiny, he glanced back at her.
And again their gazes locked. He turned, then walked
back in her direction.

He sat down in the empty chair beside her, resting his
elbows on his knees. "How are you doing?" he asked.

The deep timbre of his voice still made her heart sing.
Still swept away her natural reserve.

"I'm okay."

He frowned, as if dissatisfied with her reply. But what

else could she say? She felt especially vulnerable now
and if she said more, she would start to cry. She needed
to maintain what dignity she could. To stay aloof, calm
and in control. Nothing had changed in his life and she
couldn't put herself through that emotional wringer once
again.

"Here's your aunt," he said suddenly, standing up.

Lori came down the hallway, clutching her purse. A
nurse walked beside her, talking in hushed tones. As
they came closer Cara heard snatches of the conversation.

"He'll be on the monitors for a couple of days…good
pulse…healthy man…"

Lori nodded, but Cara knew she wasn't absorbing all
this.

Cara got up, stretching her tired muscles, and walked
toward her aunt.

"How is he?" Cara knew the question was superflu-
ous but she had to ask.

Her aunt shook her head. "He looks so awful with
all those things attached to him. You don't want to see
him yet."

But Cara needed to.

"Can I see him?" she asked the nurse.

"You two can go in," she said, gesturing at Cara. "But
only for a minute. We don't want to tire him out."

Cara realized with a start the nurse had included Nicholas in the invitation. She was about to correct her, when
the nurse turned, her shoes squeaking on the gleaming
floor.

Cara didn't look back to see if Nicholas was coming,
but as she followed the nurse, she could hear his measured tread behind her, slightly slower than her own.

The nurse motioned for Cara to come closer. "You've

got two minutes then I'll come and get you." She smiled at Cara, then past her. Cara could tell the moment her smile connected with Nicholas. Nicholas always had that effect on women, she thought dully, pushing aside the curtain around her uncle's bed, her fingers trembling.

She stepped forward, then faltered at the sight before her.

Her uncle, a large, strapping man, lay on the bed, his face still obscured by the oxygen mask. Lines attached to circular pads snaked out to a machine beeping out a regular rhythm. His arms lay beside him, bare except for a blood-pressure cuff attached to a machine. Two IVs ran out from his arms.

He looked like death.

Cara pressed her hand to her mouth, stopping the faint cry of dismay, her knees buckling beneath her.

She would have fallen, but strong arms caught her from behind. Held her. Just for those few seconds she allowed herself to drift back against Nicholas's comforting strength, thankful for his presence.

We fit so well, Cara thought, letting him support her. His touch, his smell, his warmth felt so familiar it created an ache deep in her chest.

Then, when she caught her balance, his hands settled on her waist, held a moment and then gently pushed her away.

As if he couldn't stand to touch her any longer than he had to.

Cara disguised the pain of his withdrawal by catching her uncle's hand and clinging it to it, hoping he would pull through this emergency. She stayed by her uncle's side a moment longer, then turned away.

"I want to…go," she said to Nicholas.

Aunt Lori sat huddled in the hard plastic chair, her hands kneading each other. As Cara came closer, her head came up. "Is he awake?"

Cara shook her head.

"He was working too hard." Aunt Lori's voice sounded so small. So wounded.

Cara stifled the flicker of guilt her aunt's innocent comment created. It wasn't her fault, she reminded herself. Even if she had stayed behind and worked at the clinic as her uncle had always envisioned, Alan Morrison wouldn't have slowed down. Wouldn't have done less.

"We should go home," Cara said quietly, taking her aunt's arm in hers.

"Can we come back tonight?"

"Of course we can. But you should go home and rest a bit before we do." Cara took her aunt's arm and, as they walked to the door, she leaned heavily on Cara.

The air outside smelled fresh, new. The sun shone down with a benevolent spring warmth, but Cara couldn't stop the chill shivering down her spine.

"My truck is parked over here," Nicholas said, stepping ahead of them to lead the way.

Cara acknowledged his comment with a nod, following him more slowly, holding her aunt up.

"I made him eat his vegetables. I made him go for walks," Aunt Lori was saying, clutching Cara's arm. "I took good care of him."

"Of course you did," Cara said quietly, her attention split between her aunt and the man who strode in front of them, leading the way to his truck.

He opened the door and Cara felt a jolt of dismay. The cab had one bench seat with a fold-down console.

Which meant her aunt would be sitting by the window and Cara...right beside Nicholas.

She helped her aunt into the truck, then had to walk around to Nicholas's side. She began to get in slowly, wishing she'd worn sensible shoes instead of high heels made for walking short distances, not climbing running boards of pickup trucks.

She faltered as she stepped up and Nicholas caught her, his hand on her elbow. She tried to ignore his touch, wished her heart didn't jump at his nearness.

She settled on the seat beside her aunt, and buckled herself in. Nicholas got in and Cara's senses heightened.

"Can you move over a bit," Aunt Lori asked, nudging Cara with her elbow. "I'm feeling claustrophobic."

Cara shifted as much as she dared. No matter what, though, she sat too close to Nicholas. She felt the warmth of his arm through the sleeve of her sweater and the scent of his cologne drew up older memories of other trips in this truck. Trips when she didn't mind sitting as close to him as she was now and often tried to sit even closer.

That's over, she thought.

The trip back to Cochrane was quiet, broken only by the hum of the tires on the pavement, the intermittent noise of the fan sending cooling air over the truck's occupants.

Cara kept her arms folded over her purse and tried, like her aunt did, to keep her eyes fixed on the road rolling past them.

But she couldn't stop her awareness of the man sitting next to her. Each curve in the road and each bump in the pavement brought the two of them in contact with each other.

"Did the doctor say anything about what might have

caused the heart attack?" Nicholas asked, breaking the heavy silence.

Cara took a breath. "He told me his cholesterol levels were high. And I imagine the stress of working added to that."

"Did they say how serious it was?"

"A heart attack is serious. Period," Aunt Lori said in a tone that didn't encourage any further discussion.

A heavy silence followed her remark. Cara wished she dared turn the radio on. She wished she and her aunt could share casual conversation. Anything to keep the picture of her uncle falling down the stairs out of her mind.

Anything to keep her from being so sensitive to Nicholas's presence.

The beginnings of a headache pinched her temples and by the time Nicholas pulled up to her aunt and uncle's home, Cara felt as if a vise gripped her forehead.

"Thanks for all your help," Aunt Lori said, leaning past Cara to give Nicholas a worn smile. Then she stepped out of the truck and headed up the walk to the house.

Cara slid over and from a safer distance risked a glance at Nicholas.

He draped one arm over the steering wheel, his other across the back of the seat, bringing his fingertips inches from her shoulder.

"Thanks for the ride and for all the help," Cara said. "I'm so glad you could bring Aunt Lori to the hospital."

Nicholas didn't say anything, his eyes holding hers. "Are you going to be okay?" His voice sounded cool, as if he were asking a mere acquaintance.

Cara shrugged and slipped her purse over her arm. "I don't know."

Quiet fell again and Cara didn't have anything more to say. So she slipped out of the truck and trudged up the sidewalk. But before she got to the house, she couldn't help a glance back over her shoulder.

Nicholas was watching her.

She took a chance and lifted her hand in a small wave, but he started his truck and drove away.

Cara closed her hand and pressed it to her chest, surprised at the jab of hurt.

Did you expect him to come running down the walk, pull you into his arms and beg you to give him another chance? Did you really think he was pining for you the whole time you were gone? He doesn't care for you anymore.

The words mocked her, and she turned and entered the house.

Aunt Lori sat in her usual chair in the kitchen, her arms wrapped around her midsection.

"Do you want some tea?" Cara asked, walking to the stove.

Aunt Lori nodded.

While she waited for the water to boil, Cara joined her aunt, glancing around the papers piled up on the room table, the dishes scattered over the kitchen counter. She wished she had the energy to start cleaning.

Her aunt was not a housekeeper. She always joked that she preferred to paint walls than wash them and she could always afford to get someone to do it for her.

Though she missed her aunt and uncle, she didn't miss the mess either in the house or her uncle's vet clinic. Her mother wasn't much different and at times Cara wondered if she really was a Morrison. Every time she came back to her aunt and uncle's place, either from university or visiting, she spent the first few days tidying up.

However, in spite of the chaos, Uncle Alan and Aunt Lori's home had been Cara's most stable home since Audra Morrison dropped Cara off at their place. Audra had assumed Cara was old enough to be without her while she followed her conscience and went to work overseas.

Cara still remembered the grim voice of her uncle, trying to plead with his sister, Cara's mother, to think of Cara.

Her mother's reply still rang in her ears. Cara had been raised with more privileges than any of the children she left to help. She didn't need her mother as much as these destitute young orphans in Nicaragua.

And then she left. Aunt Lori had come upstairs and had sat beside Cara, not saying anything, simply holding her close, letting Cara's tears drench the front of her shirt.

When Cara turned fifteen, everything changed. Cara's mother was killed flying into the Congo to help yet another group of lost and broken children.

And Cara was alone.

Uncle Alan and Aunt Lori were named her guardians. They paid for all her expenses, bought her a car. Put her through vet school and Uncle Alan offered her a job when she was done.

She started working for her uncle, met Nicholas and she thought her life had finally come to the place she'd been yearning for since she was a young girl.

A home of her own. A family of her own.

And now, her uncle lay in a hospital bed and Nicholas was more removed from her than ever.

"How are you doing?" Cara asked, reaching over and covering her aunt's icy hands with hers.

"I'm tired. And I'm scared." Lori looked up at Cara. "Will you pray with me?"

Cara was taken momentarily aback. How could her aunt talk about praying after what had just happened? What good would it do?

But she wasn't about to take what little comfort her aunt might derive from praying, away from her.

"Sure. I'll pray with you." Cara folded her hands over her aunt's and bowed her head.

Cara waited, then realized her aunt wanted her to do the praying.

Her heart fluttered in panic. What was she going to say? But her aunt squeezed her hands, signaling her need. So Cara cleared her throat and began.

"Dear Lord, Thank You for today…" She paused there, wondering what she could be thankful about when her uncle was so ill, but she carried on. "Thank You that we could worship with Your people in Your house…" She stopped, hearing the inauthentic words in her own ears.

She glanced up in time to see Aunt Lori looking over at her.

"Why did you stop, honey?"

Cara sighed. "I sound like Uncle Alan."

"That's not so bad."

Cara gave her aunt a quick smile. "No, but…"

"It's not from your heart." Aunt Lori finished the sentence for her.

"I don't know if I can pray from my heart." Cara tightened her grip on her aunt's hands.

"Why not?" Aunt Lori asked, her smile sad.

Cara sighed lightly, knowing she would have to be

honest with her aunt. "I don't think I've been able to pray since…"

"Audra died?" Aunt Lori stroked Cara's hand with her thumbs.

"Mom's death was the beginning."

"And what was the end?"

Cara looked down, working her lower lip between her teeth. "I know it sounds kind of funny now, maybe even a bit childish, but after Nicholas and I broke up, I haven't been able to pray at all."

"That was a hard time for you."

"Not as hard as what you're dealing with right now."

"I still have Alan's love. I know how much you cared for Nicholas and I know the hurt he caused in your life made you pull further away from God." Aunt Lori looked down at their joined hands, her thumbs still making their soothing circles around Cara's hand. "I hoped that by asking you to pray, you would be able to at least let God's love fill you. Let God break down that barrier you've put up between you and Him."

"He was the one that put it up, Aunt Lori," Cara whispered.

"God always seeks us," Aunt Lori assured her. "He never puts up walls. We do."

Cara's soul twisted and turned. "Love hurts, Aunt Lori. It hurts so much."

Her aunt reached out and cupped her cheek. "That's the risk of loving, my dear girl."

Cara let the words settle into the wrenching of her soul. She knew her aunt was right, but she also knew, for now, she wasn't going to take the chance of getting hurt again.

"I'll pray this time," Aunt Lori said, taking her hands.

Cara bowed her head and let her aunt's prayer wash over her. And for the merest moment, she felt a nudging against the walls she'd put around her heart.

She knew that everything had changed. In the space of a heartbeat, or lack of a heartbeat, her world had spun around.

There was no way she could wander around the streets of Malta knowing that her uncle, the man she thought of as her father, lay helpless and recuperating from a devastating heart attack.

She had no choice now. She would have to cancel her trip and stay in Cochrane to support her aunt. Even if it meant running the risk of seeing Nicholas and having her pain reinforced.

Though she had told her aunt she didn't pray much, she caught herself praying that when the time came she would be able to leave with her heart still intact.

Nicholas pulled up to his father's house and slammed on the brakes, dust swirling around his truck as it fishtailed then abruptly stopped. He was being juvenile and he knew it, but his anger and frustration had to find some release and driving like a fool seemed to be a part of it.

The events of the past days piled on top of each other. Seeing Cara in at the clinic then at church. She acted so cool. So remote. He knew part of it was his own fault. He'd put up his own barriers to her and he had to remind himself to keep them up.

Like you did at the hospital?

For a brief moment, when he and Cara had seen Alan lying on the hospital bed, he thought she might lean on him just a little longer. But she had quickly pulled herself together and had drawn away from his support.

Nicholas grabbed his tie from the seat and opened the door, his anger fading with each moment. He felt tired and drained. In the next couple of weeks he had to get fences fixed, his haying done and then get ready for another work trip overseas.

He sighed as he trudged up the sidewalk. He wished he could stay home, at the ranch. Wished he could get on his horse and head up into the mountains.

He thought of Cara's past insistence that he not go back to work and the ensuing fight that had sent her running.

Nicholas stopped at the top step of the house and, turning, let his eyes drift over the valley spread out before him. Cattle dotted the pasture near the house. His purebred herd painstakingly built up by him and his father over the past five years, had been paid for by the work he did.

Beyond this valley lay the land he and his father had purchased back from the bank after his parents' divorce. When missed payments led to foreclosure, this, too, had been paid for by his work. He had focused his entire life on this ranch.

He could have found work closer by, but it wouldn't have paid near what he got from working on oil rigs. The time off gave him the opportunity to work on the ranch. His father managed the ranch while he was gone. All in all it had been a convenient and lucrative arrangement.

One he wasn't in a position to change. Not yet. He knew the beating his father's pride took when they had to go, hat in hand, to the bank to refinance the ranch.

Four generations of Chapmans had farmed and ranched on this land and each generation had added to it and expanded it. Nicholas was the fifth generation and he wasn't going to let the ranch fail on his watch.

He knew Cara couldn't understand. She didn't have his attachment to the land. She didn't have the continuity of family and community he had. Though he didn't appreciate his father's puzzling antagonism toward Cara, he did agree with his father on one point.

Cara's lack of strong roots made it hard for her to appreciate the generations of sweat equity poured into this place. She couldn't understand how important the ranch was to him and to his father.

And if she didn't get that, then she wasn't the girl for him. Logically he knew his father was right about that.

He just had to convince his heart.

Chapter Three

"And how's Uncle Alan?" Cara asked, shifting the phone to her other hand as she slowed the car down and steered it around a tight corner. Dust from the gravel road swirled in a cloud behind her.

"He's still very tired, but the doctor says that's normal. How are you doing?" Aunt Lori sounded tired herself.

"I'm fine, busy, but things are going well. I'm on my way to take a stick out of a horse."

"Just another day at a vet practice," Aunt Lori said with a small laugh. "Uncle Alan asked me to remind Anita to do the supply checklist. He thinks the clinic is running low on—"

"You tell Uncle Alan that Anita has already sent in the order and everything at the clinic is under control." *Except my driving,* she thought, as she pushed the accelerator down, hoping she didn't hit any washboard on her way to the next call.

The Chapman ranch.

The last call she'd been on had taken too long. A sheep with trouble delivering her lambs. Something that could have been dealt with at the clinic, but the woman insisted someone come out to look at it.

Then the woman wanted her to check out her dog's gums and have a quick peek at her laying hens.

Which now meant that in spite of keeping the accelerator floored, she was twenty minutes late.

So it was easier to blame her heavily beating heart on the pressure of trying to get there on time rather than possibly seeing Nicholas again.

"But I gotta run, Aunty Lori. Tell Uncle Alan I'll be there tonight and give him a full report of how things are going."

"You take care, sweetie. I'll have supper ready for you when you come."

Cara smiled as she hung up. She was busy, sure, but there was a lot to be said for coming home after a hard day of work to supper cooking on the stove.

While she enjoyed cooking, many of her suppers back in Vancouver consisted of pizza or a bowl of cereal in front of the television. Hardly nutritious, despite the claims of the cereal manufacturers.

Cara made the last turn up the winding road leading to the ranch. She allowed herself a quick look at the mountains edging the fields. The bright spring sun turned the snowcapped peaks a brilliant white, creating a sharp relief against the achingly blue sky.

When she and Nicholas were dating, they seldom came to the ranch. This suited Cara just fine. Every time she came, she received the silent treatment from Nicholas's father, which created a heavy discomfort. Cara knew Nicholas's father didn't approve of her, though she was never exactly sure why.

All she knew was each time she saw Dale he glowered at her from beneath his heavy brows and said nothing at all.

So she and Nicholas usually went to a movie, hung out at her uncle and aunt's place or visited Nicholas's best friend, Lorne Hughes.

So when she found out the call came from Dale Chapman, she was already dreading the visit, and running late just made it more so.

She parked the car and, as she got out, she heard Dale Chapman speaking.

She grabbed a container with the supplies she thought she might need out of the trunk of the car. Then she headed around the barn to the corrals, following the sound of Mr. Chapman's voice.

Dale was holding the horse's head, talking in an unfamiliar gentle tone to his horse.

Just for a moment, Cara was caught unawares. She wasn't used to gentleness from Dale Chapman in any form.

"Good morning, Dale. Sorry I'm late."

His cowboy hat was pulled low on his head, shading his eyes, but when he looked up, his mouth was set in grim lines.

"I came as soon as I could." Cara knew trying to explain to him about unexpected problems with her previous case would be a waste of time.

Cara set the kit down in what seemed to be a safe place, pulled a pair of latex gloves out and slipped them on as she walked toward the horse.

She knew from the phone call that Dale had found the animal with a stick puncturing the muscles of its leg.

From here she could see the stick hanging down between his front legs. As she bent over to get a closer took, her mind skimmed frantically through her anatomy lessons, trying to picture which muscles the stick could have injured.

Watching the horse to gauge its reaction, she gently touched the leg, feeling for heat. But he didn't flinch.

"When did this happen?" she asked, looking up at the wound. There was surprising little blood on the stick, which led her to believe it hadn't punctured anything important.

"Um…let's see…" Mr. Chapman hesitated, as if trying to recall.

"I found Duke this morning in the new pasture."

The deep voice behind her reverberated across her senses. Then Nicholas crouched down beside her and she caught the scent of hay and the faintest hint of soap and aftershave.

She couldn't stop the quick flashback to another time when she was at the ranch watching her uncle working on one of Nicholas's horses. It was the first time she met him.

Too easily she recalled how attracted she had been to him. And when his eyes had turned to her, the feeling of instant connection that had arced between them.

And right behind that came the memory of his father, watching her with narrowed eyes. *He still doesn't like me,* she thought, wondering once again why.

Not that it mattered. The way Nicholas acted around her, she was sure the son and the father were finally on the same page as far as she was concerned.

"Doesn't look like any veins or arteries are punctured," Cara said, gently touching the stick. It slid easily to one side. "I'm guessing it slipped between the muscles."

Duke shifted its weight and the stick moved down a bit more.

"I'm going to pull this out, but before I do, I want to give him some anesthetic," she said as she went back to the kit for a syringe and a needle. "How heavy is he—"

But as she spoke, Nicholas gave her the weight, as if anticipating her question.

She drew up the proper amount, pleased to see her hand held steady. She walked back to the horse but Nicholas was already at the Duke's head, brushing the mane back, giving her a clear injection site.

"Are you sure you should just pull that stick out?" Dale's voice said over her shoulder as she found a site for the needle. "That's going to be trouble."

"The stick is simply inserted between the sheaths housing the muscles. Pulling it out won't cause more problems."

Cara stifled her momentary irritation with Nicholas's father. When she had worked for her uncle before, she had occasionally encountered resistance from people who didn't think a woman was tough enough to do large animal work. And while she knew Nicholas's father never particularly cared for her, she didn't think that dislike extended to her capabilities as a vet.

"You haven't been doing this for a while—"

"I'll need a hose and water," Cara said, interrupting his questions. "Could you get that for me, Mr. Chapman?" she asked, gently tugging on the stick.

He grumbled a moment, but left, giving Cara room to breathe.

Cara eased the stick the rest of the way out, moving more carefully than she might have with someone else's horse, with someone else watching. She wanted to prove herself to Nicholas—to prove she wasn't as incompetent as his father seemed to think.

The stick came out without too much exertion. It was exactly as she had said. It had slipped between the muscles and had only punctured the skin.

"Thankfully the injury isn't major." She stood up and held out the stick to Nicholas, who took it from her without a word.

She got a large jug of distilled water and a bottle with a squirt cap from the car.

She gently ran her hands over the wound, then, pulling apart the skin, began to rinse. "I'm just doing an initial cleaning of the wound to make sure everything is okay," she said, intent on her task. "The rest will have to be done with a hose."

"Won't that be too cold?" Nicholas asked.

Cara shook her head, gently cleaning away a few bits of wood she had rinsed out of the wound. "The cold water will probably be soothing and help reduce any inflammation."

"And it will heal on its own? You're not going to stitch it up?"

"The wound needs to stay open so you can irrigate it. It will heal better that way."

"Really?"

"Are you questioning my abilities, as well?" she asked, as an edge entered her voice.

"What do you mean, 'as well'?"

Cara didn't reply. The words had spilled out in a wave of frustration with Mr. Chapman and Nicholas, but mostly with herself for her silly reactions to their presence.

"Duke is my father's favorite roping horse. You can't

blame him for making sure he's being taken good care of." Nicholas frowned at her. He seemed surprised at her anger.

And he should be. When they were dating, she never lost her temper. She had always done what was expected. Been the one to keep the peace.

Fat lot of good that had done her.

Now, despite her simmering anger, she still couldn't break an age-old habit of avoiding confrontation, so instead of defending herself, she simply turned back to her patient and kept working.

"Here's the hose," Dale called out as he climbed over the corral fence. "You sure this will work?"

Cara didn't bother to answer. She just held her hand out for the end.

"You want to be careful with the angle of the hose. You don't want to be streaming the water directly upward into the wound," Cara said, demonstrating what she meant. "And keep the pressure low. You don't want to reinjure any regenerating tissue." She handed the hose to Nicholas and straightened, easing the crick out of her back.

"How will I know when I'm done?"

"Just do it for about ten minutes at a time. You'll also want to rinse the edges of the wound to keep it clean and to prevent it from scabbing over."

"It will never grow together." Dale planted his hands on his hips as if challenging her expertise. "You'll need to stitch it."

"I've seen a horse with a foot-long gash in its side that healed up on its own," Cara replied. "It's quite surprising how the body heals."

Dale didn't reply, and Cara hoped he was finished questioning and doubting her abilities.

She crouched down again, getting a closer look at what Nicholas was doing.

"Just keep doing that," she said, gently prying aside the skin. "I don't see any more bits of wood coming out and the water is running clean, so I think the bleeding has gone down."

She gently ran her hands down the leg, to double-check. "I'll give him some long-acting penicillin and I think that's all I need to do."

Nicholas stayed where he was and shot her a quick glance. As soon as their eyes met, she felt a lightness in her chest, as if someone had pulled her breath away.

Stop. Stop.

She caught her breath again, wishing her heart would settle down. How would she last until Gordon Moen, the new vet, came if a few glances from Nicholas could create such a strong reaction?

Cara closed the kit, latched it shut and drew a long, steadying breath, thankful she was just about done. "Do you have any more questions?"

Nicholas held her gaze and she saw a question in his eyes. It seemed as if he was going to say something, but then he drew back and shook his head. "If I do, I guess I can call the clinic."

She nodded, then turned away, surprised at a little flare of disappointment.

When she got to her car she was dismayed to see that Mr. Chapman had followed her.

"So you're all done?" he asked, staring at her from beneath his cowboy hat.

"The wound is clear and it looks like it should heal up just fine. I'll come by next week to double-check if I have time." Cara kept her tone professional. Detached, even, as she wondered why Dale had followed her.

Dale folded his arms over his chest, frowning. "He's over you, you know." His voice was quiet, determined. "He's started dating again."

She shouldn't care. Of course Nicholas would date again.

"That's good. I'm glad for him."

"He's got his own plans and his own life," he said, and though his voice had a threatening edge, as he spoke Cara caught the faintest note of desperation. Did he think she had any influence over his son's behavior?

"Again, I'm glad for him and you," she said, keeping her tone even. "Now if you'll excuse me, I have another call to make."

She pushed past him, her heart pounding with a variety of emotions. Frustration with Dale and her own silly reaction to Nicholas.

Too emotionally draining, she thought on the car ride back. Give it time.

She walked into the clinic and glanced at the clock as her stomach growled.

"Bill, you here?" she called out.

"He went out on a call," Anita replied from the front of the office. Anita came to the back of the clinic where Cara was replenishing her kit, wiping her hands on a towel.

"Did he say when he'd be back?"

"He had to go to Hunt's place and you know what a zoo that is."

"So, not until this afternoon." Cara sighed. Her workload just got heavier. She had a few appointments after lunch and she hoped no emergencies cropped up in the meantime.

Anita gave her an apologetic smile. "I know you've had a busy morning, but I have to run to the bank and deal with an overdraft. Do you mind covering the office for me?"

Cara didn't want to, but she didn't feel like telling Anita that. "If I get an emergency call, I'll have to call you back," Cara warned.

"Yeah. Sure." Anita flashed her a smile. "You're a dear. I'll make it up to you sometime."

Cara nodded as she closed the lid of the kit. Anita already owed her two lunch hours and a coffee break, but Cara wasn't about to get fussy about collecting on them. Once Gordon arrived, her job here was done.

Then, two minutes after Anita left, the buzzer to the front door sounded.

Of course, Cara thought, wiping her hands.

Trista Elderveld stood in the foyer, holding aloft two plastic bags and a tray of coffee. Her trim suit made her look far more professional and put together than Cara knew she actually was.

"Hey, girlfriend," Trista said with a quick grin. She put down the bags and coffee and gave her old friend a hug. "I'm so sorry to hear about your uncle."

Cara returned the hug. "Thanks. It's so good to see you again."

Trista pulled back and tugged at Cara's hair. "I like the longer length. Looks romantic."

"I was going for 'easier to care for,'" Cara said, deflecting Trista's loaded comment. "What do you have there?" she asked, pointing to the bags on the counter.

"Coffee and sub sandwiches from Hortons."

Cara's stomach groaned as she caught the scent of roasted onion. "You are a lifesaver. I just got back from a call at the Chapman ranch and thought I'd have to miss lunch."

"Really?" Trista angled her a curious glance. "And how did that go?"

"I was working. That's how it went." Cara's stomach reminded her again that she hadn't eaten anything since the banana she gobbled down on the way to work this morning. "Why don't we go eat in my uncle's office so the front doesn't smell like a deli."

"Did you see Nicholas at all?" Trista asked as she followed Cara down the hall to the back office. "Did you talk to him? I heard he went to the hospital with you and your aunt."

"We're not talking about Nicholas, okay?" Cara said, keeping her tone firm, just in case Trista didn't get the hint.

"Changing subject, now." Trista unwrapped her sandwich. "How's your uncle doing?"

"He wants to come home already, but the doctor wants to keep an eye on him for a while."

"You doing okay, jumping back into large animal after treating puppies and guppies at your last job?" Trista asked with a grin.

"It's a nice change of pace." Cara took another bite and sighed with satisfaction. "No one makes sandwiches like Hortons. Thanks a bunch for doing this."

"I had an ulterior motive," Trista said, popping a pickle in her mouth. "I had stuff I needed to talk about without your aunt or uncle around. Anita told me Bill is gone on a call, so I hoped I could catch you alone."

"Sounds mysterious," Cara said, pushing an errant onion back between the slices of bread.

"Not so mysterious." Trista finished her sandwich, balled up the paper and tossed it in the garbage can. "I'm getting married."

Cara almost choked. "What? When?"

"A couple of weeks."

This time Cara did choke. Trista bounced across the room and pounded her friend on the back.

"What's the supersonic rush, girlfriend?" Cara gasped as she reached for her water bottle, struggling to gain her breath and composure.

Trista rubbed the side of her nose, then sighed. "Well, I'm pregnant."

Cara almost coughed again and was about to say something when her friend held up her hand.

"Before you say anything, you need to know that this isn't, well, wasn't a regular thing." Trista was blushing now and Cara was still speechless. "It just, well, happened. And we were talking about getting married anyway, so this just hurries up the process."

Cara sat back, still trying to absorb this information.

"Lorne's a great guy," Trista hastened to explain. "And I know he and Mandy used to be engaged, but that was different because she never liked his parents and they never really liked her."

Which sounded exactly like Nicholas's father, Cara thought.

"…but I love him and I know he loves me and I know we'll be happy together."

"That's good, I guess," Cara said, wishing she could be more enthusiastic about the situation.

Trista's smile trembled a moment and her eyes shone

as if with tears. "I wish you could be happy for me. I know I'm happy in spite of how things are going."

Cara got up and gave her dear friend a quick hug. "If he makes you happy, then I'm happy for you."

"He will and he does," Trista said, her eyeblink releasing a tear. She brushed it away and sniffed lightly. "I love him more than I ever thought I could love someone, and he'll be a great husband and a fantastic dad."

Trista's enthusiastic defense of Lorne created a genuine smile in Cara.

Trista sniffed again, then looked back at Cara. "So now, I'm wondering how long you're sticking around?"

Cara felt a peculiar warmth as she guessed exactly where this was going. "I guess long enough to be at your wedding."

"So will you stand up for me at my wedding?"

Cara's smile blossomed. "Of course. For all the times you stood up for me when I first came here and for all the times you stuck up for me, yes, my dear friend, I will stand up for you."

Trista laughed aloud. "I'm so glad. You know your being here is an answer to prayer." Then a horrified look crossed her features and she held her hand up. "Not that I think your uncle's heart attack is an answer to prayer, but the fact that you're here and that you're not leaving and—"

"I know what you meant," Cara said with a melancholy smile as her own emotions veered from a tinge of jealousy to genuine pleasure. "And I would be honored to be your maid of honor."

Trista heaved a satisfied sigh. "I'm so, so glad. I know the wedding is sudden, but we both knew we wanted to get married and figured why waste time on a long engagement, which worked out perfectly because that means you're here for the wedding and everything seems to be falling into place…and I should stop talking so much, shouldn't I?" Trista gave a short laugh as she twirled a strand of hair around her finger. "You know I always talk a lot when I'm nervous and I was so worried you'd say no."

"Why would I do that?" Cara tossed her own sandwich wrapper in the garbage can and leaned back to smile at her friend.

Trista flapped her hand, as if erasing the question. "Nothing. I'm just babbling."

"You can stop babbling. I will do all that is in my power to be the best maid of honor ever." Cara couldn't stop a quick glance at the clock, figuring she could spare Trista a few more minutes. After all, they had a wedding to plan.

"What's the first thing you need my help on?" Cara asked.

"Lorne and I decided we wanted an outdoor wedding so tomorrow night we're checking a place out."

"An outdoor wedding." Cara sighed, thinking of the plans she had made. Her plan had also been an outdoor wedding on a hill overlooking the mountains on Nicholas's ranch. "Where did you have in mind?"

Trista gave her hair another twirl. When she looked down, avoiding her gaze, a trickle of premonition chilled Cara's neck.

"Nicholas said we could get married at the ranch."

Her words fell like stones. No. She couldn't plan someone else's wedding at Nicholas's ranch.

"And one other thing," Trista said, clearing her throat. "Lorne asked Nicholas to be his best man."

"Trista—"

"It's not a setup," Trista rushed to say. "Honestly. I knew you wouldn't be crazy about the idea and you can turn me down if you want, but I really, really could use your help and I want you to be my bridesmaid. Though you've been gone for a while, you're still my best friend. You're the only one who gets me." Trista sighed. "And you know how my mother is when she's flustered. She's no help at all and of all my high-school friends, you're the only one I stay in touch with and the only one who is organized enough to help me out."

Cara held Trista's earnest gaze while her practical nature fought with her rising emotions.

Trista had been her dearest friend since she moved to Cochrane. All through college and vet school, Trista was the only one Cara kept in contact with. It was Trista who had listened to her long-distance sorrow when Cara ran away from Nicholas.

If her friend wanted her help, then Cara knew she had to get past her own problems and do this.

"Okay. I'll be there."

"Tomorrow night. Eight o'clock. We're meeting at the ranch." Trista got up then gave Cara a hug. "I know this could be awkward, but hey, it's been three years and you're moving on, right? Like you told me?"

Cara nodded her agreement. She had to make Trista believe what she had told her all along. She was well and truly over Nicholas. "Of course I am. It will be fine."

But as she waved goodbye, her mind slipped back to that moment in the hospital when Nicholas had stood at her side at her uncle's bed.

Fine was too small a word to cover the emotions that

could still grab her. She'd tried praying, but it was as if God, as He had before, didn't listen. Or didn't care.

You've got to take care of yourself, her mother's voice mocked her.

And you've got to guard your heart, her own memories told her.

Chapter Four

He's built a new shed, Cara thought as she took inventory of the main yard of Nicholas's ranch. And torn down the old one. The barn had gotten a new coat of paint and the fences of the corrals were painted, as well.

A faint breeze moved across the yard and Cara wrapped her thin sweater around her. Cara and her aunt had gone to the hospital to visit her uncle and as they were heading home Cara finally mentioned where she was going afterward.

She'd seen the questions in her aunt's eyes, but thankfully Aunt Lori said nothing.

Cara walked farther, her eyes moving from the buildings to the fields and pastures. The land, broken by swaths of evergreens, flowed upward to the blue-gray mountains with their jagged, snow-covered peaks guarding the ranch.

She'd seen the place for the first time when her uncle came here to do a Cesarean on one of Nicholas's purebred cows. Cara came to assist and learn what she could. Uncle Alan had walked briskly toward the barn, a man intent on his work while she had dragged her feet, unable to look away from the craggy peaks capped with snow. She had wondered what it would be like to wake up every morning and see this breathtaking view.

And for a little while, when she and Nicholas were serious, the wondering moved toward reality.

Don't venture down that path, she reminded herself, pulling her thoughts back to the job at hand. *Stay in the present, the now.*

Cara glanced around the yard, dismayed to see that neither Trista nor Lorne had arrived.

She walked around the wooden fences of the corral, to see better, and as she did, the sound of hoofbeats caught her attention.

She looked toward the noise.

And her heart did a slow somersault.

A horse and rider moved toward her. Nicholas and Two Bits, she thought, recognizing the distinct blaze on the horse's dun face.

Nicholas had his cowboy hat pulled low over his face and he looked toward the mountains, as well, away from Cara. He held the reins loosely, moving easily with the chestnut horse as it cantered toward the corrals. Dust covered Nicholas's faded blue jeans. The tan shirt, with its cuffs rolled up, was also caked with dust.

Nicholas pulled Two Bits up short, then, with a subtle movement of his hands on the reins, turned his horse toward her. As horse and rider came near, Cara steeled herself. Seeing Nicholas on the horse, in his natural environment, resurrected a wave of nostalgia and unwelcome emotions.

Two Bits whinnied and Nicholas glanced up, a quick movement of his head.

In that moment, their eyes met and Cara felt it again.

That connection she thought she'd moved beyond. The attraction she thought she'd pushed aside.

"So, what brings you here?" he asked, pulling up beside her, curiosity edging his voice.

Had she come on the wrong day? Had she misunderstood?

"You come to check on Duke?" he continued.

"How is he?" she asked, seizing on the question as she tried to get her bearings.

"Good. I have to give him another shot tomorrow." Nicholas seemed to sense her puzzlement as he pushed his hat farther back on his head. "But you didn't come for Duke, did you?"

"Trista said we were meeting here to talk about the wedding. Her and Lorne's wedding, that is." Cara clamped her mouth shut, angry at the flush staining her cheeks. She took a step back so she wouldn't have to crane her neck to look up at him.

Nicholas frowned, then, in one fluid motion, got off the horse. He pulled his hat off and hit it against his pants, releasing a cloud of dust. "Today?"

"That's what I understood." She was fairly sure she hadn't gotten the date wrong. Yesterday Trista had called her twice to confirm.

He ran his hand through his thick, dark hair, as if trying to dredge up the memory, his gray eyes looking confused. "I forgot completely about it."

Cara watched his hands, then swallowed, forcing herself not to take another step back.

"They're not here yet," Cara said, "but I'm pretty sure we had agreed to meet here today."

"And you came because you're the maid of honor," Nicholas said, a faint edge to his voice.

The hairs on the back of her neck rose up at his tone. "I hope that's not a problem?"

Nicholas shot her a frown. "Not unless it is for you."

"It's been three years. Long enough to have moved on," she said, thankful she sounded so casual and in control.

"And you have," Nicholas added.

His comment made it sound as if she had caused the breakup.

However, she could be an adult about this. She was only around for a while and then moving on.

"Looks like you've been busy with some improvements to the ranch," she said, striving for an airy tone of interest.

"Dad and I did a bunch of painting last time I was home. I'll have enough money to do some reno on the house when I come back from my next job."

Next job. A good reminder to Cara about where his priorities lay.

The growl of a diesel truck broke into the moment and with relief Cara looked around to see Trista clambering out of Lorne's truck.

"Hey there," she called, waving as she strode toward them. "Sorry we're late. Lorne had a flat tire on the way here."

Lorne, a tall, slender young man, his baseball cap shoved over dark hair, followed Trista, his walk an easy-going lope.

"Hey, bud," Lorne said, sending a grin Nicholas's way. "Were you out riding?"

Then before Nicholas could answer, Trista heaved a heavy sigh. "Don't tell me. You forgot."

Nicholas's gaze flicked from Trista to Lorne then back to Cara. "I did. Sorry."

"Honestly, Nicholas. How many messages do I have to send you?" Trista complained.

"I was out riding fences the past couple of days."

"I told your dad."

"I got the message. I just forgot. Sorry." Nicholas slapped his hat against his ripped pants, releasing another cloud of dust. "Give me twenty minutes."

"I'll put Two Bits away for you," Lorne said, taking the reins of the horse from his friend as he shot a frown at his friend. "You might want to rethink the wardrobe."

"Yeah, yeah. I'll be right back."

Trista shook her head as she watched Nicholas jog toward the farmhouse. "That guy never changes. This ranch is his everything, that's for sure."

Which was something Cara had to keep in mind if she wanted to keep her heart whole.

Ten minutes later, Two Bits was rolling on his back in the pasture with the other horses, looking ungainly and undignified but happy. Cara laughed at the sight.

Then Nicholas joined them, shoving the tails of his plaid shirt into his blue jeans.

"Sorry. Again," he said, pushing his still-damp hair away from his face. A fan of pale lines radiated from his eyes, which were steel gray against his already tan skin. The eyes of a man used to squinting at the sun, looking out over pastures and hills.

"I know I forgot all about today, but I thought about the wedding and I had a few places in mind for the ceremony," Nicholas said, dropping a clean hat on his head. "One of them is close by, the other we'd have to drive to."

"Let's check the close one first," Trista said, pulling out a digital camera.

"It's over here. Past the barn and down the hill a bit."

As they walked through the yard, Cara felt a tremor of recognition, fairly sure they were headed to the same place she'd had in mind for her own wedding. The same place where Nicholas had proposed to her.

They headed around the barn, past a few tall pine trees and as they came into the open, Trista squealed with delight.

"This is perfect. Absolutely perfect," she said.

Cara followed, closing her mind off to her own memories, erasing the vision of herself standing on the grassy knoll overlooking a broad valley edged by trees flowing upward to the blue-peaked mountains.

"What do you think, Cara?" Trista exclaimed. "Isn't this gorgeous?"

"It is. Absolutely gorgeous," Cara said, looking out over the view, hoping Trista didn't catch the wistful tone in her voice.

She shot a quick glance at Nicholas, who was frowning at her, as if he had heard it. She held his gaze for a heartbeat, then her eyes slid back to the valley spread out below them. "You could put an arbor here with potted flowers tucked up against it," she said, walking to the edge of the hill. "That way you keep the view and you delineate the space for the ceremony."

"Oh, I like that," Trista said. "What kind of arbor?"

"Why not get your father to make one out of willows or something like that? You could buy some preplanted pots of flowers from the nursury and stagger them along the edges of the arbor and hang them from the top bar. Right about now they'd be clearing out their inventory and with a bit of pruning and repotting, they'd be in great shape by the wedding."

"I knew you'd be able to help me out," Trista said. "You seem to know exactly what to do."

That was only because, at one time, these ideas had been for her own wedding.

"We could rent chairs from the church," Cara added, walking slowly around the open area, gently teasing out her own memories, her old plans. "We can hang some pots on shepherd hooks stuck in the dirt beside the chairs. Sort of like living pew markers."

"You are so good at this," Trista said with a satisfied note in her voice. "I knew I got the right person when I asked you."

"The grass will need to be mowed," Nicholas said, "and I'll need help setting everything up."

"I could get my brothers to come out and help with all that stuff," Lorne said.

"Who is doing the service?" Cara asked.

Trista pulled a small book out of her purse. "Pastor Samuels said he'd be willing to do the service, but he wants to meet with us a couple of times before the wedding."

"I still think we should check out the church and that hall my mom was talking about," said Lorne.

Cara frowned. "But I thought having the wedding here was—"

"Lorne's mom wants a church wedding," said Trista.

"She just said it would be easier," Lorne said, his tone becoming defensive.

"Everyone has their wedding at a church and their reception at a hall. I don't want to be everyone."

Lorne tugged on the brim of his hat with a jerky motion. "And she thinks that not getting married in a church is like admitting—"

"That we made a mistake?" Trista's voice rose a notch and Cara felt their tension from here.

Obviously the bride and groom needed some space, so Cara walked to the edge of the knoll and wrapped her arms around herself as she looked out over the valley.

Below her, a dirt road snaked along the edge of the fenced field, then disappeared into a cut in the hills.

She knew the road led to the higher pastures where the cows were grazing. She had never been there, but every time Nicholas talked about the high pastures, his voice grew quiet with reverence.

Then the hairs on the back of her neck bristled and she didn't need to look around to know Nicholas stood right behind her.

How, after all this time, could she still be so aware of him? And why was he seeking her out?

The longer he stood there, the more aware of him she became.

"I was wondering how Alan was doing?" he finally asked, his voice quiet. "I meant to go and visit, but I had too much to do here."

Her mind cast back to that moment they had shared as they stood beside her uncle's bedside. How she had leaned against him and allowed him to support her.

That had been a mistake. In the past few years she had learned that while one may be the loneliest number, it was also the safest.

Cara felt the silvery flash of the beginnings of a headache. The week had been too busy, she thought. She'd had too much on her mind—that was why she felt so vulnerable.

"He's doing okay," she said. "The doctor said he could come home tomorrow. I'm hoping to visit him tonight."

"I'm glad he's okay. Must be hard on your aunt."

Cara thought of Aunt Lori's quiet stoicism, which almost cut her more than any fussing and fretting would have.

"She's concerned, of course," Cara said. "But we're both very thankful he's doing so well."

"And the clinic?"

"He won't be able to return to work full-time for a while."

"I heard he and Bill had a new vet coming?"

Cara nodded, her eyes still staring sightlessly at the view below her. "He's not here for another three weeks."

"And you're staying until then?"

Was she imagining the faint hint of disappointment in his voice? Or was she simply projecting her own misgivings onto him?

Had he missed her? Had he thought of her after she left?

"I'll have to. I can't go to Europe knowing that Uncle Alan can't work."

"I hope he can get back to it soon," Nicholas said. "It would be a shame if he has to slow down. He enjoys his work."

"He must," Cara said, shooting Nicholas a quick glance. "He's been here forever."

"You sound surprised."

"I can't imagine what it's like to be tied down to one place," she said, hoping her wistful feelings didn't enter her voice.

His eyes narrowed and she didn't imagine the frown

shoving his eyebrows together. "No. I didn't think you could."

She caught a note of anger threading through his voice and then he turned and walked away from her.

He had misunderstood her.

And she knew he saw her the way his father did. Rootless. Unwilling to commit. The thought kindled her anger. She wouldn't have said yes to marrying him if that was the case, but if he couldn't see that, then she couldn't change his opinion of her now.

Just as well, she thought, turning back to the scenery in front of her. Anger was an easier emotion to sustain around Nicholas than the yearning winding around her heart each time she saw him.

Cara waited a moment, then followed him to where Trista and Lorne were still talking, hoping she could sustain her emotional distance from him over the next while.

"I don't think we need to look at the other place," Trista was saying, her smile as bright as the summer sun shining down on them. "Lorne agrees with having the wedding here. This is the perfect spot. We've got lots of room for guests to park and the view is stunning." Trista flashed a grin at Cara. "What do you think?"

"If you two agree on it," she said.

"My mom will just have to get over the fact that we aren't having a church wedding," Lorne said. It looked as if their differences had been ironed out. "If this is what Trista wants, then that's good enough for me." Lorne looked down at Trista with such love and devotion that Cara's heart faltered at the sight.

They looked so happy and Cara knew she had to set her own feelings aside for the sake of her close friend's happiness.

Trista released a sigh of satisfaction as she tucked her arm into Lorne's. "I can't thank you enough, Nicholas, for suggesting this. It's absolutely perfect for a wedding."

"Yeah, I thought so, too," Nicholas said.

"And I want to let you know that my mom and dad are putting on an engagement party for us at our house on Saturday," Trista said. "We'd like you two to come."

You two. As if they were still a couple.

"I'll be there," Cara said just as her phone started to buzz. Cara pulled it out and glanced at the number on her screen.

"Sorry, people, I gotta go," she said.

"Is it your uncle?" Nicholas asked, his concern giving her a surprising lift.

"No. It's a vet call." She gave him a tight smile, then walked swiftly to her car, as if outrunning her own emotions.

Chapter Five

The Elderveld place was a zoo, Nicholas thought, watching the aimless movement of bodies from the house to the decorated yard. Minilights twinkled from the branches of the shrubs and trees surrounding the large front lawn. Tables and stacks of chairs filled one corner of the yard. Some older women were directing the movements, contradicting each other from the sounds of the complaints being registered by the men by the chairs.

He waited a moment before descending into the chaos, catching his breath from his mad drive over. His hair was still damp from the quick shower he'd taken to wash off any hay dust that had accumulated while he'd been swathing the hayfields.

Thankfully he'd gotten all the hay cut. But just barely.

"Are you sure you want the cake out yet?" one female voice called out.

"What do I do with the fruit platter?"

"If I get asked one more question I'm going to scream," Trista's mother called from inside the house. "When is Cara coming?"

The sound of her name made him take another breath.

He felt as if he teetered on the edge of an unpredict-able wave that had the potential to swamp him. And it wasn't the number of people milling around the yard or the decibel level that bothered him.

Cara was going to be here.

The other day on the ranch, he'd caught a hint of their old relationship, of that unusual rapport he and Cara shared from their first "hello."

And he realized that he had missed her.

She's not staying. She's leaving as soon as she can, he reminded himself.

And if he wanted to move on, he had to get used to seeing her and keep old emotions from clouding his judg-ment. She wasn't a part of his life or his life's plan any-more.

Nicholas took a breath and headed toward the yard just as one of Trista's teenage sisters came stomping down the sidewalk toward him. Her T-shirt was a neon storm, matching the flurry of color in her hair, and her blue jeans were ripped at the knees. "I'm not changing," she yelled. "You have to take me as I am." Then she looked ahead and her bright-pink eyelids narrowed over her eyes.

"What are you staring at, mister?" she snapped.

"Nothing," he said, feeling intimidated by her strident teenage attitude.

"Like the shirt, Twyla."

Though the voice behind him was quiet, the sound gave him an unwelcome jolt.

"Hey, Cara, about time you came," Twyla said, her voice holding the faintest note of insolence.

"Hey, yourself. Why are you smart-mouthing Mr. Chapman?" Cara now stood beside him, facing down the impudent young girl.

Today her hair hung loose, a golden cloud that rested on her narrow shoulders. She wore a flowing kind of sweater over a pink tank top, strung with a couple of necklaces, and slim blue jeans.

She looked amazing.

Twyla folded her skinny arms over her equally skinny waist, ignoring Cara as her gaze slipped up and down Nicholas as if inspecting him. "Is this Nicholas, Uncle Lorne's best man?"

"Yes. He is."

Twyla's eyes took on a peculiar glint. "He's pretty hot. Trista said you used to date him," she said, sounding catty. "Why did you dump him?"

Despite his decision to act casual, Nicholas couldn't stop the sideways slide of his gaze toward Cara, wondering what she was going to say.

"This isn't a reality television show, so I don't have to tell you." Cara gave her a quick smile.

Twyla rolled her eyes and strolled away, leaving Nicholas and Cara by themselves.

"So, I guess we're supposed to help out with this thing," Nicholas said, hoping he sounded cool and composed. "Do you have any idea what we're doing?"

"Trista told me to show up early, that's all I know."

Nicholas pushed his cowboy hat back on his head as he glanced around the chaos of the yard. Mr. Elderveld was talking to Mr. Hughes. Lorne and his brothers were leaning on a stack of chairs, laughing. And from the house, Nicholas could hear more complaining.

"I'm getting nervous about this wedding," Nicholas said.

"Has Trista talked to you about any of her plans?"

"Other than the fact that they're getting married on

the yard, no. And Lorne keeps telling me Trista is in charge. He's a great guy, but he keeps talking about letting go and trusting, which doesn't make for good wedding planning."

"You're taking this pretty seriously," Cara said with a light laugh.

"Marriage is serious," he said.

She caught a faint undercurrent and wondered if he was referring to his mother. Or her.

Cara pushed out her lower lip and blew out her breath. "I'm worried Trista has taken too much on. I don't know how she'll pull all this together in the time they have left."

"Lorne doesn't even know how many people they're inviting."

"I guess I'll have to help her a bit more."

"You don't have time for that, do you?"

"I owe Trista a lot, so for her, I'll make time."

"I'll have to make time, too. That wedding is taking place on my yard and I don't want a fiasco on my hands."

"Fair enough." She gave a delicate shrug of her shoulder. "So what do you want to do?"

"I'd like to get together tomorrow with Lorne and Trista and make a few plans," Nicholas said.

He didn't imagine her slight withdrawal, and he wondered if he shouldn't have offered to help. But what could he do?

It was either get involved or have potential chaos on his hands and on his ranch in a couple of weeks.

Neither option was great.

Then Cara nodded. "That'd be good. Bill is on call tomorrow."

"So we'll talk more then."

He could tell she wasn't crazy about the idea either.

That didn't matter to him. There was no way he was having a disorganized wedding at his place.

"Hey. Chapman. Over here." Lorne was calling him.

"I gotta go," Nicholas said, jutting his chin in Lorne's direction.

"Let me know what time you want me there tomorrow."

"Come after church," he said. His father would be at some horse clinic that day, so it would be safest to have everyone come then.

Then he turned and walked over to where his friend stood chatting with his brothers. Lorne winked at Nicholas when he came near.

"So, I saw you talking with Cara?"

Nicholas gave him a dry look. "Yeah. What of it?"

Lorne held his hands up. "I'm guessing…you're still ticked at her?"

"I'm guessing people will get hungry soon so we should start putting chairs out."

"Oh, yeah." Lorne looked at his watch. "Looks like we are running a bit late."

"Why don't you get your brothers to put out the tables, and we can put chairs around them. The women will want to put cloths on them or some such thing."

Lorne shrugged. "Who knows."

Nicholas shook his head and started unstacking the first set of chairs. But as he worked and against his will, Nicholas glanced over his shoulder and each time he saw Cara organizing things on her end.

Lorne caught the direction of his gaze, frowned, and drew Nicholas aside by the shoulder. "Are you sure you're okay with this? I mean, with Cara and all?"

Nicholas forced a laugh. "It's over, Lorne. Has been for three years."

Lorne shrugged. "Maybe, but I know you cared about her and I didn't get the whole attraction thing until I met Trista. If what you had with Cara was anything like what I have with Trista—"

"If what I had with Cara was the same, we would have been married already," Nicholas said, unable to keep the sharp note out of his voice.

"But it's still gotta be hard to see her like this. I told Trista she had to ask someone else, but she wouldn't and neither would I, so here you two are. Stuck with seeing each other. Sorry."

Nicholas shrugged. "I'll deal. It's sort of like that horse I used to have. The one that spooked every time something brushed its stomach."

"I remember the time he dumped you in the patch of thistles," Lorne said with a laugh. "But I don't get the Cara connection."

"Remember how I fixed the problem?"

Lorne nodded, but still looked puzzled.

"I took it in the corral. Brushed it with sticks and sacks and my hand and kept at it until it got desensitized. Until it didn't jump each time it saw a stick or something coming at it." Nicholas lifted one shoulder in a slow shrug. "I just have to do the same with Cara. Get desensitized."

Lorne nodded slowly, as if he didn't quite get it but was willing to go along with the idea. "Desensitized. Sure. Whatever."

"And the more I see her, the less spooked I'll get."

"Just make sure you don't get spooked the day of my wedding."

"I'll be there." Nicholas slapped his friend on the

shoulder. "Now let's finish with those chairs before the women start nagging. Then we can get going on those lanterns I see piled by the trees."

Half an hour later, chaos had fled and order had been restored and Mr. Elderveld was calling out for people's attention. Both sets of parents of the bride and groom stood side by side, fidgeting and tossing quick glances at each other.

Nicholas knew Lorne's mother, Mrs. Hughes, hated fuss and hated being the center of attention. Yet there she stood in her party clothes, smiling at her son and Trista, who sat at a table beside them.

"We'd like to thank everyone for coming here," Mr. Elderveld was saying once the noise settled down. "I'm hoping the weather for the wedding is as cooperative as it has been for this party." He glanced down at his daughter and gave her a loving smile. "I'm so thankful we can celebrate this special occasion and though I know the wedding is only a couple of weeks away, we wanted to do things right and in this family that means we have an engagement dinner." He glanced over at Lorne's father. "I'd now like to ask Mr. Hughes to say a blessing on the food."

Lorne's father stepped forward. "My wife and I would like to thank Mr. and Mrs. Elderveld for hosting this party. This means a lot." Mr. Hughes tucked his hands in the back pockets of his pants, glancing at his son and future daughter-in-law. "We all know this is a difficult situation for you two, but we want to show you that we support you both and are thankful you are taking this step. You are a blessing to us from the Lord in so many ways. Your future wedding is a celebration and, as Mr. Elderveld said, this engagement dinner is part of that." He paused a moment, glancing around the crowd as if making sure everyone there understood. "Now if you could all bow your heads, I'll ask God for a blessing on this evening and on the bridal couple and their future plans."

As Mr. Hughes spoke, a peculiar sensation curled through Nicholas's midsection.

He thought of his own father. Dale Chapman had openly struggled with his feelings toward Cara. How would he have reacted had the two of them been in the same situation as Lorne and Trista?

Would he have been as supportive? As encouraging?

Would he have been able to thank the Lord for them and to pronounce a blessing on their plans?

The thought settled, creating a restless current of uncertainty.

Was his father one of the unspoken reasons Cara had left?

Nicholas knew exactly where Cara was and he chanced a quick glance her way.

Cara was looking at Trista and her face was etched with a sorrow so strong Nicholas had to fight the urge to go to her, put his arms around her and hold her close.

And he wondered what, exactly, had created her sadness.

Cara swiped at her eyes and before she bowed her head, she looked over at him, as well.

Their gazes met and eyes held and it seemed as if time slipped backward. As if the angry words spoken about the ranch and his risky work—her sudden disappearance and long silence afterward—as if none of that had happened.

Because in that moment, awareness, as tangible as a touch, arced between them and everyone around them faded away.

For that moment it was just he and Cara as time hovered.

Then Cara jerked her head to the side, breaking the connection.

And as she did, Nicholas knew that putting his relationship with Cara behind him was going to be harder than he thought.

Just get through it. Just get through this wedding stuff and then both of you will be going your separate ways. She to Montreal and you to Kuwait.

The thought depressed him, but he pushed it aside. The ranch was doing well, but every bit of money he made brought it further along.

When everything was exactly the way he wanted, then he would quit and ranch full-time.

And he hoped, when that happened, he was going to find someone he could love as he once loved Cara.

Chapter Six

"It's good to be home." Alan sat back in his chair, glancing around the living room with a satisfied sigh. "I can't believe it's been a week already."

To Cara, he still looked pale. And his shirt and jacket hung on his large frame. She stacked up the old magazines that had gathered on the couch and added them to the pile of newspapers she had put on the coffee table.

"And everything is still okay at the clinic?" he asked Cara. "Do you need me to stop in?"

"Everything is still under control. Don't you dare drop in," Cara said, snapping open a garbage bag. "You need to rest."

"Like you're resting?" he teased as she dumped the magazines in the bag.

"I'm not the one who had a heart attack."

"You might get one the way you've been going. You haven't sat down since I came home," he said. "Just relax."

But Cara couldn't. When she came back from the hospital she had immediately started tidying. She'd made some progress, but she'd had to ignore the disorganized pantry. She would have loved to tackle the kitchen, but her aunt was there now, making up a snack for them.

"I want to get a little more done before I go," she said, tying the handles of the garbage bag.

Uncle Alan caught her hand as she bent over to pick up the discarded coffee cup from the floor beside him. "You didn't want to go to church with your aunt? You could have easily picked me up afterward."

Cara didn't meet her uncle's eye, feeling a nudge of guilt at the concern she saw there. "No. I...wanted to get you home as soon as they released you." That was a lame response, but it was mostly the truth. She didn't want to tell him that last week she'd felt uncomfortable singing songs about drawing closer to Jesus and about trusting in Him.

She preferred to trust in herself. Just as her mother had always taught her. She realized the benefits of that now. There were fewer disappointments in your life when you didn't count on others for happiness. Love was too risky. Either love of God or love of others. They required too much trust and that trust was too often broken.

"I don't mind being home earlier. I get tired pretty quick. It's frustrating," he said.

Cara curled her hand around his, squeezing it gently. "You don't have to worry about anything. The clinic is doing fine."

"I'm trying not to worry," Alan said, shifting in his chair. "But the doctor says I'll be back at work soon," he said, returning Cara's hand squeeze.

Cara didn't reply because she knew better. The specialist had been fairly emphatic about Uncle Alan making drastic changes in his lifestyle.

And the most drastic had to do with his work. He was

too old to deal with the stress of late-night calls, which meant his work would slow considerably.

"Have you talked to that new vet, Gordon?" Cara asked. "Is there any way he can come sooner?"

"I called him and he said he might. Depending on how things go with the job he's working now."

"So are you ready for dessert?" Aunt Lori asked, coming into the living room, carrying a tray of fruit and three small bowls.

Uncle Alan pulled a face at the fruit and Cara stifled a smile. Uncle Alan loved his sweets and she could see future battles with her aunt once he felt better.

She glanced at the clock, then got to her feet, grabbing the garbage bag as she left. "Sorry to bail on you, but I have to meet Nicholas."

Uncle Alan's frown made her smile.

"We're planning Lorne and Trista's wedding," she assured him. "They'll be there, as well."

He relaxed visibly. "Okay then. You go."

Cara brushed a kiss over his forehead. "And you make sure you take care of yourself."

But as she straightened, he caught her by the hand, squeezing it as if to catch her attention.

"And you take care of yourself, too," he said, his serious voice holding another undertone.

"I will."

But as she got into her uncle's car, his warning rang in her ears.

Uncle Alan knew exactly the struggle Cara had with Nicholas. It was he who had told her sometimes hard choices needed to be made and that it wasn't wrong to think of herself. Uncle Alan knew better than anyone else how much Cara had been hurt by her mother's decisions and by her mother's choices. And it was he who had held a sobbing Cara in his arms when she had come back from Nicholas's ranch, after breaking up with him.

And now she was heading right back there.

She had changed, she thought as she turned onto the road leading to the ranch. Her heart wasn't as easily ensnared. She'd been on her own for three years and had developed some independence and a tougher crust.

But as she parked her car beside Lorne's truck, she couldn't stop the fluttering of that supposedly free heart.

Remnants of old emotions, she told herself as she got out.

"Hey, Cara, over here," she heard Lorne's voice calling out from beyond the barn.

Frowning, Cara walked in the direction of his voice. What were they doing at the corrals?

She came around the corner. Lorne was stroking one of Nicholas's horses and grinned up at her when she came closer.

"I thought we could go for a ride up into the mountains after our meeting," Lorne said.

"Where's Trista?"

"She and Nicholas are in the barn, checking out if it's big enough for the wedding reception in case we have rain."

"So if we go with a barbecue, we could do it standing up," Trista was saying as she and Nicholas came out of the barn. Then she glanced over and saw Cara. "You're here. Thank goodness."

And Cara didn't imagine the look of relief on her friend's face.

"So why don't we go to the house and get a few things set out," Cara said.

"What's to talk about?" Lorne said. "We got the place, we got the minister, the other things can wait—"

"No, they can't," Nicholas said. "And Trista's been taking care of the other things all on her own." The slightly angry tone of his voice surprised Cara. He was taking this wedding seriously.

Which created a lingering, twisted pain. Had he shown as much commitment to their relationship, things might have been so different.

She pushed the feelings aside.

"Before we head up into the mountains, lovely though that may be, we need to do some basic planning," Cara said, underlining Nicholas's opinion.

Lorne glanced at Trista, and then, thankfully gave a light shrug. "Okay. If that's what you think should happen."

"As the maid of honor, I do."

As Cara spoke, she caught Nicholas's relieved gaze. And then a smile.

As she returned it, a sense of equilibrium returned. It was going to be okay. *I'll get through this just fine. We're just two old acquaintances helping friends plan a wedding. Nothing more.*

"We can go up to the house and work there," Nicholas said, leading the way. "Dad's gone so it will be quiet."

As Cara followed, she looked behind her at the beckoning mountains, feeling a moment of kinship with Lorne. The sun was shining and she had some time off, so she would much sooner have ridden up into the mountains than sit inside and plan a wedding that should have been hers.

The past year, in her last job, most of her work had been inside, working with small animals. She had often thought of the wide-open spaces of Alberta when she was casting broken limbs and stitching and dosing in the confines of the vet office.

She pushed the yearning aside.

If she was going to be a part of this wedding she couldn't let it just "happen" as Lorne seemed to think it would. For Trista's sake, she needed to help.

"Sorry about the mess," Nicholas was saying as she stepped into the kitchen.

Cara blinked. Mess? All she saw were some coffee cups on the table and a couple of magazines.

If Nicholas truly wanted to see a mess, he should come to her aunt's place.

This kitchen, though showing signs of age, was clean and tidy. The countertop gleamed and the stove shone. The old wooden table, though scarred and worn, held a ceramic bowl with a bunch of apples.

Cara's mind flashed back to the modern, expensive furniture filling her aunt and uncle's home. The money, which was no problem for Aunt Lori and Uncle Alan, couldn't replicate the homey comfort of this worn but clean kitchen.

This could have been mine, she thought, the idea lacerating her hard-won composure.

Cara pressed her lips together and marshaled her defenses. Over. Past.

She pulled a wooden chair back from the table, dropped into it and pulled out a pad of paper from the briefcase she had taken along.

And then, almost against her will, she glanced in Nicholas's direction.

He wore an old shirt, his sleeves rolled up as he measured coffee grounds into a coffee press. While she watched he rinsed a cloth and wiped the already clean counters. He poured boiling water into the press, set out cups, found a plate in the cupboard and a bag of cookies and put that out, as well.

She tried to imagine her uncle working as efficiently in her aunt's kitchen. The picture didn't gel.

Lorne and Trista were huddled together, whispering and giggling like a couple of teenagers, their previous tiff obviously forgotten. Cara cleared her throat to get their attention. "So how many people will be coming?" she asked.

Trista pulled away from Lorne, then bent over, pulling a folder out of a bag she had taken along. "We're keeping it small. Just family and close friends."

"And how many is that?" Cara asked. As Nicholas set her mug in front of her, she noticed he had put cream in it. Just enough to give it a faint caramel color. He remembered, she thought, the idea giving her heart a silly lift.

Old acquaintances. That's all.

"Not sure," Lorne said.

"Let's see your list?" Cara asked. Trista handed her a paper from the folder.

"We don't really have time to send things out in the regular mail," Trista said, "so I thought we could email whoever has an email address and phone the people who don't."

"So how many people would that be?" Nicholas asked as he sat in an empty chair beside Cara. She caught the scent of his cologne and the faintest hint of hay and straw from the barn, and she noticed the silvery line of a scar along his forearm that she didn't remember being there before.

An accident at work? Or at the ranch?

Focus, you silly girl.

"About sixty, we guessed?" Lorne said.

"I'd like to ask some girls from work," Trista said.

Lorne frowned. "I thought we were keeping the wedding small."

"Well, yeah, but I've worked with them for the past four years—"

"Then I should ask some friends from my work, too," Lorne put in.

"Of course," Trista said.

"So that makes it, what, eighty now?" Cara wrote the number down at the top of page one.

"Only if my brothers don't bring escorts," Lorne added.

Cara couldn't help a quick glance at Nicholas, who was rolling his eyes.

"Let's get a firm list down now. Trista, you send out the emails as soon as possible and give people a week to reply," Cara said, feeling like a schoolteacher. "Then we'll follow up with the people we haven't heard from. In the meantime we need to think about the meal."

"Nicholas suggested we have a barbecue," Lorne said. "Do it ourselves. Get the relatives to all bring something—like a bit of a potluck."

Cara stifled a groan and chanced a look at Nicholas. "Did you suggest that?"

Nicholas shrugged, looking a bit baffled himself. "I did, when we were talking about only thirty people."

Cara imagined herself, in her bridesmaid dress, whipping up a taco salad between the ceremony and dinner. "I think if we can get someone else to do the meal, we should definitely look at that." She made another quick note.

An hour and a half later they had a list of people who would be attending, a tentative plan for the service and a rough concept of how Trista wanted the yard decorated and set up.

"So, is that good enough for now?" Lorne asked, shifting in his chair.

"What about the supper menu?"

Lorne blew out his breath and got up. "If you're getting a caterer, they can take care of that, can't they?"

Cara bit back a sigh and chanced a look at Nicholas, who was rolling his eyes again. Then their gazes caught and she let slip a smile of commiseration.

"We live a ways out of town for a caterer to come," Nicholas said. "We could get one of those people with a portable barbecue thing."

"Sounds good." Lorne looked relieved.

"It's a bit casual," Nicholas warned.

"Casual is what we're going for, right, babe?" Lorne said, with a wink in Trista's direction.

She smiled back, nodding. "Yeah. But I still want it nice."

"It will be nice," Lorne said. "Nice and easy." He glanced from Cara to Nicholas. "So what else do we need to talk about?"

"The ceremony?" Cara asked.

"We're meeting with the minister on Tuesday."

"Sound system?" Nicholas put in.

"My brother has one. From his band days."

Lorne seemed to have an answer for everything, Cara thought, but his remarks were so glib and offhand. As if he were simply going through the motions of planning this wedding so he could get on to other things.

"And photographer?"

"That's why I wanted to go riding," Lorne said. "So we could find a place to take pictures. I don't want the usual studio stuff."

"But you'd have to bring the photographer out there, too," Cara said, puzzled at his insistence that they go out on horses to find the perfect spot, when there were some equally lovely places here on the ranch.

"That's fine," Trista added, seemingly okay with the plan. "The photographer suggested it himself when he found out where we were having the wedding."

"So you're good with all of this?" Cara asked.

Trista nodded, but Cara could see faint lines of tension around her mouth.

"Then I think we got everything we need," Cara said, sensing her friend needed a break. "I guess you guys can go look for your picture spot."

"I want you to come, too," Trista said to Cara.

"Why?" Cara hadn't figured on that.

"I need your advice. Maid of honor, remember?" Trista tossed Cara a pleading look.

Cara remembered another time she had gone riding with Nicholas. They had ridden up into the mountains and had a picnic overlooking a lake nestled in the valley. And had shared numerous kisses, which had more than made up for the slight fear she had felt while riding. She loved working with horses on the ground, not so much in the saddle.

"I don't think—"

Trista cut of her protest. "Please come. Please?"

Cara pushed down the memory of the kisses, avoiding looking at Nicholas for fear he would notice the flush in her cheeks.

"Okay. I guess I can come," she conceded, sensing Trista needed the emotional support.

"Are you sure we got everything covered?" Nicholas asked.

"We can talk a bit more on the ride if we need to," Cara said.

"Lorne and I will get the horses ready then," Nicholas said, getting up from the table. "So you're coming riding?" Nicholas glanced at Cara.

She nodded, wondering if she would regret doing this.

"That's great. I'll saddle up Two Bits," he said, a smile teasing one corner of his mouth. "You'll be okay on him."

"I hope so," she said.

"You can trust him."

She knew he was talking about the horse, yet sensed an underlying meaning that created a tiny frisson of expectation.

"You coming, Chapman?" Lorne called out from the porch.

"Trista and I will clean up," Cara said, gathering up the mugs.

Nicholas held her gaze a split second longer than necessary and then left.

Trista was already filling the sink with water, staring out the window overlooking the yard. Cara could see Lorne and Nicholas walking toward the corral, Nicholas's long strides easily catching up to Lorne. It looked as if he could be talking to Lorne and Cara hoped, for Trista's sake, he was asking him about his offhand treatment of this wedding.

Because the frown on Trista's face ignited Cara's concern.

"Is everything okay?" Cara gently asked.

Trista tugged her gaze away from the men and gave Cara a quick smile. "Yeah. Just feeling a bit confused."

"Over the wedding?"

Trista turned off the taps and dropped the mugs into the soapy water. "A bit."

"And how about Lorne. How does he feel about it all?"

"He's just…well…he doesn't like all this planning stuff."

"Does he like all this marrying stuff?" Cara slowly wiped a mug, wishing she knew how to proceed.

"Of course he does. Lorne loves me."

Cara didn't imagine the tone of indignation in Trista's voice, but behind that she also heard a hint of fear.

"I'm sure he does." Cara fought her own urge to caution her friend. But she knew she had to talk to Nicholas later. Find out if he knew what was going on with Lorne.

"And if you're insinuating he's only marrying me because I'm pregnant—"

"No. I'm not." Cara caught Trista by the shoulder, concerned by the sparkle of tears in Trista's eyes. "I just…I just want to make sure everything is okay with you two."

Trista swiped her eyes and gave Cara a trembling smile. "This pregnancy is making me really weepy and emotional and I'd be lying if I said I didn't feel overwhelmed."

"Let me take care of some of this," Cara urged.

Trista sniffed. "I can't do that. You've got enough going on—"

"Tell me what still needs to be done," Cara urged. "I want to help."

Trista sighed. "The cake needs to be done. Mom's sister was going to bake it, but she's not feeling well and begged off. I loved your idea about the buckets of flowers, and the nursery is clearing out their stock this week but I don't have time to go get the plants and take care of them. And I need to figure out if I want to put something on the tables." Then she sniffed again. "I just feel like it's all getting to be too big and too much."

Cara thought of her own busy schedule, but then looked at Trista's face and made a quick decision. "Tell you what. Aunt Lori and I will take care of the cake. I'll go to the nursery this week and pick up the plants."

"That's too much—"

"No. It isn't. Things are getting a bit quieter at the clinic and I know Aunt Lori would love to help out." Cara gave her friend a quick smile. "And if we get Uncle Alan to water the flowers every day he'll have something to do, as well."

Trista looked down at the soap bubbles clinging to her hands. "That would be great."

Cara wiped the last mug and set it on the counter. "We're done here, so let's go outside and enjoy this beautiful day," Cara said, hanging the dish towel on the bar of the oven, glancing around the tidy kitchen with the smallest flicker of envy. This place seemed more like a home in some ways than her own uncle and aunt's place.

By the time Cara and Trista joined the men, the horses were saddled and ready.

The sun's warmth surrounded them, the air held a soft breeze and as Cara looked up, a flock of sparrows swooped and played on the wind. A perfect day for a ride.

"You should shoot those things," Lorne was saying, looking up at the sparrows. "You've got tons of them."

"They don't bother me, I don't bother them." Nicholas laughed.

Lorne saw the girls and grinned. "Let's get going,"

Lorne said, looking and sounding a lot more cheerful than he had inside the house.

He helped Trista into the saddle and as he adjusted her stirrups, he was laughing up at her and smiling as if everything were fine.

And maybe it was, Cara thought.

Nicholas stood holding Two Bits, another horse tied up to the fence behind him.

"So you ready to go?" he asked, leading Two Bits toward her.

Cara looked at the huge chestnut with some trepidation. The one time she had gone riding with Nicholas, she had been on a much smaller horse, a mare named Blossom. Nicholas had ridden Two Bits and his horse had dwarfed Cara and her mount. But she'd felt quite at ease not being so far from the ground.

"He's a great horse. I trust him with my life," Nicholas said by way of encouragement. "And, more important, I trust him with yours."

Thus assured she stretched up to grasp the pommel but couldn't lift her leg high enough to reach the stirrup. Then before she could think of how to solve this, Nicholas had her foot in his hand, his other hand on her waist and he lifted her easily up.

Cara fussed needlessly with the reins, hiding the twinge of pleasure his touch gave her.

"Looks like Lorne and Trista are eager to be off," Nicholas said, untying the other horse and swinging easily into the saddle.

"Do they know where to go?" Cara asked, as they disappeared into the trees crowding the trail they were following.

"Lorne knows the place." Nicholas glanced her way, frowning. "You okay?"

"Yeah. I'm fine." But as she chanced a look down, *fine* was replaced by a quiver of apprehension. Two Bits stood about sixteen hands high and the ground looked too far away.

"He's a good horse," Nicholas assured her. "He'll be fine."

"Fine is good. Let's go then," she said, trying to project calm into her voice.

"Okay." Nicholas clucked to his horse and turned its head. "Let's go, Bud."

His horse gave a tiny jump, but then settled down and started a steady walk in the direction Trista and Lorne had gone.

Two Bits obediently followed Bud, his movement causing her to sway lightly in the saddle. Cara tried not to grab the pommel and forced herself to keep from squeezing Two Bits with her legs.

The saddle will keep you on, she reminded herself. *Just relax. You're not running a horse race.*

She took a few calming breaths. The warm summer air, the faint buzzing of insects and the regular footfalls of the horse's hooves on the packed ground lulled her into a sense of security.

She chanced a look ahead, watching Nicholas from behind.

Nicholas glanced sideways at the fields they rode beside, a smile curving his lips.

This is where he belongs, Cara thought, looking at him now silhouetted against the mountains. *This is his natural setting.*

Pain twisted Cara's heart.

And where do you belong?

Before she met Nicholas, the question had resonated through her life. Then, for those few, magical months with Nicholas she thought she had found her place.

And now?

Tomorrow will worry about itself. Each day has enough trouble of its own.

The passage from the Bible leaped into her mind, as if to underline her resolve. She was expending too much energy wondering how to react to Nicholas and thinking of how to behave around him.

They were outside on this beautiful day and were headed out into the hills. *Just enjoy it. Don't put extra burdens on it.*

Nicholas sat easily on his horse, his one hand on his thigh, the other loosely holding the reins. He had rolled his shirtsleeves up over his forearms, and as he rode, she could see his broad shoulders moving ever so slightly in response to the movement of the horse.

He's an extremely good-looking man, she thought with a touch of wistfulness.

And he doesn't belong to you anymore.

Chapter Seven

Cara and Nicholas reached the end of the field and turned on the trail where Trista and Lorne had gone moments before.

The trail started climbing almost immediately, winding through the dusky coolness of towering spruce and pine trees. In the light-strewn openings between the foliage, Cara caught glimpses of hayfields below them. The swaths Nicholas had cut were green and lush, thanks to recent rains. She knew, from talking to other farmers and ranchers, that this year would be productive.

"How much of this belongs to you and your father?" Cara asked, raising her voice so Nicholas could hear.

Nicholas glanced back and pushed his cowboy hat farther up on his head. "What you see below you is ours up to the river. Beyond that is Olsen's land." He pointed with one gloved hand.

Cara leaned to one side to see better, squinting a little until she saw the river.

"That's quite a lot of property."

"That's the hay land. We have pasture farther up the trail and we lease a bunch of land, as well."

Cara easily heard the pride in his voice as her eyes followed the contours of the land.

She knew, oh, how well she knew, how much this land meant to him. Hadn't he chosen this over her?

She tried to look at it through his eyes, to understand why she had been second choice.

The land was beautiful, the setting almost postcard perfect.

"Are your other cows up there?" she asked, thinking of the herd she saw close to the ranch.

"The purebred herd is in the pasture by the barn and the commercial herd is farther up," Nicholas explained. "I like to keep them separate as much as possible. And because I'm shipping heifers from the purebred herd, I wanted to keep them closer to the house so I could monitor their feed better."

"Did you buy this land or did it come with the ranch when your father took it over?"

Nicholas stopped his horse and Two Bits kept going until the two horses were side by side.

"My great-grandfather provided one quarter and bought a few more from the neighbors who were struggling. He started there, by the river, using a horse and his own manpower." Nicholas pointed to a small peninsula of land. "My grandfather expanded on that using an old tractor and my dad used a bulldozer to clear it all the way up to the fence line you see."

She nodded, still looking at the land. For the first time since Nicholas chose the ranch over her, she got a tiny inkling of why this meant so much to him.

"My great-great-grandfather started with a small herd of cattle and a horse-drawn plow for the grain land, and it's been growing since. My grandfather thought he'd try exotics and dabbled in Charolais and Simmental, but my dad and I went back to Angus. And now I'm breaking into purebreds. And we've always grown grain and canola on the river-bottom lands."

Cara didn't imagine the note of pride in his voice as he spoke of the ranch and she envied him the history. Her grandmother was also a single mom and had moved around as much as her mother had. She had passed away before Cara moved in with Uncle Alan and Aunt Lori. She didn't know who her father was—her mother had told her repeatedly that he died working overseas and that was all she needed to know.

All she had was her uncle and aunt, a few faded photographs and some stories that Uncle Alan would dredge up if pressed. Nicholas had a ranch steeped in history and generations of ancestors who were buried in a local churchyard.

"With each generation the ranch got a bit bigger," Nicholas said. "And with each generation it got easier to find a way to feed more cows and farm more land without hiring a whole bunch of people."

"And now it's just you and your dad."

"Yup."

She knew his history but because of Nicholas's work and because of his father's antagonism toward her, she'd caught only glimpses of the rest of the ranch. They had started dating in September, then Nicholas went away to work for a couple of months. When he came back, winter had arrived.

During his time off, their dates consisted of going out to movies, going out for coffee, some ski trips to Banff and visits with Uncle Alan and Aunt Lori. When Nicholas left again for work and returned with a broken leg, Cara thought he would quit.

But when the leg healed and spring came, he got a call for another job and took it.

As a result, she had never seen the ranch like this.

Would things have been different between them if she'd seen this earlier?

She pushed the question aside. What was done was done. Nicholas's choices were still difficult for her. That much hadn't changed.

"Did any of your ancestors ever think about moving somewhere else?" She knew the answer to this one, too, but she liked hearing him talk about his ranch. When he did, his voice softened and he became the Nicholas she remembered, the Nicholas she had fallen in love with.

"I've told you about Lily, my dad's sister who lives in Idaho," Nicholas said. "And my great-grandfather had a brother who moved back to England, but the rest of us stayed here."

"You told me once about your grandfather building a house somewhere else."

Nicholas stopped his horse and pointed through the trees to a small building tucked in some trees and edged with lilac bushes.

"Can you see that?" he asked. "That's it, right there."

"So why did he abandon it?" She knew his great-grandfather had moved the main residence to where it stood now, overlooking the valley.

"Too close to the river," he said. "They got drowned out once and my great-grandmother insisted on the move. She was a feisty one. I never knew her, but my grandfather and dad had a bunch of stories to tell about her."

"Like what?" Cara asked, intrigued by this unexpected chapter in the Chapman family history.

"I guess a porcupine was hanging around the yard one day chewing on some apple trees she had just planted. So she was going to get out the gun and kill it, but when she saw it looking at her, she couldn't. So she shot over its head to chase it away. Had to do that for the rest of the summer. She went through a lot of bullets chasing it away. Claimed she missed seeing it when it didn't show up one day." He smiled at the memory and Cara's heart hitched at the sight. Nicholas looked more relaxed than he had since she had come to Cochrane. The ranch agreed with him. It was where he belonged.

She shifted in the saddle, forcing her attention back to the land below them. "It's beautiful. I can see why it means so much to you."

Nicholas shot her a puzzled glance. "Can you?"

"It's been a part of your family for a long time."

Nicholas leaned on the pommel of his saddle, and as he looked out over the open fields, his voice tinged with pride. "We put a lot of ourselves into this place. When Mom left—" Nicholas stopped there.

As he often did.

Cara didn't know much about Nicholas's mother, Barb, only that she had suddenly left his father and Nicholas one day. Left a note on the table and a casserole in the oven.

"When your mom left," Cara prompted, wondering if she'd hear a bit more from him.

Nicholas sighed, his movement causing the saddle to creak. "Doesn't matter. That was a long time ago."

He straightened and it was as if a shutter dropped over his face. Cara experienced a glimmer of frustration. When they were dating she'd tried to get him to open up about his mother and his relationship with his father. But every time the conversation veered close to his parents, he shut down.

She had always assumed they would have time to find out more about each other. To encourage each other in their faith.

To grow together.

But that didn't happen.

"It's a terrible thing when a marriage falls apart," Nicholas said. "That's why I'm worried about Lorne and Trista."

Cara felt as if gears in her mind were grinding with the sudden shift in topic.

Obviously still not ready to talk about his mother and father's relationship, she thought. Or maybe Nicholas didn't think she warranted a glimpse into his private life.

"I'm concerned, too," she said, going along with the conversation, aware that Nicholas's concerns were hers. "Do you think he's getting cold feet?"

"I'm not sure." Nicholas tugged on the reins, turning his horse on another trail, leaving the open fields behind them. "I haven't had a chance to talk to him. I want to make sure Lorne doesn't go through the same thing I did."

Though he tossed the words out casually they wounded with precision.

"I think he and Trista are pretty committed to each other," Cara said quietly, trying to mask her own hurt as she kept her eyes on the landscape below them. "They've both made some sacrifices to make this relationship work, regardless of how it's starting out." She chanced a quick sideways glance and caught his frown. As if he didn't understand.

A relentless current of frustration washed through her. This lack of understanding of the sacrifices necessary for a relationship had dogged their own.

"At any rate, Trista seems nervous," Nicholas said.

"She doesn't do pressure well."

"None of us do."

It's just a casual comment, Cara reminded herself. *Don't read more into it than what's on the surface.*

But as their eyes connected, she caught a glimmer of an older, deeper emotion that made her wonder just how off-the-cuff this, and his previous comment, actually were.

"I know she loves Lorne and wants to marry him," Cara said, determined to keep this conversation on their friends. "But there's something else going on."

"We better figure out what it is before things go too far and I end up stuck with a bunch of guests and a caterer and no bride and groom."

"I doubt it will get that far," Cara said. "I think they've got a lot to deal with, but I have a feeling they'll find their way through this. I think they love each other enough."

Nicholas sighed heavily and his horse jumped a little to one side. He settled it down, then shot her a quick, sideways glance. "I guess that's always enough." His voice sounded wry.

Cara's heart began a slow, heavy beating and her face grew flushed. "What do you mean?" Cara said, wishing her voice didn't sound so strangled.

Nicholas slashed the air with his hand. "Nothing. Just slipped out."

Cara's hands clenched a little tighter on the reins. And

then she felt a shiver of frustration. Until this wedding was done, they would be spending more time together.

It might make things easier for both of them if they confronted what had happened.

And how would that help? Nicholas had made it clear that their relationship was over.

But the few glances they had exchanged, the few moments of connection hovered in her mind. And she had missed that so badly when she left. Though she had gone on a few dates herself, she had never found the same rapport, the same connection she and Nicholas had shared.

She was leaving, so why not get some of this out of the way? What could it hurt?

"Do you think we didn't love each other enough?"

Cara wasn't aware she had voiced the question aloud until she saw Nicholas's head spin toward her.

"Why do you ask?"

"That came up in our last conversation," she said, keeping her attention on the trail winding ahead of them. She eased one foot out of the stirrup, thankful for the cramp in her foot to distract her.

"That wasn't a conversation, Cara. That was a conflagration."

Cara turned to him. "What else could I say? I asked for something from you that you couldn't give. Something I thought was important for our future relationship."

"Did you have any idea how much your request would cost me? Would cost the ranch?"

"Or would cost your father?"

Nicholas frowned. "What do you mean by that?"

Cara knew she had ventured into territory she had never dared set foot on when she and Nicholas were dating.

But that was when she thought she had something to lose. Now nothing was at stake except her own wounded pride and an inexplicable desire to have Nicholas see the situation from her viewpoint.

"I think it's easier for your father when you work so much."

Nicholas's frown warned her, but she had gone this far, she may as well keep going. She struggled to articulate her thoughts without sounding as if she didn't like his father.

She was about to speak when a coyote bolted across the trail.

Nicholas's horse startled, reared and bumped into Two Bits.

And everything went crazy.

Cara saw the world spin once as her horse twisted. She made a quick grab for the saddle horn, but missed.

She flew sideways and hit the ground with a bone-jarring crack. An electrical charge jolted up her head into her neck. Her vision went dark.

"Cara. Cara. Are you okay?"

Was that Nicholas sounding so angry? She blinked, trying to get her bearings, pushing herself up by her elbows. She heard a thumping of hooves and turned just as Nicholas's mount bolted back down the trail. Its stirrups flapped and its feet pounded out a mad rhythm in time to the thundering in Cara's chest.

Then Nicholas crouched at her side, his hands pushing her hair back from her face. "Are you okay?" he repeated, his fingers moving over her head, his arm supporting her shoulders.

She tried to move away but he held her down.

"Don't move. I want to make sure nothing's broken," he said, his voice firm.

She chanced a look up at his face, inches from hers, his eyes dark with concern.

"I'm okay," she said, feeling as if someone had robbed her breath.

"You don't sound okay," he said, his fingers grazing her temple, fingering through her hair.

It was his gentle touch and his arms around her that caused her voice to sound so strained. So unsure.

"Really, I'm fine." She struggled to her feet, swaying as she tried to regain her balance.

But he was there to catch her. She leaned against him, and once again let him hold her up.

Just until I get my balance, she promised herself, her hands resting lightly on the front of his shirt. *Just for the smallest moment,* she thought as her fingers curled against the warmth of his chest.

She closed her eyes, fighting the sudden wave of longing threatening to sweep her hard-won independence away.

She couldn't give in. Nothing had changed and she would only endanger her heart again.

And slowly, feeling as if she were pulling herself back from a dangerous precipice, Cara lowered her hands and drew back.

"Really, I'm fine," she said.

But Nicholas kept his hands on her arms.

"I want to get you back to the house."

"What about Lorne and Trista?" she asked.

"They'll figure things out soon enough." Nicholas's eyes flitted over her features. Then he frowned and brushed his fingers over a tender spot on her one temple. "I'm more worried about this bump."

Cara wanted to protest one more time, but then a wave of dizziness hit her and the concerned look on Nicholas face told her he saw it, too.

He whistled, Cara heard the sound of hoofbeats and then Two Bits came up beside Nicholas.

"Why did that other horse run away?" Cara asked, blinking hard to get her eyes into focus as Nicholas caught the reins. "Did you get bucked off?"

"No." Nicholas sounded insulted at her question. "I bailed when I saw you hit the dirt. And while I was distracted he reared and pulled the reins out of my hands."

Cara nodded, then wished she hadn't. The ache in her forehead was spreading.

"Here. You're going to ride," he said, looping Two Bit's reins over his head.

"I don't think so. I'll walk." She wasn't ready to get back on a horse again.

"It's too far and I don't want you falling over."

Cara was about to protest again when, in one smooth motion, Nicholas had her up on the saddle and then he was right behind her.

She felt as if she should put up some token resistance, but realized that was foolish. If she had a concussion, she couldn't walk, nor could she ride on her own. Nicholas was being practical.

But her pragmatic analysis couldn't explain away the increased tempo of her heart, and the tingle rushing to the tips of her fingers at his nearness.

"Relax," he murmured, slipping one arm around her waist and pulling her back. "You'll get a headache sitting all tense like that."

"I'm not tense." But in spite of her protestation, she had to force herself to rest against his chest.

His chin rubbed the side of her head and if she peeked up, she could see the brim of his hat and a piece of his hair hanging down over his face.

As if he sensed her attention, he angled his head downward. "Do you have a headache?"

"Just a bit." She forced her gaze ahead, watching the trail as the horse walked down it.

"Double vision?"

"So you're a doctor now?" she joked, trying to find equilibrium in humor when she was far too aware of the strength of his arm holding her close and the warmth of his chest against her back.

"I've taken a few spills. Had a concussion once."

"I don't think I have a concussion. I fell on the dirt."

He nodded and she didn't know what else to say.

So they rode in silence. Each second added to her mental and physical discomfort as the silvery beginnings of a headache made itself known and the nervous knot in her stomach tightened with each footfall from the horse.

"So how—"

"When do you—"

They both spoke at once, as if each were trying to pierce the same discomfort.

"Sorry—"

"Go ahead—"

Silence again.

"When do you have to bale the hay?" she asked, needing to talk about something.

"This week sometime, if the weather holds. We've got about one hundred and sixty acres to roll up and it's running pretty heavy, so that should keep me busy."

"Do you do it all up in round bales?"

Oh, listen to you, sounding all rancherlike.

She ignored the mocking inner voice. She was simply making conversation. Nothing more. Trying to sound interested in what Nicholas was interested in.

"I have an old square baler from my grandfather that I use to make up small square bales for the horses. The rest I do up in the large round bales."

"How many horses do you and your father have now?" Good job. She sounded much calmer.

"Ten. Dad sold four last year."

"Why?"

"So he could buy more horses."

Cara wasn't sure if she imagined the edge of frustration in his voice. "But you still have your dad's roping horse, Duke."

"Yeah. He'll be staying on the ranch until he's dead. Probably put him beside Jake, his brother. He died two years ago."

"Most people bury hamsters and goldfish out back," Cara joked.

His laughter rumbled up his chest as she stared at the trail ahead, a soft breeze teasing her hair. "Those we bury closer to the house," he said. "Don't take up as much space."

"You had hamsters?"

"A couple. I was better with big animals than small ones."

"I know the feeling. I don't care for working with smaller animals as much as horses and cows."

"So why do you work with small animals then?"

She felt caught on the barbs of her casual comment.

"Well, it's easier to find a job in small animal care. And I can move around a bit easier."

"Which is important to you?"

She bit her lip, unsure of how to answer him and thankfully, he didn't follow up on the question.

They rode quietly for a while and his chest rose and fell, then again, as if he was about to ask her a question.

But nothing.

They were back to the beginning and she didn't want to return there. For a few wonderful moments, they had shared the easy rapport they had before their breakup and, despite her caution to herself, she was drawn again to this man.

You're moving on, she reminded herself.

Yes, but wouldn't it be easier if she left on better terms with Nicholas than she had the last time?

"When your great-great-grandfather came, was there much of a town?" she asked. She knew the best way to draw Nicholas out was to talk about the land beneath their feet.

Nicholas shifted in the saddle, the arm holding her close to him loosening a little, as if he had released some tension.

"Cochrane was just a small outpost when he came from England."

"That was about 1887?"

"Yeah." She sensed his puzzlement but pushed on.

"So did he come with a wife, or did he meet her here?"

"Actually, she was a mail-order bride."

"And how did that work out?"

"Good, I guess. Apparently she wasn't crazy about the ranch at first. She was from London, but she had chosen to come and made the best of it. Later the land drew her in and she grew to love it."

"Like I said, I can see why."

A heavy silence fell between them.

"Could you have?" he finally asked.

The question hung between them and Cara wasn't sure how to answer it.

"I guess we'll never know," was all she could say.

"I guess."

Did she imagine the wistful note in his voice? Did he miss her as she had missed him?

She took a chance and angled her head so she could see him better. And her heart hammered in her chest when she caught him looking down at her.

Their faces were mere inches apart. She could feel his breath, warm and gentle on her cheek.

The moment trembled between them and then, slowly, Nicholas's head shifted, she turned her face and their lips brushed each other.

Cara closed her eyes, as Nicholas kissed her again, her hand coming up to cradle his jaw, then slipping up to touch his cheek.

Her breath left her as her emotions veered between doubt and longing, between yearning and common sense.

She wasn't staying here and neither was Nicholas. Yet...

She waited a moment. Just one more moment to treasure this kiss and store it away.

"Cara, what's happening?" he whispered.

And his quiet question jolted her back to reality.

What they had done was a dangerous and costly mistake. Once again things had altered between them but where could it go? Nothing in either of their lives had changed.

And yet, in this moment, it was as if the ground beneath her had shifted.

She pulled her scattered emotions together, withdrawing back into herself.

Thankfully they were out into the open and heading toward the corrals. The ride was coming to an end.

They arrived just as Nicholas's father pulled into the yard with his truck.

Cara caught the angry look on Dale's face when he saw the two of them astride Two Bits. What would he have thought of the kiss she and Nicholas had shared?

What was she to think of it?

Chapter Eight

Nicholas helped Cara off the horse, and tried not to let his hands linger on her waist as she got her feet under her.

"You sure you're okay?" he asked. "I feel like we should take you to the hospital."

"I'm fine," she said.

"So, what's Bud doing, hanging around the corrals with the saddle still on?" Dale asked as he walked toward them. His narrowed eyes flicked from Cara to Nicholas as if looking for any hint of indiscretion.

Nicholas felt like a kid caught with his hand in the candy jar, then he dismissed the feeling. He was an adult. He'd held the woman he was once supposed to marry in his arms.

That he kissed her was simply a throwback to old, unresolved emotions.

Yeah, he could tell himself that but deep down he knew better. He knew something had dramatically altered after that kiss. At least it had for him.

"Had a little spill up on the hills," Nicholas said, fighting down a beat of frustration at his father's unexpected arrival.

Usually his dad spent at least ten hours at the auction mart. He had counted on that when he and Cara went on their ride.

"The two of you went riding?" Dale asked.

"We were going with Lorne and Trista to check out a place to take pictures," Nicholas said. He turned to Cara. "I'm driving you home."

"I'm fine. Really," she protested. "No headache, no dizziness."

"But that bruise—"

Cara put her hand on his arm to stop him. "I'll get my aunt to bring me to the hospital if necessary. You should go get Lorne and Trista sorted out."

He saw the necessity of that. "You'll let me know if anything changes?"

"I will." She didn't look at him as she walked to her car and got in. Was she regretting their kiss?

Should he?

"You going to unsaddle Bud?" his father said.

Nicholas pulled his attention away from Cara. "Why don't you do that?" he said. "I've got to take Two Bits back to find Lorne and Trista."

And before his father could ask him anything more about Cara, Nicholas was on his horse and gone. He had too much to think about. Too much to process.

And he wasn't about to do that in front of his father.

Fifteen minutes later he found Lorne and Trista heading back down the trail.

"Where's Cara?" Trista asked, as soon as she saw him.

"She had a spill and went home."

"You let her go on her own? You didn't bring her? What if she has a concussion?" Trista's questions hammered at him as they rode back to the ranch.

"She said she felt fine. She insisted on going on her own. What else could I do?" Nicholas said, his guilt making him testy. "You know how stubborn Cara can be."

"I suppose," Trista said with a sigh. "Did she talk to you about picking up plants from the nursery Tuesday?"

Nicholas glanced back at her. "No. What plants?"

"For the wedding. The nursery is having a closing-out sale, but she didn't think she would have enough room in her car to get them," Trista said. "I told her to ask you for help."

They'd had other things on their minds obviously.

"I don't know. I've got hay to bale and I have to move my cows to another pasture. The tractor needs an oil change and I've got to work on the corrals."

"I'll do the oil change tomorrow night," Lorne said. "And help you with the corrals. Your hay won't be ready to bale until Wednesday, which means you'll have time to help Cara with the plants."

"Why are you so eager to help?" He'd been getting a weird vibe from Lorne and Trista and harbored a faint suspicion they were playing matchmaker.

"Hello? Wedding? Here?" Lorne spread his hands out in an innocent gesture. "The more I can help you with, the more you can do."

So why didn't he go and get the plants? But he knew if he asked, he wouldn't get a straight answer.

"Okay, find out when she's going and I'll meet her there," he said.

Trista's grin gave him pause but he didn't want to speculate on what caused it. He had a faint suspicion that he knew what Trista was up to.

And the trouble was, he didn't mind.

* * *

"So as a friend, I need to ask. You absolutely certain Trista's the one for you?" Nicholas picked up the two-by-six, glancing across the pile of wood to his friend. He had been mulling over the questions he and Cara had discussed yesterday and knew he had to talk to his friend.

Lorne moved the piece of straw he'd been chewing on to the other side of his mouth and picked up the other end of the board. "Yeah. I am."

"And you two are happy together?" Nicholas set the board in place and braced it with his hip as he pulled his hammer out of the loop on his pouch.

"A lot happier than I was with Mandy and about as happy as you were with Cara."

Nicholas chose to ignore that last comment. Ever since the aborted ride yesterday, Lorne had been dropping hints about Cara as heavy as the board they were maneuvering into place.

"Just make sure you protect yourself," Nicholas muttered, pulling a handful of nails out of the pocket of his carpenter pouch. "You're starting a new business. If this marriage doesn't work—"

"I'm not going to lie, I have my concerns, as well, but Trista and I really love each other and we want to get married. And sometimes you just have to dive in. Take a chance. Love is a risk, but I think it's a risk worth taking."

"I took a chance with Cara. Getting engaged after seven months. Look where that got me." He easily pounded the nails in and Lorne followed suit.

"But you never set a wedding date, man."

Nicholas shrugged Lorne's comment aside. "That was only part of the problem."

Trouble was even though he had loved Cara, he had

his own embers of misgivings. Misgivings fanned into flame by his father's concerns.

It wasn't part of the plan, his father had advised. Things needed to get done on the ranch first.

"Taking a chance can have serious repercussions," Nicholas said, walking back to get another board. "You're starting a business and you're not set up yet. Don't you think you should wait?"

"No. What Trista and I did was wrong and I want this baby born into a marriage."

"But you don't seem committed. You're letting Trista and Cara do most of the work."

"Hey, I'm committed to the marriage—the wedding is just what I have to do to get there. It's just a tradition."

"But it's a good one," Nicholas said as they carried the board back to the corrals.

"Says the guy who knows all about it," Lorne said as he grinned.

Nicholas ignored him. "If I was getting married I'd want things done proper and in order. Things need to be ready. In place."

"And that's why in a few days I'm getting married and you're still single."

"What do you mean?"

"You wanted everything just so before you and Cara got married. Bills paid, bank account solid, debt paid down. Corrals fixed, barn painted, all that jazz. But things get in the way and things happen and it can all be gone in a flash." Lorne snapped his fingers to underline his statement. "So maybe I'm taking a chance, but if you never take a chance, you never get to experience the thrill of jumping off into the void without a net." Lorne's voice held a touch of amusement.

"You, my friend, have been reading too many motivational books. Next thing I know you're going to tell me I need to release myself from the bonds of earth and fly free."

Lorne grew quiet and for a moment Nicholas thought he might have hit a nerve.

Nicholas glanced up in time to see his friend looking at him with a steady gaze, his hammer hanging at his side.

"What?" Nicholas asked.

"You go to church, dude. You know that God wants us to do justice, to love mercy and to walk humbly with Him—at least that's how I remember it. I'm taking care of my responsibilities so I'm doin' that. I know you don't wanna talk about Cara, but you made a megamistake with her. And I figure you got a second chance, now that she's back."

"She's got her own plans, Lorne. And they don't include me."

Lorne gave no reply and for a while the only noise that broke the quiet was the ringing of hammers and the occasional bellow from the herd of heifers close to the barn.

But as they worked Lorne's words as well as his confidence in what he was doing spun around Nicholas's mind.

"Oh, brother. What's this doing on here?" Lorne brushed some sparrow droppings off the boards. "Those birds are getting to be a pest. You really need to do something about 'em."

"And a million other things," Nicholas said. "I can't keep up."

"Have you ever thought of quitting your job?"

"You sound like Cara used to," Nicholas muttered.

"So what happened with you and Cara?" Lorne asked.

Nicholas missed the nail he was hammering and bent

it over. "Nothing. We just had a spill. She fell and then Bud took off. So I thought I should bring her back. So, nothing happened."

Lorne snickered and Nicholas straightened the nail. "I was talking about how you two broke up, dude."

"I…I told you," he said, wishing he didn't sound so flustered. "We had a fight about my job."

"So I'm guessing something else happened between you and Cara on Sunday," Lorne asked, his voice full of innuendo.

Nicholas pounded the nail home in three swipes. He had never been a kiss-and-tell kind of guy and wasn't spilling his guts to a friend in wedding mode. "She had a spill. Nothing else happened."

"Else?"

He clamped his lips together. Best not to say anything more.

But as he fitted another nail in the board, his mind slipped back to that fateful kiss. He wished he could rewind that moment. He should never, never have done that. It was a mistake and he had to make sure he got through this wedding with his heart whole.

Chapter Nine

"And I'll take two dozen of these gerberas," Cara said to the greenhouse attendant, leaning over the wooden table to point out the one she wanted.

The swish of the sprinklers, the abundant greenery and the humid warmth of the greenhouse created a sense of wonder and expectation in Cara.

She wished she had her own place, a garden and flower beds. She let her mind wander to Nicholas's house, imagining plants nestled against the wooden step leading up to the house and flowers hanging from the porch. The place looked immaculate, but it needed a woman's touch. Some flowers, some shrubs. A kitchen garden—

"And you wanted a dozen of the prepotted arrangements?" the clerk asked, his question breaking into her runaway and foolish thoughts.

She tapped her finger on her chin, considering. "Actually, make that fifteen."

She did some mental calculations, figuring what plants she would need where, and then her phone rang. She glanced at the call display. Trista.

"Hey, Cara, are you at the nursery already?" she demanded.

"I got off work early."

"Okay. Okay, that should work. Let me think."

Cara frowned as she pinched a dead flower off one of the plants. "What should work?"

"I got Nicholas to meet you at the nursery. I thought we should bring the plants to the ranch right away. That way they don't have to get moved twice."

Cara swallowed against the anticipation that filled her at the sound of Nicholas's name. She didn't want to see him so soon. Not after Sunday.

Of its own accord her hand drifted up to her mouth. It was as if his kiss still lingered on her lips. His touch still warmed her.

"That won't work," she protested. "Who is going to water them?"

"Nicholas said he didn't mind."

A picture of Nicholas wielding a watering can flashed into Cara's mind. "He doesn't have time. Any day now he's baling his hay."

"And you know that…how?"

Cara chose to ignore the innuendo in Trista's voice. "When is Nicholas coming?"

"He should be there in about five minutes. He's taking his flatbed truck so you should be able to put all the plants on it. I gotta run. Thanks a ton for doing this." And then Trista broke the connection.

Cara put her phone away, disappointed to see her hands trembling. Nicholas was coming.

She had hoped to avoid him for a few more days. At least until her heart didn't do that silly pounding thing every time she thought of him. At least until her emotions could settle down.

She'd just have to speed up the process.

She was paying for the plants when, in the edge of her vision, she caught a shadow in the doorway of the nursery. The fine hairs on her arm rose up, her neck grew warm and she knew, without looking up, that Nicholas stood there.

"Do you need help with these?" the clerk asked as he handed over her change.

"I'll help her." Nicholas now stood beside her, his presence filling the room.

She glanced up at him, disconcerted to see him looking down at her. A slow smile teased the mouth that had kissed her yesterday and as their eyes met, a shiver spiraled up her back.

"How's the injury?" he asked, a callused finger lightly touching the bruise on her forehead.

"The doctor said everything was fine." She forced her gaze away, forced her emotions under control.

"Do all of these need to come out?" Nicholas asked, gesturing at the plants.

"Every single one," she said.

Nicholas grabbed the handles of four plants and headed out the door, Cara holding only two plants, right behind him. Thankfully he had parked his truck right out the door.

"Why don't you stay here," he said, placing his plants on the truck bed, "and I'll bring the plants up to you."

"Sounds like a good idea." She was about to put her foot on the tire and climb up, when he grabbed her by the waist and hoisted her up.

She caught her balance, then turned away from him,

busying herself with arranging the plants on the truck bed. This was ridiculous, she told herself. *Get a grip, woman.*

When he came out again, her control had returned and a few minutes later, all the plants were set out on the truck, ready to be moved.

"I'm glad I came," Nicholas said, glancing over the assortment of greenery and flowers. "It would have taken you forever to move these on your own."

"I could have managed," Cara said, trying mightily to create some emotional distance from the man looking up at her. "But, yeah, it's nice to have the help."

She made her way through the plants to the back of the truck determined, this time, to get down on her own.

"So do you want to follow me?" Nicholas asked when she was on the ground again.

Cara wanted to say no. She wanted to tell Nicholas to unload the plants himself and leave her alone. She didn't want to fall into the feelings swirling around her. Feelings that had the potential to overwhelm her and make her lose her footing once again.

And yet…

She looked up into his gray eyes and, for a moment, felt peace.

"I'll follow you," she said.

While she drove behind Nicholas's truck she phoned Aunt Lori to tell her she wasn't coming home for dinner. She assured her aunt that she would grab a bite to eat in town.

Twenty minutes later she pulled up behind Nicholas's truck. He was already taking the plants off the bed.

"I thought we could put them here," he said, pointing with his chin to the porch. He hung up one pot, the pink petunias and blue trailing lobelia creating a bright spot of color and friendly welcome.

Her heart did a slow flip as he hung the second pot on another old hook beside the first one. The house now looked like a home.

She shook aside the feeling. She was here to work, not daydream.

In no time, plants hung from every available hook and were placed along the foundation of the house, brightening the drab wood siding and filling the empty flower beds.

"Hey, that looks great," Nicholas said, brushing the dirt off his hands, grinning at the brightly colored plants. "I might have to get into gardening next year. Spruce the place up."

"You'll have to water them regularly," Cara reminded him.

He shot her a quick smile. "I irrigate one hundred and sixty acres of hay. I think I can remember to do a few plants."

"Just saying, is all," Cara said, sharing his smile.

He stood, his hands on his hips, glancing from the plants to her as if not sure what to say next. "Trista asked if we could make a bit of a plan—figure out what you wanted where."

Cara glanced over toward the site. From here she could see the arbor already in place and a sense of sorrowful déjà vu drifted over her. This was exactly how she had imagined her own wedding site.

"Did Mr. Elderveld put hooks in the top bar of the arbor?" Cara asked as they walked toward the site. "We'll need them to hang plants." Cara did a slow turn, thinking out loud. "I'd like to create some groupings of flowers of different heights, but I'm not sure what we can use."

"I have an old cream separator and a couple of cream cans we could put plants in," Nicholas suggested.

"Sounds great. Why don't you get them and we can figure out where to put them."

While he was gone, Cara put stakes in the ground where she wanted plant pots situated.

She heard the putt-putt of a small engine and turned, wondering what was going on.

Nicholas pulled up beside her, astride a green ATV, pulling a trailer. "I found two old wagon wheels, as well," he said, looking very proud of himself. "Thought we could use them somewhere."

Cara walked over to the trailer, her mind spinning with the possibilities. "Where did this come from?" she asked, running her hand over the antique machine. She didn't know how a cream separator worked. She did know that the large metal bowl on the top of the column would be a perfect holder for another plant. She bent over and read the plate. "Renfrew Machinery Company. 1924."

"My grandfather and great-grandfather milked cows." Nicholas gestured toward the red hip-roof barn. "My first memory of my grandmother was watching her clipping a cheesecloth on the basin and pouring milk from the cows into the separator. The skim milk would come out here, and the cream out here," Nicholas said, pointing to two spouts offset from each other. "Then she'd haul two five-gallon pails of milk off to the pigs." Nicholas smiled as he ran his hands over the machine. "She was a pretty tough woman, my grandmother."

"And your grandparents live in an old-age home now? In Calgary?"

"You remember?" Nicholas shot her a puzzled frown.

"I remember you talking about visiting them, yes." It hurt that he thought she had brushed away every conversation they'd ever had.

"I still go see them whenever I can."

"But no milk cows now?" Cara asked, trying to imagine Nicholas as a young boy watching his grandmother working on the same place he still lived. Cara had met her grandmother only once as she and her mother crisscrossed the continent. Her grandfather had died before Cara was born and Cara's grandmother passed away fifteen years ago, but Cara hadn't grieved the death of a woman she barely knew.

"My dad got rid of the cows as soon as he took over the place. Gramps wasn't fond of them so he didn't mind. He just kept them around for Gramma's sake. They never made a lot of money off them. The real money was in cattle and grain." Nicholas brushed some dust off the large silver bowl mounted on the top, a melancholy smile edging his mouth.

"And working away from the farm." No sooner had the words slipped out than Cara felt like smacking her head.

Silence followed that and Cara turned her attention back to the job at hand.

"So, let's decide what we should put where," she said. "I think we could put the cream separator by the guestbook table and put one of the plants with the trailing lobelia in it."

"And the guest table is where?"

Cara walked to the spot and pushed a stake in the ground. Nicholas followed her with the ATV and hauled the separator out of the trailer.

"Next, we'll figure out where we want the chairs."

As they paced out, measured and planned, Cara drew on the plans she had made for herself for the brief months of her own engagement to Nicholas. She'd had it all figured out, down to where the guest book would be located and what would have been on the table.

"This is going to look great," Nicholas said, looking over the site.

"So, do you think this will all go through?" Cara asked, thinking of the dozens of cupcakes in her aunt's freezer. She and Trista had decided to forego the usual wedding cake in favor of a cupcake tower.

"Yeah. I really do."

Cara shot a quick glance Nicholas's way. "Did you talk to Lorne?"

"He's committed to her and to being married. I think his biggest problem was the hoopla surrounding the ceremony."

"I can understand. Most guys don't like the planning part of weddings." But even as she spoke, she thought of all the work Nicholas put into this wedding.

He was meticulous and he liked things done in good order. All part of his personality and one of the reasons they were standing here, planning someone else's wedding instead of their own.

Don't go there. Don't go there.

"I feel like things are coming together," Nicholas said, slapping some dirt off his blue jeans. "You seem to know exactly what to do. How did you figure it all out?"

Cara crossed her arms, looking around the still-empty yard, seeing it the way she thought it would look when done. "I used the plans that I…" Her voice faded on the summer breeze sifting over the yard.

"Plans that you what?"

She shrugged, then figured she had nothing to lose and completed her sentence. "That I had in mind for… our wedding."

He said nothing and she didn't want to turn to catch his reaction. She didn't want to know if she'd see relief on his face because her plans never reached fruition, or if she'd see regret.

"You had actually thought that far?"

"I'm like any other girl," she said. "I made plans. Even bought a bride magazine."

She thought of their shared kiss, the tender way he had held her, and her heart stuttered with a mixture of pain and regret.

Should she have been so insistent on his staying away from his work?

But now, after seeing his love for the ranch, she knew more than before he would never put her needs before the needs of the place he loved so much.

"At least I get to use the plans now," she added, fighting a surprising wave of sorrow.

Then, to her alarm, Nicholas came to stand in front of her and his finger brushed over the bruise on her forehead.

"So how come we didn't get that far?" he asked.

Cara avoided his gaze. If she let herself be beguiled by him, she'd be headed down the same path they'd traveled before and she knew where that would end.

Nicholas would leave and she'd be left behind, afraid and worried.

So her and Nicholas? Dead end.

"Maybe we weren't meant for each other," she said quietly. "Maybe it wasn't meant to be."

"That sounds pretty vague to me."

Cara shrugged. "Maybe vague is all I can give you." She looked up at him then, taking a chance. "Maybe I can't give you any more than I already did."

Nicholas's eyes narrowed and for a moment she wondered if he understood what she meant.

"You left," he said, anger threading his voice. "You took off without a word. I thought you didn't want to marry me and now I find out that you were actually planning our wedding. So it wasn't the proposal that sent you scurrying away?"

Cara hardly dared to look at him, not sure he would fully understand. "No. It was your work. Your job."

Nicholas took a step back. "So we're still back to that?" He released a humorless laugh. "Back to where we started."

"Has anything changed?" she asked.

He opened his mouth, as if to speak, but she didn't want to hear it. Didn't want to hear him say that yes, he had to leave. Had to go work his dangerous job. Had to put the ranch ahead of everything.

"We're done here," Cara said, managing to keep her voice even as it broke into the awkward stillness drifting into the moment. Then she walked toward her car, quickening her pace, before the tears filling her eyes spilled over.

Chapter Ten

Cara sat cross-legged on her bed, her Bible on her lap flipping idly through it when she heard a knock on the door.

"Come in," she said, looking up from the book, but not closing it.

Her uncle put his head in the room. "I saw your light on. Everything okay?"

"Yeah. I'm okay." She gestured for him to come in and he grabbed a chair, carried it closer to her bed, sat down and caught his breath.

Though he claimed he was fine, Cara knew his recuperation was taking longer than he hoped.

"How was your day?" he asked. "I was napping when you got home."

"Long. Tiring." But not all her exhaustion had to do with the vet work she'd done today. Her thoughts kept edging toward the conversation she and Nicholas had on Tuesday then circling back to their time together on Sunday.

And every time she had to pull herself back to the present she felt a tiny sense of loss.

"I spent an hour with Anderson's mare, trying to deliver a colt and then spent three hours taking it apart so I could remove the body."

Uncle Alan patted her hand in commiseration. "Surgeries like that are disheartening and draining."

"I know. And that poor mare kept straining." Cara's voice hitched.

"At least you won't be doing that kind of work in Montreal," Uncle Alan said.

"No. Thank goodness." Cara tried to inject a note of relief into her voice, but in the past two weeks she'd been happier at work than she'd been for the past three years.

As to what that meant for her job in Montreal, she didn't want to ponder.

Uncle Alan gestured toward the Bible. "So, you started reading that again?"

Cara looked down at the book. She'd received it from her aunt and uncle when she graduated from high school. She had read it once in a while, but after her mother's death, she had put it away.

"I don't know if it's going to help," Cara said. "But lately I feel like I'm stumbling around in the dark—"

"God's word is a lamp unto my feet and a light unto my path." Uncle Alan gave her a gentle smile.

Cara laughed lightly. "Yeah, I guess I'm at the right place then."

"What are you reading?"

"I'm just paging through the Psalms."

"What are you looking for?"

Cara sighed as she flipped another page. "Guidance. Direction." She ran her fingers lightly down the page, as if trying to read the words by touch. "I don't know what's happening in my life anymore, Uncle. I have a plan. I know what I'm going to do and yet feel…lost."

"Are you talking about your job in Montreal?"

"It's a good job, Uncle Alan. I'll be able to do some traveling and I'll be challenged and there's lots of room for upward movement and career advancement." But as she spoke, Cara kept her eyes on her finger, still tracking the words in the Bible.

"Who are you trying harder to convince? Me or you?" he asked gently, leaning back in the chair, the light from her bedside lamp reflecting off his glasses.

Cara looked down at the Bible again and laughed. "I don't know. Both, I guess."

Uncle Alan heaved a heavy sigh. "If that Gordon fellow wasn't coming I could give you a job here—"

"I don't want a job here." The words fairly jumped out of her.

"I hope you're not so adamant because you don't want to be working with me," Uncle Alan joked.

Cara riffled the pages of the Bible with one hand. "Of course not. I would love to work with you."

"So then I'm guessing it's Nicholas?"

Cara's head snapped up. Uncle Alan just smiled.

"I may be recuperating from a heart attack, but I'm not blind."

"I never thought you were."

"Be careful, Cara," he said. "Don't let your past feelings interfere with your current situation."

"You don't have to worry," Cara said. "In fact as soon as his cattle are tested he's going on an overseas job. Something more hazardous than the offshore rig work he used to do." Her voice caught, the emotions and weariness of the day piling on her.

Thankfully Uncle Alan didn't say anything. Instead he reached over and gently took the Bible from her unresisting hands. He angled his head up so he could see through his bifocals, licked his finger and turned a few pages. Then he handed the Bible back to her.

"Read this, my dear. Psalm 139 up to verse 18. Maybe that will give you some comfort."

Then he got up, bent over, brushed a kiss over her forehead and left.

As the door closed softly behind him, Cara swiped at the lone tear trickling down her cheek, blinked the rest away and bent her head to read.

"'Oh, Lord, You have searched me and know me,'" she read, "'You know when I sit and when I rise. You perceive my thoughts from afar.'" Cara stopped there, her mind ticking back to a time when the idea that God knew her thoughts frightened her. But now she realized God now knew her confusion.

And her fear.

She read on, letting the poetry of the words nourish and seep into her soul. "'Where can I go from Your Spirit? Where can I flee from Your presence? If I go up to the heavens, You are there; if I make my bed in the depths, You are there.'"

As she read, it was as if hands rested on her shoulders, easing away the burden she carried there.

She thought of what her aunt had told her, that though she may have turned her back on God, He was still there. Still waiting.

Deep in her soul, she had always known that.

She closed her eyes and let her heart rest in God and rest in His love.

He had to be enough for her, she realized. She had to stop thinking she needed more than God.

"Forgive me, Lord," she prayed. "Help me not to look for happiness and contentment in other people. Help me to only seek You first."

And as she slowly released her hold on her plans, her life and her heart, peace stole over her soul.

And slowly she struggled to release her changing feelings for Nicholas into God's care.

Chapter Eleven

"Are you okay?" Trista held Cara by the shoulders, staring into her eyes.

Cara adjusted the gauzy veil on Trista's head and frowned. "Why are you asking me? Today is your wedding day." She knelt and fluffed up the dress, then stood back to admire her friend.

Yesterday she was wound as tight as a spring, making last-minute calls to the caterer, to Nicholas, to the minister, to Trista's mother. But it had all come together.

"I just want to make sure you're okay with Nicholas and all that."

"I'm fine. Trust me." And just to underline her statement, Cara gave Trista a bright smile, then turned her to face the mirror. "Look at you. You look amazing."

Trista's dress had been worn by her mother and altered to fit. The style was simple, but elegant. Raw silk gathered on one hip by a jeweled pin, then fell in rich folds to the ground. The veil belonged to Lorne's mother. Just a simple layer of gauzy netting and a bandeau covered with a remnant of silk taken from the dress.

Cara looked over her friend's shoulder, smiling at their

shared reflections—her blond hair pinned back on one side with a single flower, Trista's dark hair surrounded by a halo of white. "Remember the wedding plans we used to make?" she whispered, as if unwilling to disturb the moment.

"You always knew what you wanted," Trista said, reaching behind her for Cara's hand. "And just for the record, this should be you. You used to talk about getting married way more than me."

"Just silly games," Cara said, trying to laugh off Trista's concern. Dredging up old dreams and memories was a waste of time.

Trista turned and caught Cara's other hand and gave them a light shake. "I still believe you'll find the right person."

"Thanks, Trista, but today is your day." Cara adjusted her veil and wiped away a tiny smudge of mascara from her cheek. "And we're not discussing me anymore." She glanced around the room, looking for the bouquet.

Nicholas had cleared out an empty bedroom in the house for Trista's changing room and had found an old, full-length mirror. Probably an antique, Cara guessed, from the aged wood framing it. Probably something his great-grandmother used.

Trista ran her hands down the raw silk of her dress and placed her hands on her stomach. "I don't show yet, do I?"

"Not even the tiniest bump," Cara assured her.

She saw a florist's box on the bed and pulled out Trista's bouquet. The bouquet was made of white roses offset with blue larkspur tied loosely together with a blue silk ribbon matching the blue silk of Cara's dress.

Cara's bouquet was made up of blue larkspur.

"So you go first, then I do, right?" Trista asked with a grin. "Or is it the other way around?"

"I told you we should have had a rehearsal," Cara said.

"As Lorne says, what's to rehearse?" Trista leaned closer to the mirror and dabbed at her lipstick. "We're not doing anything fancy." She pressed her lips together then inhaled deeply, her hand on her stomach. "Besides, there wasn't time. Lorne and I barely got the marriage classes done."

"We've been to enough weddings. I'm sure we'll figure it all out," Cara said, though on one level, she was thankful there hadn't been a rehearsal either. Spending an evening with Nicholas at a wedding that had been based on her own plans was difficult enough. Two nights in a row would have been too hard.

You've got a good job waiting, she told herself. *A job that will finance any trip you might want to make. You can go anywhere and do anything.*

Just like your mother did.

Cara ignored the mocking voice. Her mother had a child that she left behind. She was leaving no one behind in her life. No hearts would break when she left.

And after she had spoken to Uncle Alan, she had drawn more comfort from the Bible. God would not leave her and that was enough for her.

A knock at the door made them both jump. "Are we ready?" As Trista's father came into the room, he shook his head in amazement.

"My girl," he said, with a little hitch in his voice. "You look so beautiful." He embraced his daughter and Cara caught the shimmer of tears in his eyes.

And she would be lying if she said she wasn't jealous. She had Uncle Alan and Aunt Lori and she was thankful she still had both in her life. If she were to get married, he would walk her down the aisle.

Yet that didn't seem the same as a father who had raised her from a baby, who had seen every step of her growth, looking with pride at his own daughter on this momentous day.

Trista's father pulled back and he shook his head, as if he couldn't understand himself how the years had slipped away.

"I'm so proud of you, honey," he said. "You've been a blessing to me and your mother and I pray you will be a blessing to Lorne."

Trista wiped a tear and Cara's throat thickened at this precious moment.

"Now, let's deliver you to your future husband." Mr. Elderveld patted her shoulder and gave her a bright smile.

They walked together down the stairs of Nicholas's house and down the wooden steps of the verandah. Ahead of them were the rows of chairs where the guests were seated. Pots of flowers lined the grass aisle, flanked the arbor and hung from the crosspiece, creating a riot of color set against the stunning backdrop of the mountains.

Soft music played from hidden speakers, adding to the ambience.

And as they approached, Cara saw the minister, Lorne and Nicholas already waiting.

Nicholas wore a navy suit and light blue shirt, echoing the colors of Cara's simple sheath. The shirt softened the gray of his eyes, giving them an azure tint.

The music changed, and Cara walked slowly toward the front. She kept her focus on the people in the audience smiling their encouragement as she walked past. She saw her aunt and uncle sitting in the crowd. Uncle Alan gave her a wink and Aunt Lori just smiled.

Then as she came to the front and took her place on the other side of the pastor, she chanced another quick look toward Nicholas.

This time he looked directly at her. His features were impassive and she wondered what was going on behind those gray-blue eyes of his that shifted away so quickly.

And why did that bother her?

Then the music changed to a solemn wedding march, everyone stood and Cara forced her gaze back to Trista. The gauzy veil framed her serene face and her white dress shimmered in the afternoon sun.

The smile on Trista's face transformed her and joy for her friend rippled through Cara. She looked so peacefully happy that Cara couldn't stifle another small jolt of jealousy.

That could have been me and Nicholas.

Cara gave Trista an encouraging smile and then Trista had eyes only for Lorne. Lorne met Mr. Elderveld, then took Trista's hand and led her to the arbor.

A soft breeze and the faint buzzing of bees sifted through the air as the pastor looked around the gathering as if to underscore the solemnity of the occasion.

Then he faced Lorne and Trista.

"Dearly beloved, we are gathered here to celebrate the marriage of Lorne Hughes and Trista Elderveld. That we are all gathered as friends and family is important…"

It had all come together, Cara thought as the pastor spoke, her eyes ticking over the plants hanging from the arbor, nestled against the sides and hanging from hooks down the aisle. Though she hadn't been here to supervise, everything looked exactly as she had planned.

After that emotional moment with Nicholas, she had stayed away from the ranch, preferring to give instructions via Lorne and get updates via Trista. While she and her aunt decorated cupcakes and helped make table runners from the safety of her aunt's home, Cara heard the lawn on the yard had been mowed and the arbor set up.

An excited phone call from Trista had told her the wedding dress was finished and the bridesmaid dress had arrived at the store in Calgary. She had heard that Nicholas rented a tent and got the chairs from the church. Nicholas was taking good care of the plants. The hay was baled but Nicholas was still crabby.

Yesterday Cara had told Lorne's brother how she wanted the chairs arranged and where she wanted the hooks and which plants to hang on them.

She'd immersed herself in her work and wedding plans and, with a lot of self-discipline and prayer, had managed to keep thoughts of Nicholas at bay.

Now, the day had arrived and things were moving along just as she had envisioned.

Just as she had planned for her own wedding.

She caught her thoughts from veering back down that treacherous path. Looking ahead was the only way she would survive this wedding. She had her own future to plan.

And who is in that future?

She pushed the insidious question aside. She was going it alone. It seemed to have worked for her mother, so she would make it work for herself.

Then, unable to stop herself, she glanced past Lorne to where Nicholas stood silhouetted against the valley of his ranch. Behind him lay green fields dotted with round, fat bales and, past that, the pastures and cropland of the Chapman ranch.

Nicholas had continuity and history.

He had his great-grandparents' cream separator that had been used on this place. He lived in the same home where he'd grown up.

He had roots and stability.

And she?

Since she broke up with Nicholas, the restlessness that had gripped her when her mother died had grown. She had tried to satisfy that by moving around. A restlessness, if she were to be honest with herself, still coursed through her.

But worse, she had been gripped with a loneliness that had claws.

"'Be content with what you have, because God has said, never will I leave you, never will I forsake you,'" the pastor was saying. "Trista and Lorne chose these words from Hebrews as a reminder to us of where true love comes from. A God who lavishes rich love on us."

The words caught Cara's attention.

Never will I leave you. Never will I forsake you.

And behind those words came the ones she had read the other night.

If I rise on the wings of the dawn, if I settle on the far side of the sea, even there Your hand will guide me, Your right hand will hold me fast.

The strength she'd received from those words returned to her. Strength and the reminder that though she had turned her back on God, as her Aunt Lori had said, God had not turned His back on her. It was as if, in her weak and weary moments, God was trying to catch her attention. To show her that though she may forsake Him, He hadn't forsaken her.

"...so this love that God lavishes on us is how we, too, should live our lives and live our marriages. God is a God of abundance and rich blessings if we acknowledge that He wants to walk alongside us and surround us in our marriages...and in our lives."

He paused to give the words their due and Cara felt a stirring of the same emotion that had touched her when she'd read the Bible the other night.

God alongside me, she thought, the gentle touch of His presence surrounding her.

Trista turned to her, handing Cara her bouquet, and then they were moving on to the next part of the ceremony. As Trista and Lorne exchanged their vows and then their rings, Cara felt a gentle melancholy. Her friend now belonged to someone else.

They exchanged a kiss and walked over to the table to sign the register. Cara clutched Trista's bouquet and her own and fell into step beside Nicholas. She tried not to be aware of his presence, tried not to feel overwhelmed by his nearness.

She placed the bouquets on the table. When she returned to Nicholas's side, she stepped into a depression in the grass and faltered in her high heels, but Nicholas caught her elbow and steadied her. His hand felt warm, callused. The hand of a man who worked.

And his touch sent a shock up her arm.

"Sorry about that," he murmured. "I didn't manage to get everything smooth."

She nodded her reply, focusing her attention on Trista sitting at the table.

When it was her turn to sign, she had to walk past

Nicholas and she prayed she would keep her feet under her. As she sat down, she could feel him standing behind her.

Just help me get through this, she prayed, signing her name where the pastor showed her, pleased that her hands didn't tremble as much as her stomach did.

Then the pastor presented the new couple to the gathering and with a burst of joyous music, Lorne and Trista rushed down the aisle, as if eager to start their married life.

Nicholas held out his arm to Cara and she hesitated.

"We're supposed to do this," he said, sounding put out.

She was being silly. This was simply tradition. She slipped her arm in his and they followed the bridal couple down the aisle.

But as soon as they got to the end, he released her and walked away.

Her own reaction to him frustrated her. *Why do you have to be so touchy around him?* she scolded herself. *Why can't you act like he's some ordinary guy?*

Because he wasn't and never would be an ordinary guy to her. And in spite of the comfort she'd just received, she also knew, without a doubt, neither would Nicholas be the constant in her life that God would.

Thankfully there wasn't a receiving line so Cara didn't need to stand beside Nicholas, like some pretend couple, and receive well-wishers on her friend's wedding. Instead, people simply milled about, grabbing the opportunity to congratulate Lorne and Trista when they could.

Someone tapped her shoulder and Cara turned to see the photographer standing behind her.

In all the busyness, she had forgotten about him, she realized with a start. Trista didn't want pictures taken before the ceremony nor during and had simply told him to show up after the service.

"So, where are the horses we'll be taking into the mountains?" the photographer asked. "I might need an extra one for the equipment."

Cara's heart downshifted. She didn't want to get on a horse and ride up into the hills. Whenever she brushed her hair and touched the tender spot on her temple, she was reminded of her spill.

"Trista and I decided we're not going that route." Nicholas's deep voice spoke up from behind her. "We'll just take pictures on the yard."

Relief made her bones weak and she shot a grateful look his way, but he didn't catch her gaze.

"Could you get Lorne and Trista and meet us on the south side of the barn in about fifteen minutes?" he asked, then turned and strode away, the photographer trotting along behind just to keep up.

"I'll show you where you can set up," Nicholas called over his shoulder.

Cara felt a hand on her shoulder. "Oh, my dear, you look so beautiful." Aunt Lori gave her a tight hug, then brushed a strand of hair back from her face.

Uncle Alan hugged her next, but caught a glimmer of sympathy in his expression.

"You doing okay?" he asked, lowering his voice.

She gave him a bright smile. "I'm fine. I'm so happy for Trista."

Aunt Lori tapped him on the shoulder. "I think we should go now."

Cara frowned. "You're not staying for dinner?"

Aunt Lori glanced from Cara to Uncle Alan, as if unsure of what to say. "Alan's feeling a bit tired."

"I'm not that tired," he protested. "Just a bit…"

"Tired," Aunt Lori said firmly. She gave Cara a smile, then took Alan's arm. "You enjoy the rest of the evening. I won't be waiting up for you, though."

"Probably a good idea. I'll need to stay here until the end."

"Then we'll see you in the morning." And Aunt Lori turned, her arm in Uncle Alan's as they walked away, their steps measured and slow.

They were getting old. She was the only child they had and she was leaving them alone again. But she couldn't take that burden on. She had her own stuff to deal with.

At least they have each other, she thought, lifting up her dress and heading out to find the bride and groom.

A few minutes later she herded Trista and Lorne past well-wishers and fielded questions about the supper from Lorne and Trista's family as they went to meet the photographer.

By the time she got them to the barn, he was already set up and Nicholas looked as if he was about to come and get them.

"Finally," he said, frowning at everyone. "We've got to get this show on the road. We're already running about ten minutes behind."

Trista sent Cara a look of mock horror. "Oh, no. Ten whole minutes. Whatever shall we do?"

Cara laughed, but then caught herself when Nicholas sent her a grumpy look.

"The photographer wants to start with a group shot," Nicholas was saying. "Then he can focus on you and Lorne so Cara and I can get back to—"

"Bossing people around," Trista retorted. "Okay. Group shot. I don't want the usual standing in a row shot. I want me and Lorne together and Nicholas and Cara together."

They obediently arranged themselves as couples and the photographer fussed and adjusted with Lorne and Trista, then turned his attention to Cara and Nicholas.

"Put your hand here," he said to Nicholas, taking his hand and placing it on Cara's hip.

"We're not the bride and groom," Nicholas grumbled even as he did as he was told.

Cara swallowed as his hand dropped on her hip. This was just a show. Meant nothing at all.

"I just want to balance the shot," the photographer said, squinting at Cara, as if he wasn't sure what to do with her. "Could you move back toward Nicholas?"

She could, but she didn't want to. Already she felt too aware of Nicholas standing behind her, the warmth of his chest, the scent of his cologne. But she obediently took a small step backward.

"Good. That's better. Now if you could look down at your bouquet, hold it up a bit more, and, Nicholas, could you put your hand over hers? That's great."

Cara jumped a bit as Nicholas's fingers covered her hand. They were like ice.

She chanced a quick look up at him and their gazes met.

Just for a moment she caught a flare of another emotion in his eyes. The same emotion she'd seen moments before he'd kissed her the other day.

But he blinked and she wondered if she had imagined it.

She jerked her head back and clutched her flowers. *Pay attention to the photographer.*

Yet even as she tried, she was fully aware of Nicholas's hand on hers.

The photographer set up a few more poses. In one Cara had to sit on Nicholas's knee. In another she had his jacket slung over her shoulder.

Nicholas smiled and posed, but he seemed aloof.

She got through it all and as soon as they were done, she fled the scene. She quickly found some jobs to do and kept herself busy and out of Nicholas's way.

Chapter Twelve

"I'd like to welcome everyone here tonight," Bert, Lorne's brother, was saying as people got themselves settled at their respective tables.

Thankfully Trista had the bridesmaid and the best man flanking them at the head table so Cara didn't have to sit beside Nicholas throughout the meal, as well. She couldn't forget the way her heart stuttered at the merest touch.

She had to get over this, she thought, angry at her runaway emotions. "Before we start, I'd like to ask Pastor Samuels to give a blessing on the meal."

The pastor came to the front. He'd already taken off his tie and looked far more relaxed and approachable than he had at the ceremony.

He looked over the head table, his eyes catching and holding each of theirs in turn, and Cara returned his smile. She reminded herself to talk to him about the sermon and thank him for his encouraging words.

"Welcome everyone, to this part of Lorne and Trista's wedding. Jesus blessed the couple in Cana with His presence at their wedding, and we pray that His presence may be felt here, too." He looked around at the gathering then bowed his head.

Cara followed suit. And as the pastor prayed she joined in, struggling to reach for peace.

She was here for Trista. She simply had to get over herself.

Dinner was a noisy affair with aunts and uncles, cousins and a few friends stopping at the table to talk to the married couple. Cara smiled and nodded, reminding people who she was.

By the time dessert arrived, her mouth was tired of smiling and the low-level headache dogging her all day had become a pounding, throbbing presence.

Then a tall, blond-haired man stopped in front of her and held out his hand. His smile exposed teeth that were extrawhite in contrast to his tanned skin.

"Cara Morrison. How are you?"

Cara glanced up, her mind struggling to place the handsome man.

"Tod. Tod Hanson," he prompted. "We went on a couple of dates. I lived in Olds and we met at a football game."

And Cara remembered. "You took me to the symphony. In Calgary."

"And a movie. I didn't want you to think I was some kind of cultural snob."

Cara laughed. "That's right. That was fun."

Tod raised one eyebrow. "Was it? I had no idea you enjoyed yourself. You stopped returning my calls."

"I got busy." A flush warmed her cheeks and she was unwilling to admit that fear more than busyness had kept her away. He was attractive and fun and she couldn't understand what he saw in her. "So how do you know Lorne and Trista?"

"I'm a fill-in date for Trista's sister." He angled his head to one side, his smile growing. "Her boyfriend, my roommate, couldn't come. When I found out you were going to be here, I said I'd gladly take his place."

Cara's flush grew warmer. "Really?"

"Yeah. Really. And I'd really like to claim a dance later on."

"I think that might work," she said, forcing herself not to glance at Nicholas. Spending time with another guy would be good for her. Make her realize Nicholas wasn't the only fish in the sea.

"I'll catch you later." He pointed his finger at her, then winked and walked away.

Trista's brother walked to the podium, made a few jokes about his sister and then turned to Cara.

"I just noticed Tod talking to you, Cara. And I know there are a few other guys who have noticed you, as well. Cara, my dear men, is still single and still attractive. She works as a vet." He glanced at his paper and grinned. "Cara has been visiting Cochrane, the vet clinic for now, but rumor has it she's moving to Montreal soon. She used to live in Cochrane but before that, she and her mother traveled wherever the wind took them. So though she's single, she's a challenge to pin down." He gave her a quick grin. "Cara was also Trista's best friend when she lived here, which I understand is the longest time this peripatetic girl ever stayed in one place. Which explains how Nicholas Chapman managed to nab her. But only for a time, gentlemen, only for a time." This netted her another grin, which she gamely returned. "But enough about Cara. She is going to talk about my sister and hopefully give us some new insights into the inner workings of Trista's early years."

Cara drew a quick breath, sent up a prayer for strength and picked up her glass.

In one of her classes, her prof had said the number one fear most people had was of public speaking.

She wanted to add a caveat to that. Public speaking in front of an old fiancé in a setting that was supposed to have been their wedding created a stress level beyond that basic fear.

Just pretend he's not here. Don't look at him, don't acknowledge him. This is about Trista and your tribute to her.

She glanced nervously around the gathering, her hands clammy on her glass as all faces turned to her. She wished Uncle Alan and Aunt Lori would have stayed. They could have been her two-person cheering section.

Help me not to mess up in front of Nicholas, she prayed. *Help me not to get nervous.*

She cleared her throat and dove in.

"When I first met Trista I was a gawky teenager, new to the community and new to the school. I was in eleventh grade and had been in as many schools in as many grades. I wasn't looking forward to starting all over." She turned to Trista and smiled. "I remember standing by the fence, looking around the groups of people and wondering where I would fit in when this bouncy, cheerful girl bopped up to me and asked me my name. I was entranced by her confidence and so thankful I could have kissed her."

"I know the feeling," Lorne piped in.

Cara waited for the general laughter following that comment to die down. "Trista taught me how to put on makeup, how to dress, how to do my hair and how to talk to guys—something that I struggled with."

"I can't believe that," Trista's brother called out.

More polite laughter.

"Lorne, I want you to know that Trista is a loyal, caring, warmhearted person. Trista stood up for me when I got picked on by kids who thought I was a bit strange because I'd never stayed long in one place." Cara's eyes were on Trista but she sensed Nicholas's intent gaze, as real as a touch—caught his puzzled frown. When they were together, she had kept comments about her past to minimal jokes, adopting a breezy tone as if none of it mattered. But it had, and in her desire to show Trista what her friendship meant, she had unwittingly exposed herself.

His attentiveness made her falter a moment, but she recovered. What did it matter what he knew about her now? Nothing she said would have an effect on their lives.

"Trista stood up for me as, for what seemed like the hundredth time, I navigated yet again unfamiliar ground of new schools and new people," Cara said, soldiering on. "She stood up for me when I needed a friend and, at times, a shoulder to cry on when I felt all alone. She lent me her clothes, her advice and helped me find my place. She stood by me through thick and thin and it's an honor to stand up for her now." She looked around the room. "Could you all join me in a toast to a beautiful bride, a dear friend and a loving wife."

"To Trista," was echoed around the tent.

As she walked back to the head table, her gaze unwittingly slipped past Trista.

Nicholas stared at her, his features now an enigmatic mask.

Cara sat down, her heart pounding in her chest.

"Nicholas Chapman, best friend of the groom and also single, is well-known to most of us. He's lived here all his life, though the past number of years more than half his time is spent raking in the money on offshore rigs and, lately, Kuwait. According to Lorne he's hoping to retire early so he can sit and count his ill-gotten gains." Bert threw Nicholas a mischievous grin. "But for now he's still working. So, girls, if you want to catch him, you've got about a week until he ships out again, so no dilly-dallying."

He stepped aside to polite laughter as Nicholas made his way to the podium.

"Good evening," Nicholas said, looking around the gathering. "I've known Lorne since I was a kid. I've got more memories than we've got time but if you want to know particulars about the night the cows got into his dad's wheat crop, or how the sugar got into his brother's motorcycle's gas tank, or why the windmill stopped working, or how the graffiti got on the number two overpass…well, suffice it to say I'll be here all night." He winked at Lorne. "Trista, you and Lorne are meant for each other. I know Lorne will be a loving, caring husband. That he will treat you with respect and consideration. That he will put your needs first and that he will be a support to you in your faith journey." He lifted his glass. "To Lorne."

Cara kept her eyes down as Nicholas talked, his voice pulling at old memories. Yet his words cut when he spoke of Lorne putting Trista's needs first.

He didn't see it, she thought. He didn't see what he had done to her and her headache increased.

Cara leaned close to Trista. "I have to go get my purse. I'll just be a minute."

"You okay?" Trista asked. "You look a bit pale."

"Headache. I'll be okay."

Cara got up and left the tent, thankful for the cooling evening air. She deliberately took her time walking to the house, her frustration with Nicholas slowly easing with each step she took.

Why should his words bother her? Just because he recognized that Lorne would put Trista first, didn't mean he'd do the same.

She found her purse in the room they had changed in, popped a couple of aspirin and left, closing the door behind her.

Across the hall, the door to Nicholas's room was open. Curiosity drew her to the doorway and she took a quick look in. Pictures of various rodeo cowboys hung on the wall right above a trophy he must have received competing in a rodeo.

A small pair of cowboy boots sat on a shelf above his bed. His, she presumed. Old school pictures hung on one wall beside some older pictures of what seemed to be his grandparents. Beside them, a wedding photo of his parents, which surprised her. Though Nicholas never talked about his mother, he obviously still cared about her.

As she looked around the room filled with the detritus of a life lived in one place, a sense of homesickness nudged her.

The only place she had ever stayed long enough to collect memorabilia was at her aunt and uncle's place in Cochrane. And even then, the only things she had in her bedroom were a few mementos from the two years she went to high school here.

Once again she was struck by the fact that Nicholas had history. With a wistful smile, she turned away and went downstairs.

She closed the door of the house behind her, and just as she headed down the porch stairs, a tall figure loomed in the dark. She stifled a startled scream before she realized it was Nicholas.

"Are you okay?" He had one hand slung up in his pocket, the other tapped the seam of his pants.

She remembered too well the touch of that hand on her hip, the other on hers. And how, for a moment, she had felt safe.

"I have a bit of a headache," she said. "I was heading back to the party."

"Trista sent me looking for you. They're about to do the first dance."

Cara nodded her acknowledgment of her obligations even as her heart fluttered at the thought of dancing with Nicholas.

But before she left, he caught her hand and turned her back to him. In the gathering dusk, his glittering eyes were focused on her like a laser.

"You never told me it was hard for you coming here."

She shrugged aside his comment, adopting a breezy tone to let him know it didn't matter. "That was way in the past. I only wanted Trista to know what she did for me, that's all."

Thankfully he didn't say anything, but as they walked back, he kept his hand in the small of her back, sending tiny shivers dancing up her spine. But she didn't move away.

The music had already started when they made their way back into the tent. Trista and Lorne were already twirling around on the dance floor, eyes only for each other. Cara watched them with a smile. They made such a perfect couple.

The music changed, and Trista turned and beckoned to her. That was the signal for Cara and Nicholas to join them.

"Shall we?" Nicholas held his hand out to her, and she placed hers in his. This time his hand was warm and hers cold. His fingers tightened as he gently drew her into his arms.

Cara's hand trembled as she laid it on his shoulder, and her heart fluttered out an irregular beat. She tried to keep herself distant from him, but then his hand on her waist slipped around and drew her closer.

Once again she was struck by how right it felt to be in his arms. As if she had been lost for a time and was now where she belonged.

She closed her eyes, allowing herself to enjoy the moment. Then giving into an impulse, she slipped her arm around his back, and laid her head on his shoulder.

She drew in a long, slow breath, and eased it out, hardly daring to breathe.

Forgive me, Lord, she prayed, as her arm tightened around him. *He still means so much to me.*

His breath fanned her hair, and then to her surprise, she heard him whisper her name.

"What is it?" she whispered back.

"I missed you." His words came out in a sigh, warm on her ear. "I didn't want to, but I do."

Though he whispered the words, they thundered in her ear, creating a storm of confusion. She thought of how aloof he had looked the past hour, of how he kept his distance.

"I thought you were angry with me," she said, keeping her head on his shoulder.

"I was. I was angry because I couldn't help how I still feel about you."

She thought again of the kiss they had shared. What was happening between them? And what was she supposed to do about it?

Time and time again she was confronted with her old feelings for Nicholas. And somehow, since coming back to Cochrane, they had changed, grown deeper, more intense.

"I couldn't stop thinking about what you said the other day," he said. "About how you had planned our wedding." He drew back to look at her face. "How you had seen us with a future."

"At one time, I did."

"I did, too."

He spun her around in time to the music and then spoke again, his voice deep, intense.

"I can't get you out of my mind, Cara. I thought I could, but you keep haunting me."

His words sang through her soul. He felt the same way she did, she thought, as her heart took a long, slow dive.

She leaned back a bit as Nicholas made another turn, the twinkling minilights softening the lean line of his jaw.

"I keep thinking about you, too," she returned, holding his earnest gaze.

"I don't know about you, but I'm tired of just thinking. Do you think there is a chance for us?"

Cara nestled her head against his neck, her fluttering heart now thundering out its beat.

"Maybe," she whispered back. It wasn't much, but for

now it was all she could give him. She was still afraid of him and the emotions he easily resurrected in her.

Yet the thought of being without him seemed harder to bear than the thought of being with him.

Then, to her surprise, his lips brushed her temple, then her cheek. She closed her eyes, letting him beguile her.

Then it seemed all too soon the music stopped and the dance was over. Nicholas gently drew back, and fingered a strand of hair away from her face.

"We need to talk," he said. "But not here and now." He released her but he still held her hands. "Will you go out with me? Tuesday?"

Cara couldn't look away and knew she couldn't say no.

"I want to get things cleared up between us," he continued. "I feel like we didn't finish our last conversation."

That was because she didn't think there was anything left to say.

"Okay. Where should we meet?" she asked.

His eyes looked dark, and as Cara held his gaze awareness arced between them. "Would you be willing to come here?"

She nodded, then drifted toward him and a sudden tap on her shoulder pulled her back to reality. She blinked, then turned.

"I've come to collect my dance." Tod stood in front of her, grinning as he held his hand out.

Cara looked back at Nicholas, almost hoping he would rescue her. But he stepped aside and gestured for Tod to take over.

Tod took her in his arms. "I've been looking forward to this," he said. "Hoping maybe we could pick up where we left off."

My, wasn't she the popular ex-girlfriend tonight, she

thought, with a touch of cynicism as Tod twirled her around the dance floor.

She only listened with half an ear to Tod, gave him an occasional distracted smile. Tod was better looking but as she danced with him, her eyes continually sought and found Nicholas. And each time she saw him, he was watching her with an enigmatic expression on his face.

When the dance was over, she begged off and went to get a drink from the lemonade fountain. She looked for Nicholas and saw him standing to one side of the party, talking to someone she didn't recognize. He laughed, patted the man on the shoulder and moved on, mixing with the people. People he knew and had known since he was a child.

He belongs here. The thought settled with certainty. *This is his home and his community.*

She sat a few dances out, chatted with a few people, but her eyes kept finding his.

Each time their eyes met, she knew she hadn't imagined that surreal moment on the dance floor.

And anticipation over what would happen on Tuesday seemed to rise with each shared look across the room, each light brush of his hand as he passed her.

What would he talk about?

And would it change her plans?

Chapter Thirteen

Cara's eyes flicked over the church bulletin but she wasn't reading anything she saw.

Every time a man walked down the aisle of the church her heart started up. But so far Nicholas hadn't shown up.

This morning, when she got up in time to go to church with her aunt and uncle, Aunt Lori barely managed to hide her surprise.

Though she'd crawled into bed at three-thirty after helping the families clean up, exchanging glances with Nicholas the entire time, she couldn't sleep.

Too many thoughts were clamoring for attention. Between the sermon from the pastor at the wedding and Nicholas's sudden confession, she didn't know which way to turn.

On the one hand God promised that He'd never leave her alone. And on the other, she ran the risk of letting that promise be taken over by what Nicholas might want to talk to her about.

Did the two need to be mutually exclusive? Was she looking for signs where she should simply be looking to renew her relationship with God and let everything else fall where it may?

So she came to church, hoping to find nourishment for a soul that had kept itself far from God too long.

And hoping Nicholas would show.

The worship team came to the front and started playing a song Cara remembered from her earlier years. By the third verse, Cara had let the words of the song soothe her anticipation and put it where it should be.

The peace promised her in the song stole over her.

"Hey there."

The deep voice shivered through her, shaking her new-found serenity.

She turned to Nicholas. "Hey yourself."

He sat down beside her and, ignoring her aunt's raised eyebrows and her uncle's puzzled frown, she gave him a careful smile.

"You got up early for being out so late last night," he said quietly, leaning close to her.

"So did you," she whispered back. "Did everyone leave after I did?"

"Pretty much."

And suddenly there was nothing more to say. Either they moved directly into what Nicholas wanted to talk about or they bided their time until they could do it properly.

One step at a time, Cara told herself. She wasn't sure what lay ahead. Her plans were still in place and she had no solid reason to change them.

So why did she feel another possibility glimmering over the horizon?

Keep your focus on the pastor, she reminded herself, drawing comfort and encouragement from what he said.

Her soul drank it all in, yearning for more.

As they rose to sing the final song, a sense of contentment overrode her other feelings. She didn't know what lay ahead, but she knew God held her life in His hands.

As the notes from the final song faded away, Nicholas turned to her. "I'll call you tomorrow. Make arrangements for Tuesday, okay?"

She held his gaze and nodded as expectation quivered between them.

"Those bales are heavy," Dale said, leaning back against the bale wagon piled high with sweet-smelling hay bales. "Hay is looking good."

Nicholas took a long sip of the iced tea his father had brought out, his eyes wandering over the tight, round bales still dotting the field. The summer smell of warm hay permeated the air, creating a feeling of well-being.

"Did you check the heifers before you came here?" Nicholas asked.

His father nodded. "Crackerjack bunch of animals. That guy in Montana will be thrilled." His father pushed his hat back on his head and took another sip of lemonade. "Is that Morrison girl going to do the test?"

"Not sure, Dad." Nicholas sighed, then glanced up at his father. "Why do you talk that way about her?"

His father blew out his breath and took another sip of iced tea. "You're not getting involved with her again, are you?"

Nicholas's mind ticked back the wedding—the moment of closeness with Cara. Was he getting involved with her? But he didn't answer his father.

"You still never told me much about that day you two came riding back on Two Bits," his father said.

"Like I told you, my horse spooked, she got dumped and I was worried about her." Nicholas conveniently glossed over the kiss they had shared. The kiss that had rocked his world.

"And the wedding? You've been walking around in some kind of daze since then."

And it was a good thing his father had gone to that rodeo at Sundre the day of the wedding. Nicholas said he wanted his dad's help but now Nicholas realized his absence was for the best. His father had missed his dance with Cara.

He didn't need his father ragging on him about Cara. Not when he wasn't sure himself where things were going and what was happening. For now, he was taking things one day at a time.

"Is she starting to get to you?" Dale pressed.

"I've got things under control," was all Nicholas said, squinting at the sun as his narrowed eyes followed the contours of the land. He knew every hummock, had ridden through every valley and moved cows over every hill.

And he hoped one day he could show his own son or daughter the land that had been in the Chapman family for so many generations. He wondered what that child would look like.

Wondered who would be standing beside him.

"She's a distraction," his father continued. He just wouldn't give up.

"What do you mean?" Nicholas pulled his attention back to his dad.

"You said yourself after she left that she doesn't get your commitment to the ranch. Doesn't understand how it's in your blood and in your soul."

Nicholas had thought that at one time. But after that

aborted ride into the hills with Trista and Lorne, he wasn't so sure. As he and Cara rode and talked, he sensed she understood his attraction to the land and history that permeated his life.

"Cara left you once before, Nicholas. Not only left you, ran out on you without a word. Don't fall for her again. I can see how she looks at you. She still feels something for you. You've got to keep your eye on the prize," Dale continued. "A few more years and the ranch will be where it should be. That's a sacrifice worth making."

Nicholas thought of what Cara had said on the ride back to the ranch. How she wondered why he worked a job he didn't like when his heart was so obviously here.

He thought of how interested she seemed when he told her his family's history. How she seemed to appreciate the roots that held him firmly to this place.

And his mind cast back to Sunday morning in church when he sat beside her and how he felt, for the first time in his life, willing to step into an unknown. To stop doing the never-ending work bringing in money that was never enough.

Because each time they paid off one loan, it seemed to open the way to previously unavailable possibilities.

"I sometimes wonder if I have that in me anymore, Dad," Nicholas said finally.

His father frowned. "What do you mean?"

"You weren't in church on Sunday," Nicholas said, folding his arms over his chest. "But the pastor read a piece from Philippians that I've been thinking about the past day or two. 'I have learned the secret of being content in any and every situation, whether well fed or hungry, whether living in plenty or want.' And I got to thinking. I'm not content. Not content at work and I'm not content when I'm on the ranch. There is always one more thing to buy, one more piece of machinery to fix, one more loan to pay down. Money is flowing in, but it's not making me content."

"If you keep working that'll change."

The note of desperation in his father's voice caught Nicholas's attention.

"We have a plan," his father continued. "We sell the heifers, get a steady market for our breeding stock. Then we'll be in better shape. But we need to stick to the plan. Don't let that Morrison girl distract you."

Nicholas was tired of his father talking about Cara, but he knew if he defended her, his father wouldn't quit. Besides, he wasn't sure what was happening between them, but he knew that some spark of what they had before still lingered. Maybe he was wrong about Cara, maybe he was a fool, but he sensed she felt the same.

"I better get back to work." He pushed himself away from the tractor. "I want to have the hay off the field by tomorrow."

When he and Cara would be seeing each other.

After that he had to get the heifers—their ticket to the next step up in the ranch's economic fortunes—tested and ready to ship.

And after that?

He had a job waiting and yet…

For the first time in years he was willing to put a question mark on his future.

Could he do it? Could he make the sacrifice Cara asked him to make all those years ago?

Would Cara change her mind about him if he did?

Chapter Fourteen

Pink shirt? Blue shirt?

Cara held one in front of her, then another. Nicholas was coming in ten minutes. She'd barely had time to wash the dust out of her hair from her last job and now she had to figure out what to wear.

She would have called Trista, but her friend was on her honeymoon and Cara didn't think she'd appreciate a phone call asking for fashion advice.

Cara wrinkled her nose, tossed aside the pink shirt and slipped on the blue one. Done. Now she had to figure out what to do with her still-damp hair. Ponytail? Let it hang loose?

Nicholas had called yesterday and asked if she'd be willing to go riding again. She had reluctantly agreed, knowing she had to for her sake. And Nicholas.

Nicholas wouldn't put her in danger, she thought. She knew that as surely as she knew the color of her own eyes.

She let go of her hair and decided to let it hang loose. Nicholas had said once that he liked it down. Besides, when she was working she always pulled it back in a serviceable ponytail. And she wasn't working tonight. Bill was covering the calls.

A bit of makeup, a quick fluff of her bangs and she was done.

Aunt Lori stood by the kitchen table, a tea towel slung over her shoulder, paging through a magazine. Behind her the kitchen counter was still stacked with the dinner dishes that Cara had offered to do half an hour ago.

Obviously her aunt had gotten distracted again.

She looked up when Cara came into the room. "You look nice."

"Where's Uncle Alan? I thought he said he was going to help you with the dishes." Cara slipped her denim jacket on over her shirt and pulled her hair free.

"He went to the clinic." Aunt Lori turned another page in the magazine and then put it on the table, folding a corner of the page down. "I was looking for this recipe."

"Why don't I help do the dishes a minute?" Cara said, glancing at the clock. She wasn't early enough to finish the job, but if she could get her aunt started, hopefully they would get done.

But Aunt Lori waved her off. "Your uncle said he wouldn't be at the clinic long. He'll help me when he comes back."

"Why is Uncle Alan at the clinic anyway? Surely he's not covering calls for Bill?"

Aunt Lori shook her head as she looked up from the magazine. "He said something about meeting that new vet, Gordon Moen, at the clinic. I guess he came in today and wanted to see the clinic as soon as possible."

"Neither Bill nor Anita said anything to me when I was at the clinic this afternoon."

"They must have forgot."

Cara frowned. She wasn't a partner in the clinic and she was only helping temporarily, but surely she could have been given this rather important piece of information.

"Maybe I should stop at the clinic on my way to Nicholas's."

"Do whatever you want, my dear," Aunt Lori said, tapping her chin with her finger. "What do you think of skewers for supper tomorrow? If I grill them they would be fairly healthy, I'm thinking."

"Do whatever you want, my dear," Cara returned.

"Oh, speaking of not passing information on…" Aunt Lori gave her a guilty smile. "I got a phone call from that place in Montreal where you'll be working." This was said with a grimace as if Aunt Lori didn't want to consider this. "They want you to call them as soon as possible."

Uncertainty slipped into Cara. She knew that each day she spent here in Cochrane brought her one day closer to her departure.

It was just the past few days she had preferred not to think about that.

"You're still taking that job?" Aunt Lori asked.

"The job is a fantastic opportunity," Cara said slowly, considering her own words but not as convinced as she used to be. "The pay is almost twice what I've been making the past few years. I can pay you back—"

Her aunt slashed the air with her hand. "How many times do I have to tell you? Your uncle and I don't want that money back. It was a gift of love and you just have to take it."

Cara heard the words on one level, but still struggled with the idea on another.

"Love is freely given," her aunt continued. "It doesn't require anything in return."

"I know," she said quietly, though she still wasn't entirely convinced. "But the job will also give me a chance to travel. Like you always said I should."

"That was your uncle Alan's advice."

Cara frowned. "What do you mean?"

Aunt Lori tilted her head, scratching the side of her neck. "I think, in his heart, he was a bit like your mother. The only reason we've stayed here as long as we have is because I told him I wanted roots."

"So you think traveling is a bad idea?"

"I think traveling can be good at one point in your life, but I also think there comes a time when you need to make yourself a part of something. Get connected to a community. It's hard to nourish your faith when you don't have community—when you don't have roots." Aunt Lori gave a light laugh. "I was very happy when you and Nicholas started dating and almost as sad as you when it was over. And now you're seeing him again. I think it's a good thing, regardless of what Uncle Alan might say."

Pleasure twinged through her. "We're not really seeing each other. It's just a ride up into the mountains."

Aunt Lori smiled, as if she didn't believe Cara's protestations. "Anyway, you have a good time."

Cara bent over and gave her aunt a quick kiss. "I hope to."

She wasn't going to dwell on the phone call she had to make tomorrow or what Gordon's arrival might mean for her. And she decided she wasn't stopping at the clinic either.

Nicholas was waiting for her when she parked her car by the corrals. He wore his usual blue jeans and a blue shirt with a thin white stripe. Then she felt an opening sensation in her chest as she recognized his shirt.

Was it the one she had given him when they were dating?

"Nice shirt," she blurted out as he came near.

Nicholas gave her a crooked smile. "Thanks. An old girlfriend bought it for me."

She was right.

To hide her discomposure, she looked around the yard.

The arbor still stood beside the barn. Potted plants still hung from it and others were pushed up against it, creating a splash of color and whimsy.

"You didn't take it down yet," she said, tucking her hands in her pockets.

"It spruces up the yard," Nicholas said. He poked his thumb over his shoulder. "I've got the horses saddled up in the corral. I'd like you to walk your horse around a bit. Get used to him."

"Which one will I be riding?" she asked, following him around the wooden fence of the corral.

"I thought I would put you on one of my dad's horses." He unlatched the gate and pushed it open to let her through. "I don't trust Two Bits after that spill you took the other day."

"It wasn't his fault," Cara said, waiting for Nicholas to latch the gate again. "He just got scared and I didn't have both my feet in the stirrups."

"Nice of you to give him an out, but I'm not taking any chances." His beguiling smile didn't help her equilibrium.

One of the horses nickered as they came near and Nicholas walked over and untied a tall, gray horse. "This horse is called Sammy. She used to be a pickup horse at the rodeo. Bulletproof. I would have put you on her the first time, but Dad had her at the neighbor's to get bred."

Cara surveyed the animal as Nicholas walked over with her. "A bit old to be a mother, don't you think?"

Nicholas handed her the reins. "I thought so, too, but Dad figures she could have a couple more colts yet."

Cara held her hand out to the horse, letting the mare get a whiff of her, then gently stroked the horse's nose. The mare stood stock-still, then blew out a breath.

"Just lead her around the corral a bit," Nicholas said, untying his horse, as well. "Let her get used to you—"

"And let me get used to her," Cara finished for him.

"That's about the size of it." Nicholas flashed her a grin, his teeth white against his tanned face.

Cara grasped the leather reins and started walking, the muffled thump of the horse's feet on the ground and the squeak of saddle leather the only sounds she heard. The sound of quiet contentment.

"Make her do a few turns, then make her stop and go," Nicholas called out.

Sammy responded to the smallest tug of the reins. When she brought the horse back to Nicholas, Cara felt more comfortable about getting on her back.

"So. Ready to head out?" Nicholas asked.

"I think so."

Nicholas helped her on the horse, adjusted the stirrups, tightened the cinch then tipped his hat back to look up at her. "You sure you're okay with this?"

She sensed an underlying tone to his question that had less to do with the horse and more to do with him.

She gave him a gentle smile and nodded. "Yeah. I'm sure."

His answering grin created a feeling of expectation. "Good. Then let's go."

He swung easily up on his horse and with a twist of his wrist had the horse turned and headed toward the gate. Without dismounting he leaned over and unlatched it, led his horse through, then waited while Cara followed before latching the gate again.

Then he set his hat more firmly on his head, clucked lightly and once again they rode out of the yard and across the open field.

She heard the bawl of a cow and turned in time to see a herd of about thirty black Angus heifers walking toward them, obviously curious.

Their hides gleamed in the sunlight, their uniform faces staring back at her.

"Nice bunch of heifers you got here," she called out.

Nicholas half turned in the saddle, looking back at her. Then he reined his horse in. He was looking at the heifers, as well, when she caught up to him. "They're doing great. If the guy in Montana likes them, it's a huge deal for the ranch."

Huge enough to make him stay instead of going out to work?

But Cara wisely kept the question to herself.

"You've been working hard on the bloodlines of this herd, haven't you?" Cara asked, remembering her uncle talking about trips to the Chapman ranch to artificially inseminate the growing herd with top-notch semen from prize-winning bulls.

Nicholas pushed his hat back on his head, leaning forward in the saddle. "You're looking at almost six years of breeding and culling. And a lot of money invested in good genetics."

"They look amazing," Cara said. Her comment earned her a quick smile.

"And once we run the tests, we're good to go." His horse blew, then stamped, and Nicholas straightened. "Two Bits is getting impatient. We should get going." He pointed with one hand to the trail. "We'll go the same way we went last time. We'll end up at the place where Trista and Lorne wanted their pictures taken. It's only about a twenty-minute ride from here."

"Sounds good to me." Cara's nervousness eased with each step of the horse and by the time they were back on the trail again, she relaxed. Every now and then Sammy would twitch her ears as if checking to see if she still sat on her back, but mostly her mount was content to plod along.

The quiet and cool of the approaching evening surrounded them as the horses climbed higher and higher. The creak of leather and the plod of the horses' hooves were the only sound in the utter stillness of the day.

Cara caught glimpses of the fields below them growing smaller the higher they went. Twenty minutes later, just as Nicholas had promised, they broke out into an open area.

"This is the end of the road," Nicholas said, bringing his horse to a stop. Cara's horse sidled up to him and stopped, as well. "We'll get off the horses here and tie them up. Then we can walk to the lookout point," Nicholas said, swinging off his saddle. Cara followed suit and a few minutes later Nicholas was leading her through the small clearing to an opening in the trees.

They got to the edge and the ground fell away from them.

The tree-covered hillside sloped away, meeting hayfields and pasture well below them. Beyond that lay the creek Nicholas had pointed out the last time they had ridden the trail up here. Beyond that the land rose again, green-skirted hills meeting blue and gray jagged peaks softened by caps of snow gleaming against a blue sky.

A wave of dizziness washed over her at the vast expanse of land. "Tell me again which part is yours?" she asked, breathless with the wonder and beauty of it all.

"The fields along the river belong to us, and through that cut in the hills are the high pastures where the other cows are grazing."

Cara hugged herself, letting her gaze roam over the space. "It's absolutely beautiful," she breathed. "I don't know if I want to leave."

"I know the feeling," Nicholas said, sitting down on the ground.

Cara hesitated a moment, then followed suit. And, to her surprise, Nicholas moved closer and she didn't move away.

His arm brushed hers and she caught the scent of horse mixed with hay and the faintest hint of soap.

The smell of Nicholas, she thought.

She turned her attention back to the view.

"I don't know how you can leave this," she said, wrapping her arms around her knees.

Nicholas didn't reply and she wished she could take her ill-timed comment back. It was that leaving that had caused the tension that sang between them last time.

Then he turned to her and grinned. "And I don't know how you can work in a lab when I know that you love working with animals."

His comment spoke to her doubts. Since she had started working for her uncle, she felt anchored. Secure.

As if the land and the people and the community were drawing her into themselves and giving her the home she missed when she was working in Vancouver.

"I do love it here. I feel like I can breathe."

"So why go?"

He spoke the words lightly, but they clung to Cara, mining her own doubts.

"There isn't room for me at the clinic. This new vet is here, Uncle Alan is feeling better and I'm already starting to feel redundant." She tried to keep her voice as light as Nicholas did, but her own uncertainties hovered over her future.

And her changing feelings for Nicholas.

"I wasn't just talking about the clinic," Nicholas said quietly, a wealth of meaning in his voice.

"I know." She turned to him and as their eyes met, her concerns receded. "And what about you? Do you have to go?"

Nicholas sighed as he leaned his elbows on his knees. "Unfortunately, yes."

The finality of his statement resurrected her wavering. "Will there come a time when you don't have to leave? When the ranch can hold its own?"

Nicholas didn't answer right away and once again she wondered if she had entered forbidden territory.

"I'm hoping." He looked at her, then to her surprise, reached up and cupped her cheek in his hand. As her heart billowed and expanded in her chest, he leaned closer and brushed his lips over hers. "I'm really hoping."

Cara swallowed as his hope became hers.

He pulled back, tracing her mouth with his thumb. "So, Cara Morrison, now what?" he asked, articulating her own question.

"I'm not sure," she said, her voice breathless.

"We never had much of a chance to talk the last time we were together."

Cara wasn't sure where he was going, but she guessed he referred to the conversation that had initiated the breakup.

Nicholas moved his thumb over her lips again, then gave her a careful smile. "When I found out that you had actually made wedding plans, it made me rethink all the questions I'd had when you left the first time. Why couldn't you wait for me to come back so we could make our own wedding plans?"

The whisper of the leaves around them filled the silence following his simple question as she struggled to find the right response—to find the right words to articulate her hurt and betrayal.

Cara leaned away from him to give herself what space she could. "Why did you leave even though I asked you to stay?" Begged him to stay, but she wasn't bringing up that humiliation again.

Nicholas sighed and lowered his hand. "I told you then and I'm telling you now. The ranch needed the money."

"And now? Does the ranch still need the money?" The words fell between them like a glove being thrown down.

I need to know, Cara thought, justifying her repeat of the question she'd asked him a few moments ago. *I need to know where things are going before I follow him down that path again.*

Nicholas looked away and Cara followed his gaze, her eyes tracing the lines of the hills and valleys. She let herself get drawn into the vast, open spaces stretching out and away from where they sat.

"This ranch is part of my identity. Part of who I am

and where I came from. Some Chapman sweat and even some Chapman blood is in every square inch of this place. Those are my roots, my heritage and I have to protect that."

His passion resonated with the very thing she had been looking for in her life. Yet she heard an underlying tone that disconcerted her.

"Because of your mother?" Cara spoke the question cautiously. Nicholas seldom spoke of his mother. The other time they went riding, she thought he hovered on the verge of telling her more.

Nicholas got up, walking toward the cliff overlooking the valley. "This is all Chapman land, slowly built up over the years. When my mother left my father she got enough of the ranch in the divorce settlement that it bordered on being broke. She had no right to this land. She had no right to not only break my father's heart, but to almost break this ranch."

"And now she's gone," Cara said quietly.

When she and Nicholas were first dating, the only information she got from him was that Barb had left his father and that she had died shortly after remarrying.

"And the money with her. So I keep working," Nicholas said. "And my work on the rigs is bringing this ranch back to where it should be." He turned back to her. "I'm not doing this just for myself," he added. "I'm also doing this for my father."

Cara held his gaze and she heard it again. The faint note of urgency. As if something else was going on. And then it became clear.

"Why are you doing this for him?"

"Because he's had a hard life. Because he doesn't deserve what my mother did to him. I need to protect him."

"From what?" Cara's frustration with Dale Chapman and Nicholas merged. "He's a grown man, he doesn't need your protection."

"What are you trying to say?" His voice grew quiet, but carried a weight that made Cara want to back down.

But she wasn't the quiet, soft-spoken person she'd been before. She'd found her own way, lived on her own and made her own decisions. Nicholas had to see what was going on because it seemed no one else dared tell him.

"All the work you do, all the money you make, is poured into this ranch. And that is admirable. But did your father do the same with what was given to him?" She paused, wondering if she dared venture into the place she was heading. But if anything was going to happen between them, if anything was to be rebuilt, it had to be on a different foundation than before. Or else it would fall as easily as before.

"He worked for this place, too," Nicholas said, turning away from her. But he didn't sound as confident as he had before. As if her comment had seeded the tiniest bit of doubt in his view of his father.

"Did he?" A tiny voice cautioned Cara as she struggled to find the right words. Her intention was not to put his father down, but to give him the viewpoint of an outsider looking in. "He spent a lot of time on the road going to his rodeos, didn't he?"

"Yeah. He loved doing it."

"Don't you think you made it easy for him to continue doing that?"

"How so?" His question sounded defensive and Cara fought the urge to change the subject.

"I wonder if, by working, you enable him to keep doing something that doesn't benefit the ranch. He doesn't spend as much time on this ranch as you do and it seems to me the bulk of the work gets done when you're home."

Nicholas shot her a look that would have pierced her any other time, but they had come to an important crossroads in their relationship and she had to forge on. She stood and walked closer to him.

"When I broke our engagement, I felt as if you chose working the rigs over me. And when you made that choice, in my eyes, it also seemed that you chose your father over me. You were choosing to make the ranch viable and easy to work for him. Your priority was him. So if you think I'm attacking your father, you're wrong. I'm just bringing up my view of the situation."

"I told you, I work because the ranch needs the money," Nicholas said with a weary sigh. "I got tired of watching my father fight with bills and bill collectors. Got tired of fixing fences with baler twine instead of being able to afford new boards. I promised myself I would do what I could to help him out. And there was no way I was bringing another woman, my future wife, onto the ranch until I was set up to give her the support my mother didn't get."

"What do you mean?"

"I know my mother left because money was always so tight. I didn't want to run that risk again. My dangerous work allows me to put money into the ranch and spend time here, as well."

"But not as much as you like."

Nicholas blew out a sigh. "This is reality, Cara. My work brings in much-needed money. I refuse to constantly worry about which bill to pay and which one to let ride. I don't want to live like that, Cara. And I know you don't either."

"What are you trying to say?" A chill feathered down her spine as the old shame slipped back into her life.

He knew little from her past because shame had kept her tight-lipped about her life before moving in with her wealthy aunt and uncle.

"I remember that brand-new car you tooled around town with when you were in high school. You always wore the best clothes and could afford to do what you wanted. I know Alan paid for your education. You've had it pretty easy living with your aunt and uncle."

Anger sparked at his easy assumption. "But you don't know what my life was like before that."

Nicholas turned to face her square on. "No. I don't. You never say much about that."

She heard the challenge in his voice and before she could stop herself, her anger made her spill the words out.

"You think I don't know what doing without is like? You think I've had it so incredibly easy? My mother was so intent on living the way she wanted that it didn't matter to her what I wore or what I ate." Cara took a breath to stop herself but it was as if the words, so long suppressed, were drawn out by the way Nicholas looked at her. "While I lived with my mother I missed meals. I had to pack my stuff in garbage bags because we were getting evicted from a motel. I learned how to make a pound of hamburger stretch over four meals for two. I lived in a motel. I lived in a trailer park and even a tent on a campground. An adventure, my mother told me—" Her voice broke and she pressed a hand on her lips, halting the flow of memories.

She shouldn't have let him get her so angry. She was

telling him things she'd never told Aunt Lori and Uncle Alan.

Though she loved her mother, she struggled with guilt as she tried putting the shame of that part of her life behind her.

And when her mother died, her disloyalty and guilt were compounded.

"Cara, I'm sorry—"

Cara held her hand up to stop him. "The last thing I want is your pity. It's just that you made me angry. Thinking you have the monopoly on struggling and doing without. Thinking that money will fix all that's wrong in your life."

The only sound in the ensuing silence was the riffling of a benevolent breeze through the leaves of the trees and the sigh of her horse as she shifted her weight to another foot.

After a few minutes Nicholas spoke.

"I never knew, Cara. And though you don't want my pity, I want to tell you that I'm sorry for assuming your life was easy. I wish you would have told me sooner."

Cara ran her hand up and down one arm, staring over the hills lying below them. The hills belonging to Nicholas and his father. The land that had been in their family for five generations.

She wondered if he realized how much she envied him his roots and his stability. His history.

"Money was never that important to me," she continued. "Even though I grew up without it. I never wanted a fancy car or nice clothes, though I did enjoy them." She turned to him and caught his hands in hers. "I've lived with and I've lived without. And what made the times in my life when I had money more significant was the fact that I was cared for. The money was one of my aunt and uncle's expressions of love and sacrifice." She held his gaze, willing him to understand. "I would gladly have traded that car in, lost all the clothes, given up the paid-for education, just to have my mother back. Just to have her spend some time with me and see her eyes shine when she saw me."

Nicholas's gaze softened and he squeezed her hands back. "I'm sorry, Cara. I never knew."

She gave him a wan smile. "Just for the record, you're the only person I've ever told this to. Neither Trista nor my aunt and uncle know how poorly we lived all those years." Cara's knees wobbled and she lowered herself to the grass once again.

"Why haven't you told them?" Nicholas moved and sat down beside her.

Cara wrapped her arms around her knees and drew in a long, slow breath as if preparing herself. "I knew what they thought of my mother. Uncle Alan didn't particularly care for her and I also knew he was ashamed of her." She paused, the old guilt and the old confusion returning. "But she was my mother and I loved her. And yet…"

"You didn't know how to love her."

Cara rocked slowly back and forth as her emotions returned to the old, endless circling between disloyalty and love. "Yeah. I guess you would know about that."

"I used to think God would punish me for hating my mother. For wishing she was dead. Then when she did die…" His voice trailed off and Cara placed her hand on his arm. "When she did die, I thought God was punishing me for sure."

"I don't know if God operates that way," Cara said. "I've had my own grievances with Him, but I'm slowly finding out not everything is about me. Sometimes it's simply about the choices that people make and their consequences."

"And what about your choices, Cara?"

"Now it's my turn to wonder what you mean."

Nicholas reached out and ran a callused finger down her cheek. "What choices are you going to make in the next week? What about your job?"

Did she dare pin all her hopes and dreams on the man standing in front of her?

"I don't know what to do," she said finally. "Especially when it seems like things are changing between us."

Nicholas raised his finger to her lips and as he traced their outline, he gave her a rueful smile. "I don't know what's happening either, Cara. I feel like we're the same people and yet not. I feel like we're both in different places making decisions with new information. I don't think we're heading in the same direction as we were before. But I like to think we can go in that direction together."

Cara held his gaze, her own heart lifting in response to his comment. Had things truly changed to bring them both to the same place in this relationship? Was Nicholas really willing to make different choices?

Was she?

Even as she wanted to let go of her worries and concerns, a question still hovered. A fear she couldn't articulate.

Please, Lord, she prayed, *help us through this uncertainty.* Then she gave Nicholas a cautious smile. Reached out and caressed his face, tracing his own smile.

"I guess we'll have to wait and see then, won't we?"

Then he leaned closer and caught her lips in a warm, satisfying kiss.

* * *

Nicholas held the phone, his boss's phone number up on the screen. Did he dare make this phone call? Could he quit now?

One more year of work would pay off the tractor and give them a partial down payment on a parcel of land coming up for sale.

Stick with the plan, his father had urged.

But the thought of being gone again cut him to the core. Because he wouldn't just be leaving the ranch, he'd be leaving Cara.

He thought back to their moment on the hill. The things they had talked about. The honesty they'd both displayed, so unlike the first time they were together.

She said that money didn't matter to her. Yet the idea that his mother had left because of the tight financial situation was so ingrained in him, he couldn't shift his thoughts in the direction Cara had gone.

He walked to the window of his bedroom. From here he could see his father working in the round pen, training his newest horse. He'd picked up the bay at the auction mart while Nicholas was out piling up hay bales with the tractor.

He'd never resented his father his hobby. But, as Cara had said, it required time and dedication that took his father away from the ranch.

Nicholas's eyes drifted to the tractor sitting in the yard. Last year they'd had to put a new motor in. His father, in a rush to feed the cows so he could get to the auction mart, had used too much ether and blown the engine.

It took Nicholas a month of work to fix the tractor. Had he been home to run the tractor for the cows himself, he would have had to work one less month.

You enable your father. Cara's comment slipped into his mind and behind that, Lorne's—*Take a chance. Love is a risk, but I think it's a risk worth taking.*

Nicholas spun away from the window, wishing he could stifle all the voices running through his head.

He walked back to his bed and picked up the Bible again and reread the passage from Philippians, chapter 4. He let the words encourage him and soak into his life. When he had read it a number of times, he lowered his head and prayed for wisdom and strength to do the right thing.

Then he went outside.

His father was done with his horse and sat perched on a pail in the tack shed, braiding a lead rope. The shed was well stocked and neat as a pin. Neatly coiled ropes hung on the wall. Brushes and currycombs, hoof picks and trimming tools all had their place.

Across the far wall, five saddles hung on their respective saddle trees. One of them was the roping saddle his father had won. The other four were custom-made for his father.

Paid for by his father's horse trading, supposedly, but Nicholas knew a portion of the money he earned went into his father's hobby.

Nicholas brushed away the traitorous thought. He had made his own choices. No one was putting a gun to his head to go out and work. Nicholas would be lying if he said he didn't benefit from the high wages he got paid.

Since talking to Cara, he kept seeing his father's role in the ranch in a different light. He looked at what his father did through Cara's eyes and he realized that, to some degree, Cara was right.

"How's the new horse?" Nicholas asked, picking up a brush that had fallen to the ground.

"He's a bit jumpy, but he's willing and eager. He needs a bit of work, but then they all do." Dale gave Nicholas a wink. "Time and miles. That's what makes a mediocre horse good. Time and miles."

And his father spent enough of both on his horses, Nicholas thought.

"So, I've been penciling a few things out." Nicholas ran his thumb over the soft bristles of the brush, remembering how much he loved brushing his own horse after a long ride. Remembering how he seldom went riding anymore. "After we sell these heifers, I'm thinking I'll stay at home."

"So how do you figure that would work?" his father asked, his hands working the rope, his movements slower now.

"The ranch is coming along. We wouldn't get as much money as we used to, but we'd get by. And I'd be home more."

"You don't have to worry about me," Dale said. "I manage fine while you're gone."

"But I don't." Nicholas sighed. "I've got a fancy truck with all the options paid for by my work. We're accumulating land and vehicles and for what?"

Dale's set the rope aside and, resting his hands on his knees, looked up at Nicholas again. "You know one of the reasons your mom left was because we were broke all the time?"

Nicholas crossed his arms over his chest, his mind going back to what Cara had said. "Maybe Cara is different."

"We back to that Morrison girl again? Are you forgetting how hard it was when she dumped you?"

Nicholas's frustration with his father took wings. "Why are you so determined to think the worst of her? What has she ever done to you?"

"Dumped my son."

"But that was my pain, Dad. You didn't need to take it on."

Dale glared at Nicholas. "It was the same pain I went through. And you know why I went through it? Because it was Audra, Cara's mother, that convinced your mother to leave."

"What are you saying?" Nicholas frowned at his father, who nodded.

"Audra Morrison blew into town one day. Met up with your mother and they got to talking. Barb got to complaining. Next thing you know Audra's convincing Barb that she doesn't need to stay with me. That she doesn't need to keep living this life." His father picked up his rope again and yanked a strand through.

"And how was that Cara's fault?"

"She's just like her mother. Coming into our lives. Trying to convince you to stop working. Changing things in my life."

Nicholas stared at his father, feeling as if pieces of a puzzle were slowly falling into place. His father knew how Cara felt about Nicholas's jobs.

His mind ticked back to the last time he had talked to his father about cutting back on his hours on the job. The note of panic in his father's voice. How his father insisted Nicholas stick to the plan.

"We can't afford you quittin'," his father now said.

Nicholas leaned against the shed, the wood warm on

his back. As he watched his father's quick, jerky movements, things that Cara said slipped into his mind.

Was he really enabling his father? Was he really making it easy for his father to indulge in his hobbies while Nicholas was working?

The thought seemed disloyal, yet…

"Cara grew up with a lot of stuff," his father said after a moment of silence. "She's used to a higher standard of living than this ranch can give her."

"I don't think money is important to her, Dad," Nicholas said. "She told me she'd sooner have had her mother than the money Lori and Alan spent on her."

His father didn't answer and as Nicholas watched him, another thought spiraled up through his consciousness.

"Did Mom leave because money was tight?" he asked, giving voice to those thoughts. "Or was something else going on?"

His father stared down at the rope he'd been working on. "What do you mean?"

"You spent a lot of time at rodeos, didn't you?"

"You have to if you want to get to the qualifying rounds." Dale looked up at him, his eyes narrowed. "And if you're going to go on about the money it cost, like your mother always did, you know I often broke even."

"But was it really the money she was worried about, Dad? Do you think she might have sooner had you around every weekend?"

Dale snorted his response, threw the rope down and surged to his feet. "Your mother would have been fine with everything if that Audra had stayed away from her. Your mom wanted more…and I couldn't give her what she wanted."

He stormed out of the shed, slamming the door so hard it banged shut and flew open again.

As it swung and creaked on its hinges, Nicholas bent over and picked up the rope, fingering the unwoven ends. He sighed as he hung it back up.

He had hit a sore spot with his questions to his father and for the first time in years, other speculations about his mother's leaving colored his thoughts.

And, as always, his mind drifted back to Cara and what she had said. How she had challenged him. She knew he loved working on the ranch. She knew what it meant.

He wasn't sure what was happening between them, but he wanted to see where it would go.

Talking to his father about her was a waste of time and breath. One of these days Dale would simply have to accept her as his…what?

Nicholas didn't want to think that far. Didn't dare. For now, he and Cara were together. For now they enjoyed being with each other. It felt right. Good. And it made his heart feel whole.

As for his father?

That he would have to deal with another time.

Chapter Fifteen

The corral was filled to bursting with cows, calves and heifers.

"Can't see why we need to test the whole works." Dale Chapman underlined his complaint with a frown.

"Just a precaution," Cara said, though she also didn't know why they were doing all the cattle. Nicholas was only shipping the thirty heifers across the border, and as far as she knew they were the only animals the buyer wanted tested for tuberculosis.

"Typical vet. Make you do more work than needs to be done." Dale glanced at her, his frown deepening. "I thought just Gordon, that new vet, was coming."

"He wanted some help." Cara kept her tone even as she climbed up and over the fence and away from Dale. She zeroed in on Nicholas, as if to draw strength from his presence. But he was talking to Dr. Moen.

When Gordon had asked her to come, her feelings were mixed. One part of her hoped to see Nicholas again. To test the change in their relationship.

Things were so tentative between them, so fragile, yet

a sense of anticipation floated up within her. A sense of settling, which was both new and frightening.

She wasn't sure where this was going and she didn't know what kind of plans to make. But in the next week and a half she had to make a decision.

The job on which she had pinned so much of her hopes still waited. Yet to make a major life decision based on a few kisses and a few moments with Nicholas seemed foolish.

"You don't belong in a lab. You belong out here, working with animals."

Nicholas's comment twisted through her thoughts, shifting the foundations of her plans.

And then, there he was, standing in front of her, a gentle smile hovering around the edges of his mouth.

"I'm glad you could come out, too," Nicholas said, his voice igniting the spark of possibilities within her. "I was going to call you. See if you're free this weekend. I know you're on call all week."

"I'm not on call over the weekend."

"Great. What do you say to dinner in Calgary?"

Cara's smile started inside her and spread outward. The last time they spoke, Nicholas was leaving for Kuwait on the same day he wanted to go out with her.

"That sounds like a fabulous idea."

"Lorne told me about this restaurant. He said it would change my life."

"That's putting a lot of pressure on one restaurant." The unspoken message hovered between them and Cara's heart thudded heavily in her chest. Their eyes held as the import of his offer registered on both of them.

"No. There's no pressure at all." Nicholas's own smile

grew as he reached out and feathered a strand of hair back from her face. "It's a bit fancy—"

"So no blue coveralls?" Cara asked, looking down at her own coveralls and trying to hide the flush in her cheeks, the sparkle of anticipation in her eyes.

"I'll take you exactly as you are," Nicholas said, his hand lingering on her cheek.

Cara looked up at that and as their eyes held, older, deeper emotions kindled and grew.

And with them a sense of coming home.

"I'm glad you came," Nicholas said, his hand drifting down to her shoulder. "I feel better knowing you're on the job, as well."

Cara caught Dale glancing at her, his eyes dark. Even from here his fury was as palpable as a slap.

She wished it didn't bother her. Wished he wasn't a shadow hanging over their growing relationship. But he was. And sooner or later, she and Nicholas would have to deal with Dale's feelings toward her.

"I think Gordon knows what he's doing," Cara said, shaking her head as if to turn her focus on the waiting job. "Besides, this is just a formality. Alberta is a TB-free zone."

"How long before we know anything?" Nicholas removed his hand, his voice growing businesslike.

"Two days."

"And then?"

"Then you'll be able to ship the cows and collect your paycheck." Cara added a grin to her comment, to show Nicholas she was kidding.

He didn't smile in return and Cara wondered if her comment about money bothered him.

"Gordon said he wanted to run the heifers through

first so I better get them moved." Nicholas slipped on his gloves and jogged over to the corral without a backward glance as Cara regretted her ill-timed comment.

Though they had made plans for the weekend, he hadn't said anything about the job waiting for him in Kuwait and she hadn't said anything about her job in Montreal. It was as if they lived in a bubble, holding off reality.

But what would they do when reality intruded?

Cara looked around, taking in the scenery that was both peaceful and overwhelming. She tried to imagine staying here, becoming a part of the history permeating the house, the farm, the land.

She thought of Nicholas and how things had changed between them.

She had thought she and Nicholas had been in love the first time, but now, it seemed as if the feelings growing between them were different. Deeper. Richer.

And yes, it did make her afraid. Because she knew, this time around, if things didn't work out she would be more than hurt.

She would be devastated.

"This is an amazing place," Gordon said, turning around as if to get a better look. "These guys must be loaded to be able to afford to live here and keep it looking so good."

Cara glanced around the yard. Yes, it was tidy, but Cara knew the sacrifices that had made it so.

"Nicholas works very hard," she said, unable to keep the defensive tone out of her voice.

"He must. From what I heard, all Dale does is hang around the auction mart. I saw him there both times I went with Bill."

"Hey, let's get these animals through," Dale called out from the corrals. "Haven't got all day."

Gordon raised his eyebrows and Cara made a note to talk to her uncle about the clinic's new vet. Gordon needed to learn a bit more discretion if he wanted to work in a close-knit farming community.

A cloud of dust from the milling cattle greeted them and a few minutes later they were immersed in the work.

Gordon called out the tag numbers of the cattle as he ran them through and Cara filled them in on the form.

Cara couldn't help feeling a burst of pride for Nicholas when she saw the heifers going through. They looked sleek and healthy, with beautiful conformation. They were some of the best cattle she'd ever seen and they would definitely improve the genetics of any herd they went to. Nicholas was a born rancher, she thought.

An hour and a half later the heifers were out in the pasture again and the cloud of dust was settling in the corrals.

"So what's the next step?" Nicholas asked, pulling his hat off. He slapped it against his leg, beating the dust out.

Cara was about to speak when Gordon jumped in. "I have to come back and check the sites to see if there's been any reaction to the TB test."

"Still can't figure out why that loser wanted us to do a TB test," Dale grumbled. "Waste of time and money."

"He's the buyer and if that's what the buyer wants, that's what the buyer gets," Nicholas said. "It's just a precaution."

"You probably won't have to do this for the next group of cows you ship out," Cara assured Dale.

Dale nodded but didn't look at her, and apprehension shivered through her. Though she didn't need his approval, Dale's attitude would need to be dealt with if she and Nicholas's relationship were to deepen.

If.

The word hung over their relationship and Cara couldn't delve too deeply into it. Not yet.

"I'll only need to check a couple of the heifers," Gordon was saying as he walked with Nicholas toward the corrals. "Did you bring the other cows in, as well?"

"Because I'm not shipping them, I moved them out to the far pasture again. Besides, you said this test was a formality." Nicholas settled his hat lower on his head as the morning sun blinded him. Another beautiful day on the ranch.

"I did."

Nicholas climbed up and over a fence into the pen holding the heifers, the animals that represented the future.

Last night he had taken his horse out for a midnight ride as if hunting for some sign, some indication of what he should do. He knew his feelings for Cara were growing deeper every day and he knew he wanted to be with her.

But he also knew that she still wanted him to stay home. To work the ranch.

He'd imagined the picture and it tantalized. He thought of not having to take on work that required living in a guarded compound, watching your back while you made hard decisions about drilling, work conditions, employee discontent.

He wondered what it would be like to experience every day of every season on the ranch he loved so much.

He walked slowly through the milling heifers, glancing at their ear tags, easily recalling each of their mothers.

He had chosen each of these heifers because their births had been problem free. Not that he would have known. He had been working on a rig in Newfoundland. His father was the one who'd been home to watch the births and make the necessary notations.

By being gone, he'd missed things happening on the ranch. Missed out on some of the rewards of the hard work.

And with that in mind, he'd worked up enough nerve to call his boss this morning. To talk about maybe cutting back on his hours. Maybe even quit completely. But he only got the answering machine.

He hadn't told Cara his plans. He wanted to surprise her when they went out for dinner.

Nor had he told his father.

However, sooner or later his father would have to accept that he and Cara were together again.

He pushed the thoughts aside as he focused on the work at hand. Clambering up on his horse, he clucked to it, then easily separated the first five heifers into the sorting pen and from there into the chute where Gordon could check them.

He got off his horse, closed the gate behind the first five and leaned on it while he watched Gordon move from animal to animal, checking the sites where they had done the TB test.

"Could you send another five in?" Gordon said, sounding distracted.

"Sure." Nicholas felt a niggle of unease. Cara and Gordon had both assured him this follow-up was simply a formality.

But he sorted five more out and sent them through.

When Gordon asked for five more, then another five,

Nicholas's unease grew. They processed the entire herd and when he closed the gate on the last of the heifers, he rode his horse out through the gate and toward the other side of the chute.

Gordon checked the last five heifers, then nodded for Nicholas's father to open the head gate. The steel gate clanged and the heifers bawled as they charged to freedom, kicking up dust as Gordon pulled himself up and over the fence.

"What's wrong?" Nicholas asked. "Why did you need to check them all?"

Gordon wasn't looking at Nicholas as he pulled his gloves off. "I found three positives in the herd."

A roaring began in Nicholas's ears. "What do you mean?"

Gordon stuffed the gloves in his coverall pockets. "Sorry, Nick. Your herd has TB."

The roaring grew. "I thought Alberta was TB free. Where could it have come from?"

"Possibly some of the semen you used when you artificially inseminated your cattle."

"So what does this mean?"

Gordon glanced over his shoulder at the shining, fat, healthy-looking animals. The cream of Nicholas's herd.

"Quarantine." The word came out like a bullet and Nicholas grabbed one of the uprights on the corrals to steady himself.

Quarantine.

A word associated with diseases that killed animals and livelihoods. Quarantine was the first step to something far more serious. "And after that?"

Gordon gave a listless shrug as if his diagnosis was simply another day on the job and didn't mean the de-

struction of a herd Nicholas had spent years building up.
"All the animals on this farm will have to be destroyed."

"Horses, too?"

"Not sure about them, but my guess would be yeah."
Gordon peeled his coveralls off, stepped out of them and
bunched them up. As if he was going to dispose of them
as soon as he got back to the clinic.

"So what do we do?" Nicholas couldn't stop the note
of desperation in his voice. He couldn't imagine the herd
had to be wiped out because of one random test. "Could
you test them again? Is there something we can do?"

"Not a thing to do." Gordon shoved the coveralls under
his arm. "I have a bunch of paperwork to work through
and then I have to make the call. Meantime, none of your
animals goes anywhere."

The cattle liner was coming tomorrow to pick up the
herd.

He already had half of the buyer's money in the farm
account, and most of that was already earmarked for special projects. The rest was supposed to have been their
living money until he sold the crop.

Now he had to give it all back. And he was looking at
the destruction of years of work. Gone.

Cara parked her car by the barn and got out. As soon
as she heard the news from Gordon, she cancelled her
next appointments, jumped in the car and came straight
to the Chapman ranch.

She heard the bawling of animals and ran to the corrals where she hoped the heifers were still penned up.
Awaiting orders from Gordon.

When Gordon told her what he'd found, she could
hardly believe it. There hadn't been a case of TB in cattle

in Alberta for years. And these animals had no genetic connection to any herds in Canada or the States proven to carry tuberculosis.

She knew it was unprofessional of her, but she needed to see for herself and double-check Gordon's diagnosis.

As she came around the corner, her gaze scanned the corrals looking for Nicholas, but she only saw Dale, standing with his hands in his pockets, staring over the penned-up heifers.

Cara hesitated but then walked over to his side.

"I'm so sorry, Dale," she said.

He didn't look at her, but kept his eyes on the seemingly healthy herd. "I can't believe we have to kill them all. They're the best animals we've ever raised."

"I can't believe it either," she said quietly. She hesitated to ask the next question, but she had to for Nicholas's sake. "Would you mind if I checked them myself?"

Dale gave a short laugh. "Go crazy. Won't do any harm."

Cara wasn't sure what to think of that comment, but she climbed over the fence anyhow. The animals turned to look at her, which made it difficult to see the test sites for herself. But a few kept their backs turned to her and when one swished its tail, she saw the telltale swelling.

It wasn't quite as significant as she thought it should be. Not according to what she'd seen in her textbooks or the pictures she'd checked online before she came.

But it was a reaction and she knew they couldn't ignore it.

The animals jostled each other as they moved around in reaction to her presence. They looked so sleek and healthy. Their eyes were clear and they didn't so much as sniffle.

Cara stood, her hands on her hips, watching the cattle, a sense of something off-kilter niggling at her. But she couldn't grab hold of it or formulate it. Western Canada had been TB free for years. She knew Nicholas and his father had handpicked these animals from their own herd. They had used artificial insemination to improve the genetics.

Why here and why now in this herd?

The thought of these healthy-looking animals being slaughtered created a dull ache in her chest. What a waste.

Surely something wasn't right?

She climbed over the fence, scaring a flock of sparrows drinking from the cattle waterer. Her heart jumped as they exploded up into the sky.

"Told Nicholas he should shoot those things," Dale mumbled as Cara's heart settled. "They've been hanging around the waterer steady the past couple of weeks. Found a bunch of dead ones in the barn."

"Where is Nicholas?" Cara asked.

Dale scratched his forehead with his forefinger. "Packing for Calgary."

"Why Calgary?" And why now? They had a crisis on their hands.

"He's going back to work."

Cara stared at him as the words beat in her mind in time with the flapping of the sparrows' wings overhead. Of course. Nicholas's solution to the problem.

Then she turned and strode to the house, her hands curled into fists, her feat pounding out a hard rhythm.

Had everything he said to her been a lie? His talk about staying, about taking a chance, about putting down roots, about hating the restlessness of his life? Was it all just so he could steal a few kisses?

Steal her heart again?

She stormed up the walk just as Nicholas appeared in the doorway, a duffel bag slung over one shoulder, a suitcase in his other hand.

As soon as he saw her, he dropped both to the porch with a resounding thunk. His eyes skimmed past her, looking somewhere over her shoulder.

"So what's going on?" she asked.

"I'm leaving for Calgary tonight. I have a meeting and I'm flying out tomorrow. I was going to come over before I left."

"To kiss me goodbye?"

"Cara, I'm so sorry, but I don't have any choice."

"And us? What about us?"

Nicholas frowned. "I'm only gone for two months. I'll be back."

"How are we supposed to maintain a relationship when you're halfway across the world?"

"We can email. Phone. Internet calls. It's not that hard to maintain a long-distance relationship these days."

"I don't want a long-distance relationship. I want you."

The words flew out of her mouth before she could stop them. Great. Now she sounded like some pathetic whiner who couldn't live without her boyfriend for a couple of months.

"I have to go, Cara," was all he said, regret tingeing his voice.

"Why?"

Nicholas shoved his hand through his hair, then turned to her, and when Cara saw helplessness and fear in his eyes, her resolve wavered.

"You know what Gordon said. The heifers—they'll be destroyed. Tomorrow Dad is rounding up the rest of the cows from the far pastures and bringing them down here. They're going to be killed, too."

Cara easily heard the pain in his voice and knew how dearly this would cost him. Would cost the ranch. But was leaving the only solution?

"I could ask Gordon to do another test, to try again—"

"I talked to Gordon. He's already put in the order to slaughter the herd."

"I can't believe every problem has to be solved by you, or by you working away from the ranch. Isn't there anything else you can do?"

Nicholas turned to her and she caught a flash of despair in his eyes. "What? Carpentry work? Driving a school bus? Maybe working part-time at the Seed and Feed in Cochrane? Or how about I work at the auction mart for about nine dollars an hour? And maybe, after ten years of that, I'll be able to build up my herd again and support a family." He sliced the air with his hand. "Truth is, Cara, I make more in one tour on the rigs than I would in four years of working at any other job."

"So the money is that important to you?"

"You say it isn't to you, but that changes over time."

"I don't want you to go, Nicholas," she said.

Nicholas reached out to her, as if to help her understand. "Don't ask me to stay. Please don't make me choose again."

Cara pressed her hand against her chest as if to push down her rising fear and with that, her anger. He still didn't get it.

"If you leave again, Nicholas, we're right back to where we were three years ago. I'm not going there. I thought we were through that, I thought we had both grown and changed, but it looks like you haven't at all."

Nicholas stared at her. "And have you? You accuse me of running off, but are you still leaving for Montreal?"

"I wasn't going to."

"Wasn't?" A frown creased his forehead as he zeroed in on that vague word.

"No. I wasn't. But you leave me no choice."

"Cara—"

She held up her hand to block his protest, to put up a shield against his heartrending appeal. "Your job is too dangerous."

"I always come back, Cara."

His words snaked into her mind, an eerie echo of her mother's.

She glanced down at the leg he had broken the last time. She remembered the stories she'd heard of threats on workers' lives, thinking of the casual way his co-worker had talked about kidnappings and ransoms.

And as she turned her eyes back to him her past came crashing into her present and her throat thickened with old pain and old sorrow. "That's exactly what my mother always said."

"What do you mean?"

Cara wrapped her arms around herself, as if to contain the sorrow that she had walled in these past few years.

But Nicholas's gentle foray into her heart had softened her. Had made her vulnerable and the pain sifted too easily through the breaks he had created in her fortifications.

"Every time she left she told me the work wasn't dangerous. And when I pleaded with her to stay, not to leave me alone, she told me not to be selfish. Not to think of myself. That her work was important and that she would be back." Cara couldn't stop the hitch in her voice. "And then one time she didn't come back. And I was alone."

She swallowed and swallowed, struggling to maintain her composure as the pain she had held back so long came crashing back.

She looked up at Nicholas, at the face that had grown so dear to her. At the eyes that could melt her heart with one look. At the mouth that promised so much and the arms that gave her security and shelter.

She couldn't stay behind, waiting each time he left, wondering, as she had with her mother, if he would return.

"It took that one time to tear my world apart," she cried, her hands clutching her sides. "And I'm not going through that again. I can't, Nicholas. I can't live with that fear hanging over my head each time you leave. I can't think of losing you." She dashed the tears away, not caring that he saw her like this, not caring that she had lost control of her emotions.

Nicholas stared at her, as if finally realizing what his leaving might cost her.

"Cara, please—"

"Stop. I know the ranch is important and I know how much you've put into it, but if you leave I can't stay and put myself through that pain again."

She waited a moment, as if her declaration might change something, anything between them, but he made no move toward her, said nothing to change her mind.

Then she turned, stumbled down the steps and ran toward her car.

Every step she took away from Nicholas was like a shot to her own heart.

She knew she would never see him again.

Chapter Sixteen

"Can't sleep, honey?" Aunt Lori walked into the half-darkened living room and settled herself on the couch beside Cara as the grandfather clock in the corner rang two o'clock in the morning. "What are you reading?"

"The Psalms. Trying to find out what I'm supposed to learn through all of this." Cara's eyes were dry. She had cried all the way back from Nicholas's place, praying that she wouldn't get into an accident. Thankfully neither Uncle Alan nor Aunt Lori was home when she got here.

She had hidden herself away in her bedroom, letting the tears flow until her eyes burned.

After supper she had gone back to her bedroom but sleep had eluded her.

She'd been here for four hours already, reading, praying—anything to keep from looking into the bleak and cheerless landscape of her future.

Cara turned another page. "I thought Nicholas and I were on our way to a new and better place. I even thought, in one silly, hopeful corner of my mind, that he would propose again."

Aunt Lori slipped her arm around her niece's shoulder. "I'm so sorry, honey. I was starting to see such hope and joy in your eyes. I was starting to make my own silly plans." She squeezed Cara, offering what comfort she could. "Have you called Mr. Rousseau in Montreal?"

"He's not in the office until tomorrow. I was going to call him then and let him know I wasn't coming."

"And now?"

The words hung between them.

"I'm taking the job," Cara said finally. "It's a great opportunity. And it will take me halfway across the country."

"And away from Nicholas."

Cara didn't reply.

Aunt Lori sighed and stroked Cara's head. "I'm sure you know what you're doing. I wish there was a way to solve Nicholas's problem with the cattle. Because if that happened, maybe he wouldn't leave."

"Am I being selfish because I don't want Nicholas to work those risky jobs? I know he wants to save his ranch but if this is Nicholas's way of solving all his money problems that won't change in the future. There will always be something to fix, repair or buy."

Aunt Lori gave her a reassuring smile. "No, honey. You're not selfish. I think Nicholas feels he has no choice, which, of course, is never true. We all have a choice and it's how we make our choices that determine what is most important in our lives."

"And for him, it's the ranch. Always will be the ranch. How can I compete with that?"

"You don't have to fight the ranch or compete with it. Maybe you just have to embrace it, understand it. I know you've been looking for community and roots, but I also think you've been afraid to get too settled."

"What do you mean?"

Aunt Lori angled her head to one side as if to look at the problem from another viewpoint. "I remember telling your mother it wasn't fair to you, to move you around from place to place, and that she had to do something about it. For your sake."

"Is that why she left me here?"

"One of the reasons." Aunt Lori picked up Cara's hand and gently stroked it with her thumb. "She said something to me once that didn't sink in until recently. How she was afraid of you."

"Afraid?" What could Aunt Lori be talking about? "My mother wasn't afraid of anything."

Aunt Lori's gentle look held a shadow of pity as she squeezed Cara's hand. "I think she was afraid of getting too attached to you. You never knew your father, and though he was never in your life, your mother cared for him a lot more than she let on. When he died, it sent her into a tailspin of grief. I think she always hoped he would come to his senses and come back to her and you. And I think her reaction to his death was to throw herself into whatever work she could to get rid of the grief."

"She always told me I was lucky to be born where I was, and that she had to help these other children." Cara's heart seemed to fold in on itself, as if protecting itself once again from the pain of the past. "It was like she always chose them over me."

"That was her way of keeping you at arm's length." Aunt Lori's voice was suddenly quiet and steady. "I tried to tell her she would be the one who would lose in the end. Trouble was you were the one that lost the most. I think you lost the ability to give yourself completely to anyone because you were afraid that whatever you love might get taken away."

The tiniest crack tremored through Cara's defenses. "When I asked Nicholas not to go, I felt like I was a little girl again. Asking my mother not to go." Cara sighed. "Do you think I'm afraid of loving Nicholas, too?"

"What do you think?"

Aunt Lori's simple question placed doubt on Cara's arguments against loving Nicholas. The arguments she built to defend her heart. Then she released a heavy sigh. "Maybe."

"Do you think he loves you?"

"I don't know. If he does, why would he leave?"

Aunt Lori released Cara's hand and sat back, folding her arms around her middle, as if trying to find the best way to answer.

"When your uncle had his heart attack, I resented every minute he'd spent at the clinic. I thought if only he hadn't worked so hard he would have been fine. And maybe that was true. But I also know that your uncle defines himself through work. For Alan a large part of his significance is not only in his work, but also in being able to provide for the people he loves. I think Nicholas is of a similar character and if you care for Nicholas, you need to appreciate the things he appreciates."

"I know what the ranch means to him. I didn't get that the first time."

"Then you'll have to understand why he does what he does."

"So you're saying Nicholas is right to head off?"

Aunt Lori responded with a shrug. "I'm not saying he's right or wrong. I'm just saying that if you care about him, you'll realize his dedication to the ranch is a vital part of who he is."

"And what about me? Where do I fit in this?"

Aunt Lori's only response was a careful lift of one eyebrow encouraging Cara to explain.

"I have to protect…protect myself," she continued, pleading with her aunt to understand her stumbling answers. "It's the only way I'll survive."

"Survive?"

Cara's resolve weakened with each question her aunt lobbed her way.

"Yes. Survive." A throb of an older emotion passed through her, as the pain she had exposed to Nicholas returned.

"That makes it sound like you're on your own. Like you have to get through life on your own strength." Though Aunt Lori's words were gently spoken they held the gentlest lash of reprimand.

Ashamed, Cara looked down at the Bible in her lap and her gaze was caught by the word *strength*. She read the passage aloud. "'Blessed are those whose strength is in You.'"

"Those words are true for all of us," Aunt Lori said. "Me as well as you. I know I had to cling to that when Uncle Alan was in the hospital, and I still have to realize my strength and my trust is in God, not myself."

Cara ran her finger along the edge of the page, drawing up the old memories she had thrown at Nicholas. "When mom died, I had to think of what she always told me. That you have to take care of yourself."

"She was wrong, Cara. Taking care of yourself turns you into an island. Thinking only of yourself pushes other people and their needs away. You're a better person than that. You have a good heart. Please don't take on your mother's problems." Aunt Lori released a light sigh as she stroked Cara's hair. "When she died, I wanted nothing more than to hold you close, to let you know we were here, but you were older, so independent. So much, in some ways, like your mother. So I kept my distance, waiting for you to let me know how you felt. Waiting to hear from your own mouth how much it hurt. But you kept us at a distance."

Cara covered her mouth with her hand, holding back the trembling. "I'm sorry, Aunty. I felt so alone. And I pushed you away and I pushed God away. I was doing exactly what my mother told me to do. Taking care of myself." Cara turned to her aunt. "Just like I did the last time I left. The last time Nicholas and I fought. I'm sorry I didn't call as often as I should have. I'm sorry that I kept myself separate from you. I thought if I did, I wouldn't hurt as much."

"Did it work?"

Cara shook her head as hot tears welled up. "I missed you so much."

Aunt Lori gently brushed an errant tear from Cara's cheek. "I know you did. But I'm also guessing you missed Nicholas."

Cara sighed. "I did. Horribly."

"And you will again. I know losing your mother made you afraid, but how would you sooner live? Alone? Safe? Or would you sooner risk loving someone? When you left I was so hurt. And I'm not telling this to make you feel guilty, just to explain. I could have avoided that hurt by not taking you in at all. Your uncle and I could have kept our lives free and uncluttered." Aunt Lori's expression softened and she reached out and tucked a strand of hair behind Cara's ear. "But we would have missed out on all the good things we had having you in our home. Love causes pain and makes you vulnerable to pain, but it's worth every hurt for the blessing it gives you."

Cara couldn't say anything. She bent her head and let her aunt's words wear away the walls around her heart.

"And I hope you also realize that God loves you in spite of how you feel about Him," Aunt Lori continued. "That though we hurt Him over and over, and I include myself, your uncle and every person in this world when I say that, His love is unconditional and enduring."

Her aunt's words ignited a new sorrow. She had been so wrong to push her aunt and uncle away. To push God away.

To keep Nicholas at arm's length, blaming his work, his choices.

Tears thickened her throat. Tears of regret. Sorrow.

But this sorrow had a cleansing quality. And as she laid her head on her aunt's shoulder, she felt surrounded not just by her aunt's arms, but also by the love of God. A God who knew her before she was born. Who hemmed her in behind and before.

When the sorrow abated, she lifted her head again. The pain was still there, but now she had a companion, a support in the darkness.

She was about to close the Bible when a phrase caught her attention.

She stopped and read it again.

My heart and flesh cry out for the living God. Even the sparrow has found a home.

Something niggled at her, but she couldn't seem to catch it and pin it down.

Aunt Lori stroked her niece's cheek, stifling a yawn.

"I'm sorry, my dear, but I have to go to bed." She laid her hand on Cara's shoulder. "Are you going to be okay?"

Cara nodded. "I'm staying up for a bit. Read some more."

"I'll be praying as you make your decisions." Aunt Lori cupped her chin, then dropped a light kiss on her head. "And you know that no matter what you decide, no matter where you go, your uncle and I will always love you and this will always be your home."

As she left, her aunt's words kindled warmth and yearning in Cara.

Home.

She glanced around the familiar setting of the living room as echoes of conversations held here, memories of family games and times spent reading, hovered in the quiet.

A few memories of living with her mother slipped in, as well, but they were less clear. She had no memory whatsoever of a grandmother and nothing to remember her by.

She thought of Nicholas, and of the antiques that had been handled by his grandparents and great-grandparents. They were no mere artifacts. They were part of his history and had stories attached to them. Stories woven into the fabric of his life and rooted in his history.

And she knew despite her anger and hurt, she still cared for Nicholas and because the caring was so strong, the hurt at his choice was so great.

Was he really choosing the ranch over you?

She shook her head as if to dislodge her doubts, but other thoughts returned. Memories of the pride in Nicholas's voice as he pointed out the places on his ranch that meant so much. Places that had history and stories.

Nicholas was rooted and grounded in that place. It wasn't competition for her, it was a part of who he was. And if she were honest with herself, she would realize that if she loved him, then she had to love what made him who he was.

She felt a moment of freedom at that thought and she looked down at the Bible again. She hadn't turned the page.

Even the sparrow...

As it had before, the single word caught her attention.

Sparrow. Sparrows flying around the barn. Sparrows clustered around a waterer. Sparrows dead on the ground.

And she had a good idea of what had happened with Nicholas's cattle.

The view from the hotel was amazing. At least according to the project manager who put him up here after their meeting last night. The beds were purported to be the most comfortable in the city, guaranteeing him the best night's sleep.

But Nicholas had spent most of the night clutching his cell phone, second thoughts bouncing around his skull.

Was he doing the right thing?

Should he phone Cara? Talk things over with her?

And what could he say that hadn't been said on the porch? Things between him and Cara had been coming together. And his feelings for her were stronger than before. Deeper.

But what choice did he have? Losing the cattle meant losing income he did not know how else to replace. The ranch couldn't absorb that kind of loss. And there was no way he was going to make a commitment to Cara unless he knew for sure he could provide for her.

He'd finally fallen into busy dreams around two o'clock and had woken up an hour ago.

An airplane soared past his window and beyond that the Rocky Mountains thrust rugged peaks into a sky pink from the sunrise.

Below him, he could see the suburbs of north Calgary. A maze of houses and streets flowing over the hills and leading to the mountains. In another hour people would be leaving home for work for the day and returning at night to their families.

In half an hour he had to leave for the airport, cram himself into a seat meant for someone four inches shorter and look forward to twenty-five hours of flights and stop-overs. And after that?

Twelve-hour workdays. Evenings spent watching television with men who were also far away from their homes.

He leaned his head against the window. He was already missing Cara.

What am I supposed to do, Lord? How can I find my way through this?

Going out to do this work was the only way he could guarantee the ranch could provide for his family. For Cara.

I have learned the secret of being content in any and every situation, whether well fed or hungry, whether living in plenty or in want.

The words from Philippians that he had spoken so blithely to his father seemed to taunt him.

But that was before he found out his cattle herd and his plans for a future living on the ranch with Cara were wiped out with one visit from the vet.

Do they have to be?

Nicholas pushed himself away from the window, and grabbed his suitcase. He'd already told his boss he was leaving. Had the plane ticket in his pocket. He was committed.

And what of your commitment to Cara?

He paused, his hands wrapped around the handle as indecision dogged his every move.

He looked out the window again. The sun was above the mountains, bathing the city in a pinkish glow. Once the heifers were shipped out, he had hoped to take Cara out early one morning and show her the sun coming up over the ranch.

He'd imagined himself standing behind her, his arms wrapped around her, holding her close. Then he'd imagined himself asking her, quietly, if she'd consider making their relationship more serious. If she would consider a future with him.

And you walked out on that?

What else was he supposed to do? Stay around and watch his herd of cattle being destroyed? His plans for the future?

I have learned the secret of being content in every situation...I can do everything through Him who gives me strength.

Nicholas let go of the suitcase and dropped on the bed behind him. So if he went and made his money, he'd have his ranch.

But he wouldn't have Cara.

He tried to imagine his life without her. He'd done it before, but he knew, this time, losing her would not just break his heart, it would destroy it.

Lorne had told him love was a risk.

Maybe he didn't dare take that risk with Cara the first

time. Maybe the first time, when he chose his work over her, maybe it wasn't just about the work. Maybe, deep down, it was also about the risk of loving someone who could potentially break his heart.

Who could potentially leave.

So, simple answer to that, be the first to leave.

A chill surrounded his heart, the same heart he had unwittingly protected as the words took root. And he knew this was the biggest part of his struggle.

I can do everything through Him who gives me strength.

He had treated Cara badly. She was right to be concerned that he had chosen the ranch over her.

And behind that thought came a more chilling one.

He was just like her mother.

Just like his mother.

He lowered his head into his hands as he struggled to let go of the thoughts, the concerns, the worries.

Forgive me, Lord. Forgive my need to be in charge. To be in control. Forgive me for not putting You first in my life and for not making Cara a priority. Help me to serve You, Lord. Help me to lean on You for wisdom and for strength. Show me what I should do.

He waited a moment, as if for an answer, but as the silence of his hotel room filled his ears, a conviction grew deep within him.

And accompanying that, a sense of release.

He wanted Cara in his life. And he wanted to stay on the ranch regardless of what might come. To build a life with her there. Every day. And he had to trust and believe that she meant every word when she said money didn't matter. That she would sooner have him around every day than a financially secure ranch.

Please, Lord. Give me the strength to follow through on this.

He waited a moment, then added:

Please let Cara still be there.

Chapter Seventeen

"I think it's worth a shot. You've got nothing to lose."
Cara stood in front of Dale Chapman, stifling her frustration with the man.

"Except my time," Dale growled back.

Cara shot him an exasperated frown. This morning she had gone directly to the vet clinic with her new information, hoping to convince Gordon to hold off on the order to destroy the cattle. He hadn't budged.

Now she faced the same unyielding behavior from the man who had the most to gain from her coming here.

"I thought you wanted to save the cows."

"How do you figure you know more than that Gordon fella? He's been a vet longer than you have."

And been moving from clinic to clinic ever since he'd received his license, Cara found out.

"Because he doesn't care. He's here because he can't get work anywhere else. It doesn't matter to him that the entire herd you and your son have spent years building up could be destroyed with one stroke of his pen."

"And you do care?" Dale challenged.

"I care a lot more than he does. I don't want to see the ranch lose any more money."

"Nicholas isn't here, you know."

"I know. But I still want to do this for him."

"I still think it's a waste of time."

Cara finally couldn't stand this anymore. "Your son is heading out to a dangerous job so he can save this ranch. He's willing to put his life on the line for this place and you can't put aside your own stubborn pride or your unreasonable dislike of me to let me run one single, simple, lousy test?"

Dale looked taken aback at her anger, but she wasn't near done.

"How dare you act as if I don't know what I'm doing?" Cara's voice grew quiet. "From the first moment you met me you've judged me and made me feel like I don't deserve your son. Let me set one thing straight, my uncle feels the same way about him. Neither of us deserves the other but I know that in Christ, he and I are equal and you and I are equal. I don't know what I've ever done to make you dislike—"

"How about leaving my son? Just like his mother left me and him?"

"You disliked me even before we broke up so don't use that excuse," Cara snapped. "And you're right. I shouldn't have left him. I should have stayed. But I had my own reasons and I don't think they were wrong."

"This ranch is important to him, missy. You have to know that."

"Do you think I don't?" Cara's voice grew more intense. "I've seen how the light shines in his eyes when he looks around this place. I know how his voice gets soft whenever he talks about it. I know it's in his blood and his soul and I know he shouldn't have to leave it every time this place needs something fixed."

"His mother couldn't make the sacrifice to stay, what makes you think—"

"Don't even mention us in the same breath. I'm not like her." Cara's voice rose with each sentence and she didn't care anymore. Her anger was burning white-hot. "And if you think I can't make any sacrifices for Nicholas or for this ranch, you might want to talk to my supposed boss in Montreal, who I called this morning to tell him that I won't be coming on time because I want to do an acid-fast test on sparrow poop. And he told me not to bother coming at all, so technically, I don't have a job because I want to find a way to save Nicholas's cows."

She caught Dale looking past her and she was about to grab him to make him look at her when she caught the puzzled look on his face.

She turned and her heart stopped, then flopped slowly over.

Nicholas was striding toward them, his gaze intent on her.

"What you doing here, son?" Dale asked. "Aren't you supposed to be on a plane?"

Cara couldn't speak. She could only look at him, soaking in the reality of him standing in front of her.

"I changed my mind," Nicholas said, answering his father's questions but addressing Cara.

She continued to stare at him, unable to believe he was really here.

He took her hands in his. "I'm sorry," he said, his voice quiet, his eyes intent on hers.

She stood immobile, still struggling to believe he was here. Not winging across the Atlantic to a remote oil rig.

"Why did you come back?" she asked, her voice a breathless whisper taking in the strength of him. The very presence of him.

"I don't want to leave you alone again," he said, squeezing her hands tighter in return. "I want to stay here. With you."

Cara's breath left her in a sigh, then a tentative smile hovered at the corner of her mouth. "I'm glad you came back."

Then she gave into an impulse and reached up and cupped his jaw in her hand and, in front of his father, stood up on tiptoe and kissed him.

He swept her into his arms and kissed her back, holding her tight against him. She felt safe, secure.

Cared for.

"I'm so sorry," he murmured. "I was wrong."

"So was I," she whispered, her arms twining around his neck, her fingers tangling in his hair. She gave him another kiss, relishing the privilege.

She wished she could push the world away. Wished time could stop so she could stay here, absorbing the reality of his presence. Things still lay between them that she wanted swept away.

But reality intruded and she reluctantly pulled back.

"What are you doing here?" he asked, his finger tracing her features with a gentleness that almost melted her resolve.

She brushed a kiss over his knuckles, then reluctantly lowered his hand.

"I'm trying to convince your father to let me run some tests to prove the heifers are perfectly healthy."

Nicholas blinked, as if trying to catch up to her. "I thought there was nothing else you could do?"

"Your cows don't have bovine TB," she said, forcing her attention back to the matter at hand. For now it was enough that Nicholas was here to help her solve this problem and she needed him on board to convince his stubborn father. "But I'm pretty sure they have been exposed to avian TB, which is benign to most humans and cattle, but can show a false positive in a TB test. Gordon should have known that."

"So how…" Nicholas, still holding her hand, tried to sift this information.

"You've been holding the heifers close to the barn for the past couple of months. I'm convinced if we check the cows in the upper pasture you won't find any reaction to the TB test because they weren't exposed to the sparrows living in the barn."

"And how do you know those birds have whatever it is you think they have," Dale interrupted, his puzzled glance ticking from Nicholas to Cara as if trying to absorb this new situation.

Cara's frustration eased with Nicholas standing beside her. "A simple acid test on the sparrow droppings will confirm what I suspect. And the fact that they're showing some of the classic symptoms. When I saw the flock of birds at the waterer the other day, it raised a red flag." Which was only brought to her attention when she read the piece in the Psalms about the sparrow.

"Will that test be enough?" Nicholas asked.

"Alberta is classified as TB free. I know once I do the test and present this information to Uncle Alan and Bill, they'll corroborate my findings. We might have to do a follow-up test on the heifers, but they'll get a clean bill of health. The TB test wasn't even mandatory."

"But it caused a lot of problems."

"And the fact that your other herd won't show any reaction to the test will be proof, as well, that it isn't in the heifers," Cara continued, looking back to Nicholas.

Nicholas's smile dove into her heart and though a thousand questions still hung between them, the reality was he was standing beside her instead of sitting on a plane.

That was more then enough for now.

"Okay. Let's do this then. Tell us what we need to do and we'll do it."

Nicholas tried not to chew his lip, fidget or sigh. Cara had been busy making up slides in the vet clinic for the past half an hour. After she had come to the ranch, Nicholas and his father had ridden up to the other herd and brought them down to the corrals. Cara had gone through them all and had found no reaction to the test, which corroborated her diagnosis.

After that they had helped her gather up sparrow droppings from the barn and bagged a few dead sparrows, as well.

He still couldn't believe the sight that had greeted him when he came to the ranch from Calgary. Cara's car parked in the driveway.

Cara standing up to his father, arguing with him.

The look of surprise and pleasure when she saw him walking toward her.

He wanted to sweep her off her feet, whisk her away to a secluded place where they could talk, share and remove the debris of the last argument they'd had.

But that had to wait while she pushed another slide under the microscope, determined to prove her theory.

He couldn't read her expression at all. Her entire focus was on what she could see through the lens.

She took one slide off, and put yet another one underneath it and looked through it again.

Finally Alan spoke up.

"So? What did you see?" Uncle Alan pushed his glasses up his nose. Nicholas knew Alan needed to know the results as badly as he did. To have a positive TB test show up in Alberta cattle could be devastating for the local ranchers.

Finally Cara straightened, stretching her arms over her head. Then she gave Nicholas a grin that made him sag against the wall behind him.

"The sparrow droppings tested positive for avian TB," she said, her quiet words thundering in Nicholas's head.

"That's wonderful," Alan said.

Wonderful didn't begin to cover the relief surging through Nicholas. Though he had confidence in Cara, hearing her confirm her diagnosis pushed away the last doubt he had.

"I know a follow-up test on the heifers will show them to be clear, as well." She gave Nicholas another smile. "You won't be able to ship them until we do the next test, but in the meantime, everything is clear."

"Are you going to go by her word?" Gordon blustered from the doorway of the makeshift lab Cara had set up. "She doesn't have near the experience with hands-on vet work that I do. I should have been the one to check that other herd. It was my case."

Nicholas saw Alan shoot Gordon a withering look. Then, as if Gordon didn't matter, Alan turned to Nicholas. "I'm rescinding the order to destroy the herd."

Thank You, Lord, Nicholas thought. He didn't deserve the break, but he was thankful for it.

"But you can't go over my head—" Gordon was saying.

"I can and I will," Uncle Alan retorted.

"If you're taking her word over mine, I don't know if I can work in this office," Gordon said, his hands shoved into the pockets of his smock.

"You don't have to worry about thinking you can't work in this office. It will be a reality," Uncle Alan said in a clipped voice.

Nicholas glanced from Alan to Gordon, wondering what was going on.

Alan turned to Cara. "If you'll excuse me, I have to have a chat with Gordon and Bill." He patted her on the shoulder. "Good work, girl. I'm so proud of your dedication."

He left, closing the door quietly behind him, leaving Nicholas and Cara alone in the room.

As soon as the door clicked behind him, Nicholas spun Cara around on the chair and pulled her up into his arms.

Then he caught her mouth in a long, deep and satisfying kiss.

When he came up for air, her eyes shone up at him, and her hands clung to his shoulders.

"Okay," she said, her voice sounding shaky. "I guess we're not going to bother with words."

"They have traditionally come between us." Nicholas turned and sat down on the stool and pulled her close. "But I do have something to say."

He waited, letting the silence settle to allow the moment its full due.

"I'm sorry. I'm so sorry," he said. "I was wrong. You were right."

"Please. No. I was wrong, too. Wrong not to see that

the ranch wasn't competition. That it was a part of you—
an important and vital part of you."

Nicholas shook his head, still trying to reconcile the
fact that he was here, holding Cara in his arms.

"You know, you were right. It isn't all up to me. I
was in a mad panic to head out to go and save the ranch
when, in the end, you did it. You were the one who saved
the ranch."

She put her finger to his lips. "No. It wasn't me. I had
to learn to listen." Her voice was suddenly quiet and
steady as if she needed him to understand. "I had to learn
to let go and to not put myself first." She removed her
finger and replaced it with another kiss. "I'm so thankful God brought us together again and I want you in my
life and I'll take you as you are. Right now."

Though she spoke the words lightly, he knew their
true cost.

And his heart thrilled with possibilities.

"Will you?"

"Will I what?"

"Will you take me as I am? Right now?" He couldn't
stop himself, he had to know. "Would you marry me?"

Cara held his gaze, her smile creating an answering
burst of pleasure inside him. "Yes. I will."

Nicholas bent his head and sealed their promises with
a gentle, lingering kiss. Then he sighed. "This wasn't
exactly where I had planned to propose," he said, thinking of the hillside, the sunset and having everything just
right.

"This is as good a place as any." Cara glanced around
the tiny room with its shelves of medicine and supplies.
"You had everything perfect the first time around but
that was no guarantee of success."

"Not toward the end." He gave a rueful laugh. "You sure you're willing to give engagement to me another go?"

"I think we're getting pretty good at it." Cara clasped her hands behind his neck, leaning back to look at him. "We're starting from another place."

"You're right about that. I'm not going to the rigs again," he said. "I want to stay on the ranch full-time, though I won't make as much money."

Her look held a vestige of sorrow. "Do you think that matters to me?"

"No. I suppose it wouldn't." He released a nervous laugh. "Not like it mattered to my mother. But like you suggested, I think she was lonely and being broke didn't help. And you, living with your aunt and uncle, always seemed to have more than enough. But I never realized what you had to live with."

"Doesn't matter. It all came together to bring me here. To meet you."

"Again," he said with a laugh.

"Again."

He kissed her again, then traced the line of her lips. "You know I love you, Cara Morrison."

"And I love you, Nicholas Chapman."

The words hung between them, rife with promises and hope. Hope for today and for a future.

"Let's go tell my uncle," Cara said, tugging on his arm. "I'm sure he's wondering what's going on in here."

"Oh, I think he has a pretty good idea," Nicholas said.

"And then we should go talk to your father."

Nicholas pulled her back. "I'm sorry about him, too," he went on, realizing it needed to be said. "I'm sure he'll come around in time."

Cara slanted him a half smile. "I guess I'll have to turn on the charm, then, won't I?"

"Or tell him he can get free vet services," Nicholas said.

"Maybe I'll have to start my own business," Cara said, pulling open the door. "Be competition to my uncle and Bill." She stepped out into the hallway, almost colliding with Gordon, who shot Cara a baleful glance before slamming the back door behind him.

Nicholas looked from the door, to Cara then to Alan standing in the doorway of his office, his hands on his hips.

"Something tells me you might have a job waiting right here," he said. He slipped his arm over her shoulders and in front of her uncle, dropped a kiss on her head, then together they walked toward him to share their good news.

Together.

* * * * *

Dear Reader,

This story came to me while I was doing research for another book. That often happens to writers. It's as if our internal radar is always searching. But the concept had to be put aside while other ideas clamored to be given form, so I was glad to finally tell Cara and Nicholas's story. What I was trying to show with this book is the false idea of thinking we have control over our lives. We can make all our plans and then, like Nicholas, things happen beyond our control and everything is in turmoil. I know I struggle again and again with thinking, again like Nicholas, that if everything is exactly right in my life, then I can be happy. Whereas, instead, I've had to learn to be content this moment with where I am. To look to God and realize that the most important plans I can make are with Him in mind. I hope you enjoyed the journey Nicholas and Cara had to make to grow and change.

Carolyne Aarsen

PS: I love to hear from my readers. Drop me a note at carsen@xplornet.com or visit my website, carolyneaarsen.com, to find out what's going on in my life and my writing.

COWBOY DADDY

Come to me, all you who are weary and
burdened, and I will give you rest.
—*Matthew* 11:28

To Elin and Annely, who have brought
a new dimension of love to our lives.

Chapter One

What in the world was this about?

"Housekeeper wanted." The words were handwritten, and the notice was tacked up on the bulletin board in Millarville's post office.

Kip Cosgrove ripped the notice down and glared at it, recognizing his younger sister's handwriting. What was Isabelle doing? Where did she get the idea that he needed a housekeeper?

Kip crumpled the paper and threw it in the garbage can of the post office, hoping not too many people had read it.

He spun around, almost bumping into an older woman.

"Hey, Kip, how's your mom?" she asked. "I read on the church bulletin that she had knee surgery."

"She's in a lot of pain," Kip said with a vague smile, taking another step toward the door. He didn't have time for Millarville chitchat. Not with two rambunctious five-year-old boys waiting for him in his truck parked outside the door and a sister to bawl out. "I'll tell her you said hello."

He tipped his cowboy hat, then jogged over to his

truck. He had to get home before anyone responded to the advertisement.

"What's the matter, Uncle Kip?"

"Are you mad?"

Justin and Tristan leaned over the front seat of the truck, their faces showing the remnants of the Popsicles he'd given them as a bribe to be quiet on the long trip back from Calgary.

"Buckle up again, you guys," was all he said. He started up the truck, too many things running through his head. Besides looking after his mom and his rebellious younger sister, he had a tractor to fix, hay to haul, horses' hooves to trim and cows to move. And that was today's to-do list.

He managed to ignore the boys tussling in the backseat as he headed down the road, lists and things crowding into his head. Maybe his sister wasn't so wrong in thinking they needed a housekeeper. Even just someone to watch the boys.

No, he reminded himself. Isabelle could do that.

He hunched his shoulders, planning his "you're sixteen-years-old and you can help out over the summer" lecture that he'd already had with his sister once before. Now he had to do it again.

The road made a long, slow bend, and as it straightened, he sighed. The land eased away from the road, green fields giving way to rolling hills. Peaks of granite dusted with snow thrust up behind them, starkly beautiful against the warm blue of the endless sky.

The Rocky Mountains of Southern Alberta. His beloved home.

Kip slowed, as he always did, letting the beauty seep into his soul. But only for a couple of seconds, as a scream from the back pushed his foot a little farther down on the accelerator.

"Justin, go sit down." Kip shot his nephew another warning glance as he turned onto the ranch's driveway.

"Someone is here," Justin yelled, falling over the front seat almost kicking Kip in the face with his cowboy boots, spreading dirt all over the front seat.

Kip pulled to a stop beside an unfamiliar small car. It didn't belong to his other sister, Doreen, that much he knew. Doreen and her husband, Alex, had gone with a full-size van for their brood of eight.

Probably one of his mother's many friends had come to visit. Then his teeth clenched when he noticed that the farm truck was missing, which meant Isabelle was gone. Which also meant she hadn't cleaned the house like he'd told her to.

The boys tumbled out of the truck and Kip headed up the stairs to intercept them before they burst in on his mother's visit. No sense giving the women of Millarville one more thing to gossip about. Kip and those poor, sad little fatherless boys, so out of control. So sad.

Just as he caught their hands, the door of the house opened.

An unfamiliar woman stood framed by the doorway, the late-afternoon sun burnishing her smooth hair, pulled tightly back from a perfectly heart-shaped face. Her porcelain skin, high cheekbones, narrow nose and soft lips gave her an ethereal look at odds with the crisp blue blazer, white shirt and blue dress pants. It was the faintest hint of mystery in her gray-green eyes, however, that caught and held his attention.

What was this beautiful woman doing in his house?

She held up her hands as if to appease him. "Your

sister, Isabelle, invited me in. Said you were looking for a housekeeper?" The husky note in her voice created a curious sense of intimacy.

Kip groaned inwardly. He'd taken down the notice too late. "And you are?"

"My name is Nicole."

"Kip Cosgrove." He held out his hand. Her handshake was firm, which gave him a bit more confidence.

"I'm sorry about coming straight into the house," she said, "but like I said, your sister invited me in, and I thought I should help out right away."

She looked away from him to the boys. Her gentle smile for them softened the angles of her face and turned her from attractive to stunning.

He pushed down his reaction. He had to keep his focus.

"So how long have you been here?" Or, in other words, how long had Isabelle been gone?

"A couple of hours. I managed to get the laundry done and I cleaned the house."

In spite of his overall opposition to Isabelle's harebrained scheme, Kip felt a loosening of tension in his shoulders. He and Isabelle had had a big argument about the laundry and housework before he went to Calgary. Now it was done.

He'd had too many things going on lately. His responsibility for the boys, his mother, Isabelle. The ranch seemed to be a distant fourth in his priorities, which made him even more tense.

Maybe the idea of hiring a housekeeper wasn't so farfetched.

"You realize my mother has had surgery?" he asked, still not sure he wanted a stranger in the house but also fully aware of his sister's shortcomings in the house-keeping department.

"I've already met her." Her smile seemed to under-line her lack of objection. "Isabelle gave me some of the particulars."

"Will you be able to come only certain hours, or do you have other obligations?" He still had his reservations, but since she had come all the way here and had done a bunch of work already, he should ask a few questions.

"I'm not married, if that's what you're asking," Nicole said, brushing a wisp of hair back from her face with one graceful motion.

The gold hoops in her ears caught the sun, as did the rings on her manicured hands.

She didn't look like she'd done much housekeeping. His first impression would have pegged her as a fashion model or businesswoman.

But then he'd been wrong about people before. Case in point: his one-time girlfriend, Nancy. The one who took off as soon as she found out he had been named the guardian of his nephews.

Nicole looked back at the boys, who hadn't said a peep since she had appeared in the doorway. "I'm guessing you are Justin and Tristan?" she asked.

The boys, while boisterous and outgoing around fam-ily, were invariably shy around strangers, especially since their father, Scott's death. They clung to Kip and leaned against his legs.

"It's really nice to meet you at…meet you." Nicole crouched down to the boys' level. He caught the scent of lilacs, saw the curve of her cheek as she glanced from one boy to the other. Her hand reached out, as if to touch them, then retreated.

Something about the gesture comforted him. She seemed drawn to the boys, yet gave them space.

"My nephews are five. They'll be going to school this fall." He tightened his grip on the boys' hands. "Though I hate the thought of putting the little guys on the school bus." Why he told her that, he wasn't sure.

"I told Uncle Kip we have to stay home. To help him with the chores," Tristan said.

"I don't know much about farm chores," Nicole said, glancing from one boy to the other. "What kinds of things do you have to do?"

"We have to feed the dog," Tristan offered quietly. "She has puppies."

"You have puppies?" Nicole's eyes grew wide. "That's pretty neat."

"And we have to help with the baby calves," Justin added, as if unwilling to be outdone by his brother. "But we're not allowed to ride the horses anymore." He shot a hopeful glance Kip's way but he ignored it. The boys had been campaigning all summer to ride again, but there was no way he was putting anyone he loved on a horse. Not since Scott's accident.

They were too young and too precious.

"Now all I have to do is figure out which one of you is Tristan and which is Justin." Nicole looked from one to the other, and the tenderness in her smile eased away Kip's second thoughts.

"He's Tristan," Justin said, pointing to his brother. "And I'm Justin. We're twins."

"I see that. So how should I tell you apart?" Nicole asked.

"Justin has a little brown mark on his back. In the shape of a horseshoe," Tristan offered.

"Do you think it was because you were born on a ranch?"

"Wasn't borned on the ranch. I was borned in the hospital in Halifax." He sighed. "My daddy is dead, you know."

"Dead?" Nicole frowned. "What do you mean?"

"He died when he got on Uncle Kip's horse."

Tristan's comment was said in all innocence, but again the guilt associated with his brother's death washed over Kip.

"Your father is dead?" Nicole said, one hand pressed to her chest.

Why did she sound so shocked? Kip wondered.

"He died when the horse he was on flipped over," Justin continued. "But we know he's in heaven with Jesus. I talk to Jesus and tell him what to say to my daddy every night."

"That's...interesting." A faint note of skepticism entered her voice that concerned him.

"We go regularly to church," Kip said by way of brief explanation. "I hope that's not a problem." He wasn't about to get into a theological discussion about what Jesus meant to him. If he decided to hire her, then she'd find out that faith was woven into every aspect of the Cosgroves' life.

Nicole waved her hand as if dismissing his concerns. "No. Of course not."

"And our mommy is gone," Tristan offered, unwilling to let Justin do all the talking. "She just left us one day. All alone with the babysitter."

"Then Daddy rescued us. He was a good daddy," Justin said.

"How do you know your mommy left you?" A faint

edge had entered her voice as she glanced up at Kip. "Do you know where their mother is?"

Kip shook his head, wondering why she wanted to know.

The reality was, no one in the Cosgrove family knew where Tricia was or whether she was dead or alive. His brother, Scott, and Tricia had been living in Nova Scotia when Tricia took off without a word six months after the boys were born.

Scott and his sons then moved back to the ranch.

"Do you want to see our dog's puppies?" Justin tugged his hand free of Kip's and reached out to Nicole.

"Shouldn't you go and say hi to your Gramma?" Nicole asked.

Kip was pleasantly surprised at her consideration, but he also knew the boys would rather be outside.

"They can go." He wanted a few minutes alone with his mother to get her impression of Nicole.

Tristan grabbed Nicole's other hand and before she could lodge a protest the three of them were off.

Kip watched them head down the sidewalk toward the barn, still unsure. Hiring her would give him a break from the constant nagging he did to get Isabelle to help.

He sighed, glancing at his watch. He should go see his mother and then make sure the boys didn't get into any trouble. Then he had to see what he could do about his tractor.

What had she done?

Nicole bit her lip as she looked down at the sticky faces of the two boys looking up at her, jabbering about cows and puppies and Uncle Kip and Auntie Isabelle and other relatives.

She tried to stifle her guilt.

She was no housekeeper. Nor had she come because of an advertisement. Her real reason for coming to the ranch was to see her nephews. Her sister's boys.

That Kip's sister Isabelle assumed she was the housekeeper had been a coincidence she capitalized on.

She clung to the boys' hands as she felt buffeted by a wave of love. Justin. Tristan. Tricia's twins. A remnant of the true Williams family now that Tricia was dead.

When Tricia had stormed out of their lives all those years ago, yelling that she'd never come back, Nicole had hoped her beloved sister would someday return. Nicole had prayed and had clung to this hope for eight years. However, four weeks ago a police officer showed up at the Williamses' home in Rosedale, Toronto, with the news of Tricia's death and crushed that hope.

Three years ago Tricia had been struck by a car while out walking late at night. She had no identification. It wasn't until Tricia's roommate registered her concern for the missing Tricia that the police were able to identify her body. The roommate knew only that Tricia had recently moved to Halifax and when she had earned enough money she planned to head out west. Then Tricia had had her accident.

The years had slipped by. Then, a month ago, the roommate moved out of her apartment and in the process had found an envelope behind a desk.

Inside the envelope were letters from Tricia to someone named Scott Cosgrove, a man Tricia apparently had been living with after the boys were born. From what Nicole and her father, Sam, understood from the letters, the boys' biological father was dead. Scott, who was just her boyfriend, had somehow taken Tricia's boys away from her while she was in a drug-rehabilitation program.

These letters had been mailed but returned, marked Address Unknown. These envelopes also contained letters to her sons expressing her love for them and how much she missed them. The final paper was a last will and testament addressed to her parents, asking Sam and Norah Williams to be her sons' guardians in case something happened to her.

The roommate brought all this to the police, who were finally able to inform Nicole and her father what had happened to Tricia. It was also the first time Norah and Sam found out about Tricia's sons.

Nicole had done some detective work and had discovered that Scott had moved back to his family's ranch in Alberta. It took little work from there to discover a Cosgrove family in Millarville, Alberta. Nicole decided to go to the ranch, to talk to Scott about the boys and to see them.

Nicole's father desperately wanted to come along, but his emphysema was especially bad and his doctor discouraged him from taking the trip. So Nicole came alone.

When Nicole came to the ranch house she wasn't sure what she would do or say or if she was on the right track. She just knew she wasn't leaving until she saw the boys for herself.

When Isabelle answered the door, she assumed Nicole was the housekeeper she'd advertised for and left within seconds of her arrival.

What could Nicole do? She couldn't leave Mrs. Cosgrove, who had been sitting in a wheelchair, alone, nor could she tell the poor woman why she was here. So she stayed and cleaned up and helped where she could.

Then Kip came striding up the sidewalk with his long legs, his eyebrows lowered over narrowed grey eyes shadowed by his cowboy hat, his mouth set in grim lines, and fear clutched her midsection.

She was about to come clean.

Then she saw the boys, and she knew beyond a doubt they were Tricia's twins. Everything changed in that moment, but she couldn't tell the Cosgroves who she was. Not yet.

She didn't want her first introduction to the boys to be fraught with conflict. Because as soon as Kip and his mother, Mary, found out her true purpose for being here, there would be antagonism and battles.

"We have our own kittens too," Justin said, swinging her hand as if he'd known her for all of his five years.

Nicole tightened her grip on the boys' hands, a surprising wave of love and yearning washing over her.

How could Tricia have left these boys? How horrible her life must have been to make that sacrifice? Why couldn't Tricia have asked for her family's help?

It was because of me, Nicole thought. I sent her away.

"There are five of them," Tristan said, his innocent words breaking into the morass of guilt surrounding any memory of Tricia. "One of them died, though. Do you think that kitten is in heaven with my daddy?"

"I think so," Nicole said, hesitantly. She didn't want to destroy their little dreams of heaven or of the man they thought of as their father. But Scott wasn't their father.

As for God? When Tricia left eight years ago, Nicole's faith in God had wavered. When Nicole's adoptive mother died of cancer three years after that, Nicole stopped thinking God cared.

God, if He did exist, was simply a figurehead. Someone people went to when they didn't know where else to turn and even then a huge disappointment.

"How about we check out the kittens," she said, brushing aside her anger. All that mattered was that she had found the boys.

"I don't want to see the kittens," Justin said with a pout. "I want to see the horses."

"Uncle Kip won't let us," Tristan said, placing his hands on his hips. "You know that."

"We won't go into the corrals." Justin tugged on her hand. "Uncle Kip won't get mad if we just look."

Nicole easily remembered Kip Cosgrove's formidable expression. Best not cross him sooner than she had to. "Maybe another time," she said. "We should go back to the house."

"I want to see the horses." Justin pulled loose and took off.

"Justin, come back here," she called, still holding onto Tristan as Justin disappeared around the barn.

Nicole turned to Tristan. "You stay here, okay?" She spoke firmly so he understood.

Tristan nodded, his blue eyes wide with uncertainty.

"I have to get your brother." She patted him on the shoulder, allowed herself a moment to cup his soft, tender cheek, then turned to get Justin.

Nicole ran around the barn in time to see Justin with his foot on the bottom rail of the corral. She ran over the uneven ground and caught him by the waistband of his blue jeans just as he took another shaky step up.

"I can go up myself," he said, trying to pull free.

"If your uncle said no, then it's no," Nicole said, shifting her grip from his pants to his shirt. No way was she bucking Uncle Kip on this. She needed all her ammunition for a much bigger battle. "So let's go."

"What's going on?" Kip's deep voice, edged with anger, reverberated through the quiet of the afternoon.

Nicole's heart stuttered at the latent fury in his voice.

Still holding on to Justin's arm, she turned to see Kip standing behind her, Tristan beside him.

"Justin, get down from that fence. You and Tristan are to go back to the house right now," Kip said, his tone brooking no argument. "Gramma is waiting for you."

"I want to stay with Nicole. She said I could see the horses with her."

Nicole was about to correct that when Kip spoke again.

"I need to talk to Miss Nicole," he said. "Alone."

His anger seemed extreme for the circumstances. That could mean only one thing. He knew about her momentary deception.

Time to come clean. She had seen the boys and was ready to face him down. She had Tricia's will and the law on her side.

Justin jumped down and scampered around the barn, Tristan close behind.

Kip watched them leave, then walked toward her, his booted feet stirring up little clouds of dust. The utter stillness of the air felt fraught with uncertainty and a feeling of waiting.

He stopped in front of her, crossed his arms over his chest and angled his head to one side.

Fear trembled in her midsection, threaded with a peculiar awareness of him. She pushed her reaction aside and focused on the job she had come here to do.

"We need to talk," he said quietly.

"I know—"

"I've decided to hire you," he said.

This wasn't what she had expected when he came storming around the barn, anger and fury in his eyes.

"I've got a lot going," he said. "And I can't stay on top of everything. I really could use your help."

The appeal in his voice and the confusion of his expression created an answering flash of sympathy. When she first came into his house, she felt overwhelmed at the mess. When she saw poor Mrs. Cosgrove, trying to fold laundry from her wheelchair, she knew she couldn't walk away.

So she pitched in and started cleaning. Mrs. Cosgrove's gratitude made her momentary subterfuge seem worthwhile.

Now a man who looked like he could eat bullets and spit out the casings was launching an appeal for her help.

He held his hands up in a gesture of surrender. "So tell me what you want to get paid, and we'll see if we can figure something out."

Nicole held his gaze, and when he gave her a half smile, her heart shifted and softened. For a moment, as their eyes held, a tiny crack opened in her defenses, a delicate pining for something missing in her life. As quickly as it came, she sealed it off. Opening herself up to someone would cost too much.

Besides, he was the enemy. The one who stood between her and her beloved sister's boys. When he found out who she was, the warmth in his eyes would freeze.

She took a breath and plunged in.

"You may as well know, I didn't come to apply for the housekeeping position." Nicole spoke quietly, folding her hands in front of her and forcing herself to hold his gaze. "I'm Tricia's adoptive sister. Justin and Tristan's aunt. I've come to take the boys."

Chapter Two

Kip stared at the woman in front of him, her words spinning around his head.

Tricia's sister? Come to take his boys? His brother's sons?

"What are you talking about? What do you mean?" His heart did a slow flip as the implications of what she said registered.

He had come here to offer her a job, and when he saw Justin climbing the fence of the horse corral, he'd lost it. In front of his very attractive prospective employee.

Now, with his heart still pounding from seeing Justin up on the fence, he was sandbagged with this piece of information.

"When were you going to tell me that you weren't applying for the job?" Kip growled, unable to keep his anger tamped down.

"I just did." Nicole raised her chin and looked at him with her cool gray-green eyes. "I had no intention of fooling anyone."

Kip gave a short laugh. "So how do you figure you're taking the boys? How does that work?"

Nicole pressed her lips together and looked away. "It works because Tricia wrote up a will stating that our parents get custody and now she's…now she's dead."

Kip took a step back, the news hitting him like a blow.

"What? When?" His poor nephews. How was he going to tell them?

Nicole didn't answer right away, and Kip saw the silvery track of a tear on her cheek. She swiped it away with the cuff of her tailored jacket.

"Tricia died about three years ago. We found out only a few weeks ago." Her voice sounded strangled, and for a moment Kip sympathized with her. The first few weeks after his brother Scott died, he could barely function. He went through the motions of work, hoping, praying, he could find his balance again. Hoping, praying the pain in his heart would someday ease. Hoping the guilt that tormented him over his brother's death would someday be gone as well.

His brother had died only six months ago, and they had only recently found out about Tricia. Her pain must be so raw yet…

He pulled his thoughts back to the problem at hand. "Why did it take so long for you to find out about Tricia's death?" he asked, steeling his own emotions to her sorrow.

"She hadn't told anyone about her family. Apparently she had just come out of a drug-rehab program. Then she was going to find her boys."

"Drug rehab?" Kip's anger returned. "No wonder Scott came back with the boys."

Nicole shot him an angry glance. "According to Tricia's diary and letters, he took them away without her knowledge or permission. Tricia had moved out of the apartment she shared with Scott and had taken the boys with her. She had brought the boys to a friend's place so she could go into rehab. She was in for two weeks, and when she came back to see the boys, Scott had taken them and was gone."

Kip laughed. "Really."

Nicole shot him a frown. "Yes. Really."

"And you believe a drug user?"

Nicole's frown deepened. "I truly believe that after the boys were born, Tricia had changed. I also believe my sister would not willingly abandon her children."

"But she did."

"Scott took them away from a home she had placed them in so she could get her life together." Nicole drew in a quick breath. "Something he had no right to do."

"How do you figure that?" Kip's anger grew. "He was their father."

"According to what Tricia wrote, the boys were born before she moved in with Scott. He wasn't their father."

Disbelief and anger battled with each other. "That I refuse to believe," he barked. "My brother loved those boys. They are his. You can't prove otherwise. Your sister is a liar."

Nicole's eyes narrowed, and Kip knew he had stepped over a line. He didn't care. This woman waltzes into their lives with this complicated lie and he's supposed to be polite and swallow it all? And then let her take the boys away?

Over his dead body.

"So how do you want to proceed on this?" Nicole asked, arching one perfectly plucked eyebrow in his direction.

Kip mentally heaved a sigh. For a small moment

he'd thought this woman was the solution to part of his problems.

Not only was he was back to where he started, even if she was lying, he now had a whole new legal tangle to deal with.

Dear Lord, I don't need anything else right now. I don't have the strength.

He held her steady gaze, determined not to be swayed by the sparkling in her eyes that he suspected were tears. "The boys were left with me as per my brother's verbal request," he said. "I'm their guardian, and until I am notified otherwise, they're not going anywhere and you're not to come back here."

He turned and walked away from the corral. The corral that brought back too many painful memories.

Well, add one more to the list. Somehow he had to tell his nephews that their mother, who had always been a shadowy figure in their lives, was officially dead. If he could believe what this Nicole woman had told him then he had to tell his mother that the woman they had thought was their salvation was anything but.

He shot a quick glance behind him.

Nicole stood by the corral fences, her head bent and her arms crossed over her midsection. Dusty fragments of sunlight gilded her hair and in the silence he heard a muffled sob.

Sympathy for her knotted his chest. Regardless of what he felt, she'd found out about her sister's death only a few weeks ago. Not long enough for the pain to lose that jagged edge. Not near long enough to finish shedding the tears that needed to spill.

For a moment he thought he should go over to her side

and offer her what comfort he could. Then he stopped himself.

She wants to take the boys away, he reminded himself. She claimed they weren't his nephews. And that reminder effectively doused his sympathy.

"I'm sorry, Nicole, but I'd like you to leave," he said, hoping his voice projected a tiny bit of sympathy.

She drew in a shuddering breath and looked up, a streak of mascara marring her ethereal features.

"I have pictures," she said.

"What is that supposed to mean?"

"It means I can prove who I am." Nicole wiped at her cheeks with the tips of her fingers, a delicate motion belying the strength of conviction in her voice. "I also have a signed letter from my sister along with a copy of her last will and testament." Nicole took a few steps toward him, wrapping her arms around her waist. "So I'm not without ammunition myself."

"I'd like to see all that."

"Fine." She walked past him, the scent of lilacs trailing behind her.

Kip followed her as regret lingered a moment.

She was a beautiful woman. When he still thought of her as his future housekeeper, he had thought having her around every day might have been a distraction. He was lonely, she was beautiful. Maybe not the best mix.

But now?

Right now she was a complication he didn't know how to work his way around.

She yanked a key ring out of her coat pocket, pointed it at the car and unlocked the door. Ducking inside, she pulled out a briefcase, which she set on the trunk of the car.

Kip came closer as she drew an envelope out of the case, opened it and took out a picture.

"This is my sister, the boys and your brother. I think the boys are about six months old there."

Kip took the laminated photo, and as he glanced at it he felt as if spiders scuttled across his gut.

The picture was identical to one he'd had blown up, then framed and hung in the boys' room. The only picture the boys had of their mother.

As he handed the picture back, sorrow mixed with his anger. Two of the people in the picture were dead. The boys were officially orphans.

Nicole tucked her hair behind her ears, tugged on her jacket and looked him in the eye. "I'm leaving your ranch like you asked me, but I'm not going far. I have a room in a motel in Millarville and I intend on coming here every day to see my nephews."

"I'm not discussing anything to do with the boys without my lawyer present. So until then, as I said before, I'd like you to stay away."

She looked like she was about to protest, then gave a delicate shrug. "Fine. When do you want to see your lawyer?"

Never. He had cows to move to other pastures. A tractor to fix, a stock waterer to repair and a sister who would be peeved when she discovered they didn't have a housekeeper after all.

"Tomorrow," he said, mentally cringing. He'd just have to work later in the evening to make up for lost time. Hopefully he could get in with Ron, his lawyer. If not, well, she'd have to wait.

"What's his name and number?" She pulled out a

phone, then punched in the information he gave her. "And what time?" she asked, looking up.

"I'll give you a call." He wondered what Ron would have to say about the situation.

Nicole put the phone away, then reached into a side pocket of the briefcase she had taken the papers from.

She pulled out a business card and handed it to him.

He glanced down at the name embossed on the card.

Nicole Williams. Director, Williams Foundation. The information was followed by several numbers—home, office, fax, cell—and an email address and a website.

Very official and a bit intimidating.

"Director of the Williams Foundation?" he asked, flicking the card between his fingers.

"My adoptive parents started it."

"Adoptive?"

"Sam and Norah Williams adopted me when I was eight," Nicole said, her voice matter of fact. "My father started the nonprofit in memory of my adoptive mother."

"Admirable." He tucked the card in the back pocket of his worn jeans, hoping this wasn't the pair with the hole in the pocket. "I'll let you know what's up."

"Can I come tomorrow to see the boys?"

"Let's wait to see what my lawyer says."

Nicole squeezed the top of her briefcase, averting her eyes. "They're my nephews too," she said quietly. "My sister's boys."

"Boys she abandoned, that no one bothered to find."

Nicole's eyes grew hard. "They were taken away from her. The lack of communication is hardly my fault considering we found out about these boys only a few weeks ago."

Kip was about to say something more when a truck turning onto the yard caught his attention. Isabelle.

His younger sister pulled up beside Nicole's car, putting it between her and her brother. A strategic move, he thought, fighting his anger and frustration with her.

"Hey, Nicole. How'd things go today?" Isabelle called out as she jumped out of the truck. "Had to get groceries," she said to Kip holding up a solitary plastic bag as if to underline her defense.

"Dressed like that?" Kip asked, eyeing her bright red lipstick, snug T-shirt that sparkled in the sunlight and her too-tight blue jeans.

Isabelle's face grew mutinous. "I didn't think I had to stick around here. Especially since Nicole showed up." She pulled another bag out of the truck and flounced up the walk to the house, her dark hair bouncing with every step.

Kip bit back whatever he wanted to say to his little sister, fully aware of his audience.

Too many things going on, he thought, fighting his frustration with his sister and this new, huge complication.

"I'm going now," Nicole said, her voice quiet, well modulated. She gave him a tight smile, then pulled her briefcase off the trunk of the car. "I'll wait to hear from you."

Without a second glance, she got in, started the engine and roared away from him in a cloud of dust.

Kip pushed back his hat as he watched her leave, frustration clawing at him.

Please Lord, don't let my family be broken up, he prayed. *Don't let her take my boys away from me.*

And please don't let me lose it with my sister.

He stepped into the house just as his mother wheeled herself into the kitchen. Her long, graying hair was brushed and neatly swept up into a ponytail, her brown eyes sparkled, and the smile on her face was a welcome respite from the resignation that had been his mother's default expression since her surgery.

"Where did Nicole go?" his mother asked, sounding happier than she had in a while. "She seems like a lovely girl. I'm looking forward to having her around to help out."

Kip glanced at the clean countertop and shining sink. When he first saw how clean the house was he couldn't believe that businesslike woman had done all this. Now he knew she was simply trying to weasel her way into his mother's good graces.

"Where's Isabelle?"

"In her room."

"When did she leave the ranch?"

Mary Cosgrove tapped her finger against her lips. "About one."

Three hours to pick up one bag of groceries. He was so going to talk to his little sister. Leaving his mother alone with a stranger, even if she had come here because of an advertisement, was irresponsible.

Not only a stranger, a woman who had come to completely disrupt their lives.

"I'm so glad you decided to take on a housekeeper," his mother continued, sounding hopeful. "She seems so capable and organized."

Kip hated to burst her bubble. "I still think Isabelle should learn to pull her share of the housework."

His mother sighed. "I know, and I agree, but it's so

much work to get her motivated and Nicole seems so capable." Mary looked past Kip. "Where is Nicole now?"

"She left." Kip blew out his breath and dropped into a chair across from her mother. "Truth is, she didn't come for the housekeeping job. She came…" he hesitated, glancing up at his mother, who seemed more relaxed than she had in months. Scott's death had been devastating for her. This new piece of information wouldn't help. "Nicole, apparently, is Tricia's sister."

His mother frowned. "Tricia? Scott's girlfriend?"

"Yep. The mother of the boys."

Mary's fingers fluttered over her heart, her eyes wide in a suddenly pale face. "What did she want?"

Kip wrapped his rough hands around his mother's cold ones. "She claims she has a will granting her custody of Justin and Tristan."

"But the boys' mother…Tricia…" Mary squeezed her son's hands. "Where is she?"

"She's dead." The words sounded harsh, even though he'd never met the woman. But she had been the mother of his nephews.

The nephews that Nicole claimed didn't belong to Kip's family. Kip's heart turned over in his chest.

There was no way he was telling his mother that piece of information. He didn't believe that fact for one minute anyhow. Scott had loved those boys. Doted on them.

Since Scott died, Kip had fought to keep this family together, but lately he felt as if everything he worked so hard for was slipping out of his fingers.

There was no way he was letting Nicole take his mother's only connection to Scott away. No way.

Chapter Three

"I found them. I found the boys." Nicole tucked the phone under her chin as she sorted through her clothes. The motel room held a small dresser and minuscule closet she could hang some clothes in. She had packed a variety of clothes, unsure what she would need.

She closed the closet door and glanced around the room. It was the best, supposedly, in Millarville, and she guessed it would do. She hoped she wouldn't have to stay here long. Staying here resurrected memories she had relegated to the "before" part of her life.

Before the Williams family took her in.

"Are they okay? How do they look?" Her father sounded a bit better, as if the news sparked new life in him.

"They're fine." Nicole thought of Justin and Tristan, and her heart contracted.

She knew the Cosgroves wouldn't simply hand over the boys to her as soon as she had arrived. From what she had discovered, the boys had been at the ranch since Scott took them away.

Kip's family was the only one the children knew. A

family, she discovered, which included Kip's mother, a younger sister and a married sister with six children.

Nicole couldn't stop a nudge of jealousy at the thought of Kip's large family, then quashed it. She'd had a full life with the Williams, and she owed her adoptive parents more than she could ever repay. That Sam's natural daughter was the one gone only increased her guilt.

"Is the family treating them okay? Do they seem to have a stable home life?"

"The farmhouse is a bit of a wreck," Nicole said, thinking of the worn flooring, and the faded paint. "It looks as if no money had been spent on the house in a while."

Yet in spite of the mess, when she walked into the spacious kitchen of the Cosgrove house, she felt enveloped by a sense of home. Of comfort and peace.

Something she seldom experienced in her father's cavernous house.

"They're well taken care of." She tucked the phone under her ear, pulled her laptop out of the bag and plugged it in. Thankfully, she would be able to do much of her work for the family's foundation while she was here.

"You sound like you think they should stay." Her father's voice held an accusatory tone.

"No. I don't," Nicole assured him. "But we can't simply remove them immediately." She knew she sounded practical, however, her feelings were anything but.

When she saw the boys, a feeling of love, almost devastating in its intensity, bowled her over. She wanted to grab them, hold them close, then run away with them. She couldn't understand or explain the unexpected power of these feelings. The only time she'd experienced this before was when she saw her little sister, Tricia, for the first time.

"It was what your sister wanted," her father said, a hard note entering his voice.

"I know. It's what I want as well, but we have to proceed carefully. The boys don't remember their mother and they most certainly don't know who I am." She highly doubted Kip would tell them in the next few days.

"I should be there," her father said, his voice harsh. "I should be meeting with that lawyer." This was followed by a bout of coughing that belied his insistence.

"You know yourself that once lawyers get hold of things, the process grinds to a halt." She ignored a sliver of panic at the thought. When she arranged to come here, she had given herself three weeks to bring the boys back. Sure, she could work here, but she also needed to spend time with the boys so the transition from here to Toronto wouldn't be so difficult.

"Who do the boys look like?" Sam asked, a thread of hope in his voice.

"They look exactly like Tricia." Nicole pressed her fingers to her lips, restraining her sorrow.

"You have to bring my boys back, Nicole. They are all I have left of Tricia. Those boys don't belong there. They're not even blood relatives."

Nicole knew her father spoke out of sorrow, but his words struck at the foundations of Nicole's insecurities. Tricia was Sam and Norah's natural daughter.

Nicole was simply the adopted one.

"Tomorrow I'll see Mr. Cosgrove's lawyer," Nicole said, opening her laptop and turning it on. "We'll have to take this one step at a time."

"When you talk to that lawyer you make sure to let

him know that James Feschuk is working for us. His reputation might get things moving a bit. I also want a DNA test. If they don't believe us, then we'll get positive proof that Scott Cosgrove was not the boys' father."

"How will that happen?" Nicole asked.

"James told me that you can get DNA tests done locally. He suggested one called a grandparent's test. Get that grandmother to get tested and we'll find out. I'll get tested too. Then we've got some teeth to our argument." His voice rose and Sam started coughing again.

"I'm saying goodbye," Nicole said. "And you should go to bed. Make sure you take your medication and use that puffer the doctor gave you."

"Yes, yes," Sam said. "I'll get James to phone that lawyer. Tell him we insist on a DNA test. Give me his name and I can take care of it."

Nicole pulled out her cell phone and called up the name and number and gave that information to her father. "I'll let you know the minute I hear anything."

Nicole said goodbye. She turned back to her computer, but only sat and stared sightlessly at the screen, her work suddenly forgotten as she thought of Justin and Tristan. Tricia's boys.

Seeing them had been heartwarming and heartrending at the same time.

Again she felt the sting of her sister's betrayal when Tricia had left without a word those many years ago. Nicole had hoped and prayed for an opportunity to talk to her face-to-face, to apologize. But the only letter in the envelope was one to her parents pleading for forgiveness. Nothing for her.

Nicole glanced around the room as memories of other evenings in other motel rooms crowded in.

Nicole tried to push the memories away, but the emotions of the past day had made her vulnerable and her mind slipped back to a vivid picture of herself, sitting on a bed in a motel room, a little girl of five, waiting while her aunt smoked and strode back and forth, watching through the window.

When Nicole's natural mother died, her father, a long-distance trucker, put Nicole into the care of his sister, a bitter, verbally abusive woman.

Whenever he came into town, Nicole's aunt would bring her to a motel where they would meet her father. She would stay with him for a couple of days and then he would be gone.

That evening they waited until the next morning, but he never came. His truck had spun out of control and he had died in the subsequent accident.

After six months, her aunt had her moved to an already-full foster home.

Four years later, she was adopted by the Williams family at age eight, and her life went from the instability of seven foster homes in four years to the stability of a wealthy family. She was told enough times how blessed she was, and she knew it.

Yet each night as she crawled into her bed, she would wonder when it would all get taken away. People had always left her. It would happen again.

Then something magical and miraculous happened to her and the Williams family. Norah, who was never supposed to be able to conceive, became pregnant. When Tricia was born, Nicole bonded with this little baby in a way she couldn't seem to with Norah and Sam. Tricia became as much Nicole's child as her parents'.

Nicole took care of her with a fierce intensity. She

stood up for her in school, listened to her stories of heart-break and sorrow. Defended her to Sam and Norah whenever Tricia got into yet another scrape. She was Tricia's confidant.

Then Tricia turned thirteen. She withdrew. Became sullen and ungrateful. She started hanging around with the wrong crowd and staying out late. Nicole had tried to reason with her, to explain that she was throwing her life away.

But Tricia kept up her self-destructive lifestyle. Finally, in frustration, Nicole fought with her.

Then Tricia too left and never came back.

Nicole got up, grabbed her purse and walked out of the motel. She walked down the street, then up it again. She let the cooling mountain air soothe away the memories. She bought a sandwich, returned to her motel room and dove into her work. A few hours later she took a shower and crawled, exhausted, into bed. She needed all the rest she could get.

Tomorrow she would be seeing Kip Cosgrove again.

Tomorrow she would have other battles to fight.

"So she has some legitimacy?" Kip leaned his elbows on his knees, then frowned at the grass stain he saw on his blue jeans. He should have checked before he put the pants on. Of course he was in a hurry when he left the ranch. Of course he had to go through a mini battle to get Isabelle to agree to take care of her nephews while he was gone.

"As an aunt to the boys, she has as much right as you do," Ron Benton, his lawyer, said, leaning his elbows on the desk. "As for her claim about Scott not being the father, unfortunately it's a matter of her word against yours now that both the principals in this case are dead. We'll need more information."

"Tricia abandoned the boys, Ron. She left them with Scott. She was gone for three years."

"Well, now we know she was dead for three years."

Kip blew out a sigh of frustration at that irrefutable truth. When Nicole had told him that, he felt as if his world had been realigned. Ever since Scott showed up at the farm with the two boys, Kip had burned with a righteous indignation that a woman could leave these boys all alone. An indignation that grew with each year of no communication.

Now he found out she'd been dead and possibly didn't know where Scott was.

If what Nicole said was true.

"The trouble is we don't have a legal document that grants custody to you," Ron said. "And it sounds like this Nicole might have one that gives it to her. Though you've been the primary caregiver—and any court would look at that as well—the reality is you don't have legal backup for your case. As well, we don't know why Tricia left."

"I know what Scott told me."

Ron blew his breath out, tapping his fingers against the sleeve of his suit jacket. "She and Scott got along? He never did anything to her?"

"Of course not." Kip barked his reply, then forced himself to settle down. Ever since Nicole had walked into their lives, he'd been edgy and distracted.

He had too much responsibility. The words dropped into his mind with the weight of rocks.

How could he think that? He loved his nephews dearly. He wasn't going to let Nicole take them away. Especially not after promising his dying brother that he would take care of them. There was no way he was backing out on that. Not after what had happened to Scott.

Guilt over his brother's death stabbed him again. If only he hadn't let him get on that horse. The horse was too green, he had told him, but Scott was insistent. Kip should have held his ground.

Should have. He shoved his hand through his hair. The words would haunt him for the rest of his life.

"Trouble is, we don't have a lot to go on," Ron continued. "Your main weapon is the primary-caregiver option. You've been taking care of Justin and Tristan. That's what we'll have to go with if this gets to court."

"Court? Would it get that far?"

Ron lifted his shoulder in a shrug. "I'll have to do some digging to see if I can avoid that, but no promises."

No time. No time.

The words bounced around Kip's mind, mocking him. He didn't have time to fight this woman.

"Whatever happens, I'm not letting some high and mighty Easterner come and take the boys simply because she has some piece of paper and I don't," Kip said as the door to the office opened.

He stopped mid rant and turned in his chair in time to see Nicole standing in the doorway, the overhead lights of the office glinting off her long, blond hair and turning her gray-green eyes into chips of ice.

Chapter Four

Nicole glared at Kip Cosgrove, wondering if he could read the anger in her eyes. She doubted it. He sat back in the chair, looking as if he was completely in charge of the situation and his world.

I've got a legal will, she reminded herself.

The boys are Tricia's.

"Good morning," she said, projecting pleasant briskness into her voice. She'd dressed with care this morning. Her tailored suit was her defense in the boardroom of her father's foundation and it became her armor now.

Her gaze ticked over Kip and moved to the man sitting on the other side of the desk. He certainly didn't look like any lawyer she had ever met with his open-necked twill shirt, blue jeans and cowboy boots. She was definitely not in Toronto anymore. "My name is Nicole Williams, but I'm sure you already know that."

"Ron Benton." He stood, gave her a slow-release grin and shook her hand. At least he looked friendly, which was more than she could say for Kip Cosgrove with his deep scowl.

Ron sat back in his chair, his arms crossed over his

chest. "I understand we have a problem that we need to resolve."

Nicole shrugged as she set her briefcase on the floor beside her chair. "No problem as far as I can see. I have a will from Tricia Williams giving her parents, Sam and Norah Williams, full custody of the boys, Justin and Tristan Williams. Norah Williams has passed away, but Sam is very much alive." Nicole took out a copy of the will and placed it on the wooden desk in front of Ron. "You can keep that for your records."

Ron glanced over the papers. "This will hasn't been filed with any legal firm, or put together with the help of a lawyer?"

Nicole shook her head. "No, but it is witnessed and dated."

"By whom?" Ron kept his eyes on the papers, flipping through them as he frowned.

"I don't know the woman. Apparently it was someone that Tricia lived with."

Ron's slow nod combined with his laissez-faire attitude grated on Nicole, but she kept her temper in check. She had to stay in control.

Then Ron sat back in his chair, his hands laced behind his head. "We could easily contest the legality of this will."

Now it was Nicole's turn to frown. "What do you mean?"

"How do we know this is Tricia William's signature? And who was this friend? Anyone could have put this together."

Kip leaned forward and she couldn't help glancing his way, catching a gleam in his eye.

"So you're saying this isn't as cut-and-dried as some people think?" Kip asked.

Hard not to miss the pleasure in his voice. Nicole fought back her concern. She had too much riding on this situation. Sam was expecting her to bring these boys back. It was what she had to do.

"Unfortunately, no."

"So that makes things a bit easier," Kip said with an obvious note of relief in his voice.

"We have our own lawyer working on this case," Nicole added, just in case Kip thought she was simply rolling over. "We have copies of Tricia's handwriting and photographs of the boys."

"Birth certificates?" Ron asked, his chair creaking as he leaned forward, glancing over the will again.

Nicole had to say no. "Again, that's something our lawyer, James Feschuk is working on." Dropping James's name, however, got no reaction.

"So things are still in limbo?" Kip asked. He tapped a booted foot on the carpet, as if he couldn't wait to get out of there. Nicole wasn't surprised.

He looked as if he was far more at home on the back of a horse than sitting in an office.

Which made her wonder why he wouldn't let the boys on the horses. He seemed so unreasonably angry with her when she took them to the horse corrals.

And why did she care? The boys were leaving this life as soon as possible.

Ron tapped his fingers on the desk, shaking his head as if to negate everything Nicole had said. "I'm sorry, but I don't think anything can happen until we get all our questions answered."

"Great." Kip got to his feet. "Then we'll wait."

"Not so fast, Kip," Ron continued. "The other reality is we can't completely negate Ms. Williams's claim on these boys. She does have some rights for now."

Nicole's frustration eased off. She had been ready to do battle with this small-town lawyer.

Kip had already grabbed his denim jacket but clutched it now, his grey eyes staying on Ron, ignoring Nicole. "What rights?"

"Visitation, for one," Ron said.

Kip blew out a sigh and shoved his hands through his hair as he glared at his own lawyer. "How will that work?"

Time to take control. "I would like to visit the boys every day," Nicole said.

Kip finally turned his attention to her. "Every day? For how long?"

"I think that's something we can settle here and now," Nicole said. "I was thinking I could come and pick up the boys and take them for a visit either morning or afternoon. Whichever is convenient."

Kip made a show of looking at his watch, as if he was the only one in this room with a schedule to keep. Then he sat down and leaned back in his chair. "Okay, I'm thinking something else. I'm thinking you can see the boys every day, but the visits have to happen on the ranch and under my supervision."

Nicole frowned at that. "Why?"

Kip held her gaze, his frown and piercing gaze giving him a slightly menacing air. "I only have your word that you are who you are, and until Ron is satisfied, I'm not letting Justin and Tristan out of my sight."

His antagonism was like a wave and for the briefest

moment, fear flashed through Nicole. He reminded her of a wolf, defending its pups.

Then she pushed her fear down.

"And how would these visits be apportioned?"

"I'm guessing you mean how much time and when?"

"Precisely."

Kip raised an eyebrow and Nicole knew she was putting on her "office" voice. She couldn't help it. She felt as if she needed the defense.

"You come from 2:30 until 5:00 every afternoon. That's what works best for me."

She bit back her anger. Two and a half hours? Was that what he considered a visit?

"Take it or leave it," he added.

She didn't have much choice. Right now she may hold a legal will, but until it was proven legitimate, he had the right of possession—if that was the correct way to term guardianship of the boys.

"Those terms are…fine with me," she said, trying to sound reasonable. She wasn't fighting him over this. Not yet. In the end, she knew she would be proven right, but in the meantime the boys were in his care and on his ranch and she could do nothing about that.

"So we should draw something up," Ron said, pulling out a pen. "Just in case there are any repercussions."

Fifteen minutes later, papers were printed up and signed and everyone given a copy.

Kip folded his over and shoved them in the back pocket of his jeans. She put hers in her briefcase.

"There is one more thing," Nicole said quietly. "My father insists that we do a DNA test."

"What?" The word fairly exploded out of Kip's mouth. "What do you think this is? *CSI Alberta?*"

"It's not that complex. There is a test that can be ordered, and I've checked into the locations of the clinics where they can be brought. We would require your mother to take a test and my father, given that the parents of the boys are dead."

"Is this legal?" Kip asked his lawyer.

Ron leaned back in his chair, tapping his pen against his chin. "Might not be a bad idea. It could bolster your case, Kip."

More likely ours, Nicole thought.

Kip narrowed his eyes as he looked at Nicole, as if he didn't trust her. "Okay. If you think it will help, Ron, I'll get Mom to do it."

"I'll find out more about it and let you know what has to happen," Ron said.

"So that's settled." Kip shrugged his jacket on and gave Nicole the briefest of nods. "I'll see you tomorrow."

Nicole gave him a crisp smile. "Actually, I'd like to come now."

Kip faltered, his frown deepening. "As in today?"

"As in, I have just been granted visitation from 2:30 to 5:00 every afternoon." Nicole gave him a cool look as she too got to her feet. She didn't like him towering over her, but even in her heels, she only reached his shoulder.

"I thought we'd start tomorrow."

"I have every right to start today." She had signed a paper giving her those rights. He had no reason to deny her.

Kip blew out a sigh as he dropped a tattered cowboy hat on his head. "I don't have time today."

Nicole lifted her shoulder in a delicate shrug. "You're the one who set out the terms of the visits."

Kip held her gaze, his eyes shadowed by the brim of

the cowboy hat. Then he glanced down at her tailored suit and laughed. "Okay, but you'd better change. The boys are helping me fix a tractor this afternoon."

"Should I bring a hammer?" she said, determined not to let him goad her.

"Just a three-eighth-inch wrench and a five-sixteenth-inch socket," he returned.

"Excellent. I just happened to bring mine along."

"In your Louis Vuitton luggage?" This was tossed back at her underlined with the arching of one of his eyebrows.

"No. Coach." And how would a cowboy like him know about Louis Vuitton?

"Cute." He buttoned his jacket. "This has been fun, but I've got work to do," he said in a tone that implied "fun" was the last thing he'd been having. "See you when we see you."

When he closed the door behind him, it was as if the office deflated. Became less full, less dynamic.

Nicole brushed the feeling off and turned to Ron. "I'll get my lawyer to call you. He'll bring you up to speed on his side of the case, and the two of you can discuss the DNA tests."

Ron got to his feet and pursed his lips. Then he sighed. "I'm not speaking as a lawyer anymore, but as a friend of Kip's. You may as well know that Kip Cosgrove dotes on those boys. He goes everywhere with them. Does everything with them. He has since those boys moved to the ranch with his brother."

"They're not even his." As soon as Nicole spoke the words she regretted giving her thoughts voice. She knew how coldhearted that must have sounded to Ron.

The reality was she knew firsthand what it was like to

be the one pushed aside. She had been in enough homes as the "outsider," the nonbiological child, to know that no matter what, biology always won out. The "natural" children were always treated differently than the "foster" child.

Ron shot her an angry look. "That is the last thing on Kip's mind," he snapped. "Those boys have been in his life since they were one year old. Living on the ranch is the only life they know."

Nicole held his angry gaze, determined not to let his opinion of her matter. "They only know this life because Scott took them away from their biological mother." She picked up her briefcase and slung her trench coat over her arm. "Now all I need to know is where I can buy some tools."

This netted her a puzzled look from Ron. "Why?"

"Because I fully intend on helping fix that tractor."

Chapter Five

Kip pulled off his "town" shirt and tossed it onto his unmade bed. He grabbed the work shirt from the floor where he'd tossed it. He'd been in too much of a rush to clean up before he left for town.

He buttoned up his shirt as he headed down the stairs to where the boys were playing a board game at the kitchen table with his mom.

Isabelle stood at the kitchen sink, washing dishes from lunch, her expression letting him know exactly what she thought of this chore.

"Oh, Gramma, you have to go down the snake," Justin shouted, waving his arms in the air as if he had won the Stanley Cup.

"Oh dear, here I go," Kip's mother said, reaching across the board to do as Justin said. "This puts me way behind."

Kip caught her grimace as she sat back in her wheelchair and wondered again how long it would be before his mother was mobile. Though the kitchen was still clean from Nicole's visit on Saturday, he knew it was simply a matter of time before things slowly deteriorated.

"Isabelle, that laundry that got folded yesterday is still in the laundry basket upstairs," Kip said.

"Yeah. I know."

"So what should happen with it?"

Isabelle set a plate on the drying rack with agonizing slowness, punctuated her movement with a sigh, then shrugged. "I guess I should put it away."

"I guess," he reiterated.

"I think someone is here," Tristan said, standing up on his chair.

Kip groaned. Probably Nicole. Well, she'd have to tag along with him. He had promised the boys they could help him fix the tractor. They weren't much help, but they were slowly learning how to read wrench sizes and knew the difference between a Phillips and a flat screwdriver. Plus, it was a way to spend time with them.

"It's Nicole," Justin yelled, confirming what Kip suspected. "I'm going to go say hi." He jumped off his chair, Tristan right behind him. The porch door slammed shut behind them, creating a momentary quiet in the home.

His mother turned in her wheelchair, wincing as she did so. "Now that the boys are gone, what did Ron tell you?"

Kip glanced out of the window. Nicole was barely out of her car and the boys were already grabbing her hands. Their hasty switch in allegiances bothered him in a way he didn't want to scrutinize.

Isabelle stopped what she was doing and turned around, listening with avid interest.

"For now we have to allow her visits with the boys," Kip said, rolling up the sleeves of his shirt. "He's looking into how legitimate Tricia's will is, but nothing has been settled And..." he hesitated, wondering what his mother would think of this new wrinkle. "She and her father insist on you taking a DNA test."

His mother frowned. "Is that hard? Do I have to go to the hospital?"

"Apparently there's a test for grandparents. You can order it and then bring the results to a couple of clinics not far away. It's nothing to worry about. Just a formality so we can prove that Scott is as much a parent to the boys as Tricia was."

Kip stopped there. Until Nicole brought the news she had, Kip hadn't been able to think of Tricia without a surge of anger. She'd left her boys behind. But knowing she had been dead the past years changed a lot.

And raised a few more questions.

Kip brushed them aside. The boys were Scott's. He knew it beyond a doubt. Scott wouldn't have taken them with him back to the ranch if they weren't.

"So Nicole is really the twins' aunt too?" Isabelle asked.

"I think so."

"Is she taking the boys?"

Kip shot Isabelle a warning glance. "No one is taking the boys anywhere. They belong here."

His mother placed her hand on his arm. "But if she's their aunt—"

Kip squeezed his mother's hand in reassurance. "I won't let it happen. I promised Scott I would keep the boys on the ranch, and I keep my promises."

"You always have," Mary Cosgrove said with a wan smile. "You've been a good son. I'm so thankful for you. I still hope and pray that you'll find someone who sees past that gruff exterior of yours and sees you for who you really are." She gave his hands a gentle shake. "Nancy

Colbert didn't know what she gave up when she broke up with you."

Kip sighed. He didn't want to think about his ex-girlfriend either. "Nancy was never cut out to be a rancher's wife," he said.

"I never liked that Nancy chick," Isabelle added. "She reminded me of a snake."

"Thanks for that, Izzy. Maybe those dishes could get done before the day is over."

This piece of advice netted him an eye roll, but she turned back to the sink and plodded on.

"I still wonder, if you hadn't agreed to take on the boys, if she would have stayed with you…" his mother's voice trailed off, putting voice to the questions that had plagued Kip for the first two months after Scott had died.

"Scott begged me, Mom," Kip reminded her. "He begged me to keep the boys on the ranch. I owed him. It was because of my horse—" he stopped himself there. He still couldn't think of his brother's death without guilt. He wondered if that would ever leave. "Besides, if Nancy had really loved me, she would have been willing to take on the boys as well as me."

Mary nodded, but Kip could see a hint of sorrow in her assuring smile.

"I know you really liked her, but the reality is anyone who wants me will have to take the boys and the ranch as well—"

"And your mother and your little sister," Mary added. She shook her head. "You took too much on when you took over the ranch after Dad died. You take too much on all the time."

Kip gave her a quick hug. "I do it because I love you, and anything taken on in love isn't a burden." He heard the noise of the boys' excited voices coming closer. "And now I'd better deal with Ms. Williams."

He gently squeezed his mother's shoulder, squared his own and went out the door.

Nicole was leading the boys up the walk, holding both boys' hands. She looked up at him and Kip felt a jolt of surprise.

She had completely transformed. Gone was the suit, the tied-back hair, the high-heeled shoes. The uptight city woman had been transformed.

She wore blue jeans, a loose plaid shirt over a black T-shirt and cowboy boots. And she had let her hair down. It flowed over her shoulders in loose waves, softening her features.

Making her look more approachable and, even worse, more appealing.

He put a brake on his thoughts, blaming his distraction on his mother's mention of his old girlfriend. Though he didn't miss Nancy as much as he'd thought he would, there were times he missed having someone special in his life. Missed being a boyfriend. He'd always wanted a family of his own.

"Hello," Nicole said, her voice as cool as it had been in Ron's office.

He acknowledged her greeting with a curt nod. "Okay, boys, let's go work on that tractor."

"Yippee." Justin jumped up and down. "Let's go, Tristan."

Kip glanced at his other nephew who was staring up at Nicole, looking a little starstruck. "I want to play with the puppies," Tristan said. "Can you play with the puppies with me?" he asked Nicole.

"I thought you wanted to help me," Kip said to Tristan

with a forced jocularity. Tristan was never as adventurous as Justin, but he always came along.

Tristan shook his head still looking up at Nicole. "I want to be with Auntie Nicole."

Auntie Nicole? The words jarred him, and he stifled a shiver of premonition. She had already staked a claim on his boys.

"So do I," Justin shouted out.

Nicole glanced from Kip to the boys. "Your Uncle Kip said I had to help him with the tractor." She shot him an arch look. "Unless he was kidding."

"Nope," he said, deadpan. "Absolutely serious."

"Then I'll come," Justin said, turning on his allegiances as quickly as he turned on his feet.

"What are those," Nicole asked, as they walked past two of his wagons parked beside the barn. Grass had grown up a bit around them. He'd parked them there last fall and hadn't touched them since.

"Chuck wagons."

"What do you use them for?" Nicole asked.

"Uncle Kip used to race them," Tristan said. "Before my daddy died."

"Race them? How do you do that?"

"You don't know?" Justin's astonishment was a bit rude, but Kip didn't feel like correcting him.

"I'm sorry. I do not."

Kip wasn't surprised. Chuck-wagon racing had originated in Calgary, and while it was an integral part of the Calgary Stampede, it wasn't a regular event in all the rodeos scattered around North America. He'd grown up with it, though. His father and his uncle and his grandfather all competed in the chuck-wagon races. It was in his blood.

He knew he should be teaching the boys so they could carry on the tradition. It was in their blood too. They were as much Cosgroves as he was.

"Uncle Kip will have to show you, won't you, Uncle Kip?" Justin said.

"Maybe," was his curt reply.

Since Scott died, he hadn't worked with his horses. Hadn't competed in any of the races. Chuck-wagon racing took up too much of the time he didn't have anymore.

He felt a pinch of sorrow. He missed the thrill of the race, the keenness of competing, the pleasure of working with his horses.

"Uncle Kip was one of the fastest racers," Tristan said, pride tingeing his voice. "But he doesn't race anymore. He says it's not 'sponsible 'cause now he has us."

"Well, that sounds like a good way to think," Nicole said.

Kip shot her a glance, wondering if she was serious. But he caught her steady gaze and she wasn't laughing.

"So where's the tractor?"

"Just over here." He was only too glad to change the subject. Chuck wagons were in his past. He had enough going on in the present.

"What do we need to do?" Nicole asked as they walked across the packed ground toward the shop.

Kip gave her a curious look. "You don't have to help."

"Of course I do." She gave him a wry look, as if to say "you asked for it."

Their eyes held a split-second longer than necessary. As if each was testing the other to see who would give. Then he broke the connection. He didn't have anything to prove.

Yet even as he thought those brave words, a finger of

fear trickled down his spine. Actually, he did have something to prove. He had to prove that Justin and Tristan's were Scott's boys. That they belonged here on the ranch.

Kip pulled on the chain and the large garage door creaked and groaned as light spilled into the usually gloomy shop. He loved working with the door open and today, with the sun shining and a bright blue sky, was a perfect day to do so.

"This is where the tractor is," Justin said. "Uncle Kip took it apart and he said a bad word when he dropped a wrench on his toe."

"Did he now?" Nicole's voice held a hint of laughter and Kip made a mental note to talk to the boys about "things we don't tell Ms. Williams."

"Tristan, you can wheel over the tool chest. Justin, you can get me the box of rags," Kip said, shooting his blabbermouth nephew a warning look as he rolled up his sleeves.

"I got the rags the last time," Justin whined. "How come Tristan always gets to push the tool chest? I never do."

As Kip stifled his frustration, he caught Nicole watching him. As if assessing what he was going to do.

"Just do it, Justin," he said more firmly.

But Justin shoved his hands in his pockets and glared back at him. Kip felt Nicole's gaze burning on him. For a moment he wished he hadn't insisted that she visit the kids here. Now everything he did with the boys would be with an audience. A very critical audience who, he was sure, would be only too glad to see him mess up.

He tried to ignore her presence as he knelt down in front of Justin. "Buddy, I asked you to do something. You wanted to help me, and this is part of helping."

"But…my dad always…" Justin's lower lip pushed out and Kip could see the sparkle of tears in his eyes and his heart melted.

"Oh, buddy," he whispered, pulling Justin in his arms. He gave him a tight squeeze, his own heart contracting in sorrow. It had been only six months since they stood together at Scott's grave. In the busyness of life, he sometimes forgot that. He held Justin a moment longer and as he stood, he caught Nicole looking at them both, her lips pressed together, her fingers resting on her chin.

She understood, he thought, and he wondered if she was remembering her own sister.

Their gaze held and for a moment they shared a sorrow.

The rumbling of the tool chest broke the moment. "I got it. I got it," Tristan called out.

Kip gave Justin another quick hug, patted him on the head and turned back to the tractor with a sigh.

"What do you have to do?" Nicole asked.

"It's a basic fix," Kip said as he pushed a piece of cardboard under the tractor. "Replace a leaky fuel line, but whoever designed this tractor has obviously never worked on one." Kip bent over, squinting at the nuts holding the old line. Then he grabbed the tools he needed, lay on the cardboard and pulled himself under the tractor.

"Justin, why don't you get those rags for your Uncle Kip," he heard Nicole say. "Tristan, maybe you can clean up those bits of wood lying in the corner."

A born organizer, he thought, straining as he tried to pull off a bolt. He was still trying to wrap his head around the woman whom he'd seen in the office this morning—the all-business woman in her stark suit—

and the woman wearing blue jeans and a flannel shirt, standing in his shop.

He pushed the picture aside, focussing on the job at hand.

"Tristan, does your Uncle Kip have a broom?" he heard her asking, and a couple of minutes later he heard the swishing of the broom over the concrete floor accompanied by her quiet voice giving directions to the boys to move things out of the way.

He felt a squirm of embarrassment as he worked another nut free, imagining the shop through her eyes. He knew it was a mess. He liked his shop organized and neat but hadn't had the time to tidy it up.

Finally he got the line free, and as he pulled himself out from under the tractor he found the box of rags.

His second surprise was the clean floor and the boxes of oil and grease stacked neatly in one corner by the compressor. The shop vac sat beside it, the hose attached again and the cord wrapped neatly around the top.

"So when will you need my socket and wrench?" Nicole asked, poking her head around the front of the tractor.

Kip released a short laugh. "Right now."

"So you were serious about that?" she asked, arching a perfectly plucked brow.

"I was joking about you bringing them, but I wasn't joking about needing them." He hadn't been able to find the wrench and socket ever since the boys "helped" him the last time. In his rush to get back to the ranch after seeing Ron, he had forgotten to pick up the tools at the hardware store.

He blew out a sigh of displeasure thinking of yet another trip to town.

"Then I'll go get them," she said.

He frowned. "You have them here?"

"In my car. Shall I get them?" She gave him a wry look.

"If you've got them here, that would be great," he said, completely serious this time.

"Can we come?" Justin and Tristan chimed in.

"Ms. Williams can go by herself," Kip said.

"I'm just going to the car."

"The boys stay here."

Nicole held his gaze a beat, as if reading more into his comment than he meant. Which was fine by him.

"Okay. I'll be back."

Kip watched her go, her blond hair catching the sun, her hands strung up in the pockets of her snug blue jeans.

He didn't need this right now. He looked down at the boys who were watching her go, looking a bit starstruck. Not that he blamed them. She was beautiful, she was attentive.

Only they didn't know was that she was big, big trouble.

Nicole didn't have to look over her shoulder to know Kip was watching her. She felt his eyes drilling into the back of her neck and wished he hadn't insisted on her visiting the boys at the ranch. It was as if she was under constant scrutiny.

When she got to the car she shot a quick look over her shoulder, but she was out of sight of the shed. She pulled out the bag of tools and grabbed her cell phone at the same time.

"Pretty sweet cell phone."

Nicole jumped, then spun around in time to see Isabelle sauntering down the stairs with all the confidence of a sixteen-year-old girl.

"You got any fun games on it?" she asked.

"I don't play games on my phone."

Isabelle slanted her head to one side, her eyes narrowed. "No, but you play games with us. Pretending to be a housekeeper. You know how much trouble I got into because of you?"

"You seemed glad to leave me alone with your mother and all the work," Nicole countered.

"I don't think I like you," Isabelle said, crossing her thin arms over her chest.

"I don't think that matters." Nicole was sure she wasn't well liked by the rest of the Cosgrove family either. She wasn't here to win a popularity contest. She was here to get her father's grandchildren back to him. Her atonement.

"My brother won't let you take Justin and Tristan away from here, you know. He'll fight you."

"I know he will," she answered, checking her voice mail while she spoke. Five new messages. She hit the Answer button as she walked back to the shed, taking the bag of tools with her.

Isabelle followed a few steps behind her.

"Don't you have work to do?" Nicole asked, feeling like was being spied on.

"My mom is sleeping and I don't want to wake her up."

Nicole gave her a vague nod as she skipped through the messages from her assistant, Heather. She could deal with those when she got back to the motel, but the one from the lawyer...

"No news to report yet." Her family's lawyer's voice was brisk and businesslike, and he didn't waste any words or time. "Still working on the legalities of the will. Should have more information in a couple of days."

Isabelle took a quick step to get ahead of Nicole. "You can't do this to my mother, you know," she said, her voice intense. "She'll die if you take the twins. Those are Scott's boys and he's gone." This was followed by a dramatic sniff.

Nicole caught a flash of her own intensity in the young girl's eyes. Her own reasons for reuniting the boys with her father.

Her step faltered, but for only a moment. "I'm sorry, Isabelle, but I'm not talking to you about this."

She walked past Isabelle toward the garage, shoving her phone into her pocket. As she came near she saw Kip watching her, wiping his hands on a rag. Had he been looking at her the entire time?

"What did you say to my sister?" he asked, pointing his chin toward Isabelle.

Nicole shot a quick glance over her shoulder. Isabelle stood in the middle of the yard, her arms wrapped around her middle, staring at Nicole, her expression tight with anger.

"I told her I wasn't talking to her about the situation." She handed him the tools. "Where are the boys?"

Kip angled his head to the back of the shop and without a word to him, Nicole walked toward them.

But even as she did, her stomach twisted with old, familiar emotions. Again she was on the outside of a family looking in. Sure, she hadn't expected to be accepted and greeted with warmth, but she hadn't counted on how much their antagonism would bother her. Especially when, for a few hours, she had been welcomed by them.

"Auntie Nicole, there you are."

Nicole smiled and looked around. "I can't find you Justin," she called out, warmth flooding her heart at the sound of his voice.

Then a pair of arms flung themselves around her waist and she looked down onto the blond head of a little boy.

As she hugged him back, she felt her own heart crack open just a little wider. She could not let the feelings of the Cosgrove family stand in the way of what she had to do.

Her father's needs came before theirs.

Chapter Six

Nicole pushed the accelerator further down as her car climbed the hill. She had Vivaldi on the stereo, the windows open and her car headed in the direction of the ranch and Tricia's boys.

The highway made a curve, then topped a rise, and Nicole's breath left her. The valley spread out below her, a vast expanse of space yawning for miles, then undulating toward green hills and giving way to imperious mountains, their peaks capped with snow, blinding white against a blue, blue sky.

In spite of her hurry to get to the ranch, she slowed down, taking it all in. The space, the emptiness.

The freedom. She felt the faintest hitch in her soul.

She was a city girl, but somehow this country called to her. Yesterday she'd almost got lost on her way to the ranch because she kept looking around, taking in the view.

She took in a deep breath and let the space and quiet ease into her soul.

Yesterday, after seeing the boys, she'd come back to a raft of emails all dealing with the foundation banquet she and her assistant had been planning. Nicole first sent a quick update to her father, then waded into the work, dealing with whatever came out of them until two. This morning she'd gotten up early and finished up. Then, still tired, she'd grabbed a nap, only she forgot to set her alarm. Now she was an hour and a half late for her meeting with the boys.

The ringing of her cell phone made her jump. She blew out a frustrated sigh, glanced at the caller ID and forced a smile.

"What did the lawyer say?" her father asked.

Sam Williams may have been ill, but he hadn't lost his capacity of getting straight to the point.

"The usual lawyer stuff," Nicole said tucking a strand of hair behind her ear that the wind coming into the car had pulled free from her ponytail. "Things are going to take time. He needs to verify Tricia's will. Nothing definite."

"How are the boys?"

"I wish you could see them. They're so cute." A picture of them pushing the oversize broom in their uncle's shop yesterday made her smile. "They're such little cowboys."

Her father didn't say anything to that and Nicole guessed it was the wrong response.

"I'll try to call from the ranch today," Nicole said. "See if you can talk to them."

"The new school year starts in three months," her father said as Nicole turned onto the road leading to the ranch. "I'm looking into schools for them."

As Sam spoke, Nicole's thoughts slipped back to Kip's comment about putting the boys on the bus and his obvious regret. At least he wouldn't have to deal with that come September.

"I'm getting to a bad area and I'll be losing reception. I'll try to call you from the ranch."

"If I was feeling better I'd be there…"

The rest of her father's words were cut off when Nicole's car dropped into the valley.

As Nicole turned onto the ranch's driveway, she felt another clutch of frustration at Kip Cosgrove's insistence that she visit the boys only at the ranch.

How was she supposed to get to know her nephews in two and a half hours under his watchful eye? But as she came around the corner, her frustration gave way to anticipation at the thought of seeing the boys again.

As Nicole parked her car beside Kip's huge pickup she jumped out of the car, looked around, but didn't see anyone. She walked to the house and knocked on the door.

Nothing.

Where was everybody? She lifted her hand to knock again when she saw a note on the door addressed to her.

"In the field. Moving bales. Mom sleeping." The words were hastily scribbled on a small piece of paper and stuck to the door with a piece of masking tape.

Nicole blew out a sigh. Which field? How was she supposed to find them? She could almost hear the clock ticking down the precious seconds on her visit.

She paused, listening, then heard the sound of a tractor. Thankfully, it sounded like it was coming closer.

She jogged across the yard, past the chuck wagons. As she raced around a corner of the barn, a tractor lurched into view pulling a wagon loaded up with hay. Smoke billowed from the stack and the engine roared, a deafening sound in the once-stillness.

The sun reflected off the glass of the closed-in cab of the tractor, but as it came closer, Nicole saw Kip driving and Justin and Tristan standing behind the seat.

With a squeal of brakes the tractor came to a halt beside her and Kip opened the side door. "You're late," he yelled over the noise of the tractor's engine.

Like she needed him to tell her that.

"Yes. Sorry." What else could she say?

Justin leaned over Kip's shoulder and waved at her. "Hey, Ms. Williams," he shouted.

Ms. Williams? What happened to Auntie Nicole?

Nicole just smiled and waved, quite sure Kip had something to do with the change.

She walked to the tractor, raising her arms to take the boys out. "Hey, Tristan. You boys helping Mr. Cosgrove?" Two could play that game.

Tristan gave her a puzzled look. Nicole could tell that Kip understood exactly what she was doing.

"We just have to unload these bales." Kip closed the door before she came any closer and before the boys could get out. He put the tractor in gear and drove away.

She was left to trail behind the swaying wagon, fuming as bits of hay swirled around her face. With each step her anger at his pettiness grew. He was depriving her of valuable time with her own nephews so he could prove a point.

She easily kept up with the tractor and followed it to where she assumed he was going to pile up these bales. But neither he nor the boys got out of the tractor. Somehow he unhitched the wagon from inside, turned the tractor around and started to unload the bales. One at a time.

She was reduced to watching as the clock ticked away precious minutes of her visiting time.

Kip reminded her of her biological father and how he used to make her wait in the motel room while he busied himself with who knew what in his truck while her aunt fumed. Older, buried emotions slipped to the fore. As she had done the first few years at Sam and Norah's, she fought them down. She was here and she had a job to do for her father. That was all she had to focus on.

She waited until the last bale was unloaded and then she marched over to the tractor before Kip could decide he had to go for another load and leave her behind.

But just as she reached the tractor, Kip shut it off and the door opened.

"You finally came," Tristan called out.

The "finally" added to her burden of guilt, and she gave them a quick smile. "Yes, I'm sorry I was late," she said as Kip lifted Tristan up and over the seat.

"Got busy with work?" he asked as she reached up to take Tristan from him.

"Forgot to set my alarm," was her terse reply as she set Tristan down on the ground. He didn't need to know that to some degree he was right and she was surprised that he had guessed, at least partially, why she was late.

He made a show of looking at his watch. "You city people keep crazy hours."

"I was working late and grabbed a nap," she said trying not to rise to his goading.

"So you were working."

"I have to do something while I'm waiting around for my appointed visiting times," she snapped. "Justin, honey, tell Mr. Cosgrove that he's working on a Saturday too and we're wasting time here."

Justin frowned, then laughed. "He is Uncle Kip," the little boy said with a grin.

"He is many things," Nicole returned, her gaze still on Kip.

His eyes narrowed as if he caught the inference but wasn't sure what to do with it. Instead of saying anything, he handed Justin down to her.

"I'm taking the boys to see the puppies. Is that okay?" she asked.

"Just stay away from the horses. I'm going back for another load of hay," he said, his voice brusque. "Make sure you keep the boys away from the tractor too when I come back."

Before she could think of a suitable reply, he had closed the door and started up the tractor again.

She bit her anger back, took a breath to calm herself, then looked down at the boys. No sense in letting them know how angry she was with their uncle.

"Let's go," the boys said, dragging her by the hand toward the barn.

"We'll first go see your grandmother and then we'll go see the puppies," Nicole said.

They ran across the yard ahead of her, laughing and screaming like two young colts.

Nicole smiled at the picture of utter freedom.

When Nicole and the boys got to the house, Mary was watching television. She brightened when the boys came into the living room.

"Hey, there, my boys. Do you want to watch a movie with me?" she asked.

Nicole was about to protest.

"Can we watch *Robin Hood?*" Justin asked before she could speak.

"I'll go get it," Tristan said.

Nicole stifled a beat of disappointment. She'd hoped to

spend her time with the boys alone, just the three of them. She had looked forward to being outside with them, walking around the ranch, not sitting inside a stuffy house watching television.

But Mary was their grandmother and she was simply the outsider, so she said nothing.

The boys popped the movie in and settled on the couch to watch. Nicole sat with them for a bit but got fidgety. She'd never enjoyed watching television like her sister did. She had preferred reading and doing crafts.

"Do you mind if I tidy up?" she said to Mary.

"You don't have to do our work," Mary protested, pushing herself up as if to get up out of her wheelchair.

"I don't mind. I'm not much of a television person, and I don't mind, really. You sit with the boys and I'll wander around here."

Though she had grown up with a housekeeper, years of living in foster homes had given Nicole a measure of independence, and she had always kept her own room neat and later on, she did her own laundry.

So Nicole tidied and cleaned, washed dishes and did another load of laundry while the boys sat mindlessly in front of the television.

What a shame, she thought, wishing she had enough authority to turn off the television and make them come outside.

Finally, the movie was over and Nicole came into the living room. "I think we should go outside now."

"I'll have a nap," Mary said. She smiled at the boys. "Now don't go and tell your Uncle Kip." She winked at them and they giggled. Then she glanced at Nicole. "Kip doesn't let them watch television during the day."

If she'd known that, Nicole thought, she wouldn't have

let them. But she didn't know the politics and the hierarchy of this particular household, though she was learning.

She turned to the boys. "Now you'll have to show me where those puppies are," she said. They each took one of her hands and as she looked down at their upraised faces a wave of love washed over her.

It surprised her and, if she were honest, frightened her. Each time she saw them it was as if one more hook was attached to her heart. The pain of letting go could be too much.

But that wouldn't happen, she reminded herself, holding even more tightly to their hands. The boys were Tricia's and were never Scott's no matter what Kip might believe. She and her father had the law on their side.

They stepped outside and Nicole inhaled the fresh, pure air. It was so wonderful to be outdoors.

"I want to see the horses," Justin said as they stepped off the porch.

"Your uncle said it wasn't allowed." And there was no way she was running afoul of Kip while on his ranch.

"If we're real careful, it will be okay."

"Not on your life," Nicole said firmly.

Justin sighed. "That's what Uncle Kip always says too."

One more thing we have in common, Nicole thought with a sense of irony.

"So where are these puppies?" she asked.

"They're in the barn."

As they walked, the boys, mostly Justin, brought her up to date on what Uncle Kip had done this morning—first he cut himself shaving, then he listened to the market report and made breakfast, then he tried to get Gramma to do her exercises.

What their grandmother had done—sat and watched television.

What Isabelle had done—slept in and got into trouble with Uncle Kip.

"Isabelle is fun. Uncle Kip says she has to grow up, but she's pretty big already."

Nicole suspected that Uncle Kip had his hands full with his sister. Isabelle needed a firm hand and guidance. Something, she suspected, Kip was at a loss to enforce.

Justin pulled open the large, heavy barn door then he stopped and held his finger to his lips. "I better go in first because we don't want to scare the mommy dog," he whispered. "I'll call you when you can come in."

He walked slowly into the barn and Tristan seemed content to stay behind with Nicole.

The only sound breaking the stillness was the shuffle of Justin's feet on the barn floor and the song of a few birds that Nicole couldn't identify. She listened, and the quiet pressed down on her ears.

The silence spread out everywhere, huge and overwhelming. For the briefest moment, icy fingers of panic gripped her heart. They were far away from the nearest road, the nearest town.

All alone.

Then she looked down at Tristan, smiling shyly up at her. She watched Justin creeping into the dusty barn. They were completely relaxed here, at home and at peace.

"And a little child shall lead them."

The familiar passage drifted into her mind and she puzzled it over, wondering where it had come from.

Then she remembered. It was from the Bible. Her mother used to read the Bible to her and Tricia.

"You hold my hand almost as tight as Uncle Kip does when we're in Calgary," Tristan whispered.

Nicole started. "I'm sorry," she said, loosening her grip. "I didn't mean to hurt you."

He smiled up at her. "That's okay. Uncle Kip always says he holds tight because he never wants to let us go. That makes me feel good."

Nicole's heart faltered at his words. Of course the boys would be attached to Kip Cosgrove and he to them. This was the only life the boys had known.

But they weren't Cosgroves, she reminded herself. They were Williamses, in spite of what Kip may claim.

Yet as she followed Justin into the dusky coolness of the barn, she felt her own misgivings come to the fore. Her own memories of being moved from home to home.

But she never returned to her biological home, like these boys were going to. She could never go back to where the people she lived with were related to her by blood, but these boys could. She would give them the true family she'd never had and in doing so, maybe, just maybe—

Her thoughts were cut off by the ringing of her phone. It was her father.

"Hey," she whispered, following Tristan into the dusty pen. The floor was strewn with straw and Justin was crouched in the corner, his behind stuck in the air as he reached under a pile of lumber.

"Can you talk?"

"Yes. I'm with the boys."

"I want to talk to them. Now."

Nicole hesitated. This was the first time she'd been alone with the boys since she'd met them. She hadn't had an opportunity to let them know that not only did they have another aunt, they also had a grandfather. She highly doubted Kip Cosgrove let them know either.

"I haven't explained everything to them yet—"

"You're telling me they don't know about me?"

Her father's gruff voice created a storm of guilt in Nicole. "I haven't found the right time to tell them," she whispered.

Justin wriggled backwards then turned around with a triumphant grin. He held up a squirming, mewling puppy. The little creature was a bundle of brown and black fur with a shiny button nose.

"I got one," he squealed. Nicole knelt down, still holding the phone as Justin brought the puppy over to her. "You want to hold it?" he asked.

"That's one of them, isn't it?" her father asked. He broke into a fit of coughing, a sure sign to Nicole that he was upset. "I need to talk to them. Please, let me talk to them."

It was the please that was her undoing. She couldn't remember her father saying those words more than a dozen times in her life.

"Just give me a few seconds," she whispered to her father. "I need to explain a few things." She smiled at Justin and held out her hand. "Yes, I'd love to hold it," she said. "Why don't you hold my phone for me and I'll take the puppy?"

Justin managed to release his grip on the puppy and take the phone. Nicole gathered the warm, silky bundle in her arms, her heart melting at the sight of its chocolate-brown eyes staring soulfully up at her. She crouched down in the straw covering the floor of the pen, preferring not to think what might be living in it.

"He likes you," Tristan said as she settled down.

"Who are you talking to?" Justin asked, looking at her phone.

"Why don't you come and sit by me," she said, keeping her voice low and quiet. "I have something to tell you."

Curious, Justin knelt down in front of her, still holding the phone, Tristan beside her. She stroked the puppy and looked from one pair of trusting eyes to the other. "You know that you had a mommy, right?"

"We don't know where our mommy is," Justin said. "She ranned away."

Nicole pressed back an angry reply. Their lack of knowledge wasn't their fault. "Your mommy didn't run away," she said. "Your mommy loved you both very much, and your mommy had a father who loved her very much too. That father is your grandmother."

"Our grandpa is dead," Justin said. "Uncle Kip told us."

"Now you know that you have another grandfather," Nicole said. "And he's alive and he lives in Toronto."

"You mean like Paul and Liam and Kirsten and Leah and Emily and Jenna from Auntie Doreen? They have a grandpa," Tristan squealed. "Uncle Ron's daddy."

"That's right."

"Where is our other grandfather?" Justin asked.

"I was talking to him on the phone you're holding," Nicole said, tilting her head toward the phone Justin clutched. "You can talk to him if you want."

Justin frowned. "Uncle Kip lets me pretend to talk on his phone," he said.

"You don't have to pretend," Nicole said gently. "Now I'll hit a button and put it on speakerphone so we can all hear all of us talk." She tapped her phone, then held it out. "Justin, say hello to your grandfather."

Justin lifted his shoulders, suddenly self-conscious. "Are you my grandpa? This is Justin."

"Yes, I am. How are you?"

Justin frowned, then said, "I'm fine. How are you?"

She heard a faint cough, then her father replied that he was fine.

Nicole let Justin chatter on about the puppies and hauling hay. Her father made a few responses, but he didn't have to say much around Justin.

"Father, this is Tristan. He wants to say hi," Nicole said, taking the phone away from Justin.

Tristan was more reserved, but soon he was giving out information as freely as his brother.

The phone distorted her father's voice but it wasn't hard to hear the joy in it. Joy she hadn't heard in her father's voice since Tricia left home.

"Hey there, did you guys find the puppies?"

Nicole jumped, startling the puppy, then she craned her neck backwards to see Kip standing in the doorway.

What was he doing? Checking up on her?

"What are you doing with Ms. Williams's phone?" Kip asked, frowning at Tristan.

Tristan looked up, his smile dropping away as soon as he saw his Uncle Kip.

"We're talking to our grandpa," Justin announced. "He said we are going to stay with him. In Toronto. Can we go, Uncle Kip? Can we?"

Nicole's heart dropped when she saw the thunderous expression cross Kip's face.

"I think you should give the phone back to Ms. Williams, then go back to the house."

"I want to talk to my other grandfather some more," Justin whined.

"Tristan, please give the phone back to Ms. Williams and go with Justin to the house."

Nicole glanced at the little boy who was obviously listening to something her father was saying. Tristan looked from Kip to Nicole, confusion on his features.

"Don't go," she heard her father say. "Don't listen to him."

She had to put poor Tristan out of his misery.

"I'll take the phone, sweetie," she said holding her hand out.

"No. Nicole. I need to talk to them."

"Sorry, Father," she said quietly. She turned the phone off speaker, then walked away from Kip. "The boys have to go."

"Those boys shouldn't be there," her father said. "They should be here with me."

"I know, but not everything is settled yet."

Her father started coughing again, then got his breath. "I'm phoning that lawyer first thing Monday morning. We shouldn't have to wait for these DNA tests. We know Tricia was their mother."

Nicole glanced over her shoulder at Kip standing in the doorway of the barn watching the boys walk to the house. Obviously he was sticking around to talk to her. "We have to move slowly on this," she said to her father.

"Those boys have to come back to their home," he said quietly. "You of all people know why Tricia's boys need to come back."

As always, his words held a subtext of obligation that was never spoken directly but always hinted at. "Of course I do," she replied. "I have to go." As she said goodbye, she felt a moment of sympathy for her father, all alone back home.

She couldn't help comparing his lonely situation to Mary Cosgrove's. Mary had one daughter with six grand-children and she had another daughter and son and two more grandchildren under her roof.

The boys weren't Cosgroves. It was as if she had to drum that information into her mind. If she didn't, then she would start to feel sorry for Mary.

And for Kip.

She pocketed her phone and turned to face Kip.

"Why did you do that?" he demanded.

Any sympathy she might have felt for the man was brushed away in the icy blast of his question.

"If you're thinking I deliberately brought the boys out here so they could talk to my father on the phone, you're mistaken. He just happened to call while I was out here."

"And you just happened to let the boys talk to him."

"May I remind you that he's their grandfather?"

"That hasn't been proven beyond a doubt."

"You were willing to let me visit them based on this doubt."

Kip's eyes narrowed and she knew she had gone too far. "Only because my lawyer told me I should. No other reason."

Nicole knew Kip had not let her willingly onto the farm. She was here on suffrage only. "Regardless of how you see the situation, the man I just spoke to is Tricia's father—"

"And he was never part of the agreement." Kip took a step closer and it was all Nicole could do to keep her cool. "You're not to let the boys talk to your father again without talking to me about it," he warned, his voice lowering to a growl. "Those poor kids lost their father six months ago, and they don't need to have any more confusion in their lives."

Nicole struggled to hold his steely gaze. "Finding out that they have a maternal grandfather can hardly be confusing to any child. In fact, many people would see it as a blessing."

That last comment came out before she could stop it, as did the tiny hitch in her voice. She hoped he would put it down to her anger rather than the fact that she had found herself jealous of these boys. Jealous of Kip.

He had family that had no strings attached. A mother who doted on him and a sister who, in spite of her rebellious ways, still cared for him. He didn't have to try to earn his mother's love, try to atone for what he did.

Kip's mouth settled into a grim line and she felt as if she scored the tiniest point.

"That may be, but at the same time I'm their uncle and guardian and responsible for their well-being. Anything you do with them gets run by me. The boys are my first priority, not you, or your father."

Nicole bit back a retort, realizing that to some degree he was right. Much as it bothered her, she couldn't argue with him.

Kip shoved his hand through his hair and released a heavy sigh. "I've got too much happening right now. I can't give the boys the explanations they will need if you start complicating their lives."

Nicole held his gaze and for a moment in spite of her anger with him, sympathy stirred in her soul. Sympathy and something more profound. Respect, even. Regardless of whatever claim Nicole may have, the reality was that this man was putting as a first priority the welfare of two little boys that weren't his children. Even though his guardianship put them at odds, at the same time she respected what he was doing.

She thought of how easily her biological father seemed to give her up. How happy her aunt had been when Social Services came to take her away for good. In spite of her aunt's antagonism, Nicole had wished that she could stay, but her aunt wanted her gone.

Those boys don't know how good they had it. In fact, Nicole was jealous that they had this strong, tough man on their side. A man who had made sacrifices for his nephews. A man who was willing to fight for them.

What would have happened in her earlier life if she'd had the same kind of advocate? If she'd had someone who was willing to go to the mat for her welfare? What if she'd had someone like Kip on her side?

"I'd like you to leave now," Kip said quietly.

Nicole opened her mouth to protest.

"It's past five," Kip said.

"Of course," was all she said. "I'll be back tomorrow then."

Kip just nodded.

Nicole got up and walked past him, then got into her car. As she drove off, she could see him in her rearview mirror watching her.

He could watch and glower all he wanted. She wasn't letting him intimidate her.

She had rights and she was going to exercise them regardless of what he thought of her.

Chapter Seven

"I'm not doing the dishes again." Isabelle glared at Kip, her hands on her hips. "Sunday is a day of rest. At least that's what I thought the minister said."

As Kip tried to match her glare for glare he also tried not to feel guilty about all the work he hoped to get done today.

"I'm not your slave," she muttered.

He ignored that. "Just make sure the dishes get done," he growled. Then he turned to his mother. "And you make sure she does it and don't you even think about doing it yourself."

Mary gave him a quick nod, which didn't give Kip much confidence.

Didn't any of the women in his life listen to him? He spun around just as he heard a knock on the door.

What was Nicole doing here already?

"Tristan. Justin," he called out. "Finish up. Ms. Williams is here." He sent the boys upstairs to change out of their Sunday clothes about an hour ago and they still weren't down.

"It's not fair, you know," Isabelle whined, leaning back against the counter.

Nicole stepped into the kitchen. "Um…I think you have a problem," she said. "There are some cows roaming around the yard," she continued. "I'm guessing they're not supposed to be there."

"What?" Kip frowned, then as her words registered, he pushed past her and stepped outside, then groaned in disbelief.

Over two dozen cows and calves were milling about out of the fence.

There went the afternoon, Kip thought, his heart dropping into his gut. His mind flipped through all the scenarios why the animals would be loose. Open gate. Broken fence.

Not that it mattered. For now he had to get them away from the hay bales, and even more important, away from the granary filled with oats.

"What can I do?" Nicole asked.

Was she kidding? Kip spared her a quick glance then strode down the steps. "Just stay out of the way."

Not that he had a master plan that she could help him implement. He was pretty much winging it.

As he got closer to the moving herd he slowed his steps, planning, thinking. The gate to the pasture wasn't open, so that left one thing. Broken fences.

He shifted his hat back on his head as he glanced around the yard, trying to figure out what to do with the herd. Where to put them.

They started moving and he hurried his steps, trying to get ahead of them without spooking them.

Of course, one cow let out a bawl, spun around and

they all decided to change their focus and head down the driveway.

"No, you stupid creatures," he yelled, moving even more quickly.

Please, Lord, don't let them head down the driveway. Because once they did, they would be on the run and it would take hours and hours to get them back again.

He changed direction and ran, knowing he didn't stand a chance of getting them turned around. Not on foot and not without his horse, but he had to try.

Sweat poured down his back, anger clenched his gut and then, suddenly he heard, "Hey. Get back there."

He looked up and there were Nicole and Isabelle standing by the driveway waving dishtowels. Were they kidding? Dishtowels against two dozen 1,200-pound cows on the loose?

Miraculously the cows stopped, dust slowly settling around them. Kip caught his breath, trying to assess. Then a calf broke free from the herd but again, to his surprise Nicole got the animal turned around.

"Let's get them into the corrals," he called out. "Isabelle, can you get to the gate?"

"No," she said, glaring at him.

"This is not the time, missy," he called back.

Thankfully, Nicole moved over to the fence and climbed over it, leaving Isabelle standing guard. Even from here Kip could see the fear on Nicole's face, but surprisingly she kept moving.

She opened the gate to the pasture, then came back over the fence, staying clear of the cows.

"Start moving slowly toward them," Kip called out. "Don't get right in front of them. Work at them from the side."

Nicole nodded and started walking at an angle toward the herd. It was probably a good thing she was afraid. She moved slowly and took her time.

"Stop there, Nicole," Kip yelled.

Kip moved toward the herd just enough to get them going. Then, thankfully, the cows in the lead turned around. The ones behind them followed their example, and soon the herd was turned around and walking back to the pasture.

Please, please, he prayed as he moved slowly behind them, keeping them moving. If they turned around now, they would scatter and it could easily take all day to get them herded up again.

The cows at the head of the herd sped up the pace. It was going to be all right, Kip thought.

Suddenly one of the cows in the middle turned her head and decided to make a break for it.

Right toward Nicole.

She stood, frozen, as another cow followed the one trying to get away. This was it. They were hooped.

Then Nicole waved her arms and yelled and to Kip's surprise the cow stopped and rejoined the herd now heading into the corral.

"Isabelle, get over the fence and make sure they don't get into the pasture," Kip called out.

"Are you kidding?" Isabelle said. "I'm going back to the house."

"Oh, stop being such a selfish stinker and just do what your brother said," Nicole shouted back at her.

Kip didn't know who was more surprised at Nicole's outburst, him or his sister.

At any rate, Isabelle scrambled over the fence and headed off the cows that were eyeing the wide-open spaces of the pasture. Then, thankfully, the cows were all in the corral and Kip closed the metal gate, locking them in.

"So is that all of them?" Nicole's voice sounded a bit shaky as she joined them.

"Those were only a small part of the whole herd. Now I have to saddle up and find out where they got out and then make sure that the rest of the cows are where they're supposed to be." He dragged his hand over his face, thinking.

"I know this might sound dumb, but is there anything I can do?"

Kip glanced down at her. Some wisps of hair had pulled loose from her ponytail and were curling around her face. Her cheeks were flushed and she had a smear of dust on her forehead. She looked a bit scared yet, but she also looked kinda cute.

"Not really, but thanks for all your help. I couldn't have done it without you."

"And Isabelle," Nicole said wryly.

"Thanks for bawling her out. Nice to know I'm not the only one doing it."

Nicole laughed at that. "I'm real good at bawling out little sisters. I did it all the time with Tricia." She stopped there as an expression of deep sorrow slid over her face.

Kip wondered what she meant by her comment. What created that look of desolate sadness?

"Are you okay?" he asked.

Puzzlement replaced the sadness. "Why do you ask?"

He frowned. "You looked so sad. I'm thinking you're remembering your sister. I guess I know what it feels like."

She looked up at him then. Their gazes locked and held as awareness arced between them.

Without thinking of the implications he laid his hand on her shoulder, as if to cement the connection.

She looked away, but didn't move.

A yearning slipped through him. A yearning for things to be different between them. Involuntarily, his hand tightened.

"Nicole—"

"Uncle Kip, Uncle Kip. Isabelle said the cows got out…Did you get them in?…Can we help…Do you have to ride the horses?"

The boys burst into the moment with a barrage of questions and Nicole stepped away. As Kip lowered his hand, he experienced a surprising sense of loss. Then he gave his head a shake.

What was he thinking? This woman was simply another problem in his complicated life.

Kip dragged his attention back to his nephews. "Yeah. I'll be saddling up and heading out."

"Can we ride with you?" Justin asked.

Kip shot him a warning glance. The little guy knew better.

"Why don't we go and check out the puppies," Nicole said, taking the boys by their hands. "Have they gotten any bigger?"

"Silly, you just saw them yesterday," Justin said.

"I know, but puppies grow very fast and change quickly," she replied. "I would hate to think that we missed out on something fun that they didn't do yesterday."

Kip was sure her comment was off the cuff, but it

reminded him of all the changes he'd experienced with the boys. All the changes she and her father had missed.

You can't start going there, he reminded himself. You have a lawyer working to make sure the boys stay here. She has a lawyer to make sure the boys go with her.

Very straightforward. Cut-and-dried.

Yet just before she left she shot a glance over her shoulder, her hair brushing her cheek. Then she gave him a quick smile and things got confusing again. Thankfully he was going out on his horse. Things always got clearer for him when he was in the saddle.

He headed out to the tack shed, and as he opened the door the scent of leather and neat's foot oil washed over him. He halted as recollections of his brother surfaced from the corner of his mind where he thought he'd buried them.

He and Scott racing each other through pastures. He and Scott training the horses, racing the chucks, dust roiling out behind them, the horses' hooves pounding, the adrenaline flowing.

He grabbed the door frame, steadying himself against the onslaught of memories.

Dear Lord, help me get through this, he prayed, bowing his head as pain mingled with the memories. He missed his brother. He missed their time together, but mixed with the sorrow was the sad reality that he missed the freedom he'd had before his brother died.

The insidious thought crept into his mind. How much easier and freer his life would be if he didn't have the boys. How much simpler. The obligations of their future hung on his shoulders as well. Providing for them, taking care of their future.

Kip reached for his saddle and jerked it off the stand,

shaking his head as if dislodging the thought. They were his brother's boys, his mother's grandchildren. They were not a burden.

A few minutes later he had saddled his horse, Duke, and was riding out, leaving the ranch house and all the tangle of family obligations behind for a while.

Again he sent up a prayer for clarity of thought, and as he rode, as the sun warmed his back and the wind cooled his face, peace settled into his soul.

This was how he used to spend his Sundays, just riding around or working with the horses.

Now work piled on top of work, and quiet time for himself was as rare as a date, something else he hadn't had in months. He let his thoughts dwell for a moment on his horses. He should work with them. For their sake, if not his.

But when?

He looked around him, at the hills surrounding the ranch. A group of cows lay on one hill, beyond them another bunch. Thankfully, they hadn't decided to follow the wayward cows that had managed to get out.

Though he still had the same amount of work as he'd had before, riding out on his horse loosened the tension gripping his neck. Checking fences was one of his favorite jobs. Just him and his horse and the quiet. Oh, how he missed the quiet.

The irony was, he wouldn't have been able to do this if it wasn't for Nicole being with the boys and watching over his mother. Much as he hated to admit it, since she'd started visiting, some of his responsibilities had eased off his shoulders.

At the same time, Nicole presented a whole nest of

problems that complicated his life. He thought again of that moment they'd shared a moment ago.

He wished he could shake it off. Wished he could get her out of his mind.

"I'm just a lonely old cowboy," he said to Duke as he dismounted and stapled up another loose wire. "I've got responsibilities out the wazoo, and once this thing is settled with the boys, my life can go back to normal crazy instead of super crazy."

Duke whickered, tossing his head as if sympathizing with him.

Kip checked the wire and got on the horse again. Duke started walking, the sound of his muffled footfalls creating a soothing rhythm.

Except he couldn't get rid of the nagging feeling that things would not be settled with the boys. Not without a fight.

"C'mon, Auntie Nicole. Hurry up." Tristan's disembodied voice came from somewhere ahead of her on the narrow trail through the trees.

Nicole slowed down and stepped over an exposed rock on the trail, then pushed past a clump of spruce trees.

"Slow down," she puffed, pushing aside a spruce branch that threatened to blind her. "I can't go as fast as you." Not for the first time was she thankful she had bought some running shoes. Keeping up with the boys would have been impossible in the leather boots that she, at one time, had considered casual wear.

When she'd arrived this afternoon the boys had grabbed her and insisted she come and see something important. They wouldn't tell her what, only that she had to come right now.

She caught a glimpse of Tristan's striped T-shirt as she clambered over a fallen tree, then clambered over another one.

"Are you coming?" she heard Justin call out.

"Yes, I'm coming." She drew in a ragged breath, then, finally, she came to a small clearing. She ducked to get under a tree and as she straightened, looked around.

She couldn't see the boys. "Where are you guys?"

She heard giggling above her and looked up.

Two grinning faces stared down at her from a platform anchored between two aspen trees.

"What is this?" she asked, smiling back at the boys.

"It's Uncle Kip and our dad's Robin Hood tree house." They stood up and then disappeared again, only to reappear higher up on another platform. "Come up and see."

"Is it safe?" she asked. If Kip and his brother had been the architects of this tree house, then it had be at least twenty years old.

"Yup," was all they said.

Nicole walked around and found a ladder constructed of branches leaning up against the tree. She tested it and then slowly climbed up. When she got to the platform, she saw Justin, about six trees over, swinging from a rope.

"Justin, would you stop that," she called out.

"It's okay, Auntie Nicole," Tristan assured her. "Uncle Kip said we could play here. He helped fix it up so we could."

Nicole stepped onto the platform and, holding onto an overhanging tree branch for support, looked around.

She saw ropes and bridges and catwalks and more platforms strung between trees edging the clearing. A veritable hideout and a boy's dream come true. "You said your Uncle Kip made this?"

"Yup, he did," Justin called back, still swinging from the rope. "His dad helped him and our dad."

Nicole leaned against the tree behind her and tried to imagine Kip as a young boy working on this tree fort with his father and his brother.

A smile played over her lips as she watched the boys clambering from one structure to another like monkeys. Again she envied them their freedom. How many young boys wouldn't love to have their life?

"Come on back now," she said, glancing at her watch. It was getting close to the end of her visit. Yesterday she had stayed a bit longer and Isabelle had made a snarky comment, which she had ignored.

At the same time, she didn't want to cause any problems. Especially not when the legal status of the boys seemed to be, at least in Kip's eyes, in limbo.

"Can't we play a little longer?" Justin called out.

"No. We have to get back." Nicole tried to sound firm, but failed. She wasn't in any rush to go back either. The smell of the woods, the sun filtering through the canopy of leaves above and the gentle stillness of the woods eased away the tensions of the day.

She had spent most of her morning on the telephone playing telephone tag with caterers, trying to get a better deal from the venue and sweet-talking various sponsors for the foundation's annual fund-raiser.

More than that, she was having so much fun following the boys around the farm and exploring with them. She couldn't remember the last time she'd simply taken time off and done nothing constructive whatsoever. Even her holidays were usually slotted around conventions or business trips with her father.

She eased out a sigh and slipped down the tree, wrapping her arms around her knees as she watched the boys clamber from tree to tree, yelling and daring each other to go higher, farther, faster.

"Look at me, Auntie Nicole," Justin called out. "I'm flying."

"Me too," Tristan said, determined not to be outdone.

Nicole watched, and applauded and made appropriate noises of admiration.

Reluctantly she glanced at her watch again. Now she really had to go.

"C'mon boys. Let's get back to the house," she said, getting to her feet.

"Just a few more minutes."

"Nope. We have to go. Now." She was already twenty minutes past her visiting time. All she could do was hope Kip was still busy welding and wouldn't notice. She climbed down the ladder to let the boys know she meant business and reluctantly they followed her.

"Can we come here again tomorrow?" Justin asked.

"Of course we can." Nicole looked behind her once more with a smile. Maybe she'd stop in town and pick up some treats. They could have a picnic.

Nicole heard the hum of the welder coming from the shop as they got nearer the house and felt a surge of relief. Kip was still busy.

"What's that smell?" Justin said, wrinkling his nose. "Smells like—"

"Something's burning," Nicole said. She dropped the boys' hands, took the stairs two at a time and burst into the house.

Mary was leaning on the counter with one hand as she struggled to pull a pan out of the oven with the other.

Smoke billowed out of the oven and the smoke detector started screeching.

"Let me do that," Nicole said, grabbing a tea towel as the boys followed her into the kitchen, hands clapped over their ears and yelling questions.

Ignoring the boys and the piercing shriek of the smoke detector, Nicole rescued a blackened casserole dish from the oven, set it on top of the stove and turned the oven off.

Then she supported Mary and helped her back to her chair.

"Open the back door," she called out to the boys above the ear-piercing shriek as she slid open the window above the sink. "Where's the smoke detector?" she yelled at Mary.

Mary pointed to the hallway off the kitchen and Nicole grabbed a couple of tea towels. She flapped the towels at the detector, the noise piercing through her brain. Justin and Tristan joined her. "We'll help you," they called out, waving their hands at the ceiling.

Nicole laughed at the sight, but kept flapping. Then the smoke detector abruptly quit and peaceful silence fell on the house.

"That was very loud," Tristan said, digging his finger in his ear, as if to dislodge the noise.

"You boys were big helpers," she said, patting them on the head as they walked back to the kitchen.

"Thank you so much," Mary said. "I could smell something boiling over for a while from my bedroom, but I thought Isabelle was watching the casserole."

"I was," Isabelle said, finally making an appearance from upstairs. "I had to make a phone call." Isabelle glanced at Nicole. "What are you doing here?"

"What you should have been doing." Nicole brushed

past the sullen girl, and moved to the oven, wincing at the streaked, black goop baked onto the side of the casserole dish. From the condition of the dish and its contents, the phone call had been lengthy.

Nicole found a knife in the sink and pried the lid off the pot, making a face at the burnt mess inside. "There's not much left of this."

"Well, so much for dinner," Mary said with a heavy sigh. "Isabelle, did you forget to turn the oven down after the first ten minutes?"

"I guess."

Nicole glanced around the kitchen. Potato peelings and carrot scrapings filled the sink. The counter was covered with bowls and empty plastic bags and pots. She glanced back at Mary, who was struggling to her feet as if to start making supper all over again. The poor woman looked exhausted.

Nicole tried to imagine herself in the same situation. However, living with her father, they had a housekeeper and a cook who came in three times a week. And she didn't have a son, a teenage daughter and two young boys to cook for.

She made a sudden decision. "Don't worry about supper," she said, shooting a glance at Kip's sister. "Isabelle and I will pull something together."

"What?" Isabelle exclaimed.

"Why don't we go through the refrigerator and see what we can do?" She gave Isabelle a sweet smile, as if challenging her to protest.

Isabelle simply rolled her eyes and sighed.

"Can we help too?" Tristan and Justin asked.

"Of course," Nicole exclaimed. "You guys will be our biggest helpers."

At least this way she could spend the rest of her time with the boys, Nicole thought.

She didn't want to think how Kip would react. He would just have to accept it.

Chapter Eight

What was Nicole still doing here?

Kip glanced at his watch, pushing down a beat of anger. Six-ten. She was supposed to have left over an hour ago.

He forced his frustration back as he toed off his boots on the verandah, then stepped inside the house to speak to Ms. Williams.

The first thing he noticed was the clean counters. Then an unfamiliar but savory smell.

His mother sat in a chair directing Tristan on how to set the knives by the plates on the table, which was covered with a tablecloth. He didn't even know his mother owned a tablecloth. Isabelle was washing dishes and Nicole stood beside her, wearing an apron, her hair tied back, drying a bowl. She handed the bowl to Justin who sat on the counter beside her and he put it in the cupboard.

The kitchen was a rare picture of domestic bliss, with Nicole running point.

He glanced over at Nicole just as she looked back over her shoulder. Her cheeks were flushed, her eyes bright, and she was smiling a genuine smile that gave his heart a lift.

A smile that faded when she saw him.

He shouldn't care, he thought, pushing his reaction to the back of his mind. He had too many things going to be concerned about her reaction to him. On Monday he'd picked up the stuff for the DNA test, gotten everything done just the way the instructions had told him, then ran it all back to town on Tuesday. It was easier than he thought and though he didn't have time to do all the running around, he wanted that whole business out of the way. Now he didn't have to think about it anymore.

"I thought Isabelle was making supper," he grumbled, walking over to the table. He bent over and touched his mother's shoulder lightly. "How are you feeling?"

Mary smiled up at him as well. "Much better. I got up and around a bit. Nicole helped me with my exercises."

"Making yourself indispensable?" Kip asked Nicole.

"Just trying to help," she said with a forced sweetness.

"Auntie Nicole did help," Tristan said looking up from his work. "The house was almost burning down, but then Auntie Nicole pulled the yucky casserole out of the oven—"

"And Auntie Isabelle was supposed to watch it," Justin interrupted. "She forgot because she was on the phone and then we had to help Auntie Nicole wave at the detector."

"You little tattletale," Isabelle snapped, slamming another bowl onto the drying rack.

"It's true. You were talking on the phone and Gramma couldn't sleep 'cause the detector went off," Justin said, his face growing red. "I'm not a tattletale."

"You are," Isabelle retorted.

"I'm not. You're a tattler. All you do is tattle on the phone."

"You better watch yourself, mister," Isabelle said.

"I think we're done here," Nicole said, flashing Isabelle a warning look. "Unless you want to continue an argument with a five-year-old?"

Isabelle blew out a sigh, but to Kip's surprise, said nothing more.

Nicole pulled Justin off the counter, then slowly pulled off her apron. "And I'd better be going."

Kip wasn't proud that he felt relieved. She'd made supper, brought order to the chaos that had been the kitchen, yet he was glad that she wasn't sticking around. Besides not being a friend to this family, she was starting to slip into his thoughts the times she wasn't here.

"What? No. You can't. You have to stay." His mother and the twins all spoke at once.

"Ms. Williams probably has business to get to," Kip added.

"Of course you have to stay for supper," Mary protested. "If it wasn't for you we'd be eating peanut butter sandwiches." Kip's mother turned to him, frowning. "Kip, make her stay."

Kip glanced from his mother to the boys, feeling outnumbered.

"Please stay," he said to Nicole, relenting. "I appreciate what you did for us here."

Nicole slowly folded the apron she'd been wearing. "You don't have to go through the motions for me," she said quietly.

The thought of her going back to an empty motel room bothered him.

"No. Really," he said, projecting some warmth into

his voice. "Please stay. It's the least we can do for all your help. You made dinner. You should at least stay around to eat it."

Nicole's smile shifted and she angled her head to one side as if studying him. "Thanks for that. I believe I will stay."

Five minutes later everyone was gathered around the table. Nicole sat directly across from Kip, the twins flanking her. Usually they sat beside him, but the boys had scooted over to her side when she sat down.

He felt a pang as he watched them take her hands before they prayed. She smiled down at them and the picture eased sorrow into his heart.

They would never remember their mother. Though they had grown up with his mother and his sister in their lives, it wasn't the same.

He wished again that things were different for the boys. He wished again that he could give them all the things they missed out on.

Which made him wonder when he should tell them about their mother. An opportunity hadn't come up, and he didn't want Nicole to be the one to tell them.

Just at that moment Nicole looked up at him. Their gazes met and a peculiar awareness rose up. It was as tangible as a touch, and it not only surprised him, it rocked him. He looked down, not sure where to put feelings he had neither space nor time for. Feelings for a woman whose plans had the potential to throw his life into turmoil.

Kip cleared his throat, pulling himself back to reality. "We usually pray before our meals."

He lowered his head, waited a moment while he shifted his focus. He never spent enough time in concentrated prayer. Too often his prayers were a hurried, please, please. Or an equally rushed, thank you, thank you.

But at mealtime, he had an opportunity to slow down, at least for a few moments, and make his prayer sincere.

"Thank You, Lord for our food. For the hands that prepared it." His thoughts slipped to Nicole as he hesitated. While he was thankful for what she did, he still struggled with her presence in their lives and what might happen. He pushed on, determined not to let her dominate his life right now. "Thank You for the lives You give us and the many blessings we have. Thank You for each other. Help us to be a blessing to this family. Help us to use our gifts, our time and our lives for You. Be with us this evening. Help us to trust You in every part of our life." Help me to trust that you didn't bring the boys into our lives just to take them away, he added quietly. "All this we ask in Jesus' name, Amen."

He waited a moment, then lifted his head. Justin and Tristan began talking right away, as they usually did, but Nicole was looking across the table at him again. Her forehead held the faintest of frowns. As if she was trying to figure him out.

"I hope you like quiche," Isabelle said to Kip, her voice dripping with disdain. "Because that's what Ms. Williams made us for supper."

He wasn't crazy about it, but he wasn't about to diss food that he didn't make himself.

"Looks good," Kip said, serving up his mother.

"What is this stuff?" Justin asked, poking his quiche with his fork. "It looks gross."

"Justin, you know we don't use that word when we

talk about food." Kip shot him a warning frown to underline his reprimand.

"I like it," Tristan said, taking a big mouthful. "It's really good."

"I still think it's gross." Justin leaned back in his chair, his chin resting on his chest.

"Justin, what did I say?" Kip warned. The boy had been pushing his patience the past few days. It was as if he understood on some level the tension between him and Nicole.

Justin stared back at him, then his lower lip quivered. "I don't want to eat. My stomach hurts and I miss my dad."

Kip's anger left him like air out of a balloon. "Oh, Justin," he said, his own sorrow sliding into his voice. "Come here, buddy."

Justin slipped off his chair and walked over to Kip. Kip pulled the little boy up onto his lap and held him close. "I'm sorry, buddy. I wish I could make it better," he murmured, wrapping his arms tightly around his nephew.

He looked over at Tristan, who was still eating as if he hadn't even noticed Justin's little breakdown. Kip often wondered how could two boys could look so alike and yet be so different.

Justin was all drama and noise, just like Scott could be, and Tristan was quieter and more sedate. Which made him wonder what Tricia was like.

His gaze drifted over just enough to catch Nicole watching him. Her fingers rested lightly on her lips, as if holding back the glimpse of sorrow he caught in her eyes. Then she blinked and looked away and the moment was gone.

Justin sat quiet a moment, then sniffed. "Do I still have to eat my quiche?"

Kip sighed, feeling as if he had been played by his nephew. He wasn't sure what to say, but before he could speak his mother touched Justin on the arm.

"No, you don't, honey. I'll make you something else when dinner's over."

"Mom, you shouldn't..." but then he stopped himself. He didn't have the energy to deal with this.

"If Justin doesn't have to eat his quiche, do I?" Isabelle asked hopefully.

Kip shot her an annoyed glance. She got the hint and resumed poking at her supper with her fork.

"I'm sorry," Nicole said quietly. "I thought quiche would be safe."

"It is," Kip said. "We haven't eaten it a lot." Juggling Justin on his lap he took another bite. It tasted a bit better now that he knew what to expect.

"You should try a bite, Justin," he encouraged. "It tastes really good."

Justin lifted his head and with a sigh took an offered bite. He ate it, then laid his head down on Kip's chest again. Kip didn't mind. His nephews were getting more independent every day, so he enjoyed the moments when they needed him.

"She made this out of her head," his mother told him. "I watched her."

"I like cooking," Nicole offered. "I often helped our cook make meals."

"You had a cook?" Isabelle asked. "You must be rich."

Kip had wondered himself about Nicole's financial situation. Having a personal cook definitely put her beyond his financial situation.

"We had a cook, yes, and I liked helping her."

"If I was rich I wouldn't help cook," Isabelle continued. "Of course the only way I might get rich is to move off this ranch."

"What do you want to do when you're finished high school?" Nicole asked.

Isabelle tossed her hair. "Be an actress. See the world."

"Do you take drama in school?" Nicole asked, reaching across to help Tristan with the last of his supper.

"I wish. They don't offer it in my school."

"That's too bad. It's always helpful to get a taste of what you want to do when you're young." Nicole turned her attention back to Justin. "Do you want to try some of your own supper? It tastes the same as your uncle's."

Justin lifted his head and looked across the table at Nicole, then to Kip's surprise, he slipped off Kip's lap and scooted around the table to Nicole.

Kip wished Nicole had left Justin be. Soon enough the little boy wouldn't want to sit on his uncle's lap.

"So where in Toronto do you live?" Kip's mother asked Nicole.

"My father has a home in Rosedale."

"Where's that?" Isabelle asked.

"Rich part of Toronto," Kip said. "Lots of walls and gated yards."

"Did you live all your life in Toronto area?" Mary asked, ignoring Kip's jibe.

"My parents did." Nicole's smile tightened. "I was born in Winnipeg, Manitoba."

Kip was puzzled. "So your parents moved—"

"Sam and Norah Williams are my adoptive parents," Nicole said. "I grew up…spent the first years of my life in, uh, foster homes."

"Oh, I'm sorry to hear that," Mary said, sympathy lacing her voice. "Was that difficult?"

Nicole lifted her shoulder in a delicate shrug. "I was blessed to be taken in by the Williamses when I was eight. They've been very good to me and I owe them more than I can ever repay."

Her voice faltered, and as Kip witnessed the faint break in her defenses he felt a nudge of sympathy that was both unexpected and unwelcome. He didn't want to feel sorry for her.

It was easier to deal dispassionately with her if he could see her simply as an opponent. Bad enough that she had come into his house and blurred the lines.

"I'm done," Justin announced, shoveling more food into his mouth. The little boy's stomach couldn't be that sore, Kip thought.

"Good. You're the last one," Nicole said, getting up. "Now we can do the dishes."

"If you don't mind, Nicole, we often have devotions after supper," Kip said. "The dishes might have to wait a bit."

She immediately sat down, looking a bit flustered. "Oh. I see. I'm sorry."

"Tristan, can you get me the Bible?"

Tristan was already out of his chair. The two boys took turns getting the Bible and sitting on his lap while he read, and today it was Tristan's turn.

Tristan handed him the Bible but returned to Nicole's side, which bothered Kip more than he cared to admit.

"We've been reading through Matthew," Kip said, turning to the passage. He cleared his throat, and as he read he felt Nicole's eyes on him. He had a hard time concentrating, but then he reminded himself that he was reading God's Holy Word and let the words become part of him. "Come to Me, all you who are weary and burdened, and I will give you rest. Take My yoke upon you and learn from Me, for I am gentle and humble in heart, and you will find rest for your souls. For My yoke is easy and My burden is light." Kip stopped as the words resonated in his mind. *You will find rest for your souls'.* He lowered his head and began praying. He asked that he could learn to put all his cares and concerns in God's loving hands.

When he was done, he glanced up to see Nicole staring at him, her brow holding a faint frown.

"Can we take Auntie Nicole to see the puppies again?" Justin begged.

"We'll have to do the dishes first," Nicole said.

"After the dishes." Justin turned to Kip. "Can we? Please?"

"I don't think that's a good idea," Kip said, remembering the last time she'd taken the boys to see the puppies. Though he hadn't been proud of his reaction—part of it was plain and simple fear—he still believed he was right to insist she run anything new past him first.

Nicole glanced over at him, an enigmatic look on her face. It was as if she knew exactly what he was thinking.

"I have to call Nellie back," Isabelle announced, pushing back from the table.

"Before you do that, can you help me clear the dishes?" Nicole asked, getting up.

Isabelle shot her a puzzled frown as if wondering who this woman was who was asking her favors. She sent Kip a look of appeal.

"That's okay, Nicole. I don't mind helping," his mother said.

"See? Mom can help," Isabelle said with a triumphant note in her voice and a faint sneer in Nicole's direction.

He sighed, feeling as if he was stuck between a sister who was basically lazy and a mother who enabled her. Though Kip understood why Isabelle would resent taking orders from a woman she barely knew, at the same time he was disappointed that his little sister couldn't see that their mother wasn't able to help much.

Then he caught Nicole looking at him, as if wondering what he was going to do and he stiffened his back.

"Mom, you go into the living room and watch television," he said, coming up with his own solution. "Isabelle, you can make your phone call but keep it short. I'll do the dishes."

"Can we help you and Auntie Nicole do dishes too?" Justin and Tristan asked, their eyes lighting up.

"Of course you can," Nicole said, bringing a stack of plates to the kitchen counter.

Nicole got the boys clearing the table while she walked over to the counter, pulled on her apron again and started cleaning up.

"As you can see we don't have a dishwasher." He didn't know why he was apologizing for the lack.

"No big deal." She started running water in the sink and getting the boys to find some dry dish towels.

He returned to the table and pulled off the tablecloth, not sure what to do with it. "And where did you find this?"

"Isabelle found it in your mother's bedroom," Nicole said, shooting him a quick glance over her shoulder. "I hope that was okay."

She added a gentle smile to the glance and again their

gazes tangled. She didn't turn her head away and for a moment, neither did he.

Don't be an idiot, he told himself, breaking the connection. *You're just a lonely bachelor, that's all.*

He folded up the tablecloth with jerky movements. "That a rich Toronto thing? A tablecloth on the table?" That came out a bit more harsh than he intended. Truth was she made him uncomfortable and he had to keep things impersonal.

Of course having her in his kitchen, wearing his mother's apron after making his family supper didn't exactly create an impersonal atmosphere.

"Actually it is. All the very wealthy people use tablecloths," she snapped.

He'd made her mad. Well, that was his intention, wasn't it?

With every visit and everything she did for him and for his family, she seemed to be slowly seeping into his life.

And the trouble was, part of him didn't mind. She was helpful, capable.

And attractive.

You can't afford to go there, he reminded himself. She's trouble.

He set the folded tablecloth on the worn wooden table, noticing again how old and scarred it was. He and his brother and sisters had grown up around this table, arguing and bickering over doing the dishes, doing chores and whatever else it was that siblings argued about.

Until half a year ago, his brother sat here as well.

Kip clenched his fist, willing away the memories, forcing himself to the present. He looked over his shoulder again at Nicole, who was teasing Justin and encouraging Tristan.

And this woman, standing in his kitchen, was part of the present he didn't want to deal with.

"Weeding the garden? You sure you know which ones to pull?"

Kip's voice made Nicole look up. All she saw of him was his outline silhouetted against the blue sky. He looked larger than life and, as he had the past couple of days, the sight of him lifted her heart. Being around him gave her the tiniest thrill.

It's the whole rugged-man thing that he carries off so well with his piercing gaze and smoldering looks, she thought, trying to pull back and analyze her reaction.

And let's not forget the cowboy hat.

Yet even as she tried to be casual about it, she knew there was more to his appeal than simply looks.

"I go by height," she said airily, trying to dismiss her reaction to him. "If it's tall and healthy-looking, I figure it must be a weed."

"Gramma is helping," Justin said, pointing to his grandmother, who sat on a bench at the end of the garden overseeing the operation. "She's telling us what to pull."

Nicole glanced over the mat of green tangled plants. "It's an ongoing battle," she said.

"The curse of the earth," Kip replied. "Adam had to deal with it from the beginning."

"So why are we doing this instead of you?"

Kip laughed, then reached over and yanked out a large-leafed plant. Pigweed, Mary had told her. "Because I'm tilling the ground on a different scale."

"At least you get to use a tractor."

"Air-conditioned too," he added, pointing to a bead of sweat working its way down her temple.

She hurriedly wiped it away, suddenly self-conscious. Usually when she was talking to men she wore a suit, her hair was pinned back and she had an attitude. Usually she was in charge. Not on her knees with dirt under her nails and probably smears on her face.

In spite of that, she knew she felt more comfortable than she'd had around any man she'd met in a while.

It was a distraction she couldn't afford. She had her own plans, the culmination of which would mean her leaving with the boys he claimed were Cosgroves. That leaving would effectively kill any hint of attraction she sensed growing between them.

And why did that bother her?

"Have you ever done any gardening before?" Kip asked.

"The closest my mother came to having a garden was when I brought home a bean plant in grade six."

"In a foam cup too, I'm sure."

Nicole laughed. "You too?"

"I think it's a classic." He pulled another weed and tossed it aside. "So you know what a bean plant looks like."

"I don't know if I can think back that far." She moved forward a bit more and reached for another weed just as he did. Their hands brushed each other and she jerked hers back.

And now you're acting like you're back in grade six again.

He sat back on his heels. "I have a couple of favors to ask," he said. "Tomorrow I promised a buddy that I would go help him do some welding, so would you mind watching the boys?"

"So you won't be around?" she said. This would be a treat for her, not having him around.

"Nope. Sorry. I know you'll miss me like crazy, but a guy's gotta do what a guy's gotta do."

Nicole couldn't help a chuckle at that. "Noble of you. But no, I don't mind." It was on the tip of her tongue to ask him if she could take them to town, but she thought she could save that for another time.

He pulled out another weed, then pushed himself to his feet and walked over to his mother.

"Good to see you out here," she heard Kip say to his mother, walking over to her side. "How are you feeling?"

"A lot better. Nicole convinced me that I'd feel better if I went outside and she was right."

"That's great," Kip said. "I better get back to work. Didn't get as much done yesterday as I hoped."

"You got the fence fixed and went out on Duke," Mary said. "You haven't had a chance to go riding in months."

"Nope. I haven't. Duke was a bit out of shape."

Nicole heard the longing in his voice. She wasn't surprised. This morning Mary had told her that Kip used to practically live with the horses before Scott died.

Then she had given Nicole a bright smile. "Thanks to you taking care of the boys, he's able to go now," she had said. Then Mary had launched into further stories from the past. How Kip, an A-plus scholar, had dropped out of school when his father died so he could take care of the ranch and his mother and Isabelle.

Nicole had heard about all the work Kip took on when Scott left and how Scott had returned to the ranch with the two boys, which only made more work for him. How Kip provided for them all and how he worried about the financial well-being of the ranch.

Mary showed Nicole pictures of Kip, but the one that stood out the most was a picture that had been taken when he won at the Ponoka stampede. The photographer caught him standing on the chuck wagon, leaning forward, reins threaded through his hands as he urged his horses on.

She saw, through the pictures and Mary's stories, a side of Kip that she wasn't sure she wanted to get to know. It was a side of him that created a mixture of sadness and admiration for the sacrifices he had made for his family and for the boys.

Nicole knew she was in danger of seeing Kip as human. Caring. Compassionate.

Trouble.

"Do you think you'll have a chance to enter a team in any of the races?" she heard Mary asking Kip.

"Those times are over, Mom," Kip said with a note of finality that made Nicole think back to the pictures.

She stopped her thoughts, but even as she did, she chanced another look up. Kip was looking directly at her.

She couldn't decipher his expression and wasn't sure she wanted to spend much time trying to figure him out.

She dragged her attention back to the gardening. She had to make another phone call to her father's lawyer. Surely something had to have happened by now.

She didn't want to stay here any longer than she had to.

Chapter Nine

"How are things between you and the cowboy?" Heather asked.

Nicole tucked the phone under her ear and sat down at the minuscule table that passed for a desk in her motel room. "And a good morning to you too," Nicole said to her assistant.

"Sorry. Good morning back. I've been hanging around your dad too long," Heather said with a laugh. "I tend to get straight to the point."

"May as well, there's a lot to do. As for the cowboy, we've agreed to disagree," was all she said, preferring not to talk about Kip.

Yesterday he had been at his friend's place doing some welding, and today he'd been busy with the horses, which meant he wanted Justin and Tristan out of the way.

She had been only too happy to oblige. Being around Kip confused her and frustrated her.

"Your father's been putting major pressure on me to pressure you to find out what's happening with the boys," Heather said.

"I don't have anything to report." Last week this would

have frustrated Nicole, but part of her didn't mind the time she spent with the boys without her father around.

"This cowboy of yours. Will he give up the boys or will it get down to a battle?"

"He's not my cowboy, and even though we've come to a bit of a truce now, when push comes to shove it will be a fight." Nicole rubbed her forehead, not sure she wanted to imagine her and Kip in that situation. "He's attached to the boys and they're attached to him."

"Of course they would be. They spent most of their life with him. No thanks to his brother taking the boys away."

Nicole felt the same way, yet each day she was at the ranch gave her more insight into Kip's life, gave her a bit more knowledge of him as a person.

Made her more attracted to him.

"By the way, I stopped in at your place. Did you know your dad is fixing up Tricia's old room for the boys?"

A shiver danced down Nicole's spine. Tricia's room hadn't been touched or changed since she left all those years ago. It was left like a shrine, as if waiting for her return.

"I suppose that's a good sign. It means he's moving on." At the same time it created an extra layer of pressure that Nicole couldn't deal with yet.

"I may as well warn you, your father is doing more than fixing up the room. He's got me checking out private-detective agencies."

"That seems a bit extreme."

"Nothing else is happening. Your dad's lawyer seems to be stalling out and your dad's getting antsy." Heather sighed, and Nicole was fairly sure her assistant was on the receiving end of some of her father's frustration.

"Change of subject," Nicole said abruptly. "I'm still

waiting for a quote from the caterer, and the venue's been making noises about an increase in costs. I'm looking into a few alternatives just to keep them on their toes."

"You do realize that I'm perfectly capable of doing that," Heather reprimanded.

"I've got to do something while I'm waiting for visits."

"I'll call the lawyer again and put more pressure on him, and you should stop worrying about the fund-raiser. I do have some experience with this."

Nicole knew that, but the fund-raiser was a major source of income and prestige for the foundation. And the foundation was her father's passion, the only way he could keep the memory of his beloved wife alive. Nicole's work for the foundation was one of the ways she had found she could maintain a connection to her father.

"You just develop some kind of relationship with those boys," Heather said, "so it's not such a shock to them when they come here. I'll take care of what I can over here."

Nicole was reassured by the authority in Heather's voice. Not *if* the boys come back, *when* they come back.

Nicole said goodbye, then got up and walked over to the window. From here, all she could see was the parking lot of the hardware store beside the motel. If she stepped outside, she could see the sun setting behind the mountains beyond the town, and for the faintest moment she felt a longing to go back to the farm that had nothing to do with the boys.

But she couldn't. Things were shifting between her and Kip. Her loyalties were getting strained. She had to get back in control of the situation. Starting now.

She picked up the phone and dialed.

Kip answered on the first ring and she plunged in.

"I'd like to take the boys to the Calgary Stampede tomorrow," she said.

Silence followed her request. She chafed at the pause, feeling like she was a minion begging for favors. The boys were as much hers as Kip's. Even though Tricia was her adopted sister, she was still her sister.

"What time would you be coming for them?" he asked.

Nicole was taken aback. She thought he would fight her on this. "I was hoping to pick them up at eleven and spend the day at the Stampede, then take them on the midway."

"That's more than the usual time," he said.

"I think I'm due a bit more than the 'usual time,'" she replied with some asperity, trying to create some distance.

"I suppose you are. What time did you figure on being back?"

"I hope to be back by nine o'clock in the evening. Of course that would depend on traffic and anything else out of my control." She didn't mean to sound snappy. She didn't like feeling like a potential date being grilled by a suspicious parent.

This netted her another thoughtful pause on his end. She heard his muffled conversation. What could he possibly have to think about or consult his family about? It was a simple yes or no answer.

"Okay. That might work," he said when he came back to the phone. "I'll see you tomorrow."

Nicole heard a click in her ear and then she stared at the phone. *Well. I guess that was that.* Tomorrow she was taking the boys out. All by herself. She smiled at the thought, but behind that came the tiniest touch of regret.

It would have been kind of fun if Kip came along.

She pushed that thought aside. She had been thinking about him too much lately. Time to focus on what lay ahead.

Bringing the boys back.

Saturday morning dawned with a spill of bright sunshine and a clear blue sky. Nicole smiled as she drove to the ranch, thinking of her day alone with Justin and Tristan. She was looking forward to a break from the tension of constantly being around Kip and his family. She needed to feel like the boys were hers. Needed to spend some time one-on-one with them.

When she pulled into the ranch yard, the familiar sight of the house nestled against the tree-covered hills rolling upward to the mountains created anticipation.

She was going to see the boys, her boys, again.

As always a small part of her held back committing all her emotions. People left, she knew.

When she stepped out of the car and the boys came barreling down the stairs toward her, however, she ignored her innate wariness, bent over and pulled them into her arms and into her heart.

They smelled like hay. "Have you been helping your Uncle Kip haul hay again?" she asked, pulling back.

"We were playing on the bales," Justin reported. "Uncle Kip had to do some welding so he didn't want us around."

"That's good thinking." Nicole pulled out a handkerchief and wiped a smear of jam from the corner of Justin's mouth. "Looks like you had lunch already," she said with a touch of disappointment. She had hoped to get them something to eat at the Stampede.

"Just enough to take the edge off," Tristan said. "At least that's what Gramma told me."

"Great. Now you boys stay here inside my car and don't move an inch. I want to say hi to your gramma, and when I come back we're going."

She buckled the boys in, then fairly flew up the stairs. She was going to have so much fun. She was going to spoil these boys absolutely rotten.

Then, just as she stepped onto the verandah, the door opened and Kip stood before her. He wore a clean shirt that she remembered Mary folding the first day she had come. The day they thought she was the housekeeper.

His blue jeans were crisply new and he had shaved, making him look less gruff and more approachable. His hair, still damp from a shower, curled over his forehead and around his ears. He looked even more appealing than he usually did.

Nicole pushed down her reaction and forced herself not to take a step back. "I want to say hello to your mother," she said, hating the breathless tone in her voice. "I'll just be a minute, then I'll be leaving." She ducked around him, catching a whiff of laundry soap and aftershave. She wondered where he was headed. A date? But he was always talking about how busy he was.

Why do you care?

Nicole pushed open the door of the porch and stepped into the house.

Mary Cosgrove stood by the sink, leaning on her walker with one arm, doing dishes with her free hand. It looked awkward and uncomfortable and Nicole had to resist the urge to help her. But she was glad to see her up and about.

"Hey, Mary. I've come to say hello," Nicole said.

Mary glanced up and a welcoming smile. "Well, that's kind of you. As you can see, I'm using my walker."

"That's great." Nicole frowned as Mary washed another plate one-handed. "Where's Isabelle?"

"She's in the bathroom."

Tricia used to do that, Nicole thought. Her little sister could make a bathroom break stretch out long enough to miss loading the dishwasher and cleaning up the kitchen. Her mother always let her get away with it.

"She can easily help you," Nicole said, regretting the sharp tone her voice took.

"I know," Mary said with a gentle sigh. "It's less work to do the dishes myself than it is to make her help me."

"Kip should be helping you out."

Mary frowned. "Kip doesn't have to do the dishes. He works hard enough on the ranch."

"I meant with Isabelle," Nicole replied.

Mary shrugged. "I don't think he always knows what to do with her either."

Nicole bit back another reply, realizing that all this badgering and pushing was none of her business.

"Well, I'm leaving with the boys. You take care," Nicole said quietly. Then she left before she could offer more of her unneeded advice. The Cosgroves' problems weren't hers, she reminded herself as she closed the door of the house behind her.

The unmistakable growl of Kip's truck resonated through the quiet. Guess he was off on his date now that he didn't have to watch the twins.

She squinted against the sun then lifted her hand to shade her eyes as she looked at her car. Empty.

"Justin. Tristan. Where are you?" she called, walking

toward her car, her gaze flickering over the yard. She was so sure she had told them to stay put.

Then she heard the honk of a horn and saw Justin leaning out the back window of Kip's truck, waving at her.

What in the world was going on? And where did Kip Cosgrove think he was going with the boys?

She marched over to the driver's window and as she did, Kip rolled it down.

"I thought it would be better if we took my truck. There's more room for all of us than in that car you're driving."

"What…how…" she sputtered, trying to comprehend what he was saying.

"I'm coming along," he announced pushing his cowboy hat back on his head.

Anger washed over her. She didn't want to share her time with the boys. Especially not with him.

"C'mon, Auntie Nicole. Let's go," Tristan said, leaning out of the back window. "We don't want to miss anything."

She felt suddenly impotent, unable to speak openly in front of the boys, her own feelings a tangle of mixed emotions. She grabbed onto her anger, suspecting she would need it as a defense. "I understood the boys and I were going alone…"

Kip shrugged. "You understood wrong. Are you coming? It's a long drive. Don't want to waste any time." His steady gaze held hers and she read resolute determination.

Nicole tried to hold her ground as various emotions danced through her head. Anger, yes, but behind that a vague hungering for a chance to spend more time with this man.

She truncated that thought. She and Kip could never be anything but adversaries.

"I'll get my purse."

Ten minutes later the truck's tires hummed on the asphalt, a country song whined from the radio and the boys narrated the trip from the backseat.

"Mr. and Mrs. Ogilvie live there," Justin said. "Last year when Isabelle took us out trick-or-treating, we got four chocolate bars from them. They were yummy. But Mr. Jorritsma always has the best candy and he brings honey to the farmers' market."

They told her about trips to see friends, play dates with cousins and how cute Auntie Doreen's brand-new baby was.

The plus of all that chatter was that Nicole didn't have to say anything to Kip.

So she formed her lips into a smile and nodded, listening to the boys, all the while pretending not to be fully aware of the tall figure sitting behind the wheel. He steered one-handed, the other resting on the open window as he drove, looking as comfortable as if he were lounging on a couch watching television.

She wished she felt as comfortable. She had hoped to avoid him today, but they sat mere feet from each other, and with each mile her anger seemed more foolish. He was here. He wasn't going away. May as well enjoy her time with the boys.

"So what did you boys do this morning?" she asked, half turning in the seat so she could focus on them.

"Uncle Kip got up real, real early," Justin said.

"He said he wanted to get done on time 'cause he had a hot date." Tristan frowned. "What's a hot date?"

She couldn't stop a quick glance Kip's way. He was

rolling his eyes and a flush warmed her cheeks. She wasn't sure she wanted to know exactly what Kip meant by that. Sarcasm, most likely.

"I think it means that the day was going to be warm," Nicole said, letting him off the hook.

"And he was whistling, even though he had to get up early and work on the stupid welder," Tristan added.

"You don't need to say that," Kip said with a note of reprimand.

"That's what you called it."

"I shouldn't have, okay?"

"Radioactive hearing," Nicole murmured, shooting Kip a quick glance.

He shrugged. "I've got to learn to keep my big mouth shut."

She suspected he was referring to his previous comment but wasn't sure she wanted to analyze that too much.

"Have you been to Stampede?" Justin asked, unbuckling his seatbelt.

"No. I've never been, and what do you think you're doing?"

"Justin, get back in your seat and buckle up," Kip said at exactly the same time.

We sound like parents, Nicole thought, forcing herself to keep looking at her nephew.

Justin glanced from Nicole to Kip as if trying to figure this arrangement out.

"Justin—"

"Now—"

"Okay, okay. You both don't have to be so bossy."

Nicole was about to reprimand him again, but held back in case Kip had the same idea. At least when it came to the boys' safety, they agreed.

"I'm bored," Justin grumbled after he buckled up.

"Then let's play a driving game. We can play I Spy."

"How do you play that?" Tristan asked.

Nicole explained the rules and soon they were guessing all kinds of things from the feather in the hatband of Uncle Kip's cowboy hat to the pattern stitched into their little cowboy boots to the color of Nicole's eyes.

"I think they're blue," Tristan said, leaning forward as if to get a better look.

"Nuh-uh. Gray," Justin announced.

"What color are they, Auntie Nicole?" Tristan asked.

"I don't know. One of my foster mothers said they were the color of dishwater," Nicole said with a light laugh. She didn't really want to talk about her eyes. Not with Kip sitting next to her, smiling and glancing at her from time to time as if trying to decide for himself on their color.

"What's a foster mother?" Justin asked.

Trust him not to miss the slightest slip of the tongue, Nicole thought.

"A foster mother is someone who takes care of children when they can't live at their own place," Nicole said with a smile. "Now it's my turn. I spy with my little eye—"

"You said you had foster mothers," Justin interrupted. "How many did you have?"

"Doesn't matter how many—"

"How could you have more than one? Didn't you have your own mother?"

"My mother died when I was very little," Nicole said. "So I went to live with another family—"

"Didn't your dad take care of you?" Tristan asked.

"My father…was a busy man. He was gone a lot."

"Did your dad miss you when he was gone?" Justin asked.

Nicole wasn't sure how to answer that question. She often wondered herself. Her father never seemed excessively eager to return to her, and when he did come it was usually a brief appearance, then he was gone again.

"I hope he did," she said quietly.

"Where did you live when he was gone?" Justin asked.

"I lived with my auntie for a while."

"Was she a foster mom?"

Nicole wished they would get off this topic already so she simply said yes.

"But you had lots of foster moms."

They weren't going to quit. She sighed and knew she had to give them the entire rundown.

"I lived with my auntie for a while, and when my dad died and she couldn't take care of me anymore she put me in a foster home. When they couldn't take care of me anymore, they put me in another one. Then I got adopted by the Williams family. So that's my story. Now why don't you tell me yours?" she said. Though she knew it well, she wanted to stop talking about her past. It was over and done with, thanks to Sam and Norah Williams.

Besides, she didn't like the way Kip was looking at her. The faint frown on his face as if he was trying to figure out what to think of her now that he knew more about her past.

"Our dad died too," Justin said. "But he took care of us all the time and so did Uncle Kip."

"You had lots of mothers and had lots of fathers but we have a mommy and we don't know where she is," Tristan said, a gentle sadness entering his voice.

Nicole didn't want to look at Kip, knowing they were

both thinking about Tricia and when they should tell the boys, but at the same time, like a magnetic force, their eyes met. In his gaze she saw concern and, at the same time, an indefinable emotion that called to her loneliness.

She tore her gaze away as she struggled to be analytical about the situation. He was a single, attractive man. She was a single woman. They were spending a lot of time together. So something was bound to happen.

"Uncle Kip used to race chuck wagons, but he doesn't anymore. He gots trophies. Lots of trophies."

"Can we watch the chuck-wagon races tonight, Uncle Kip?" Justin asked, suddenly excited.

Kip shrugged and shot another glance at Nicole. "I don't know if Nicole is interested."

"I've never seen a chuck-wagon race," she said. "It sounds very exciting."

"We'll see." Then Kip straightened, his attention focused on his driving as they entered Calgary. The traffic got busier and he turned off the radio, and soon they were hemmed in by vehicles all racing toward the next traffic light. They made their way slowly up the McLeod Trail. Though Nicole travelled in traffic when she lived in Toronto, she found the sudden busyness disconcerting and, surprisingly, annoying.

Funny how used she had gotten to driving quiet roads from the motel to the ranch and how much she enjoyed it. Well, she'd have to get used to traffic soon enough when she and the boys moved back to Toronto.

After numerous intersections and hundreds of vehicles, Kip pulled off into a huge parking lot and drove around until he finally found an empty spot big enough for the truck.

Nicole got out before he even had the truck turned

off and was opening the back door to let the boys out. Tristan was already unbuckled and he jumped into her outstretched arms. Justin, however, went to Kip.

As Nicole walked around the truck she heard the squeal of people, the pounding music from some of the rides and the general hubbub emitted by fairgrounds the world over. She felt a peculiar sense of anticipation. She'd been to a fair only once in her life.

"Before we go any farther, I have to say something to you boys." Kip caught the boys by the hand and knelt down so that he was face to face with them. "We're going to a very busy place. You have to remember to stay close. You're not to run off. You have to be holding either Nicole's or my hand. Do you understand?"

They both nodded.

"Do you both understand?" he repeated again.

"Yes. We do," they both said again.

"Okay, then, as long as that's clear, let's go."

Tristan grabbed Nicole's hand, Justin caught Kip's and then the boys held each others, anchoring the adults.

Just like a family.

Nicole wanted to push the thought aside, but at the same time, she was tired of juggling her feelings. Trying to ignore her attraction to Kip and her appreciation of who he was.

This was supposed to be a fun time, and she intended to enjoy herself. This was like a little holiday. She wasn't thinking past today. She was with a good-looking man and she was free from responsibilities for the day.

Why not simply enjoy it?

Chapter Ten

It had been years since he'd been to Stampede. Everywhere Kip looked he saw cowboy hats, blue jeans and cowboy boots. Most were the brand-new hats of the once-a-year cowboys, but a lot were well-worn. The tinny sounds of carousels and blaring music from busy rides mingled with the oily scent of funnel cakes and hot dogs.

Though he'd crawled out of bed at some ridiculous hour so he could get done with the farm work on time, it was worth every minute of lack of sleep to see the looks of wonder on the boys' faces as they stood in the center of this milling crowd.

He glanced over at Nicole, who was glancing around with a bemused look on her face. He thought of her comments in the truck and wondered how many fairs she'd been to in her life. He doubted very many.

Though she'd spoken quietly and unemotionally about her past, Kip had sensed a hidden pain and sorrow that made him see her through different eyes. Her life hadn't been so privileged after all.

"So where do we start?" Nicole asked.

"For now we just wander around, and take it all in."

"We should buy Auntie Nicole a cowboy hat," Tristan said.

"I don't know if Auntie Nicole can pull off a cowboy hat." Kip glanced at Nicole's distressed blue jeans and silk shirt.

"I chased cows the other day," Nicole protested. "I think I'm a good candidate for a cowboy hat."

"I don't know if that's enough of a qualification," he said, responding to her humor.

"I also know how to ride a horse," she said with another grin as she stepped aside to avoid a man pushing a baby buggy.

"And you probably ride English," Kip said, giving Tristan's hand a bit of a tug, reminding him to stay close.

"It's not as easy as it looks," she replied.

"Auntie Nicole should ride the horses at the ranch," Tristan said, jumping with excitement. "Then we can too."

Kip shook his head. "I don't think so, buddy."

Nicole shot him a puzzled glance, and though he wasn't about to elaborate, he got the feeling that sometime or another she would ask him more about it.

They wandered through the crowds and past rides, working their way to the events' barns. They turned a corner and came upon a group of people in a circle cheering on three children riding pedal tractors racing each other to a finish line.

When Justin saw this he tried to break free of Kip's hand. "Can we race? Please?"

Kip frowned as he looked over the crowd.

"I'm here too, you know," Nicole said.

"What do you mean?"

"I can watch the boys too." She added a crooked smile which made him wonder if she was teasing him just a bit.

He couldn't help but smile back. A relaxed Nicole was, he had to admit, fun to be around. "Okay. I guess it'll be fine."

"Goody." Justin grabbed Tristan's hand.

Kip let them go to stand in line while he and Nicole moved in closer. People walked around them and gathered ahead of them, yet Kip felt so aware of Nicole it was as if no one else existed.

"So tell me a bit about your chuck-wagon racing. Do you miss it?" Though her question was quiet, he sensed her sympathy.

"Yeah. I do." He let his mind slip back, pulling up memories and he smiled.

"What do you miss the most?"

"I don't know," he said, shrugging her question aside.

"You must miss something," she pressed.

Kip shot her a puzzled look. "Why does it matter?"

Nicole held his gaze for a moment, then looked away. "Because I'm guessing you gave it up for the boys, and…I think that's admirable and, well, I'd just like to know."

"Okay. Let's see." He scratched the side of his nose with his forefinger, trying to formulate his answer. No one had ever asked him what he missed, so he had to think a bit.

"I guess I miss the challenge and the thrill. The sound of the horn and then trying to jockey for first place after running the figure eight. The feel of those hooves thundering on the packed dirt and how you sense every shift of the horse in the reins, trying to read them and keep them working as a team." He stopped, feeling a touch of embarrassment at his enthusiasm. "That's in the past now."

"Still, it must have been hard to give up dreams," Nicole said quietly.

"Yeah. It was," he admitted. "Hanging around on the circuit gets expensive, and I need to think about the boys' financial future."

"I take it Scott had no life insurance?"

"Or a will." Something Nicole and her father did have granting them custody of the boys. Tricia may have been irresponsible in some areas but not in that one.

"I'm surprised Scott didn't ask your married sister to take Justin and Tristan," she said quietly.

"Scott wanted the boys on the ranch, and my sister was expecting a baby. I was too attached to them to let the twins go anywhere else." He gave her a careful smile, surprised to feel his reaction to the softening of her features. A wayward breeze tossed her hair, and a strand got caught in her lip gloss.

Before he could stop himself, he reached over and loosened her hair, his fingers lingering on her cheek.

His heart gave a little thrum and he wondered, just for a moment—

"We're going to race now," Tristan shouted out.

Kip dragged his way emotions back to reality. This was crazy. He had to keep his focus on the boys.

The boys she was planning to take away.

Nicole followed Kip down the concrete stairs of the arena to their seats, clinging to Tristan's hand. The excited voices of people echoed in the yawning space.

This was supposed to have been a time alone with her

and the boys, she thought, trying to work up her resent-
ment. Kip wasn't supposed to be along.

The trouble was, the more time she spent with Kip,
the more confused she grew. The more attracted she became to him.

Which definitely complicated her life. The purpose
that had brought her here grew foggier with each day that
she saw the boys with Kip and his family on the ranch.

This was the only life the boys had known. Could she
really take them away from that?

She closed her eyes willing her mind to stop its cease-
less whirling and circling back. She was here with an attractive man experiencing something she could talk to
her friends back home about once it was all over.

A date. Something she hadn't gone on for a while. So
just enjoy it, she told herself.

"We're up in the nosebleed area, but we'll be able to
see the whole track this way too," Kip said as they followed him to their seats. Below them lay a large open
area surrounded by other bleachers and ringed by a racing track.

"I sit with Uncle Kip and Tristan sits with Auntie Nicole," Justin announced.

Auntie Nicole would have preferred to keep the boys
between her and Kip, but the boys were already in their
seats, leaving two open between them.

Just go with it, Nicole thought. Stop overthinking.

"So how does this race work?" she asked, determined
to be casual about the situation.

"You see this space below us where the barrels are laid
out?" Kip swept his hand over the large open area ringed
by other, smaller bleachers. "That's where the first part of
the race is. There's eight barrels, two for each team. The

teams line up at a designated spot marked with chalk in the dirt, do a figure eight around each barrel in the open space, and then they have to head around the half mile track and come back to the finish line right below us."

"Looks complicated," Nicole said, trying to imagine what would happen.

"Then there's the four outriders," Kip added.

"What do they do?"

"They have to stay with the chuck wagons," Tristan said, clutching the teddy bear Kip had won for him in a shooting gallery.

"Each chuck wagon is assigned four outriders," Kip continued. "When the horn goes, they have to throw a stove and a couple of sticks into the back of the wagon, mount up and follow the chuck wagons through the pattern." Kip grew animated as he spoke, and he was grinning, leaning forward in his seat as if he could hardly wait for the races to start. "If they're too far behind their chuck wagon when he crosses the finish line, the team gets a penalty. Those outriders really give 'er to keep up."

Nicole was struggling as well to keep up, but she simply smiled and nodded, surprised at the excitement in Kip's voice.

"Here they come," he said, pointing to the track. Four teams of horses pulling what looked like a small covered wagon with wooden wheels came trotting down the track toward the place where other men were putting up the barrels.

"What's on the covers of the wagons?" Nicole asked.

"Sponsors' names. Costs a lot to keep a team of horses and a wagon racing in the circuit. Especially to get to the Stampede. Technically the chuck-wagon races are called the Rangeland Derby, but it's always part of Stampede."

Kip clasped and unclasped his hands, his eyes tracking the movement of the chuck wagons. "Nick is here. Awesome." Kip shot her a quick grin. "Every time we competed he said he would quit, but he didn't and now he's here." He laughed, turning his attention back to the teams. "And Pete Nellisher. Huh. I never thought his team had it in them to get this far." The hunger in his voice was reflected in the expression on his face as he leaned forward.

He misses this more than he lets on, Nicole realized.

She remembered the smile of contentment on his face when he had come back from fixing the fences the day the cows got out.

He'd given up a lot to take care of the boys. She thought of the parked wagons and the dozens of horses the boys were supposed to stay away from. Kip made sacrifices that never came up in any conversation they'd ever had. From the way the boys talked, she knew they had no inkling of what he relinquished so he could be there for them. Kip could have easily left them with his mother every weekend. Could easily have carried on racing.

But he didn't. He gave all this up for the boys.

"See, each team has their starting position marked out," Kip said, leaning closer to her as he pointed to the teams moving into position. "This is one of the trickiest parts. See how antsy those horses are? They know what they have to do, but you have to make sure you get them to the starting position at exactly the right time. You get too close and they jump the horn. Too far and you lose valuable real estate." Kip's voice grew more intense, his full attention, like a laser, on the action below. He leaned closer to her, laying one hand on her shoulder, pointing with his other hand. "See how hard the guy at the head of the team has to work to keep the team back? The driver can't pull up too hard or the horses won't be ready."

A horn blared, Nicole jumped and Kip's hand dropped from her shoulder. He jerked forward as if the sound itself triggered an automatic reaction.

The outriders let go of the lead horses and jumped on their own, and soon the area around the barrels was a confusion of wagons and horses as four teams wove a figure eight.

"C'mon, Nick, not too tight. Ease up. Ease up." Kip bit his lip, watching. "Yeah. Like that. Like that." He nodded his approval of his friend's work, inching to the edge of his seat. "See, Nicole, he's got to lean way over the side of the wagon to help the wagon move sideways. You've got to get into that inside lane right off the mark." He clasped his hands, nodding his approval of his friend's tactics. "Now lean left. Get those horses over to the inside. Lean. Lean," he yelled as his friend did exactly what Kip urged him to do. "Like that." He turned to Nicole, catching her hand in his. "He's doing it, he got the lead."

Nicole's attention was torn between the race and Kip's undivided attention to what was going on. He was more animated and alive than she'd ever seen him.

And his hand still clutched hers.

Then, when the racing wagons thundered around the last bend, outriders trailing behind the wagons, madly trying to keep up to their wagon, Kip jumped to his feet. "C'mon, Nick. C'mon."

Nick was standing up, leaning way ahead, urging the team on. He shot a glance over his shoulder as if to check where his outriders were, then he gave the horses another slap with the reins and they sailed across the finish line.

Kip hollered, waving his hat. "Yeah. Nick. Way to go."

Then Kip turned to her, grabbed her and gave her a bear hug, lifting her off the ground. "He won. Nick won." He pulled back, grinning and to her surprise and shock, planted a kiss on her mouth.

When he drew back, the astonishment Nicole felt was mirrored on Kip's face. For a moment they stared at each other, as if unsure of how to react or what to think.

Kip blew out his breath, then bent over to pick up his hat. "I'm…I'm sorry," he muttered. "I got carried away."

Nicole wished she could make a casual joke, but she was still trying to catch her breath. Trying to reorient herself.

Kip's kiss was unexpected but, to her surprise, not unwelcome.

"I was excited for your friend too." She drew in a quick breath, willing her heart to stop pounding.

"Did you give Auntie Nicole a kiss?" Tristan asked, his voice holding a teasing note.

"Shame, shame, double shame, now I know your girl-friend's name," Justin chanted in the sing-songy voice of the schoolyard.

Nicole ignored them as she sat down, her cheeks flushed and her heart beating erratically against her ribs.

It was the excitement of the moment, she reminded herself as the competitors trotted away, passing the next set of teams heading toward the starting position. The kiss was spontaneous and spur-of-the-moment…

And nothing like she'd ever experienced before.

Nicole folded her trembling hands together. She kept her eyes on the horses, but for the rest of the races, her attention was distracted by the man beside her.

Chapter Eleven

That wasn't the dumbest thing he'd ever done, but it ranked right up there, Kip thought as he sat down. What had come over him, grabbing Nicole's hand like that? Kissing her like that?

It was the excitement of seeing his friend compete. Seeing him grab the lead, then win. That was all.

As awkwardness fell between him and Nicole. Kip knew his feelings and awareness of her were tied in with other factors. Her love for the boys even though she had just met them. The way she helped his mother, the way she handled herself with Isabelle.

Family was important to her. She was willing to do whatever it took to make her adoptive father happy and to bring her sister's boys back. Though this put her in opposition to him, her affection for the twins showed him a side of her that he respected and appreciated.

Justin poked Kip in the side. "Does kissing Auntie Nicole mean you love her?"

It means I'm an idiot, Kip thought.

"I was just excited to see Nick win," Kip said, shooting

his nephew a warning glance. The teenager sitting beside Justin gave Kip a smirk as if he didn't believe him either.

"Why are you frowning?" Tristan asked. "Kissing should make you smile."

It made him confused.

"Kiss her again. Kiss her again." Justin slapped his knees in time to his chanting.

Kip wasn't even going to look his way because that meant looking at Nicole.

"Look, the next group is getting to run. Why don't we watch them? After all, that's what I bought the tickets for." He clasped his hands together, leaning forward and away from Nicole. He tried to focus on the riders, but he could smell her perfume, hear her talking quietly to Tristan. In his peripheral vision he saw her tuck her hair behind her ears, pull her jacket closer against the gathering chill of the evening.

Then the horn blew and he was drawn into the race.

They watched the races until the sun went down. When the last wagon crossed the finish line followed by the last of the outriders, Kip stood up. "Let's try to beat the crowd out of here," he said, wishing he felt as casual as he hoped he sounded.

Nicole got up and caught Tristan by the hand. Without a backward glance, she headed toward the exit.

"We didn't have a ride on the Ferris wheel like you promised," Justin said, trotting alongside him.

"I never promised you a ride," Kip contradicted him.

Tristan looked back, leaning past Nicole. "Yes, you did. You said that when we go to Stampede you would take us on the Ferris wheel."

He might have. He couldn't remember. But it was getting late, and he wanted to get back to the ranch and away from Nicole. She was spinning him around in circles.

His messy life had no space for a woman. Especially not a woman like Nicole who was leaving, and leaving with his boys, if she had her way.

"We need to get back to the ranch," he said firmly.

"But you promised," Tristan wailed.

"If Uncle Kip says we have to go back then that's what we have to do," Nicole said quietly, backing him up.

He wasn't surprised that she did. She probably didn't want a repeat performance of that kiss.

Thankfully, there was no more opportunity for conversation as they made their way down the noisy concrete stairwell to ground level.

When they stepped outside, the cool evening air had eased away the heat of the day. In the gathering dusk, the lights of the rides sparkled and beckoned in time to the raucous beat of rock music. People were laughing, screaming, having fun.

He paused by the midway, unable to ignore the longing look on his nephews' faces.

Justin, ever looking for the tiniest chink in his uncle's armor, homed in on Kip's hesitation. "Please Uncle Kip. We've never been on a Ferris wheel. Never."

Tristan added his pleas to his brother's. "Our dad always said he would take us and now he can't."

Kip sighed. They were really pulling out the heavy artillery by bringing up Scott. He couldn't help a glance Nicole's way, as if to get her take on the situation.

She gave him a quick smile. "If you don't mind, I don't mind. I'm not in any rush to bring the boys back."

Of course she wouldn't be. When they got to the ranch she knew that would be the end of her visit with the boys.

"We can take another walk along the midway," Kip said.

"And we can find the Ferris wheel?" Justin asked.

Like a terrier with a toy, just like Scott used to be. "We'll just walk for now," he said.

The mixture of smells made him realize they hadn't had anything to eat since the hot dog when they first arrived. "Anyone for something to eat?"

"Can I have a pretzel?" Justin asked in a fakely innocent voice.

Kip shot him a warning look. Did the little guy know the only pretzel stand was clear across the fairgrounds?

"How about a piece of pizza?" Nicole suggested.

"Mini donuts," Tristan shouted, pulling away from Nicole. Kip was about to call him back when Nicole managed to grab his hand and pull him back.

"We stay together," she said sternly. "Don't take off like that again."

Tristan looked down, suitably chastened.

"I'd love some mini donuts," Kip said. "Nicole? You game?"

"Yeah. I'm game. I don't think I've ever had mini donuts."

"And the Ferris wheel?" Justin pressed. "Have you ever been on the Ferris wheel?"

"Actually, no," Nicole said.

"You've never been on a Ferris wheel? Don't they have fairs in Toronto?" Kip asked.

"I've never been on one. I'd like to try a ride."

"Yay. You're the best, Auntie Nicole," Justin shouted.

Kip shot her a frown and she gave him a look of mock consternation. "What? I've never been on a Ferris wheel."

"Never?"

"No. Never."

That seemed odd to him. "I guess I'm outnumbered," he said with a sigh of resignation.

"Obviously good at math too," she said with a flash of a smile.

"Never been my strong point. I did drop out of high school, after all." Kip wasn't sure where this playful Nicole was coming from, but he was willing to go along.

Kip ordered a bag of donuts, paid for them and handed them out. Nicole took one and then glanced up at him. "I think that was a very admirable thing to do."

"Buy donuts or become a dropout?" He added a grin so she would know he had no regrets.

"Make the sacrifice." She popped a donut in her mouth. "And I'm not talking about donuts."

"Well, it wasn't a huge sacrifice." Kip pulled a hanky out of his pocket and wiped the sugar off Justin's cheek.

"That you even say that tells me a lot about you," Nicole said with a bemused look on her face.

"Like what?" He caught Justin's hand again as they made their way through the crowd. The fairground took on a magical quality in the evening. The outside world faded away and it was him, Nicole and the boys surrounded by nameless people. The boys were too busy looking around to pay attention to what he and Nicole were discussing.

"It tells me how much you value family, and what you're willing to do to keep your family together." The lights of the Tilt-A-Whirl sent flashes of orange, red and blue across her face, making her eyes sparkle. "The boys are very blessed to have you in their lives. You've done an amazing job with them."

Kip was taken aback at her comment, but he couldn't

look away from her. Her words were like a balm to his soul. A recognition that what he had done was, at times, worth all the frustration and all the uncertainty.

"Thank you," he said releasing a slow smile.

She returned it. "When I saw how excited you were, when I heard you talking about the chuck wagons, I sensed that you missed it more than you let on."

Kip tried to push her comment aside with a shrug. "It had to end eventually."

"You've still got your horses, though. When I see what those teams can do, I'm trying to think of the hours of training you've put into them." She touched his shoulder, as if trying to convince him. "I can't imagine that you can stand to be away from that for long."

"I've got the boys," he said, gripping Justin's hand as they meandered through the crowds. "They're my responsibility. Like I said, I can't be leaving them alone every weekend." His words came out a bit harsher than he intended. He got the feeling that she was trying to make him wish he didn't have Tristan and Justin.

"Your mother can take care of the boys, and Isabelle can do more."

Kip was surprised by her reply. He was so sure she was going to tell him how much easier his life would be without the boys, which would bolster her case.

"Isabelle has had her own troubles," he said, defending his little sister.

"You lost a brother too."

Darkness entered Kip's soul. "Whatever happened to me is my own fault."

"How so?"

"Doesn't matter." He struggled to keep his emotions in check, flashes of that horrible day coming one after the other, the tangle of the reins, the horse struggling to pull free, Scott lying underneath.

"I understand from your mother that you blame yourself for what happened to Scott."

She spoke quietly, but her words laid his soul bare.

"Why do you care?"

"I've seen what guilt can do," she said, shooting him a quick glance. "And how it can distort a person's view of himself."

She hadn't answered his question, but he suspected she wouldn't. He thought of what she had told him the other night and wondered if she regretted telling him all she had.

"I understand it was your horse he was riding," she added.

Didn't look like she was quitting. With a sigh, he gave in. "Yeah. It was mine. A green-broke horse that Scott shouldn't have been riding."

Nicole nodded. "He chose to ride it, didn't he?"

Kip frowned. "You sound like my mother."

"That's not a bad thing." Nicole shot him a sideways glance, her mouth lifted in a faint smile. "Your mother is right."

Kip shrugged aside her comment. "You can color it anyway you want, the reality is he'd still be here if he hadn't gotten on that horse."

"Could you have stopped him from getting on that horse, and would you have?"

Her quiet question set him back.

"He was an adult, and he made his own choices," Nicole continued. "I don't think you need to carry that responsibility. No one else seems to think you should."

Her softly spoken words rearranged thoughts and ideas

he'd held for the past six months. Guilt he had carried since he pulled Scott out from underneath the horse.

Then, to his further surprise, he felt her hand on his arm. "You're a good man, Kip, and you're an even better brother. I don't know many men who would let their brother and two little boys move in with him when he already has a mother and a sister to take care of."

He glanced over at her, her soft smile easing into his soul. Then puzzlement took over. "Why are you telling me this? Aren't you supposed to be making me out to be the bad guy?" His eyes ticked over her face, then met her gaze.

She didn't look away. "You're not the bad guy."

Kip didn't reply, not sure what to make of her. Was she flirting with him?

"You just happen to be caught in a bad situation." Then she looked away.

What was she doing? Was she playing him?

He blew out his breath, not sure what to think. Then he glanced over at her. She was watching him again. That had been happening a lot lately, but this time as their eyes met, he felt a deeper, surprising emotion.

More than appeal. More than attraction. Her story the other night had shown him a glimpse into the inner workings of Nicole Williams. And yes, he felt sorry for her, but at the same time he'd been given something precious. He suspected that someone as private as she didn't share her history with too many people.

"Why are you guys talking about our dad?" Justin said, suddenly speaking up.

"We're just remembering things." Time to change the subject. "And you have sugar on your face." Kip brushed away the shiny granules clinging to his lip.

"So does Auntie Nicole," Justin said, pointing with one sugar-coated hand.

"So she does."

"Where?" Nicole asked, brushing at her face.

"There." Kip pointed it out to her with a smile.

Nicole wiped her cheek, then the other one. "No, I don't."

"It's right here." Kip brushed the sugar from her chin. Then his fingers slowed; lingered an extra second.

She swallowed and her free hand caught his, her delicate fingers encircling his wrist. "Thanks," she whispered, her smile settling into his soul.

"You're welcome."

"Hey, there's the Ferris wheel." Justin pulled on Kip's hand, breaking the moment. "Let's go for a ride."

"Here goes," Kip said, letting Justin pull him along.

The Ferris wheel towered above them, buckets swinging and people laughing.

"I'll get in line, you get the tickets," Nicole suggested. She pulled out her wallet, but Kip waved it off.

"My treat," he said.

"Thank you." She gave him another smile and Kip almost started whistling as he walked to the ticket booth. But he didn't. Justin was looking up at him as if trying to figure out why his uncle Kip was in such a good mood.

It was just a fun evening, he told himself as he paid for the tickets. Just a casual time with an attractive woman and his nephews. Their nephews, he corrected.

When he returned, the line behind them had grown. When they got to the front, Kip saw that the seats held four people. He had assumed that he would go on one seat with Justin and Nicole and Tristan on another. From the looks of the line, he doubted each would be allowed to have their own seat.

"Move along, go sit down," the operator called out. "Four to a seat, please."

"I want to sit on the outside," Tristan said, scurrying to the far side of the bench.

"Me too." Justin added, dropping into the other side.

Which left the middle for Kip and Nicole.

Kip didn't look at Nicole as they sat down. The operator lowered the bar, they were secured in, and the wheel moved ahead to let the next group of four on.

"We're going to be real high," Tristan said, his voice full of awe. "It's like we're in another world."

Kip sat back. Nicole did the same, just as the wheel jerked forward pushing them against each other.

"Sorry," Kip said, trying to give her some space.

"Uncle Kip, you're hogging my space," Justin said.

There was no getting around it. He and Nicole were spending the next few minutes sitting close together. He looked over at her to gauge her reaction only to find her grinning at him.

"I guess we're stuck together," she said.

Kip grinned back. "I guess." He didn't look away, his mind flicking back to the kiss he had given her. He thought of her hand, encircling his wrist.

Then, before he could change his mind, he slipped his arm around her shoulders. "May as well get comfortable," he said, and she didn't pull away.

The wheel turned slowly around, each movement bringing them closer to the top. When it stopped there, the boys were speechless. Their seat swung a bit, suspended above the fairgrounds, removed from the noise and music. Like Tristan had said, it was as if they were in another world.

Nicole shivered, and Kip capitalized on that and pulled her closer. Her face, framed by her golden hair, was a pale silhouette against a starry sky.

Everything slipped away and it was as if they were the only two people in this endless space.

He leaned closer and she met him partway. Then he kissed her. Gently. Slowly.

He pulled away, a gentle sigh easing out of him. She didn't look away. Neither did he. Their silence extended the moment. Then, with a jerk, the Ferris wheel moved along one more time.

Kip kept his arm around her and she reached up and caught his hand, as if anchoring him to her.

"Wow, this is so awesome," Justin said, still looking over the edge.

"I love this," Tristan replied from his seat.

"I know what they mean," Kip murmured.

Though Nicole looked away from him, she tightened her grip on his hand.

The wheel was full and then they were moving steadily and with each revolution, at the top, Kip looked at Nicole and she looked at him. They didn't repeat the kiss, but each time their eyes met it was as if they had.

And each time their eyes met Kip's heart beat a little harder and his optimism burned a little brighter.

Could he and Nicole have a future?

Did he dare think that far?

Chapter Twelve

"Here's your cowboy hat." Kip took the white straw hat he had bought from the kiosk and dropped it on Nicole's head. He lifted her chin with his knuckle, his rough skin rasping on hers. "There you go, Nicole Williams. Now you're an Alberta cowgirl."

"That sounds official." Nicole pushed the hat further on her head, wishing her heart didn't jump at his every touch.

"Auntie Nicole is a cowgirl." Tristan jumped up and down.

"Now she has to go riding horses," Justin said hopefully.

Nicole didn't say anything to bolster his cause. She'd said quite enough to Kip already. And she had let Kip Cosgrove do quite enough, kissing her on the Ferris wheel.

She tried to remind herself that Kip wasn't her friend.

She had discovered in the past few days, however, that he wasn't her enemy either. He was simply a man doing what he was asked to do. A man living up to his responsibilities.

But the memory of that kiss and the utterly spontaneous one earlier lingered both in her mind and on her lips.

"We're not talking about the horses now," Kip said with a note of finality. "We're going home. It's way past your bedtime."

The boys were obviously tired because they didn't even argue as they trudged back to the truck. They got in and settled down for the long ride back.

Nicole tried not to look at Kip as he drove, his face illuminated by the glow of the dashboard lights. She tried to push the kiss to the back of her mind as she pulled herself back into reality mode.

She took her hat off and held it on her lap, as if easing away from the day—turning back into Nicole, the girl who wore business suits and high heels and attended business meetings. Not a cowgirl in blue jeans who let a man kiss her on the Ferris wheel.

"I was wondering if we could discuss my visit tomorrow," Nicole said quietly after they reached the city limits. "I have a conference call in the late afternoon. Would it be possible to come in the morning?"

"You can't," Justin piped up from the backseat of the truck. "We go to church on Sunday."

"Of course." Nicole tapped her fingers on her arm, thinking. They'd gone last week while she was at the motel sending out flurries of emails about work.

"Why don't you come to church with us?" Justin asked. "Then you can sit with us."

"I'm not so sure—"

"Please come," Tristan added. "It's kind of long sometimes, but then we can see you in the morning too."

Nicole's resistance softened as she looked back at the boys, considering the invitation.

"You're welcome to come," Kip said quietly.

The last time Nicole had been in church was for her mother's funeral. That service had been full of sorrow, regret and a heavy layer of guilt.

Though attending church would mean she'd see the boys, it would also mean seeing Kip.

That's a dangerous place to go, she reminded herself. This evening was supposed to be a blip on your radar. An experience—a date—that she could put away in the memory chest.

"I'd like it if you could come," Kip added, his voice quiet.

His comment, combined with his tender smile, swept away her resistance. "What time does the service start?"

"Ten o'clock."

"I'll see how my morning goes," she said cautiously.

It was just church, she reminded herself as she sat back in the truck. Going back to church could be a good thing.

"I'm bored," Justin said from the backseat. "And I don't want to play I Spy again."

Nicole twisted in her seat. "Do you guys know any songs? Maybe you could sing them for me."

"I don't like to sing," Tristan said.

"I'm really bored," Justin repeated.

Nicole pulled out her phone. "If you guys can share, I can show you a game that you can play on my phone."

Their eyes grew to four large circles of surprise. "Really?"

"Cool." Justin had his hand out for her phone.

"You can't have it, I want it."

Nicole hesitated looking from Justin to Tristan.

"You started something now," Kip said. She could hear the smile in his voice.

"You'll have to take turns," she said. She turned on a timer function, started up the game and handed it to Tristan. "When this bell dings, then it's Justin's turn."

"How come he gets to go first?" Justin whined.

"Because we love him more," Kip said.

Nicole shot him look of shock. What was he doing? What was he saying? She was about to reprimand him when she heard Justin's giggle.

"No, you don't, Uncle Kip," he said, completely unperturbed by the comment.

"Oh, yes, I do," Kip said, glancing in his rearview mirror at his nephew.

"You love us both the same," Tristan chimed in, quickly figuring out how to play the game.

Nicole tried to absorb what had happened. The boys were so utterly confident of their uncle's love that his outrageous statement was greeted with humor.

Did those boys have any idea of how blessed they were, Nicole thought, her heart contracting with envy?

"Oops. I think I pushed the wrong button...hey, is this your house?" Justin held out the phone to Nicole. Somehow he had gotten into her picture file.

"Yes, that's where I live. Here, let me find that game for you again."

"Uncle Kip, look at Auntie Nicole's house." Justin held the phone toward Kip who dutifully glanced at it.

"Very nice. Very impressive," he said in a tone that implied anything but.

"Do you have any other pictures?" Justin asked.

Nicole thought of the one photo she had of her father on her phone but felt a surprising reluctance to show them. Some of that had to do with the man sitting across the truck from her, frowning now. The other part was a reluctance to bring that part of her life into this moment.

"I'll get you the game again," she said, taking the phone and getting them back on track.

The boys took a couple of turns with her phone, their chatter slowly fading away. Half an hour later the phone lay between them and the only sound in the truck was their deep, rhythmic breathing. Nicole glanced into the vehicles passing them, the stores beyond the traffic—everywhere but at the man driving the truck.

The man who had kissed her twice.

She'd been kissed before. It was nothing new. She'd be kissed again. Someday by the man she would marry.

Which wouldn't happen anytime soon, she reasoned. Not when she had so much happening. The boys. Her father. Her job.

"I want to thank you," Kip said, his deep voice breaking into her thoughts and pulling her attention back to him.

"For what?"

Kip was looking ahead at the flow of traffic, his face illuminated by the glow of the streetlights.

"For what you said about Scott and about guilt." He turned his head, his eyes catching her gaze. "I guessed you know a bit about that too."

Nicole sighed. "I do, or rather, I did." What happened between her and Tricia was in the past.

"I'm guessing you're talking about your sister."

Nicole nodded.

"How did you two get along?" he asked, gently prying.

Nicole shrugged. "Tricia and I got along really great when she was a little girl."

"And later?

"That's when we started fighting."

"About the usual girl stuff?"

She wished. "No. It was bigger than lipstick and borrowed blue jeans."

"I'm guessing she was a rebellious person."

Nicole shifted down into her seat, her eyes following the road. Against her will, scenes from the last time she saw her sister edged into her mind. The angry words she'd said. The accusations. Things she should never have said. "We had a nasty fight, and the next morning she was gone. I never heard anything from her after that."

"She didn't write your parents either. That must have been hard for them."

"It was. My mother cried every night for months after Tricia left."

"And your father?"

"It was especially hard for him. Tricia was his daughter and she was gone."

"You make it sound like she was his *only* daughter."

"I know she wasn't…" Nicole shifted in her seat, wishing he would stop this line of questioning. "But I was his adopted daughter. Tricia was his natural child. Of course it would hurt that she chose to leave."

"What are you trying to say?" Kip sounded like he really wanted to hear what she had to say.

Nicole paused, searching for the right words to formulate her thoughts. "I was eight years old when Sam and Norah adopted me. I know it's hard to bond with children that aren't yours. I experienced that with my aunt and in most of the foster homes I stayed in. That's the reality. Tricia was Sam and Norah's biological child. Of course it would hurt my father more when she left."

"What…why would you say that?"

Tricia was surprised at the thread of anger in his voice. "Like I said, it's reality, Kip. If you found out that the boys…" she paused as she shot a quick glance over her shoulder. Thankfully both Justin and Tristan were still fast asleep, heads at awkward angles, mouths slightly open. Utterly innocent and utterly adorable. She cleared her throat and tried again. "If you found out that the boys weren't Scott's—" and he would, she thought "—weren't your nephews, wouldn't that make a difference for you?"

"What? Are you kidding?" Kip sounded incredulous. As if he couldn't believe she would even speak those words aloud.

"No. I'm not."

Kip leaned forward, a deep frown furrowing his brow. "I love the boys. They were always as much mine as Scott's, even though they were his boys." He thumbed his hat back on his head and shot her a frown. "They're woven into my heart. They're a part of me that I can't imagine living without. That's not because of biology. It's because I made a choice to take care of them and to take them in, and weaved through that choice came love."

Nicole's heart stuttered at the sincerity in his voice. At the intensity of his gaze.

"Even if I found out they weren't Scott's boys that wouldn't affect how much I love them. That wouldn't change anything." He sighed and turned his attention back to the road. "I love them. With all my heart."

Tears pricked her eyes at the sincerity in his voice. Each word he spoke dove into her heart and attached itself, creating another connection to this man. A connection that she had yearned, since she was a little girl, to have with her own father.

"I don't want to turn everything into a battle over the

boys," Kip added, his voice growing quiet. "You know where I stand on that matter." He sighed. "You need to know that these boys are a part of me that I can't live without."

He looked at her again and she held his gaze a moment. She gave into an impulse and covered his hand with hers. "I know that." She gave his hand a light squeeze, then drew away before he could see the tears threatening in her eyes.

She blinked, reasoning the moment of sadness away. She had always accepted that as the adopted daughter, she wouldn't have the same connection to Sam as Tricia had.

However, in spite of her practical reasoning, the lonely-little-girl part of her wished that for even a moment, she could have heard Sam say about her what Kip had said about his nephews. That she could have received even a particle of the affection Kip lavished so freely on children that weren't his.

As Nicole stared out the window, her thoughts drifted back to her father. To the moment she had with him before she left for Alberta.

He had clung to her hand with a strength she had never felt before, the frustration with the illness that kept him in bed burning in his eyes. He would settle for nothing less than the boys coming to Toronto and he would do what he could on his end to ensure that happened. At the time she'd taken on the cause, feeling it was another opportunity to atone. To earn his love.

And now?

Nicole wasn't so sure of the rightness of their claim anymore.

You know what it's like to be uprooted.

But she also knew what it was like to yearn for a place

where she belonged, body and soul. A place where she was a blood relative. Because no matter what Kip might say, she knew from personal experience that blood truly was thicker than water.

Tricia had been blood. Nicole had been water.

Nicole's mind drifted back and forth, her thoughts wearing on her as she slowly spun down into a half sleep. Her mind drifted from thoughts about her father into vague thoughts of Ferris wheels and Kip's kiss...that wonderful kiss...

"Hey. Nicole. We're here." Kip's voice came from far away and Nicole blinked, trying to orient herself. Her mouth felt dry and her eyes full of sand. She blinked as she looked up at Kip's face as he stood in the open door of the truck.

He touched her cheek and with her dreams still clouding her mind, Nicole caught his hand. His eyes were softly lit by the half moon above and she couldn't look away.

"You were sleeping," he whispered, his hand cupping her cheek.

"I'm sorry," she mumbled, struggling to pull her thoughts back to reality. She shivered as the cool night sifted over her. Then she looked up at him and smiled. "Thanks for a fun evening."

Kip's fingers caressed her cheek. "I enjoyed it. A lot."

She should look away and end this connection, but the moment seemed surreal. Ethereal. Then, with the kiss he had given her on the Ferris wheel still vivid in her mind, and with her soul yearning for the closeness she'd experienced, she leaned forward and brushed her lips over his.

Kip whispered her name, then drew her into his arms and they kissed again. A kiss born of longing and connection. A kiss that anchored them in a way that nothing else had.

A kiss that rocked Nicole's world.

She pulled away, her heart thrumming in her chest. What was she doing? This was dangerous. And confusing. And...

Wonderful.

Kissing Kip was like coming home.

Chapter Thirteen

Nicole smoothed her hair, checked her lipstick in the rearview mirror of her car and took in a deep breath.

It's just a gathering of people, she reminded herself, pushing aside memories of a God she used to think cared about her. You're only here so you can see your nephews.

She slung her leather purse over her shoulder and strode across the parking lot to the white stucco church, her high heels clicking on the asphalt. The summer sun warmed her shoulders, and for a moment she regretted the suit and silk shirt she had chosen for today.

When she had gone to church with the Williams family, Norah had insisted on wearing their best clothes. A sign of respect and consideration she had said, as Tricia fought putting on the cute dress that always matched Nicole's. Only Nicole was allowed to brush Tricia's dark hair and tie it up in a ribbon, and once they were all ready, only Nicole was allowed to help Tricia put her coat on.

Nicole's steps faltered as the old memories surfaced. On the heels of that came the reminder of her beloved sister's last wishes.

That the boys be with their father and with her.

A young father and mother and their two children came out of a car ahead of her, and as they got out, the woman smiled at Nicole and wished her a good morning.

Another elderly couple did the same as she neared the church building.

Friendly, Nicole thought, as she pushed open one of the large glass doors of the building. The buzz of conversation greeted her. People young and old milled about the entrance, chatting and visiting with one another. She held back for a moment, assessing and looking around. People knew each other. She didn't belong.

She pushed the thought aside as she worked her way through the gathering to the double doors she saw past the people. Once she got to the main auditorium, things were a little quieter, but not much. People were settling into pews, still talking amongst one another.

The front stage area held a lectern, a set of drums, a piano and a few guitars standing upright on stands.

"Welcome to our church," a young man said, handing her a piece of paper. "I hope you like the service."

Nicole glanced at his blue jeans topped with a T-shirt and open shirt and felt overdressed.

"You visiting here?" he asked.

"Yes, I am." She looked over the people already seated, that out-of-place feeling returning. She didn't know anyone. "Is the Cosgrove family here yet?"

"They're sitting where they always sit." Nicole looked in the direction he was pointing and immediately recognized Kip's tall figure and his broad shoulders. Justin and Tristan sat on either side of him.

Kip's mother sat in her wheelchair in the aisle beside him, which made Nicole frown. Why wasn't she using her walker?

She brushed the questions aside and with a nod to the young man strode down the aisle. She came at the pew from the other side and slid into the empty spot beside Justin.

Kip, who had been talking to his mother while Nicole sat down, turned suddenly. As their eyes met, Nicole felt that sudden jolt of awareness that not only surprised her but disconcerted her.

In spite of her mental warnings, she let her smile linger and shift.

Kip's returning smile softened his features and created another, more peculiar tingle.

"Auntie Nicole, you came." Justin grinned, tucking his warm, slightly damp hand inside hers.

"I want to sit by Auntie Nicole too," Tristan whined.

"Okay, go ahead, but be quiet," Kip warned.

Tristan scooted past Justin and sat triumphantly on her other side.

"You guys look really spiffy," she said, glancing from one to the other. She hardly recognized the shining faces, the slicked-back hair and the white shirts and dark pants she remembered ironing the other day.

Justin made a face. "Gramma always makes us dress up for church. Says it's a sign of respect."

Nicole felt a touch of melancholy at the words, so similar to what she'd just been thinking. Her mother used to say the same thing whenever they went to church and Tricia would argue about what to wear.

Mary leaned forward and waved to Nicole. "Hey, Nicole. Good to see you here. I didn't think you'd come."

Nicole hadn't thought she would either, but here she was. She returned Mary's smile, but as she sat back, her eyes naturally drifted to Kip, who was still watching her. His expression had grown serious, his eyebrows pulled together in a frown of, what? Concentration? Disapproval?

Nicole turned her attention back to the boys, trying to keep their high spirits reasonably under control. This was church, after all.

"We told Gramma about the Stampede," Justin said. "And the midway and the Ferris wheel." Nicole's heart jolted at that. Had the boys seen their kiss? "She said it sounded like fun."

"Can I play with your phone again?" Justin asked.

"It's my turn. You played with it last time," Tristan said.

Nicole shook her head. "It's not respectful," she said, building on what Mary had already told them.

They looked like they were about to argue when a figure dropped into the pew beside Justin.

Isabelle.

She wore a skirt today, short and snug, and under that leggings with lace at the bottom and ballet flats with bright orange flowers. Her shirt was a riot of pink and purple overtop of an orange tank top. A white scarf was draped around her neck.

Obviously still trying to find a personal style.

Isabelle shot Nicole a frown. "What are you doing here?"

"And a good morning to you," Nicole said with a bright smile, determined not to let Isabelle push her around.

"Auntie Nicole, when can we talk to our Grandpa on the phone again?"

Nicole shot a frown their way. "What Grandpa are you talking about?"

"The one in Toronto, silly," Justin shot back.

"You don't have a Grandpa in Toronto." Isabelle spoke the words with smug authority.

"Yes, we do," Tristan said. "Auntie Nicole let us talk to him."

"Why are you telling them that?" Isabelle gave Nicole a look that was supposed to be disdainful, but in her eyes, Nicole caught a hint of fear. "My dad was their only Grandpa."

Though she treated the boys like they were nothing but a nuisance, Nicole sensed Isabelle would be just as upset as her mother was if the boys were to leave.

Nicole looked away, the moment of vulnerability creating an unease.

Things were getting complicated, she thought, her eyes drifting over to Kip and beyond that to Mary. Complicated and confusing. She wasn't as sure of what she needed to do as when she first came here. She wasn't so sure she wanted to take the boys away from this home.

Or Kip.

She brushed the second thoughts aside. She was letting her emotions interfere with what she knew was right. Tricia had wanted her parents to take care of her boys. What Nicole thought of the situation had nothing to do with that.

The music started up and everyone stood. The leader announced the song they were going to sing and words flashed up on a screen in the front of the church.

The song had a catchy tune and soon she was singing along, surprised to find herself enjoying the music. The song segued into another, quieter song.

The words to this song were familiar to her. It was an older hymn, and the combination of music drew up pictures of Tricia and her parents standing in church together. The memories created an unwelcome thickness in her throat

She stopped singing, pulling back from the emotions and the memories. By the time she had everything under control the song, thankfully, was ended.

They were greeted by a minister who welcomed them all and led them in prayer, followed by another song.

As they went through the service, Nicole's self-control returned. Besides, she was distracted enough keeping the boys from fidgeting too much or talking too loudly.

"You boys have to be a little quieter," she whispered as they sat down after another song.

Justin sighed. "Uncle Kip always says that too."

"Uncle Kip is right," Nicole said, slipping her arms around the boys' shoulders as the minister encouraged them to turn to 1 Corinthians 13.

Tristan pulled a Bible from the pew ahead of him, laying it on Nicole's lap and gesturing for her to look it up.

She felt a moment's panic as she opened it and flipped through the pages. The name of the book was familiar and she remembered that it was in the New Testament, but that was it. The minister started reading, but she still hadn't found the passage.

"Don't you know where it is, Auntie Nicole?" Tristan asked.

"No. Sorry." Flip, flip. Still no luck. She knew the book, not where it was located.

Then Kip leaned past Justin and turned to the right spot.

Nicole's cheeks burned and for a moment she felt like she didn't belong here. Couldn't even find a book of the Bible.

Her eyes flew over the page trying to catch up to the minister. There it was.

"...If I give all I possess to the poor and surrender my body to the flames, but have not love, I gain nothing.

"Love is patient, love is kind. It does not envy, it does not boast, it is not proud. It is not rude, it is not self-seeking, it is not easily angered, it keeps no record of wrongs." The words came at her in a steady rhythm. Her mind slipped back to her father and how she'd yearned every day for not only his respect, but even more, his love.

"...Love does not delight in evil, but rejoices with the truth. It always protects, always trusts, always hopes, always perseveres." A haunting tune wove itself through the words as he read. The tune was from a song she remembered Norah Williams singing when she was a young girl. It was a song about how deep the Father's love, how vast beyond all measure. The song had spoken to her then, had called to the part of her that had longed for her biological father's love, then, later, tried to earn Sam's love. Then Tricia left and the song and the feelings they evoked were buried in the barrage of pain and sorrow that followed.

"...And now these three remain. Faith, hope and love, but the greatest of these is love."

The sorrows of the past beat at her, yet, in spite of that, below the turmoil, the words of the passage offered something more.

The love of God. The steadfast and faithful love of God.

Then the minister closed the Bible, leaned on the podium and started speaking.

"This passage is not simply about love. To put it in context, the people of Corinth wanted one thing—certain spiritual gifts—but needed something even more important. Love. Love is just a small word," he continued. "A word that has been thrown about so often, we've sucked all the power out of it. Love is a word that the Creator of the world not only invented, but embodies."

His words drew Nicole on as he spoke of God's faithful love and how it satisfies all our needs. How love is such a small word for the powerful thing God had done when He gave up His own life for the sake of sinful beings.

"Who would put the needs of someone else before such imperfect beings? Only God has that kind of love. The love our parents have is powerful, but not as powerful as God's love for us. This love comes to us as a gift. Freely given. We don't deserve it and we can't earn it."

Nicole listened to the pastor, seeking the hope and love he claimed was hers for the taking, just as Kip had told her the other night. A love that didn't need to be earned because it could never be earned. Love that was freely given, in spite of the cost, and meant to be freely received.

The words slipped into the empty spaces in Nicole's heart. It seemed she had spent all of her time at the Williamses' home feeling as if she had to earn their love. Her father reinforced that feeling with each expectation he had of her—work at his side in the foundation, live at home and now make sure that Tricia's boys come to where he thought they should be.

What else could she do? It was her reality.

Then, it seemed too soon, the service was over. They stood for the final song, and as the notes rang away, Tristan tugged on her hand.

"It's time to go," he said, dragging her out of her circling thoughts.

They were stopped at the end of the pew by the flow

of people all exiting at once. As Nicole was drawn back into reality, she pulled Tristan back as he tried to wiggle his way through the crowd. "Why are you in such a rush?" she asked.

"We have to get to Auntie Doreen's right away," Tristan said. "So we can get the best toys."

"Auntie Doreen's? What are you talking about?"

"We always go to Auntie Doreen's for lunch," Justin said, in a tone that implied she should know this.

Nicole glanced back over her shoulder, but Kip was exiting the other aisle, pushing his mother's wheelchair. She'd have to wait until he caught up to her to find out what was going on.

The boys had their own plan. They pulled her along, and as they exited the auditorium, someone called the boys' names.

"Oh, brother," Justin said, throwing his hands up in an dramatic gesture. "Now we're going to be late." But he stopped and turned around.

A young woman carrying a tiny baby in one arm and leading a little girl roughly the same age as the boys walked up to them. "Hey, guys. There you are," she said to them.

The woman's hair was the same shade as Kip's and her eyes the same color. Her features were closer to Isabelle's than her brother's. When she smiled at the boys, Nicole could see Mary Cosgrove in the shape of her mouth.

"I'm guessing you're Nicole," the woman said. When she met Nicole's eyes, her smile tightened, as if she had to force it.

Nicole wasn't surprised. She didn't think Kip's sister would be thrilled to meet the woman who was laying a claim to her nephews.

Alleged nephews, she reminded herself.

"Hello, I'm Doreen. Kip's sister." Doreen raised her chin by way of greeting, her hands otherwise occupied with two of her children. "Would you like to join us for lunch?"

Doreen knew who she was and what she hoped to do, yet she was asking her over?

She was about to give the very polite young mother an easy out when Justin blurted out, "You have to come, Auntie Nicole. You have to."

"Please, come. Please," Tristan added, pulling on her hand as if he hoped to physically drag a response from her. "We can ride with you and tell you where to go so you don't get lost."

"I don't know—" she hesitated. If she didn't go along, this time in church would be her only time with the boys.

"Come and join us," Doreen added. "Kip asked me to ask you, but it would be our pleasure if you came." Her smile held a bit more warmth, and Nicole relented.

"I'd be glad to." Truth was, the thought of returning to the stark and plain motel room held little appeal. It reminded her too much of the times her aunt would bring her to her father when he was working near the town.

It had nothing to do with the fact that Kip had asked Doreen to invite her. Nothing at all.

Fifteen minutes and some rather convoluted directions later, Nicole was parking her car beside an older house on an acreage outside of Millarville. Trucks and ride-on toys dotted the lawn. Flowers spilled out of pots hanging from brackets on the side of the house and set up against a crooked concrete step. Shrub-filled flower beds nestled up against the wooden siding of the older home. The entire place looked homey and comfortable and welcoming.

"Let's go, Auntie Nicole," the boys called out as they ran up the walk.

As she got out, Kip pulled up his truck beside her. Mary Cosgrove sat in the front seat.

"You go inside," she told the boys. "I'll help Uncle Kip."

The boys didn't even look back as they raced over the lawn to the house.

"Where's Isabelle?" Nicole asked as Kip got out of the truck.

"She rode with Doreen." Kip pulled a wheelchair out of the back of the truck.

Nicole frowned. "Where's your mom's walker?"

"She said her knee was really bothering her," Kip said as he snapped open the chair. "So she's taking a break."

"She'll never heal from the surgery properly if she doesn't keep working her legs."

Kip gave her an odd look as he wheeled the chair to the door of the truck, and she wasn't sure what to make of it. Then he held her gaze and smiled a slow-release smile. She wasn't sure what to make of that either.

"Why don't you tell her that?" he said quietly.

"I will." Nicole waited until Kip opened the door of the truck, then watched as Mary worked her way into the chair.

"So you found your way here," Mary said with a grunt as she settled into the chair. "I thought for sure those boys would try to take you through the shortcut and get lost."

"We made it okay. Why aren't you using your walker?"

"My knee has been bothering me," Mary said with a quick glance back at Kip as if hoping he would intervene.

"If you don't keep moving, then all the pain from the surgery will be for nothing and you'll be back to where you started before your surgery."

"Well, I suppose." Mary bit her lip, as if thinking. "But I don't have my walker now."

"Kip and I can help you to the house. You can lean on our arms, and then you can sit on a normal chair and not look like such an invalid."

"I guess so," Mary said with a heavy sigh. She looked up at Nicole with narrow eyes. "You're a bit bossy, you know."

"So I've been told." Nicole caught Kip's gaze and tried not to roll her eyes. Kip grinned.

They walked slowly up to the house just as Isabelle came to the door. She glared at Nicole, then back at her mother.

"Wow, Mom. You're not using the wheelchair," she said with an admiring tone.

"Nicole told me I could do it, and I guess I can."

Isabelle shot Nicole a frown, but then reached out for her mother's arm. "I'll take over from here."

Nicole relinquished her hold as Isabelle ushered Mary into the house.

Kip blew out his breath and shot her a quick smile. "Thanks for the help. For some reason she won't listen to me."

"You have to be firm."

"You sound like a mother." Kip's smile widened.

"I used to boss Tricia around something awful." Nicole felt a momentary pang at the memory. "I guess I'm a natural."

"You are that." Kip touched her face, his fingers lingering on her cheek.

Nicole's heart stuttered in her chest and, cheeks burning, she stepped into the house.

Mary was already settled in a chair, looking quite satisfied with herself, a cup of tea beside her on a TV tray. Isabelle was lying on the couch, reading a magazine.

"Hey, Kip, you made it." Doreen called out as she came into the living room, carrying her baby. She reached up to give Kip a one-armed hug that he reached down to return. Then he bent over the baby curled up in his sister's arm and touched its tiny head with one finger.

"Hey, little one," he said quietly. "How are you?"

Nicole swallowed at the sight of this big, tough cowboy bent over this little baby, a look of tenderness on his face.

Doreen glanced over at Nicole. "I hope this isn't too overwhelming. Kip told me that you're used to a little more sedate lifestyle."

Nicole wondered what else Kip had told his sister.

"I'll be fine. I like kids."

Doreen's gaze flashed from Nicole to Kip. "That's good." She jostled the now-fussing baby.

"What's her name?" Nicole asked.

"Emily."

Nicole gave into an impulse and held her arms out. "Can I hold her?"

Doreen's frown was fleeting, but then she nodded. "That'd be great."

She handed the little bundle over with all the confidence of an experienced mother. Nicole felt a little awkward as the baby squawked a protest, but when Emily settled in Nicole's arms, her tiny mouth stretched open in a yawn. Her delicate fingers stretched and with a sigh as gentle as a cobweb, she drifted back to sleep.

"She's so beautiful," Nicole whispered, stroking her petal-soft cheek with one finger.

"I think we'll keep her around for a while. At least until the terrible twos. Might have to see if we can farm her out then—" Then Doreen sucked in a quick breath. "I'm sorry…I didn't mean…that was thoughtless."

"Why don't I help you and Ron get lunch on the table," Kip said, taking his sister's arm. "Just make yourself at home," he said to Nicole.

Nicole presumed that Kip wanted to have a "chat" with his sister. She also presumed that he had told her about her past, which surprised her.

"Come sit over here," Mary said, brushing a stuffed duck and a book off the chair beside her. "Don't worry about Doreen. She tends to talk before she thinks. The hazards of being a mother."

"That's okay. It didn't bother me." Nicole just smiled as she slowly lowered herself into the chair. Little Emily pursed her lips and rolled her head, then settled again. Nicole touched her face again, then let the baby curl her tiny fingers around hers. "Look how delicate her fingernails are. Like little grains of rice," she remarked, taking in the wonder of this brand-new person.

"Pretty amazing," Mary said quietly. "It never gets old."

"Did you want to hold her?" Nicole asked, realizing that she was taking this baby away from her own grandmother.

Mary waved away her offer. "I get to see her enough."

Nicole was secretly glad. She didn't want to relinquish her precious burden. It had been years and years since she'd seen a baby, much less held one.

As she looked down at Emily, she wondered about

her biological mother's love. Wondered how she had felt when she held her. Wondered how Tricia felt when the twins were born.

Her heart contracted at the thought.

She heard lowered voices coming from the kitchen and she presumed Kip and his sister were talking. About her plans? About the boys?

"Don't worry," Mary said quietly. "He'll be back."

A flush worked its way up Nicole's neck. "I was just… it's not…"

Mary patted her on the shoulder. "He's a good man, my Kip. Please remember that," she said, lowering her voice.

Nicole caught Mary's gaze. Did she know what was building between Nicole and her son? "I know he is a good man," she said, her voice full of conviction.

Isabelle glared at her over the top of her magazine. "Then why are you taking the boys—" Isabelle stopped herself, threw her magazine down on the couch and got up. "I'm going outside."

But as she left, Nicole caught a glimmer in her eyes. She suspected the glimmer came from unshed tears and the sight tangled her emotions even more.

The longer she stayed here and the more she got to know the Cosgrove family, the more confused she became about what she had come to do. She wondered if, when the time came, she could do it?

Chapter Fourteen

"So the boys tell me you went to the chuck-wagon races yesterday, Kip," Alex said, reaching across the dining room table for another bun. "That must have been interesting."

If he only knew, Kip thought, slicing up a bun for Tristan and avoiding Nicole's gaze.

The entire family was grouped around the dining room table, kids interspersed between the adults, and conversations zipped back and forth and through each other.

"Yeah. Nick won his heat."

"Uncle Kip was so excited that he kissed Auntie Nicole," Justin piped up.

Kip wanted to elbow the little guy, but that would only draw even more attention to the situation.

"Do you miss it?" Alex asked, feeding another spoonful of soup to his youngest daughter, tactfully ignoring Justin's little outburst.

"What? You kissed Auntie Nicole?" Jenna, one of Doreen's older children, called across the table.

"Yeah. I missed racing the chucks." Kip ignored Jenna and tried not to catch Nicole's reaction to both the comment and his niece's reference to her as "Auntie Nicole." She sat across from him, and it was hard not to look over her way from time to time only to catch her looking at him.

"You beat Mike a bunch of times, didn't you?" Mary said. "Paul, don't blow your nose in the napkin, honey."

"I tied with him once at the Ponoka Stampede and I think I beat him at a race in Lethbridge." Kip stood up and helped himself to another bowl of soup from the huge pot in the middle of the table, then served up for two of Doreen's children as well.

As he did, he thought of the pictures of Nicole's home that the boys had found on Nicole's phone and so generously shown to him. The photos were small, but it wasn't hard to see the size of the house and the grounds surrounding it.

He doubted Nicole had ever had soup served to her out of an industrial sized pot plopped unceremoniously on an old wooden table, scarred from the doodlings of six children.

He doubted she ever ate with a group of kids so noisy and rambunctious that half of the conversation consisted of reprimands and reminders to eat.

"I think you should do it again," Kristen, Doreen's second oldest daughter, said. "I loved watching you race."

"Uncle Kip takes us every year, at Christmas, on a sleigh ride," Jenna said to Nicole. "But he didn't this year."

Kip wished they could move to the usual topics of conversation. The weather, the kids, the crops, the kids, the neighbors, the kids.

"Have you ever ridden, Nicole?" Doreen said, wiping the face of a little child beside her while she spoke.

"Quite extensively. My parents owned a number of horses that my sister and I rode, though I spent more time with them than Tricia did. We were fortunate enough to have a barn that we could ride in all year round."

Some barn, Kip thought, remembering the pictures of the arena and painted wooden fences. That barn looked in better shape than their house.

"You really should take Nicole out on the horses," Doreen said. "Or at least take her out in the wagon."

"I don't think I have time."

"You always had time before," his mother said.

Kip wasn't going to point out the obvious. That "before" was before Scott died. Before he didn't trust other people around his horses anymore.

Scott made his own choices. Nicole's comment echoed in his head at the same time as she focused her gaze on him.

"Wouldn't you love to go on a wagon ride with Kip's horses?" Doreen asked Nicole, pushing the point.

"Doreen…" Kip warned.

"I think it would be wonderful to do something so idyllic." Nicole spoke quietly, but her subtext was clear as was her choice of words.

Idyllic indeed.

Doreen clapped her hands like a little kid. "Why don't you take Nicole out and then, tomorrow after school, I'll drop by with the kids and you can take them on a ride too? To make up for them not being able to go on their sleigh ride at Christmas."

Kip shot his sister an exasperated look, but she stared him down, looking as innocent as her little baby.

"I think it's a great idea and I'd love to go," Nicole said, adding one more layer of pressure.

Though he had other work waiting for him, Kip knew what he'd be doing tomorrow.

Unbidden, his gaze slipped to Nicole, only to catch her looking at him. For a moment he couldn't look away. For a moment, it was as if he'd lost himself in her eyes.

And that was a dangerous place to be.

"Are you sure you're okay with this?" Nicole glanced over at Kip as they walked to the corrals. She didn't want him to feel pressured, but at the same time the thought of going out on the wagon with him created a little thrum of excitement.

Kip sighed. "When my sister starts bossing me around, I just pull my hat lower, and smile and nod."

"Seems to be your default position around the women in your life."

Kip laughed. "That and keep a low profile."

Tristan and Justin were back at the house with Mary and Isabelle. To Nicole's surprise, Isabelle had been willing to watch the boys while Nicole went with Kip to get the horses and hitch them up. She suspected it might have something to do with the comment she made at Doreen's on Sunday. As if she suddenly realized what the implications of Nicole's presence would mean to the boys she had grown up with.

Seemed she wasn't as self-centered as she came across.

"I feel like you were railroaded into this," Nicole added. "Are you sure you're comfortable with the idea?"

"I wouldn't be comfortable working with my horses with anyone else," he said, surprising her with his comment.

She tried to read his expression, but he was looking ahead, his eyes shadowed by the brim of his cowboy hat.

"I haven't worked with horses for a while," Kip added. "If things don't go the way I want right off the bat, then we're not doing this at all."

"I understand," Nicole said. "Though I don't have my heart set on going out, I do think it's a good thing for you."

Kip pushed his hat back and glanced at her. "And you care for my welfare because?"

Nicole stopped, looking directly at him. "I care because I saw how much racing those horses meant to you. I care because I have the feeling you're not complete unless you've got a team of horses ahead of you, leather reins threaded through your hands, and the wind in your face."

Kip slowly shook his head, smiling at her. "You seem to spend a lot of time looking out for other people."

Nicole shrugged. "Not really. I just…care."

"Do you ever look out for yourself?"

"Of course I do." Nicole released a short laugh.

"That's why you're doing conference calls on Sunday afternoons and trying to juggle your work at home with your time here."

"It's my reality."

"And you worrying about my mom? Is that your reality? And the way you're not afraid to tackle Isabelle? And how you're always fussing about the boys?"

Nicole frowned at him. "What are you talking about?"

Kip's expression grew serious. He tapped her on her forehead. "Doesn't this ever get full of other people's things, other people's stuff, other people's problems?"

"I'm not sure…"

Kip released a slow smile. "Of course you're not. And that's part of the problem."

"What problem?" She wasn't sure what he was talking about.

He brushed her cheek with his knuckles, sending a frisson of pleasure up her spine. She gave into an impulse and caught his hand by the wrist.

What are you doing? You're playing with fire.

Nicole dismissed the accusing thoughts. Being with Kip felt right and good. She had never felt this way about any man before, and that had to mean something.

"I get the feeling that you have a hard time thinking about yourself, Nicole Williams. Sometimes I think you should."

His words wound around her heart creating a gentle warmth but she wasn't sure how to reply.

He gave her an enigmatic look, then stepped back.

"Let's go get those horses," Kip said quietly.

Thankfully the horses were already in the corral when they came, so it took no time to bring them into the barn. Nicole held them at the head, while Kip began harnessing. When he had the first buckle done up, the horses sensed what was happening and they stamped and snorted with impatience.

"It's like they missed all of this," Nicole said, steadying the one horse.

Kip grunted as he got out from underneath the horse. "I hope they settle down once we get them going."

He looks worried, Nicole thought.

"I trust you completely," she said quietly.

Kip gave her an enigmatic look then he shook his head lightly. "I sure hope you're right."

The horses danced around, jingling the harnesses, while Kip backed them up to the wagon. A couple of times Nicole was sure he was going to call the whole thing off, but she said nothing, quietly following his instructions, soothing the horses when she could.

"You're pretty good with the horses," Kip said as he clipped and fastened.

"I like horses, and I think they sense that."

"Not many women would feel comfortable handling four horses at the same time," Kip said taking the reins from her. "I've got them now."

Nicole stroked the neck of one of the more jumpy horses, spoke a few soothing words, then carefully climbed onto the seat of the creaking wooden wagon.

She realized too late that the seat was small and narrow, and she would be sitting right up against Kip.

The horses stamped and tossed their heads, as if eager to get going. Kip climbed onto the wagon, holding the horses back.

"It's been a while since I've taken them out," Kip said as if apologizing for their behavior. His lips were pressed together, and his eyes narrowed. "Last chance," he said adjusting the reins in his hand.

Nicole gave into an impulse, and squeezed his knee. "I'm not worried at all."

Their gazes met and held. Kip lifted the corner of his mouth in a gentle smile. "Thanks for that."

He eased off on the reins, and with a jerk the horses took off, though Kip held them back to a trot.

The wooden wagon had no suspension, and every bump on the ground vibrated up through the wagon seat. That didn't matter. Nicole felt exhilarated watching the four horses move in unison and watching Kip controlling them. He made it look easy, but she could see by the whiteness of his knuckles and the way his elbows locked that he was using a lot of strength to hold them back.

"Why don't you take them onto the tracks?" Nicole suggested. "Maybe they need to get rid of some energy."

Kip shot her a nervous glance. "Are you sure? If they hit the track they'll try to go flat out."

"Like I said, Kip. I trust you to take care of these horses."

Kip drew in a long slow breath then turned the horses toward the beaten oval track on the other side of the horse corral.

As he eased off the reins a bit, one of the leading horses tossed his head and with a jump headed out, the other horses going along.

Nicole grabbed onto the side of the wagon with one hand as the horses gained speed, the beat of their pounding hooves coming closer and closer together. Then they were thundering on the packed ground, manes flying, tails up. Nicole's hair whipped back from her face, and dust roiled around them. Kip narrowed his eyes and leaned forward.

As the horses gained speed, the grin on Kip's face grew wider.

Though she wanted to watch the horses, Nicole could not keep her eyes off him. It was as if he transformed right before her eyes and she saw yet another part of him.

Then, on the second time round the track, she saw Isabelle, Tristan, Justin and Mary standing by the fence watching. Their faces were a blur as they ran past, but she saw the boys waving at them.

They went another time around the track and Kip eased the horses down to a trot, his grin a white flash against his dusty face. "You okay?" he asked Nicole.

"That was fantastic," she said, pushing her hair back from her face.

"Looking good," Mary called out giving him a thumbs-up.

"Can we go for a ride?" Justin yelled.

Kip shook his head. "Nicole and I are taking them out for a bit more. They're still kind of antsy."

Justin pushed his lips out in a pout, Tristan crossed his arms over his chest as if expressing his frustration, but Kip didn't seem moved by the display.

Nicole felt guilty that she was the one to take the first ride out. The grim look on Isabelle's face told Nicole the young girl felt the same. But Mary was grinning. It wasn't hard to see how happy she was to see her son driving the horses again.

"We'll be back in a couple of hours," Kip called out as he eased off on the reins and the horses headed out again, but at a slower pace than before.

Fifteen minutes later, Kip had them eased down to a gentle walk. The creaking of the wagon and the steady plod of the horses hooves filled the silence that sprang up between them.

Nicole was content to simply look around, and enjoy the space and the quiet in his company. That the swaying of the wagon bumped her shoulder up against Kip's from time to time was a nice benefit.

"I'm surprised how much I've missed this," Kip said quietly, finally breaking the silence.

"I can see why. This is beautiful." Nicole's gaze shifted to the mountains edging the field they rode along. "So peaceful. It will be difficult to go back to the city."

Kip sighed lightly and Nicole glanced over at him.

"What's wrong?" she asked.

Kip's only reply was to pull back on the horses, bringing them to a stop. He pushed on what she assumed was the brake of the wagon, then wrapped the reins around the handle of the brake, holding the horses back.

They stamped and snorted, but settled down.

Nicole's heart fluttered in her chest as Kip turned to her. He grazed her cheek with his knuckle, his eyes flitting over her face.

"Do you have to go back?"

Nicole's breath hovered in her chest, as if unsure of where to go.

"You know I do."

"No. I don't." He spoke the words quietly, but Nicole heard an edge of frustration in them.

Her feelings for him were changing every day they spent together. He was easing into a part of her heart that she had kept closed off for a long time, and she sensed he felt the same.

Though it frightened her, it also created tantalizing possibilities, and now he was putting voice to her own questions.

She looked away, her feelings wavering. Staying would make things easier. Staying would be the best solution.

"And what about my father?"

"What about him?"

"He can't be dismissed that easily. He needs to see the boys."

Kip tucked his knuckle under her chin and gently turned her face back to his. "Let's not talk about the boys for now. Let's talk about you and me."

That was even scarier.

"I don't know…"

Kip brushed his knuckle over her skin. "What don't you know? How you feel?"

Nicole pressed her trembling lips together. She knew

how she felt about him. She simply didn't dare tell him. Not with so many things hanging between them.

Then Kip leaned closer and brushed a kiss, light as the breeze that toyed with her hair, over her lips. "I think you know how I feel about you."

Nicole caught his hand, hardly daring to think that this man, in spite of who she was, could care for her. Hardly daring to allow herself to take what he was gently offering.

It meant becoming vulnerable and giving Kip the ability to hurt her. To break her heart.

"I'm a stable guy," Kip said, as if reading her thoughts. "I don't say things I don't mean and I do what I say I'm going to do."

Nicole knew that all too well. Taking care of his mother and sister, taking care of the boys. He was stable and sure.

"I don't know how you can," she said quietly, unable to simply take what he was offering. It was a dream. It wasn't possible. "I can't stay. I'm taking the boys—"

Kip silenced her with another kiss. "Don't go," Kip whispered, his lips touching her cheek, her forehead. "Stay here. With me and the boys."

Nicole closed her eyes, his words drawing out her deepest yearnings. Yearnings for a place she belonged. A home. A family.

Oh, how she wanted to give in and say yes.

"You know I care for you," Kip said, pulling back, his fingers trailing down her cheek. "I think you feel the same way, because I don't think you're the kind of woman who would let someone kiss her casually."

They had only spent a few weeks together and already he knew her that well. "I'm not," she said quietly, clinging to her hands. "You've come to mean more to me than…" she let the sentence trail off, the implications of her words ringing in her mind.

If she acknowledged her true feelings, what would that mean for her? It would tear apart everything she had come here to do.

"I have to bring the boys back to my father."

"Do you really think you can take them away from all of this?" Kip flung his arm out, his movement encompassing the length and breadth of the country surrounding them—the fields, the hills and the mountains beyond that.

His question hit her own doubts with deadly accuracy. She wanted to be able to say without hesitation, yes. Yes, she could.

At one time she'd been able to. But now?

Now she'd seen the boys running free, helping Kip, working with the cows. She could easily see them in the future riding horses once Kip got past his own guilt. She could see them running pell-mell through fields, as free as the horses that Kip raised.

"I don't know," was all she could say.

"Then why do you want to?"

She looked up at him and that was her undoing. Faint lines radiated out from his eyes. Eyes used to squinting against a prairie sun. Eyes that could probe deep into her soul and make her bare secrets she'd told no one.

"I have to. I owe it to my father."

Kip caught her by the shoulders. "Why do you think you owe your father so much? Why do you think his love comes with so many burdens attached to it?"

Nicole wished he weren't holding her. Her own lonely

soul yearned for his touch, for his nearness. But she had to explain one more time.

"Sam and Norah took me from a life of uncertainty and gave me security. Gave me a life. They gave me a little sister who I..." Nicole's voice broke on that last word. She fought her tears back. She took a steadying breath. "I owe my father more than I can ever hope to repay."

"And you hope to repay part of that debt by taking the boys away from the only life they'd ever known?"

Nicole wanted to pull away from his touch. It confused her. His hands on her shoulders made her second-guess convictions that weren't as single-minded as they were when she first came.

"Sam gave me a family. He gave me a job. He gave me my life."

"How much is enough to pay that back?"

His words cut her. "How can you ask that?"

"I'm using your language. You're the one talking about owing and repaying."

She didn't know how to answer him.

"Love is a gift, Nicole. It isn't about weighing and measuring and repaying. Love isn't earned. Like the pastor said on Sunday, love is God's great gift to us, and it comes without a price."

"But the boys—"

Kip narrowed his eyes and slowly nodded his head. "It always seems to come back to the boys. I'm wondering if you think bringing them back will earn you your father's love."

Nicole's eyes narrowed. "Is that what you think I'm doing?"

Kip shrugged, pulling away. "Why don't you tell me?"

"It's so much more than that."

"So explain."

"I can't keep the boys away from him, Kip," she snapped, his accusation making her angry. He didn't know. He didn't realize. "I can't. He gave me everything and I took...I sent his only daughter away."

"What? How do you figure that?"

Nicole's anger eased away as her shame, buried so deep, so long, slowly worked its way through the crack created by her emotions. Like the weeds in the garden she'd been tending with Mary the past few days, the secret was pushing up through and couldn't be hidden.

She bit her lip, looked away, trying to regain the anger. Anger was better. Anger was like an offense. It pushed people away.

But she couldn't find it as easily as she used to.

"Nicole, what are you talking about?" Kip's voice softened and he lifted one hand to cup her cheek.

"I can't...I can't..."

"Please. Tell me."

Nicole took a breath, her own emotions threatening to overwhelm her.

"Tricia...I loved her, you know. She was my sister. My little, adorable, loved and protected sister. She was the daughter that Sam and Norah had waited so long for." She swallowed, struggling to stay on top of her emotions. "She was their only child, but she didn't get it. She didn't understand how good she had it. I tried to tell her. Tried to make her understand. She always fought with our parents. Always rebelled. Then, one day, I found out she'd been hanging out with a bad crowd. Doing drugs. I got mad and yelled at her." The memories came in waves now, relentlessly washing over her. "We had a huge fight. I told her she was treating our parents poorly. She told me that I was jealous of her." Nicole bit her lip and looked down, still ashamed of her actions. "I told her I was. I told her that every day, when I was a little girl, I wished for parents like she had." Nicole clenched her fists, struggling, fighting. "Then I told her she didn't deserve to be a Williams. That she didn't deserve this family and if she couldn't be a loving daughter, if she couldn't appreciate all the good things she'd received from this family, then maybe she should go."

"And then she did leave."

Kip's quiet voice gave substance to the reality that had haunted Nicole from the morning she went to her sister's room.

"She left me a note. Just me." She paused, remembering.

"What did it say?" Kip's gentle voice drew the deeper confession out of her.

"It said that if I thought that our parents were so wonderful, then she was leaving. Leaving me to have them to myself. She told me that she didn't want to be a Williams. That she had never chosen to be a part of this family. That was it. That was the extent of what she wrote." Her voice broke. It was all she could to keep the sorrow inside. "She left because of me. The adopted daughter. The one that was brought into the family. She was the real Williams and she left. I drove her away. I didn't deserve what Sam and Norah had done for me. Sam was right when he told me that. Sam was right when he said that I didn't deserve to be a Williams." A sob crept up her throat and she swallowed it down. "Now Tricia's dead and Norah's dead and I don't know how to fix what I broke. I don't know how except to bring Tricia's boys back. Back to their family...back to Sam..." She stopped as another

sob washed upward followed by another. "I owe him so
much. He gave me so much, and I'm not even his natural
daughter. Bringing the boys back to him will fix everything I did." Suddenly she couldn't hold it back anymore.
Sobs racked her body, tears streamed down her cheeks
as her shame and pain finally found release.

Next thing she knew she was in Kip's arms and he was
holding her tightly against his chest, a haven in the storm
of sorrow and pain that she had held back for so long.

"Nicole, oh Nicole, how could you think that?" Kip
murmured, his head pressed against hers, his strong arms
holding her close.

"I loved them, I did," Nicole sobbed. "I loved them
all. But Tricia left and Sam blamed me…I didn't mean
to hurt Sam and Norah. I was trying to help. I don't deserve the good things they did for me."

Kip silenced her with another kiss, then he held
her close.

"It's not your fault, Nicole. It's not your fault," Kip
murmured. "Tricia made her own choices and your father was wrong to drop those choices on your shoulders."

Nicole wanted to believe him. Oh, how she wanted to
believe him, but she had clung to that guilt so long, she
didn't know if she could let go.

"It's not your fault," Kip repeated, more firmly this
time. "You are a good daughter, and you keep saying
that you owe Sam Williams. Well, he owes you. You are
a faithful daughter. You are a better daughter than Tricia. Any parent would love more than anything to have
a daughter as good and faithful as you."

His words eased part of her sorrow. Then he pulled
back, framing her face with his hands. "You are an amaz-

ing person who has made good choices. You don't need to earn your father's love."

"I didn't really belong—"

"You belong in the Williams family as much as the boys belong in our family." Kip couldn't keep the anger out of his voice. "I don't love those boys more or less because they're not my biological sons. They are a part of me because I chose to take them in. I chose to take them into my heart. They may not have been born to me, but they grew to become a part of me. And I want what's best for them. I want nothing but good things for them."

Nicole heard the conviction in his voice, and her tears slowly subsided and she closed her swollen eyes. Her aching head rested on Kip's shoulder. She didn't want to be strong anymore. She didn't want to be responsible, and she didn't want Kip to let her go.

She stayed there a moment longer, letting his strength hold her up and support her.

He murmured her name again and she looked up at him. His head was a silhouette against the blue prairie sky. Then he lowered his head and his lips touched hers.

She reached up to him, wrapping her arms around him, returning his kiss, letting herself be drawn closer, letting him into her heart.

His lips touched her cheek and then he buried his face in her hair, his one hand caressing her head.

"Don't go, Nicole," he said. "Don't go."

She hardly dared wonder what he was saying. Hardly dared let his words enter her soul.

Instead she stayed in his arms, her own clinging to him, the sun pouring down on them both like a benediction.

She didn't want to go either, but reality seeped into

the moment. The boys and the reality of their legal status still stood between them. She knew that she didn't want to take them away from here either. She knew they belonged here.

"We should go back," she said quietly. "I'm sure your mother is wondering what's happening."

"I think she knows." Kip gave her another quick kiss as the wagon jolted. The horses were getting antsy.

Nicole didn't want to go. She wanted this moment to stay forever, this time out of time. She didn't want to go back to the ranch and the boys and the cold, hard reality of the decisions she had to make.

She lowered her arms and drew away.

"Let's go, then."

When they got back to the ranch, Doreen and her kids had arrived, so Kip took the boys and Doreen's kids for a couple of tours around the track while Doreen and Nicole hung over the fence and watched.

"Kip looks good driving the team again," Doreen said quietly, her arms folded over the top rail of the fence.

Nicole wasn't sure what to say in reply, so she just nodded.

"I love watching him with the horses. He hasn't done it for a while and I know he misses it." Doreen's eyes were on Kip, watching his progress around the track, smiling at the sounds of the children's laughter drifting back to them. "Thanks for helping me push him into this."

"I didn't really do much," Nicole protested.

Doreen shot her a wry glance. "You've done more than you might think. I haven't seen Kip this relaxed in a long time." Her voice seemed to hint at something Nicole wasn't sure she wanted to examine. At least not with Kip's sister watching her.

Half an hour later Doreen helped the protesting kids out of the wagon.

"We should go see Grandma," she said as she and Nicole herded the whole works toward the house. "Nicole, you're the horse person. Why don't you help Kip with the horses while I get these kids cleaned up."

And before Nicole could say anything, Doreen was gone, the children trailing behind her.

Thankfully Kip hadn't heard the exchange. She hesitated, but only a moment. The thought of spending more time with Kip was greater than her self-consciousness over what Doreen had hinted at all.

She walked back to where Kip was, helped him lead the horses back to the barn, then helped him unhitch them.

They worked together in silence, but Nicole was aware of every brush of their hands, every time they bumped against each other.

It was like slow torture, she thought. Thankfully, the boys stayed away, letting her and Kip have this moment.

Nicole helped him hang up the harnesses and when everything was done, when there was no job left to do, he turned to her and rested his hands on her arms.

"So, Nicole Williams, where do we go from here?"

She didn't want to think about that. She wasn't sure herself. It made her heart hurt.

Kip's hands lingered on her arms, drifted down to her hands and caught them in hers. The calluses on his hands were rough against hers. The hands of a working man. The hands of a man who cared so much for his family that he was willing to make all the sacrifices that each callus represented.

She chanced a look into his eyes, then brushed her

fingers over his cheek, his whiskers rasping against her hand.

"I don't know." She couldn't give him anything more than that. "I simply don't know anymore. The truth is your brother rescued the boys. He saved them when he brought them here."

Kip gave her a sad smile, as if he understood. "They were his boys. What else could he do?"

"But the will. I don't know what to do about the will. If it's proved to be Tricia's…" She wasn't sure where to go anymore. At one time everything was laid out so clearly. Her obligations. Her work. Her plan to bring the boys back to her father where she had, at one time, thought they belonged.

Now it was as if that everything that had given her life meaning was no longer as valid as it had been.

It's not your fault.

Kip's words comforted and frightened her at the same time. Because if Tricia's leaving wasn't her fault, if she was absolved of what Tricia had done, then where did that leave her with her father?

Their entire relationship during the past few years was built on the foundation of Nicole's obligation to her father—first by way of the adoption, then by way of the repercussions of her "talk" with Tricia. The talk that drove Tricia out into the world.

It's not your fault.

"I'm willing to wait," he said quietly. "I'm willing to give you time to sort things out."

His tenderness and consideration cradled her soul.

"You are an amazing man, Kip Cosgrove," she said quietly, squeezing his hand.

Kip's smile created an answering happiness.

Tell him. Tell him that you think the boys should stay.

She held his gaze, wondering what he would say if she told him that. Wondering what would happen.

Kip's words wound themselves around her weary soul, then his arms held her close. She rested in the shelter they offered, laying her head against his chest, drawing from his quiet strength.

You are a good daughter. You are a good daughter.

She had thought bringing the boys to Toronto could change everything between her and her father, but she also wondered if Kip was right. Was she pinning too much on the boys?

They should stay.

Nicole let the words drift through her mind, testing them.

They belong here.

As Nicole let the words settle, peace entered her soul. And even more important, Kip was offering her something even more.

Did she dare take that too? Wasn't that too many underserved blessings?

And then her phone jangled a tune.

"You were carrying your phone around with you?" Kip laughed.

"I forgot about it," Nicole said with a gentle smile as she pulled the phone out her pocket.

Kip caught her hand. "Just leave it, Nicole. Don't let anything else come in right now."

But as he spoke, her eyes slipped down, as if they had no power of their own. It was her father calling.

Kip didn't let go of her hand, and as she looked back a him, he didn't let his gaze leave hers as he gently shook his head.

She looked from him to the phone, torn. But years of obligation drew harder on her than her recent moment with Kip.

"I'm sorry. I have to take this." She took a few steps away from him and answered the phone.

"Nicole. Have you spoken to that cowboy's lawyer yet?"

Trust her father to get straight to the point. He must be feeling better, she thought with a measure of relief.

"No, and I don't believe Kip has either."

"You may as well know, we got the first DNA test back today."

"Which one?"

"Mine won't come for a couple of days, but we got Mary Cosgrove's. And we got good news. Mary Cosgrove is not the boys' grandmother."

Nicole pressed her hand to her chest, her emotions in a sudden tailspin. A few weeks ago she would have welcomed this news.

But a few weeks ago, Kip was a hindrance to her goal. A few weeks ago Kip was simply an annoying, attractive complication getting in the way of her plan to take the boys back to where she thought they belonged.

How much had changed in the past week. The past few days.

Nicole didn't want to let her mind dwell on that. Her father's phone call and the hard reality of the boys' parentage were what she had to face now.

She tried not to look at Kip, refocussing her emotions. She knew her father well enough to understand what his next step would be.

"So that means…"

"Scott Cosgrove is not the boys' father. The boys belong to me. I want you to bring them back here as soon as possible. I've got the lawyer coming tomorrow afternoon. He's filing the papers and after that I want the boys back here."

"How can you—"

"I'll use the police if I have to," Sam growled.

Nicole rubbed her forehead with her fingers. He would, she thought. Once Sam Williams had an idea in his head, there was no stopping him no matter how he felt.

Nicole glanced back at Kip, who was watching her. Again her obligations to her father pulled on her.

She looked away from him. She had to make a choice. Had to make a decision.

But how could she go through with it?

Chapter Fifteen

Kip watched the interplay of emotions on Nicole's face while she spoke to her father on the phone.

Panic shot through him when her eyes widened and she glanced at Kip. The expression on her face wasn't encouraging.

Then she walked away from him, talking in low, urgent tones.

He wanted to grab the phone out of her hands and tell her to put her father aside. To put the boys aside. To focus on what she needed and wanted.

Kip stood, his hands on his hips, watching as she wilted in front of his eyes. Her shoulders dropped, her head lowered and she seemed to turn in on herself.

Did she even realize what effect her father had on her?

A few minutes later she was finished with her call. She stood with her back to him, her head lowered, and Kip felt as if everything he'd told her had been erased with that one phone call.

She turned back to him and he read the anguish on her face.

"I have to go back," she said quietly.

Kip started. This was not what he expected to hear. "Go back? To Toronto? Is something wrong with your father?"

She shook her head. "He's feeling much better." She bit her lip and Kip's heart dropped into his gut.

"So why do you have to go back now? Just as things are changing for us?"

"I know, but..." She lifted her hands toward him, then clenched them into fists. "The situation is different."

"How? What did your father say to you that could possibly have made such a difference?"

Nicole pressed her fists against her forehead. Kip wanted to drag her hands away and tell her how much he hated seeing her like this.

Nicole lowered her hands, but still didn't look at him. "My father got the first of the DNA tests back."

Kip's breath left him in a rush. His heart vibrated erratically, like it always did before a big race when he thought about the uncertainty of what lay ahead and where events would take him.

At least, when he was racing, he had the reins in his hand. He was in charge.

"There were no DNA matches between the boys and your mother. From what the lab could figure out, Scott wasn't the boys' biological father."

Kip could only stare at her. It was as if her mouth was moving but he couldn't figure out exactly what she was saying. Something about Scott not being the boys' father? "How...how can that be? That's impossible."

Ron was supposed to have heard about the tests the same time as Mr. William's lawyer. Why hadn't Ron called him?

"Why would Scott…he mustn't have known…" Kip's voice drifted off as the implications of this slowly sank in.

"It was what I had told you from the beginning," she said.

Kip could only stare at her. Was that all she had to say? "Are you kidding me?"

Nicole frowned as if she didn't understand. "Kip, why is this such a surprise? I told you that Tricia said—"

"And Scott told me they were his kids." Kip shoved his hand through his hair and spun away from her. He couldn't pull his thoughts together into a coherent sentence.

When Nicole had first come with her far-fetched story of the boys not belonging to Scott, he'd never, for one moment, believed her.

His thoughts sped back and forth as he tried to think. To plan.

"She left them," he growled, his pain and frustration seeping into his voice. "She abandoned those boys and Scott saved them." He turned back to her. "That has to mean something."

Nicole didn't reply.

"He did what he was supposed to, even if the boys weren't his. Nicole, tell me what you're thinking." He wanted to pull her close. He wanted to go back to where they were before her father intruded into her life again. "Tell me what's on your mind."

She reached out and touched his face, her cool fingers trailing a light caress down his cheek. "I have to go," she said quietly.

"Don't do this, Nicole," Kip said. "Don't throw what we have away."

She took a step back.

Away from him.

"Don't go, Nicole. Don't make me your enemy."

She gave him a sad smile. "You'll never be my enemy."

"If you try to take my boys away, you will be. I'll fight you tooth and nail for them."

As soon as the words left his mouth, he regretted saying them. It wasn't about the boys. It was about her. He didn't want her to go. He didn't want to lose her.

But he wasn't sure he could say that yet.

She paused, the hurt in her eyes obvious. Then she turned and walked away.

This wasn't where they were supposed to end up, but he didn't know how to get back to where he wanted to be.

Go after her. Don't let her leave you like this. Tell her how you really feel.

He took a step toward her, then stopped himself. No. She had made her choice. In spite of everything he had told her, everything he had offered her, she'd chosen her father over him.

He had to stay back here and fight for his boys and let her go back to where she thought she belonged.

"I'm sorry, I don't have the best news, Kip," Ron said.

Kip clutched the telephone, glancing over at his mother, who stood by the sink, peeling potatoes.

Since Nicole had left two days ago, his mother had been working harder and harder on her exercises. It was as if she wanted to get strong enough to stand up for her grandsons.

But they're not her grandsons.

Kip pushed the traitorous thought away. The boys were as much a part of his family as they were part of the Williams family. More, in fact.

"They've filed for legal custody of the boys." Ron's voice was a disembodied sound as Kip realized what had happened. No wonder she took off so quick.

After Nicole had left, some part of him had nurtured the faintest hope that she would come back and tell him she had changed her mind.

But he heard nothing. No phone call, no email. Just a long, frustrating silence that grew more oppressing each day. A silence that choked off the brief moment of enthusiasm he'd experienced when he hitched up the horses.

A silence that slowly eroded at the hope she would come back and tell him she would help him fight for the boys.

Instead she had chosen her father over them.

What did you expect? A few kisses and a few declarations of affection and she was going to throw over nearly a lifetime of obligation to a man who required more than she could give?

"So what do we do now?" Kip asked, fear and frustration and confusion warring in his gut.

"We can fight back," Ron said. "Claim that Scott acted in the best interests of the boys when he took them. I'm still working on the validity of her will, but I'm warning you, it's uphill now that it's been proven the boys aren't Scott's."

Kip sighed and tunneled his hand through his hair.

"So what do you want me to do?" Ron pressed.

"I can't think right now. I'll have to get back to you." Kip disconnected the phone and released a heavy sigh.

"I take it that's not good news," Mary said, her voice small.

Kip glanced her way, wondering how much to tell her. "Nicole's father has filed for custody of the boys." Kip said, preferring to break things to his mother one piece of bad news at a time.

His mother flipped her tea towel over her shoulder and came to sit beside him. "What are we going to do?"

"I don't think there's anything we can do," Kip said. "I'm sure that's why Nicole hightailed it back to Toronto so fast. She didn't want to be around when everything imploded."

Mary laid her hand on his arm. "I know that you cared for her," his mother said quietly.

Kip sighed. "Yeah. I did."

"Did?" his mother pressed.

"Do." He tapped his fingers on his arm. "I don't know what to do. Don't know what to think."

"Why?"

Kip held his mother's gaze, then looked past her to the kitchen with its worn cupboards, stained linoleum and scarred countertop. He had only seen pictures of the outside of Nicole's home, but he was sure the countertops were granite, the floor solid hardwood and the cupboards crafted from some exotic wood that he'd never heard of.

"Even before Nicole came, I often wondered how I would take care of everyone." He hated to admit this to his mother, but he had to be honest with her. "I wondered especially about the boys. Would I be able to give them the life I thought they should have." He looked up at her. "I don't think I can give them the life that I know the Williams family can."

His mother gave him a tired smile. "I know how you feel. I've thought the same."

Her admission gave Kip some measure of relief. At least he didn't feel like he was giving up on the boys.

"You've taken on a lot since your father died. You've

always taken everything on yourself." Mary put her hand on his shoulder. "Now you've got the boys."

"Not for long, it seems."

He caught a glimmer of tears in his mother's eyes. "I don't want to see them go either, but you can only do so much." She caught his hands in her own, turning them over. "We've all depended on you a lot. Depended on you to take care of us. To do what needed to be done. Then Nicole came and it was as if a burden shifted off your shoulders. She seemed to take some of what you were carrying on herself. The boys, me. Even Isabelle." She released a short laugh and squeezed his hands. "What is more important, I saw you smile. I saw you happy. I saw you falling in love again. That hasn't happened in a long time."

"I was in love with Nancy."

Mary shrugged. "I never saw you smile at Nancy the way I see you smile at Nicole, and I never saw you as upset about Nancy leaving the way you have been since Nicole left."

Kip eased out another sigh.

"I don't know what to do, Mom."

His mother squeezed his hands. "You can't 'do' anything anymore. Now, I think you have to let go and let God."

The familiar adage had always seemed lame and empty, but now, in the face of a situation that Kip could not control, he knew he had to do exactly what his mother suggested.

"Can we pray together?" his mother asked.

He nodded and together they bowed their heads.

"Please Lord, You know what is in our hearts. You know that we are concerned over what will happen to our boys, but at the same time, You know better what they need. Help us to trust that You will take care of them. Help us to realize that they were Yours before they were ever ours. Amen."

Before he raised his head, Kip added his own prayer for Nicole. For his own feelings for her. Because right now he was having a harder time putting her into God's hands than he was the boys.

Chapter Sixteen

The room was everything a little boy could want and, Nicole guessed, no expense was spared. Nicole adjusted the pillows of the bed, shaped like a car, then eased out a sigh. The past couple of days she'd felt as if she were hurtling down a road she had no control over.

I can do all things through Him who strengthens me.

The verse of the Bible resonated through Nicole's mind. Since arriving here, she had found an old Bible of her mother's. She had brought it into her room and read it whenever she had the chance. Yesterday she had read this quote.

Nicole clung to the words. She knew she would need the encouragement she had gotten from reading that in the next couple of days.

She gently closed the door of the large room and walked down the carpeted hall and down the stairs, her hand trailing over the wooden banister. Tricia used to slide down it, but Nicole never dared be that rebellious.

She glanced around the large foyer with its sparkling chandelier and windows that stretched up two and a half floors. Her mind slipped back to the jumbled porch of the Cosgrove household, the worn flooring in the kitchen and the faded paint on the outside of the house. In spite of the general air of neglect, that house felt more like a home than this house ever did.

Her heart faltered. Though she had been gone from the ranch only two days, it seemed like two weeks. She hadn't dared call Kip, but he had not called her either.

She missed him so much it hurt her heart. She wondered what he was thinking right now. She wondered if he thought of her. If he missed her as much as she missed him.

She wanted to talk to him, and chances were good she would one way or the other. The boys still had to be dealt with. But before she talked to Kip, she had to try one more thing.

Please Lord, help me through this, she prayed, one hand clutching the wooden banister. Then she took a breath, and strode down the long hallway to the sun room where her father waited for her.

"What do you think of the changes I've made for the boys?" Sam asked, looking up as she came into the room.

Her father sat in a wicker chair, his cheeks shining and his eyes bright. He looked better than he had in months.

And no wonder. He had a project and a purpose. Making plans and getting the house ready for Tricia's boys, as he'd been calling them since Nicole came back. He'd already managed to find a school they could attend come fall and had looked into various sports programs they would be able to participate in.

He was like a one-man freight train, pulling everyone along.

"I love the playroom, and I'm sure they would too,"

Nicole said quietly, settling into the padded wicker love seat across from her father.

"Would?" Of course Sam would have caught that tiny slip of the tongue. "What do you mean by that?"

Nicole wound a loose thread around the button on her cardigan, inarticulate words and thoughts piling up in her mind as she tried to sort out how to voice them.

She was about to speak when her father gestured to the pile of envelopes sitting on the table between them. "Heather brought this for you to look at."

Nicole frowned. "I had asked Heather to take care of the mail at the office."

"Heather did mention something like that when I asked her to bring it." Her father frowned. "You know all the ins and outs of the foundation's correspondence better than she ever will."

"I won't always be around," Nicole said, trying to lead into one of the things she wanted to talk to her father about.

"Nonsense. You're my right-hand man."

I would prefer to be your daughter, Nicole thought.

Instead she picked up the mail and started sorting through it.

She glanced at the return address of a large envelope, wondering what this was about. The corner was emblazoned with the name of a clinic that was unfamiliar to her.

She held up the envelope. "What's this?" she asked. "Test results?"

Her father looked up from the papers he was going over, then nodded. "I think that's the DNA test I had to do. The same test that messed up the expectations of that Cosgrove family."

Nicole's heart beat heavy in her chest at the contempt in her father's voice.

"That test didn't mess up that family that much," Nicole murmured, struggling against years of training that taught her to never, ever talk back to her father either as father or boss.

"What do you mean?" her father growled, then began coughing.

Nicole jumped to her feet and handed him a glass of water. He took the glass, took a drink, then stared up at Nicole. "They thought they had a biological claim on the boys, but they didn't. We won." He coughed again and took another drink.

Nicole put the glass back, then returned to her seat. She picked up the letter and stared at it. "Won what?" she asked.

"What is going on with you? Ever since you came back from Alberta you've been distracted. Like your mind is somewhere else."

It was, Nicole thought, slitting opening the envelope with her father's silver letter opener. Her mind was with Kip and Tristan and Justin and Kip and Mary…and Kip.

"I think you need to do something other than foundation work this afternoon," her father said. "Why don't you go out to one of those toy places and buy some kind of jungle gym for the yard," her father said. "Get something for the boys to play on."

Nicole glanced through the windows of the sun room to the yard beyond. Though it was large by Toronto standards, it suddenly looked small and restrictive compared to what she knew Tristan and Justin were used to.

"Would they love it?" she asked.

"What do you mean?"

Nicole pulled the letter slowly out of the envelope, still staring at the yard. "The only place those boys have known is the ranch. I wonder what it will be like for them to be uprooted from that."

Her father waved his hand, as if erasing her concerns. "You said yourself the Cosgroves were broke."

"I never said that. I said it didn't look like they had an abundance of ready cash." Which, when they thought the Cosgrove family might be willing to fight them in court, had been a concern.

"You know we can give the boys a better life."

"In one way, yes we can, but I don't think it's a good idea to uproot them."

Her father almost snorted. "You were moved around a lot and you turned out fine. Because we gave you a better place than any of the places you lived before. We gave you the best home you ever had."

Something that had been pointed out to her daily.

Something that never happened at the Cosgrove home. Tristan and Justin would grow up never knowing what Kip had sacrificed to be a father to them and to give them a home.

She thought of his chuck-wagon racing and her mind ticked back to her ride with him. How his eyes, no, his entire face lit up with excitement and the pure pleasure of working with the horses. He gave all that up for the boys, but she never got any sense of regret from Kip.

She riffled the papers in her hand, forcing herself to meet her father's piercing gaze. "I'm not sure we can do the same for Tristan and Justin," she said, quietly.

"What do you mean?"

Nicole kept her eyes on his, putting voice to the uncertainties that had grown in intensity in the past week.

Uncertainty that had grown into a reality. "I'm not sure we can give them a better home than they have in Alberta. I think they have everything they will ever want or need there. They belong in Alberta. With the Cosgroves."

"What are you talking about?" Her father looked baffled, as if he wasn't sure he had heard her properly.

"They've lived with that family for four years. They are the only family they know." Nicole's voice faltered as she tried to articulate what she had to say.

"What does that matter? Those boys don't even belong to them. Never will, no matter what they may think. They belong here. They belong to me. They're my only daughter's sons."

Only daughter. Why, after all this time, could those words still hurt so much?

Because she'd seen something else. She'd seen another kind of love. A kind of love that didn't depend on biology. The kind of love that was pure gift.

Just like God's love.

"I don't think Tristan and Justin belong to anybody," Nicole said carefully. "We have been treating them like they are possessions. They are people. Little boys, who only know what it's like to live on a ranch, with wideopen spaces, an uncle who loves them and a huge family who cares for them deeply. I think it's selfish to take them away from all of that."

"Are you saying I'm selfish for wanting to have my daughter's children living with me? Especially after this is what she wanted?" Her father's voice rose with each question, as if he could hardly believe that she would question him.

Please Lord, help me find the right words, she prayed. *Sam is still my father.*

"I think we have to step back from the situation, and forget about what Tricia wanted, what we want, I think we need to look at the boys' situation for their sake, not ours."

"Are you daring to question me?" Her father struggled to his feet, staring at her as if she didn't understand who she was talking to. "What kind of daughter does that?"

For a moment remorse clung to her.

You're a good daughter. You're a good daughter.

Kip's words resonated through her mind, washing away the guilt her father could so easily resurrect in her.

Love does not delight in evil, but rejoices with the truth.

She clung to those words as she turned to her father.

"The kind of daughter who thinks she should tell the truth. I can't support you in your fight to bring the boys back here. I can't help you with that and I won't."

Her father stared at her, as if he didn't recognize her. "Are you saying you would fight me?"

"I'm saying I would fight for what is best for Tristan and Justin," she amended. "If that puts me against you, then that's the way it has to be."

"You would choose that family over me?"

"It's not about choosing, Father. It's about doing what's best for the boys."

Sam's eyes narrowed and his expression grew thunderous. "After everything I've done for you, after all I've given you, this is how you repay me?"

"Repay you?" Nicole spoke quietly. "I didn't think love came with a cost."

Her father looked taken aback, but changed tactics. "You've done much damage to this family—"

"Tricia made her own choices, Father," Nicole said

quietly, drawing on the words Kip had told her. Words she had held close in the past few days.

"You pushed her."

"You pushed her too," Nicole snapped back. Her outburst surprised her as much as it surprised her father judging from the shocked look on his face. "I think she was leaving regardless. My fight with her was simply bad timing," she continued, suddenly tired of her father's endless condemnation.

In the shocked silence that followed Nicole's outburst she looked down at the letter she still held in her hands. She skimmed over the words, giving herself something to do other than face her father's anger. She came to the end of the letter.

What in the world?

She read it one more time, to make sure she had read correctly.

"What's wrong?" her father asked, obviously distracted by her puzzlement. "What's in the letter?"

She cleared her throat and looked at her father. "It says that the DNA from you doesn't match the boys' either."

Sam snatched the papers from her hand, his eyes racing over the letter. Then again. "I don't understand." He looked up, his once ruddy face, ashen. "The boys didn't belong to that man Tricia was living with and we know they are Tricia's. The detective's reports showed that."

Nicole frowned. "Detective's reports?"

"I hired a private detective to find a few more things out about Tricia and Scott."

This was news to her. Not that it mattered anymore. Now they were faced with an entirely different puzzle.

Sam looked down at the papers, shaking his head. "I

don't understand. I simply don't…" His voice faded as he read the papers again, his hands clenching.

Then his face grew hard, his eyes glinted and his nostrils flared as his head moved back and forth as if in denial of facts he couldn't absorb.

He flung the papers to the ground, glaring at them.

"Norah, how could you?" he called out.

"What are you talking about?" Nicole asked, catching him by the arm. "What's going on?"

He spun to face her, his eyes glittering with anger, his breath coming in short spurts. "I should have confronted her. But no. I thought Norah and that Bart fellow were just friends."

Nicole's confusion grew with every word. "I don't know what you mean. I don't know who Bart is."

Her father looked everywhere but at her as he seemed to gather his thoughts. He took a few breaths, then, as if the life was sucked out of him, his shoulders sagged down, his head lowered.

"Just before we adopted you, we found out I wasn't able to father a child. But Norah wanted a child so badly. I didn't. Then she started spending time with Bart and his wife. Finally, I gave in and she adopted you. Then, a few years later, when Norah had Tricia, it was like a miracle. That happens sometimes." His hands trembled as he dragged them over his face. "She told me Bart was just a friend and I believed her. Turns out, if this report is true, it seems he was a whole lot more."

"You can't know that for sure," Nicole said, stroking his shoulder, her pity for him coming to the fore.

"I always suspected." Sam pushed at the papers with the toe of his slipper. "This proves it." He stumbled back to his chair and dropped his head in his hands. "How could she have done this to me?" Her father sighed, then looked up at Nicole. "If my DNA doesn't match the boys, then this means that Tricia isn't my daughter either."

The "either" was like a small, indifferent slap.

"That means those boys don't belong to me."

Nicole was set back on her heels, trying to absorb everything she'd heard in the past few minutes. Tricia not her father's biological daughter. Her mother cheating on her father?

She couldn't put it all together.

Sam sighed, pushing his hands through his hair. "Tricia wasn't my daughter. She wasn't my daughter and I raised her. Paid for everything she had. What a waste."

On one level Nicole felt sorry for him and tried to realize that he was speaking from his pain, but on another level his words underlined the insecurity she'd felt ever since coming to this family.

He had paid for everything she had done. Was she a waste too?

Sam took another breath, then straightened and looked directly at Nicole. "So you said you would fight me over those boys?"

Puzzled as to where he was going with this, Nicole could only nod.

"You would really choose them over me?"

"It's not a matter of choice, but if that's how you want to put it, then I would put their needs over yours because I think Kip Cosgrove is the best person to be taking care of those boys." She still wasn't sure what was going on, but she stuck to what she knew to be right and true.

Sam emitted a bitter laugh. "That cowboy? What could he possibly give them?"

Anger surged through Nicole at the contempt in his

voice and she stepped away from her father. "That cowboy has made more sacrifices for Tristan and Justin than you ever have for me or Tricia. That cowboy is a kind and considerate man who I respect more than I've ever respected any man, including you. That cowboy is the best example of a father's love that I could ever imagine. I'm jealous of those boys because that cowboy is the best thing that has ever happened to them. Right now I wish I was with Kip, that cowboy as you call him, instead of here with you."

Her father stared at her, then he got up and walked over to the papers that still lay on the floor. He bent over and picked them up. Then he glanced over her shoulder.

"Looks like you might get your wish after all," was all he said.

What did he mean?

Nicole felt a prickling at the back of her neck, then slowly turned around. Her eyes widened.

How did he...? When...?

Kip stood in the doorway of the sun room, his cowboy hat pulled low on his head, his hands on his jeans-clad hips. She blinked, wondering if she was imagining things.

As she tried to pull her mind around his presence, her father grabbed the papers and walked over to Kip.

"You want those boys?" he asked. Then, without waiting for an answer, Sam Williams shoved the papers into Kip's hands. "You can have them. They don't belong to me."

Kip glanced from Sam to Nicole as he took the papers, his expression unreadable. Then he looked back at Sam. "Those boys don't belong to me either."

"What do you mean by that? I thought you wanted them."

"I do, but they aren't a possession, just like Nicole isn't your possession. The boys are a gift, like Nicole is a gift."

Sam glanced back over his shoulder, frowning as if trying to see her that way.

Then, without a backward glance, he walked slowly over to his office and closed the door behind him.

Nicole clasped her suddenly trembling hands together, still trying to absorb his presence in her home.

Kip took off his hat, and glanced around the sun room. "So this is a nice place you have here," he said.

"What are you doing here?" Nicole asked.

He took a few steps closer and dropped his hat on the chair beside her. Then his warm rough hands were covering hers. "I could be all manly and say I've come to claim what's mine. That might be partly true, but mostly I came because I wanted to see you."

Nicole closed her eyes, as if by doing so she could better absorb what he was saying. Then his lips brushed her forehead and her eyes flew open.

"Did you mean what you said to your father before I came in?" he asked, his voice quiet, but intense.

Nicole clung to his hands, her gaze clinging to his. "Every word."

He squeezed her hands. "I spent half the flight here practicing what I would say. I even wrote it down so I wouldn't forget." He took in a long, slow breath and blew it out, as if gathering his strength. "I want you to know that whatever you decide about Tristan and Justin has nothing to do with how I feel about you. I want what's best for the boys, and if you think that having them here is best for them, I'm willing to go with that."

Nicole could only stare at him, his speech in direct contrast to what she had just heard from her own father.

"You would give up the boys?" she asked.

"Like I told your father, I think I've had to realize they aren't mine, or yours or his to give up. But I do have to let go of what I want and put their needs first."

Nicole could only stare. This amazing, wonderful, caring man was willing to do something her father couldn't even conceive of doing. "Why?"

"Because I love them."

Back to love again.

"Because they are God's children first," Kip continued. "When I think that, I realize that what they need is more important than what I want."

"That's amazing," was all she could say.

"Not really." He blew out his breath, his hands kneading hers. Then he cleared his throat and continued. "I also want you to know that I care for you more than I ever cared for anyone. I don't know how it happened, and I don't know why, but for some reason I seem to have fallen in love with you."

Nicole's throat thickened with emotion as she stared at Kip. This wonderful, loving and caring man had fallen in love with her? She couldn't absorb it, couldn't take it in. It was too much.

Kip inclined his head toward her and gave a nervous laugh. "Usually a declaration like that requires some kind of response."

Happiness and gratitude and love washed over her in a cleansing flood. She fought back tears as she slipped her arms around his neck, pulled him toward her, and pressed a firm kiss to his lips. Then she drew back, her fingers tangling in his hair, then tracing the contours of his face as if making sure he was really here and really telling her all these wonderful things. "I've fallen in love with you too." Her words came out a lot shakier than his as she blinked away unexpected tears. "I can't believe that this is happening."

"Me neither." Kip kissed her again pulling her close to him. "I didn't know how this would turn out," he murmured stroking her hair as he tucked her head against his shoulder. "I only knew I couldn't stay on the ranch one moment longer without letting you know how I felt about you. I need you in my life. I need you at my side."

Nicole's heart could hold no more happiness. "I need you too," she murmured. "The past two days have been so hard. I needed to talk to my father, to try to convince him that the boy should stay where they are."

Kip kissed her again. "I don't want to talk about the boys right now. They've been too much a part of all of this. In spite of what I said before, my main reason for coming here was for you, and only you."

Nicole's first thought was that she didn't deserve such happiness. Maybe she didn't, but that didn't matter. It was being given to her, freely and without strings attached.

She kissed Kip again. "I love you so much," she whispered, stroking his face. "Though you didn't come here to talk about the boys, you may as well know that I believe my father is repealing his claim to them."

"Why would he be willing to give them up without a fight?"

"He just found out that his DNA doesn't match the boys' either."

Kip frowned. "I'm not sure I follow."

Nicole smiled at him. "Given the way my father operates, I think once he found out that the boys weren't biologically his, they didn't mean as much to him." She paused, biting her lip. "That's important to him."

Kip stroked her arms, his eyes narrowing. "I said this before, and I'll say it again, that man was blessed beyond blessing to have you as his daughter. He doesn't deserve you."

Kip's heartfelt words pierced her soul, and made a home there.

"Of course I don't deserve you either," he continued. "But I'm hoping I can persuade you to come back to the ranch." Kip's smile was tentative, as if he didn't dare believe she would take him up on the offer. "And once you're back in Alberta, I'm hoping I can persuade you to marry me."

Nicole threw her arms around Kip's neck her heart bursting with love. "I won't take much convincing. In fact, I've already got my suitcases packed."

Kip stared at her openmouthed. "For what?"

"Before you came, I was going to tell my father that I'm moving out. I didn't get the chance once the letter came. And then you came and now…"

"You should tell him now and I'm coming with you." Kip kissed her again. "I have a few things I have to discuss with him too."

Nicole opened the door of her father's office. Sam stood at the window, looking out over the yard, his shoulders slumped, his hands clasped behind his back.

Was he imagining Justin and Tristan playing there? Was he regretting the loss of the dreams and plans he had made?

Then he turned and simply stared at them as if waiting for them to talk.

"I've come to say goodbye," Nicole said quietly. "I meant to tell you earlier, but I'm moving out."

Sam glared at Kip, as if he was to blame. "And what about him?"

Kip stepped forward, his hat in his hand. A sign of respect, Nicole thought. He really was a good man.

"I want to let you know that I've asked Nicole to marry me. She's coming back to Alberta with me now. We will notify you of the wedding date." His words came out clipped, precise. As if he was making some kind of business deal.

"Aren't you supposed to ask my permission? I am after all her father."

"That's good to know," Kip said quietly.

"What's that supposed to mean?" Sam asked with a frown. But he didn't give Kip a chance to answer. He turned to Nicole. "I don't deserve to be treated like this."

Kip laid his arm over her shoulder and squeezed, encouraging her. Nicole gave him a quick smile, then walked over to her father's side.

"Someone told me once that I was a good daughter," she said quietly. "I believe them now. I've always tried to earn your love, but I'm not doing that anymore. Love is a gift. Kip taught me that," she said glancing over her shoulder at the man she loved. "I'll always love you, and I'll always be thankful for the family you've given me. However, it's time for me to start my own family." She gave her father a kiss. "I've left instructions to the housekeeper about what is supposed to happen with the things I couldn't take along. If there's any problem, let me know and I'll call you once I'm back in Alberta." Her father didn't reply. Nicole then turned and walked back to Kip, taking his hand in hers.

A few minutes later they walked out of the large double doors to a small car waiting outside.

"You couldn't get a truck?" Nicole asked as Kip opened the trunk and dropped her suitcases inside.

"This was all they had left at the airport," Kip said. "Once we're back in Alberta, I'll have my truck back again. And it can't come too soon." He shuddered. "Driving in Toronto is like pulling out my fingernails. Slowly."

Nicole could imagine. "Do you want me to drive back to the airport?"

"That's a direct affront to my masculinity," Kip said as he slammed the trunk shut. He jingled his keys as he looked up at the house. "Are you sure you won't miss all this?"

Nicole glanced behind her at the place that had been her home for the most of her life, trying to see it through Kip's eyes.

It was imposing compared to the farmhouse, but it was simply bricks piled upon bricks. Just a house.

"I might, just a bit," she said quietly, then turned back to Kip and smiled. "I think what I'll miss the most is having my own housekeeper."

"We could always put up a notice advertising for one at the local post office," Kip said with a grin, as he helped her into the car.

"Are you kidding?" Nicole said, wrinkling her nose. "You never know who'll show up on your doorstep."

"No, you don't," Kip said dropping a kiss on her forehead. "But you never know what might come of it."

Nicole cast another glance over her shoulder at the place that had been her home. Then she got into the car and turned to Kip.

"And now, let's go home."

Epilogue

"C'mon. Let's go. C'mon," Kip yelled, slapping his reins on the backs of the horses, squinting into the dust raised by dozens of hooves pounding into the ground and sixteen wagon wheels churning up the dirt.

Yokes clanked, wheels rumbled and above all that he could hear the roar of the crowd as his horses stretched out, doing the best and gaining foot by foot.

Just a bit more. Just a few feet more and they'd be ahead of the leader, Willard Kelly.

Kip braced himself against the rocking of the wagon, leaning ahead as far as he dared urging his horses on. The spectators lining the rails were a blur. Kip knew Nicole and the boys were watching, but he kept his focus on the horses and on the finish line.

A bit more. Just a bit more.

Then they were across the chalked line and the race was over.

Kip drew back on the reins, pulling his horses back. They tossed their heads, unwilling to stop. They had done well, he thought. They had done their best and he was thrilled they had come this far.

The Rangeland Derby. Even to qualify had been thrill enough for him.

"And the winner of the heat, back in competition after a long break…Kip Cosgrove."

The words of the announcer blared above the noise of the crowd and Kip dropped back onto the seat of the chuck wagon, his heart pounding.

He won his heat. He actually won his heat.

The reins slipped through his hand because of his moment of inattention and he gathered them up, slowly bringing his horses to a quick walk.

He'd won his heat. And, even better, he won in front of Nicole and the kids.

"Good race, Kip," Willard called out as he turned his team around. "Good to see you back on the circuit."

Kip nodded his acknowledgment, his entire focus on getting his horses turned around. The next group of wagons were coming around for their heat and he needed to get out of the way.

When he got his horses turned, his sponsor's rep, Aidan Thomson, jumped into his wagon to join him in the victory walk past the stands.

"Good race, Cosgrove," he said, slapping Kip on the shoulder, then waving to the people as they drove past the grandstand. "Your father-in-law will be happy to know he's getting a return on his sponsorship."

Kip just grinned, rubbed the dust out of his eyes with his arm and glanced over the people gathered at the rail.

Then he saw them. Nicole waving, Justin sitting on the rail whistling, Tristan yelling with his hands cupped around his mouth.

Mary and Isabelle stood to one side madly waving as well. On Nicole's other side stood Nicole's father, arms resting on the rails, eyes narrowed as if still trying to figure this whole chuck-wagon-racing thing out.

Sam gave Kip a curt nod of his head, and from Sam Williams that was high praise indeed.

Sam had kept his distance for a while until Kip's mother had taken things in hand and called him. She'd told him in no uncertain terms he could either die a lonely, miserable old man or he could accept the family he had and see it as a blessing.

It had taken a few letters, a few pictures and a few phone calls from Nicole for Sam to come around. But eventually he had. During his first visit to the ranch, the twins had been enthusiastic and charming and he had thawed under their spell. Seeing Kip working with the horses had sealed the deal and Kip had gotten a new sponsor.

Then Kip caught Nicole's gaze.

She pressed her fingers to her mouth and blew him a kiss, grinning and waving. I love you, she mouthed.

I love you too, he returned.

"Nice little family you got there," Aidan said.

"The best," Kip said, bunching his reins into one hand and waving back, his grin almost hurting his face. "The best family this cowboy could ask for."

* * * * *

Dear Reader,

The burden of obligation can lie heavily on someone's shoulders. Especially when carrying that burden makes a person feel they are less. Nicole struggled with the fact that she was adopted, and therefore she felt an obligation to earn the love of her parents. And to some degree, her father reinforced that idea.

Kip, in spite of his own shortcomings, was an example to her of love that gives without expectation of a return. The kind of love that God gives us every day. I know there are times that I don't feel I deserve God's love. That I have to earn it and work for it. But the reality is that God's perfect love cannot be earned. It can only be received. I pray that you may feel God's awesome, powerful love in your life, as well.

Carolyne Aarsen

We hope you enjoyed reading
this special collection.

If you liked reading these stories,
then you will love **Love Inspired**® books!

You believe hearts can heal. **Love Inspired**
stories show that faith, forgiveness and hope
have the power to lift spirits and change
lives—always.

Enjoy six new stories from
Love Inspired every month!

Available wherever books and
ebooks are sold.

**Uplifting romances of faith,
forgiveness and hope.**

Find us on Facebook at
www.Facebook.com/LoveInspiredBooks

STEPLI

COMING NEXT MONTH FROM
Love Inspired®

Available May 19, 2015

THE COWBOY'S HOMECOMING
Refuge Ranch
by Carolyne Aarsen

Abby Newton knows she should stay away from the charming cowboy blamed for her family's downfall, but when she's roped into working with Lee Bannister on his ranch, will they rediscover the romance they've never forgotten?

A MOTHER TO LOVE
by Gail Gaymer Martin

As she helps coworker Rick Jameson gain custody of his little girl—and falls for both dad and daughter—can Angie Bursten forgive the mistakes from her past and open her heart to a new future?

THE AMISH WIDOW'S SECRET
by Cheryl Williford

Desperate for help with his children, widowed dad Mose Fischer proposes marriage to widow Sarah Nolt. Could this be their chance for true love, or will Sarah's secrets rock the foundation they've built?

HEALING THE LAWMAN'S HEART
Kirkwood Lake
by Ruth Logan Herne

Midwife Julia Harrison never imagined she'd clash with state trooper Tanner Reddington when opening her women's clinic, but when they join forces to save a baby girl, they might find their chance at forever—together.

SAFE IN THE FIREMAN'S ARMS
by Tina Radcliffe

Coming to the rescue of Maggie Jones is no hardship for hunky fire chief Jake MacLaughlin, but when the shy girl suddenly has a line of suitors, Jake will have to prove he's her perfect match!

A RANCHER FOR THEIR MOM
Rodeo Heroes
by Leann Harris

Cowboy Joel Kaye is back on the rodeo circuit to find glory, but when he starts to work on single mom April Landers's ranch, he'll find a new purpose—one filled with love and family.

———————

LOOK FOR THESE AND OTHER LOVE INSPIRED BOOKS WHEREVER BOOKS ARE SOLD, INCLUDING MOST BOOKSTORES, SUPERMARKETS, DISCOUNT STORES AND DRUGSTORES.

LICNM0515

SPECIAL EXCERPT FROM

Love Inspired®

Can a widow and widower ever leave their grief in the past and forge a new future—and a family—together?

Read on for a sneak preview of
THE AMISH WIDOW'S SECRET.

"Wait, before you go. I have an important question to ask you."

Sarah nodded her head and sat back down.

"I stayed up until late last night, thinking about your situation and mine. I prayed, and *Gott* kept pushing this thought at me." He took a deep breath. "I wonder, would you consider becoming my *frau*?"

Sarah held up her hand, as if to stop his words. "I…"

"Before you speak, let me explain." Mose took another deep breath. "I know you still love Joseph, just as I still love my Greta. But I have *kinder* who need a mother to guide and love them. Now that Joseph's gone and the farm's being sold, you need a place to call home, people who care about you, a family. We can join forces and help each other." He saw a panicked expression forming in her eyes. "It would only be a marriage of convenience. The girls need a loving mother and you've already proven you can be that. What do you say, Sarah Nolt? Will you be my wife?"

Sarah sat silent, her face turned away. She looked into Mose's eyes. "You'd do this for me? But…you don't know me."

"I'd do this for us," Mose corrected, and smiled.

LIEXP0515

The tips of Sarah's fingers nervously pleated and un-pleated a scrap of her skirt. "But we hardly know each other. What would people think? They will say I took advantage of your good nature."

Mose smiled. "So, let them talk. They'd be wrong and we'd know it. I want this marriage for both of us, for the *kinder*. We can't let others decide what is best for our lives. I believe this marriage is *Gott*'s plan for us."

Sarah's face cleared and she seemed to come to a decision. She smoothed out the fabric of her skirt and tidied her hair, then finally took Mose's outstretched hand with a smile. "You're right. This is our life. I accept your proposal, Mose Fisher. I will be your *frau* and your *kinder*'s mother."

Don't miss
THE AMISH WIDOW'S SECRET
by Cheryl Williford,
available June 2015 wherever
Love Inspired® books and ebooks are sold.

Copyright © 2015 by Harlequin Books, S.A.

LIEXP0515

JUST CAN'T GET ENOUGH OF INSPIRATIONAL ROMANCE?

Join our social communities
and talk to us online!
You will have access to the latest
news on upcoming titles and special
promotions, but most important,
you can talk to other fans about your
favorite Love Inspired® reads.

 www.Facebook.com/LoveInspiredBooks

 www.Twitter.com/LoveInspiredBks

Harlequin.com/Community

LISOCIAL

Love the Love Inspired
book you just read?

Your opinion matters.

Review this book on your favorite
book site, review site, blog or your own
social media properties and share your
opinion with other readers!

Be sure to connect with us at:
Harlequin.com/Newsletters
Twitter.com/LoveInspiredBks
Facebook.com/LoveInspiredBooks

HLIREVIEWSR